THE LEAVES ARE FALLING

LUCY BECKETT

The Leaves Are Falling

IGNATIUS PRESS   SAN FRANCISCO

Cover photograph by X. Sean Gao Photography

Cover design by Riz Boncan Marsella

© 2014 by Ignatius Press, San Francisco
All rights reserved
ISBN 978-1-58617-894-9
Library of Congress Control Number 2013916530
Printed in the United States of America ♾

For my grandchildren
Rufus, Joe, and Matilda Brooks
Emily and Max Warrack
Alfred Warrack

Herbst

Die Blätter fallen, fallen wie von weit,
als welkten in den Himmeln ferne Gärten;
sie fallen mit verneinender Gebärde.

Und in den Nächten fällt die schwere Erde
aus allen Sternen in die Einsamkeit.

Wir alle fallen. Diese Hand da fällt.
Und sieh dir andre an: es ist in allen.

Und doch ist Einer, welche dieses Fallen
unendlich sanft in seinen Händen hält.

Rainer Maria Rilke

Fall

The leaves are falling, falling as from far,
as if in distant skies gardens were dying;
they fall reluctantly, denying death.

And through the nights there falls the heavy earth
from all the stars into forsakenness.

We all are falling. This hand here is falling.
And look, the other: all that is, is falling.

And yet there's One who gently in his hands
holds to eternity all things that fall.

The Singular

The Prince of This World governs number.
The singular is the hidden God's dominion,
The Lord of rescues and exception's Father.

Czeslaw Milosz

Prologue I

One day not long ago she received a letter which surprised her very much. The letter was written in a foreign hand, a little uneven but with no mistakes or corrections, and not difficult to read. It was perhaps a fair copy.

> *Dear Madam,*
>
> *(Or possibly Doctor or Professor—please forgive me. I do not know which is correct.)*
>
> *I have yesterday finished reading your book. It has very much moved me, as you will imagine when I tell you that I am the son of Dr Jacob Halpern. I understand, naturally, that you have told only a story, a story which it must have cost you much labour to write, since so long a time has passed. Such things did happen, however. Not only such things but these things, so far as I know, which is not so far.*
>
> *I would be most grateful to meet you, most grateful and also most privileged. I live, as you see, in west London, and I am sorry to say that I am too lame to travel because stairs in the Underground and in the station are difficult for me. If you should by chance be in London and could spare for me a short time, would you possibly be so kind as to visit me here one day? I could tell you of some later things that happened which would, I think, interest you. I remember much, which for many years I did not understand, which I do not altogether even now understand, and I have myself had many hours to read. My eyes, thanks be to God, as the old are still permitted to say, see well.*
>
> *You will forgive this letter from a very old stranger, and you will perhaps visit me if you should have the opportunity.*
>
>

With apology and many thanks,
Joseph Halpern
>

Five days after she read this letter, they were sitting in shabby, comfortable chairs that did not match, on either side of an ancient gas fire in a sitting room lit by the evening sun. His flat was the ground floor of a house in a quiet street between the Uxbridge Road and the Goldhawk Road. The street had taken her some time to find; she had walked from the tube station with an old A to Z open in her hand. She liked the street, wide, peaceful, with brick and stucco houses, probably early Victorian, set back in pairs. There were roses, not out yet, shrubs, dead daffodils, and sometimes tulips in the small front gardens except where cars, instead, were squeezed into now-paved spaces. Outside the two windows of his sitting room, facing the street, there was no car but a lilac bush coming into bloom and a straggly forsythia, its flowers over, that no one had pruned for years. Then a low wall. Then the pavement. And the sunshine. His room—bookcases stacked with too many books, an upright piano with piles of music and a violin in its case—also had the basics of a small, tidy kitchen in one back corner. Did the door in the other lead to his bedroom, his bathroom, windows onto the garden? From trees she had seen from the street, she knew there were long gardens behind the houses.

The street was going up in the world. Most of the houses were still quite scruffy, like his, but a few were smartened up with newly painted stucco and security devices in their bright front doors. Several had skips on the road in front of them, full of debris from demolished walls and the odd ripped-out fireplace or dismantled cupboard. Builders, Poles perhaps, or Ukrainians, with power tools, lengths of flex winding out of windows, and strong lights here and there, were working, or not. It was the middle of the afternoon as she walked down the street looking at the house numbers. Three workmen, smoking as they lounged against a wall, had taken a break to watch the women, young and not-so-young, mothers or nannies, black, white, Asian, some with babies in pushchairs and three-year-olds on scooters, as they walked to wait for older children outside a primary school at the distant end of the street. She lived in a village a long way from London. She liked his street.

She liked him. Standing an hour ago at his front door, listening as someone—he—came slowly to let her in, she was reassured—was she a gullible fool to have believed in that letter?—by the label beside the lower of the two bells at the door: "Halpern", typewritten on a yellowing piece of paper under slightly bulging cellophane in a small brass frame. It had been there for years, decades probably. When he opened the door, he was so exactly what she had expected, hoped, that she smiled, could not for a moment speak.

8

"Come in, please."

"Thank you."

Small, thin, an old, wrinkled face. Black, intelligent eyes, smiling, inquisitive. A black beret. White hair under the beret. An old, dark jumper. The collar of a checked shirt that looked too English for him. A stick.

"Come. Follow me, please. I am slow."

He limped, his stick keeping him upright, a yard or two along a passage to an open door. His back was straight, his left leg obviously unreliable and probably painful.

"Here. I am sorry my house is not so tidy. Sit down, please. I will make coffee."

Slowly, he did. She sat still until she saw him pour the coffee.

"Do you like sugar?"

"No, thank you. Let me carry the cups."

"Thank you."

They sat.

"It is kind of you to come. My letter surprised you?"

"Of course. And pleased me very much. I was so glad—I had thought—"

"You had thought that there was no one of my family alive. Very nearly there was no one. Why I was alive at the end of the war I did not know then. I do not know now. Chance, luck, providence, God—they become more favourable, you see, as one wonders—but chance, I think, colourless chance, is all I can be sure of."

"But how very good that you were, alive at the end of the war. That you are alive now, and well. Are you reasonably well?"

He laughed. "That is an excellent English question. You mean to ask how old am I, and given that I am so old, how do I do? But you are too tactful to use such words."

"I'm sorry."

"No. By no means. You must not apologize. It is the obvious question you should ask. I shall be eighty-two in September."

He smiled as he watched her do the sum in her head.

"Yes. I was born in 1929, a year and a half or so after my father left Breslau. You did not know—or, if you allow me to say more exactly, you did not guess—that my father had a girl he loved in Breslau, a girlfriend, you would say. She was a nurse in his hospital. Doctors love

9

nurses, nurses love doctors—it is universal, I think, and why not? She
was a Jewess of course, but German, not Russian or Polish or whatever
my father thought he was by then, though always he was a Litvak, a
Lithuanian Jew I should say, and she was not. She followed him to
Vilna. It was easy for a well-trained German nurse to be given a job in
the Jewish hospital there. So, soon they married, and one year later or
so, I was born."

"Was your grandfather still alive?"

"He was. I remember him. He died in 1936, thanks be to God. He
simply died, as one does. As one should."

"And how long have you lived in England?"

"More than sixty-five years." He watched her do another sum. "Not
long after the war I arrived. Again, chance, providence, et cetera, whichever it has been. There is here a story, a complicated story, which ...
May I offer you some more coffee?"

"No, thank you. Your coffee is very good."

"One of my last indulgences. Another is ... Do you mind if I smoke?"

"Of course not."

"I smoke very little these days. I promised the doctor. She is a good
girl. But now and then a cigarette is very good."

He got to his feet with some difficulty, took a nearly full packet of
Gauloises and a box of matches from the mantelpiece, sat back in his
chair, and lit a cigarette.

"Yes. Very good."

"Which—you were saying—a complicated story which?"

He looked at her with his bright, smiling eyes.

"Which I want you to tell."

"What? But—"

"I know. You are busy. You have other books to write. You are not
so young. Not so old as I am, naturally, but not so young either."

"It's not that, not at all. It's just that—"

"I shall guess. Allow me. You do not know me, as you knew Max
Hofmann, even though you were only a schoolgirl when he died, again
simply died, like my grandfather, in his own bed. Many books you will
have to read so as to understand a time and a place which are lost and
which have never been interesting in England—not now, I fear, interesting to anyone, anywhere, except to a few very old people, like me.
The time perhaps to historians is interesting. The place perhaps to those

who live there. But not both together. For example, a nice girl, whose name is Ona, comes twice a week for one hour to help me a little—to tidy me up, iron my shirts, and so forth. This girl is Lithuanian. She was born in Vilna—to her of course it is Vilnius—in the 1980s, I suppose, so in the USSR. She is happy now to be a citizen of the European Union so that she may work in London and send every month a little money home. But she has no idea, not the least little idea, of the past of her own city, the glorious, the terrible, past. Perhaps that is good. Why burden the young with knowledge when they live quite happily without it? She thinks I am English, more or less, like all the different people she might meet in London, in the streets, in the shops, and by now I admit I am even to myself English, more or less. Less, you think? You are right. I do not tell her I am a Jew. I think this is still not a word that is"—he paused—"welcome in Lithuania.

"As for the English themselves—I know from my grandchildren, who do well, who have been to English schools, who are as English as anyone else, as English as you, for example, that in school they have learned exactly nothing of the eastern Europe that there was. Of Hitler they learn a lot; of Stalin they learn a little; of Auschwitz they know; of Churchill and the Blitz and El Alamein and D-day of course. But of the fact that between Germany and Russia a world was destroyed—of that they learn nothing. They do not know even the map. And when I try to tell them, my grandchildren—who are grown up now so it is too late—only a very little of the old time, of how things were when I was a boy, it is to them as if I talk of ancient history, something in a book they are not interested to read. And yet I think that possibly—"

"You think that possibly in the story, your story, there is something not to be lost?"

He looked at her for some time before answering.

"Your question makes me ashamed. These different people in the streets and the shops in London—in every one of them, and most of all in the old, like me, is a story. The old Sikh in his turban whom I meet in the paper shop. The old black woman, with her beautiful Jamaican speech, who takes her three grandchildren every day to school along this street—the naughty boy who runs ahead is called Michael. The old Italian who has a stick, like me, not that he is so lame; he has flat feet. On a bench in the park one day he told me he was a waiter all his life, in the Savoy, so grand. From a village, from a back street, somewhere in the world, they came once upon a time, these old people, and at last they are in London, where the tide has floated them to this beach, a beach which is not so bad. Often not so good, but always not so bad. Every one a story. So why does mine deserve to be told when theirs, most likely, will never be? I don't know."

"Maybe because it is yours? I think that is a good enough reason—as it would be for any of them. For anyone."

Another long look.

"All right. Yes. You have understood, I think—as you also understood once before. But there is something else. This story is not so much mine but the story of some others, better and braver than I. There is a line of Mickiewicz ... Do you know Polish?"

"I'm afraid I don't."

"Let me think. Yes. 'If I forget about them, then you, God in heaven, forget about me.' His line, more or less. I know you understand. Yes?"

"I think so."

"So—"

"So will I try, again? Perhaps I will. But it must depend on you, on what you can tell me."

"Ah."

He lit another cigarette.

"This is against all my rules, this cigarette. But this is a highly exceptional day."

She waited, again.

"I will give you some names, some dates, some facts. Among these facts are some which for many years I did not discover—and one or two which are guesses only, and so will stay. I think it is better if I write them down. There are memories of which I have never spoken. Of them I could not now speak without ... without difficulty."

"Your wife?"

A steady look.

"I am sorry ... I shouldn't have ..."

Then a smile.

"Do not apologize. My wife, yes. She died a long time ago, twenty years or so. She had cancer. It was a cruel death, but the cruelty was not the cruelty of people. There is a very great difference. The people were most kind. Only the disease was cruel. Yes, my wife knew me, loved me of course, as I was. She did not know me as I had been; nor in those days did I know myself. I wished to forget. I did not discuss with her what I wished to forget. Also—how can I say?—she was so much an English woman, so beautiful also when she was young, and even she inherited some money that was her own. It was a miracle that she wanted me, married me. I did not wish her to pity me also. I was no longer the boy in the forest. I was not yet the old man who remembers the forest. Do you perhaps understand?"

"Perhaps. I think I may." She hesitated. "The forest?"

"A real forest, very far from England. Also a forest of the mind. You will imagine."

"And your children. Do they know the story? Have you . . .?"

"I have not. My son—I have one son only. He has made much money in a business I do not understand. He belongs to the new world. In airports he talks to two people at the same time on different telephones. I know because occasionally one of them is me. Old Europe does not interest him. God, with his ways deep in mystery and grief, does not interest him. He has two children, grown up now; I said I have tried, when they were children, and intelligent children, to interest them a little in old Europe, but I could not. It is for them too far away, too long ago, too full of things they cannot understand and do not wish to learn. My granddaughter tells me I should buy a computer. Then she can e-mail me. Why? I prefer to see her if she has a little time. She is the one who will read your book."

"But . . ."

"But you do not think you have agreed to write this book. I think you have." He smiled, his winning smile. "Curiosity. Is not this the first step? You know, I met him, Max Hofmann."

"You knew him? I had no idea. How did you find him?"

"He found me. It was chance again, luck, whatever you like. He came into the shop where I worked. It was not an ordinary shop but a shop for music, old music, old books about music, composers' letters, all sorts of stuff." He waved a hand at the crowded shelves. "And so not very surprising that he, a musician, should come in. He asked my name because he thought . . . well . . . you will see all this, and much more. So easily I might not have been myself. But I was. In its way another miracle."

The doorbell.

He looked at his watch.

"Ah. This is Ona, the good Lithuanian child who will wash the cups and sweep the floor and iron two shirts today. Be so kind—will you open the door? Before Ona comes—a moment."

She stood, and turned towards him. He looked at her with the full force of his eyes—his soul, she thought later.

"I thank you for your visit. And for what you will do. The much work, and the book. I will write to you these facts."

She saw he looked very tired.

"Don't get up. Good-bye. And it is for me to thank you. For your letter, for allowing me to come to see you, for asking me—thank you so very much."

They shook hands.

The doorbell again.

"Good-bye."

As she turned in the doorway for a last look, he smiled.

"No e-mails." she said.

"No e-mails."

Chapter 1

Later, when he had for some time been living more or less alone in London, he was grateful—to what? to whom?—that for his first two years in England he had found himself in the north, in the country. One reason was that it was there—because it was quiet and the days and weeks and months went by in a safe pattern—that he did actually find himself. Not suddenly, not all at once, but bit by bit, with much left unfound for other times, other places. To find oneself: it was more than a turn of phrase, a spent metaphor. Much more—it was a verb, to find, with an object, oneself, to be found. Afterwards he thought he began to find himself the morning he woke in an unfamiliar place and slowly remembered how and why he was there, wherever it was—he hadn't heard the name properly and so couldn't remember it—and realized that he was neither cold nor afraid.

Keep still. Don't move. Can it last? If it lasts even for a few weeks, that will be very good.

That morning, in that warm bed, he came to. Another English phrase. Came to what? The day? The world? Himself, again? Anyway, he came to, and he discovered, tentatively and then surely, that what he had come to was warm, and it was quiet.

What a language. Which then, of course, he had very little of. Some words and phrases he had learned at the lake, from an old Jewish woman who had lived in England for many years. She came every day for three weeks and taught some useful bits of English to the children whose only language was Yiddish. He knew, more or less, four languages, but it didn't seem necessary or sensible to say so, and Yiddish was one of them so he joined the others. He learned how to greet people, thank people, ask people to explain slowly; the days of the week; how to count; about pounds, shillings, and pence. Not that they had seen any English money except for the coins and notes she showed them, passing them round among the children, who sat on chairs arranged in a circle three rows deep in what seemed to be some kind of big classroom. The youngest children learned the fastest, and after a few days she could even get them to laugh. One little girl of five or six reminded him of his sister—but his sister would have been much older by then, ten years old if only she had lived. The little girl cried when the others laughed, so the old woman picked her up and sat her on her knee, took a handkerchief from her pocket, dried the child's eyes, and told her to blow her nose, which she did. The room was still. He and the other children watched. There was not one of them who had not lost his mother, her mother, somewhere, at some time in the war. The little girl sobbed, sniffed, stopped crying, sniffed once or twice more. Had there been someone to comfort his sister when she cried?

One day not long before they all left the lake, climbing into buses with their new clothes in bundles, the Jewish woman called over to her table the oldest of them, about a dozen boys and girls. He thought he might be the oldest of them all, though it was hard to guess. She told them that her friends in Manchester would like to give each of them a dictionary so that, wherever they were going in England, they could learn more of the language, look up words they didn't understand. "What language would you like?" she asked each of them. "Yiddish? Polish? French?" But when he said, "German", she shook her head, so he said, "Polish. Thank you." He didn't try to explain that German was the language of his home because it was his mother's, that Yiddish and Polish were the languages of his world and his city, and that everyone in his family had always known some Russian, for survival among enemies. Without each of these languages, suddenly necessary as each had happened to be now and then—and then again, in the forest—he would certainly have been dead.

Instead of alive, as he found himself this morning, this real morning, warm and comfortable as he kept his eyes open and pushed back sleep and its nightmares, which, in the few weeks since the aeroplane and the knowledge (which he didn't yet trust) that he was safe, still seemed more real than the day because they were memories, not dreams one could choose to end by awakening. But now, this morning, he could lie still—wait for the bell on the alarm clock to ring, as the woman had said, then get up—and feel and think nothing except that he was warm and comfortable. It was the eiderdown, not that he knew the word for it, that made the morning like a gift. The eiderdown was thinner than the heavier quilt of his childhood, but he was comfortable because there were clean white sheets, and warm because there were blankets, thick woollen blankets, tucked in over him and then the eiderdown on top. He sat up in bed. The surface of the eiderdown, stitched in large squares, had a swirling pattern—blue and red, pink, dark blue, black and white, in curious shapes like large drops of water, which reminded him of the patterns on old shawls he had seen hanging outside certain little shops in the alleys of Vilna. The shawls had been dusty and soft. This quilt, whatever it was called, was bright and clean, smooth cotton under his hands. Who had given it to him? To this foreign boy who had arrived from so far away, who for such a long time had had no bed, no room to sleep in that was his own?

After his sister was born, his father had made half the attic of their house into a room for him, with his books, his violin, his music, the stool he sat on to practise. The attic had a small window from which he could look down into the narrow street, busy with old women with shawls over their heads and shopping bags; children playing; peasants from the country selling potatoes, apples, cabbages, beets from handcarts and baskets; carpenters, tailors, tinsmiths, shoemakers, and saddlers, all working outside their shops if it was fine.

At the lake each of the children had a narrow room, so at least he was alone at night, but they had said at the beginning that they would not be there for long. Under one worn blanket, though it was clean, he was cold on his bed. And the walls were thin, made of some kind of board. The girl in the next room cried every night. Through the wall he could hear her. On the first night he went to see if he could comfort her, but a woman in a uniform had seen him go into the girl's room, and she marched quickly down the corridor to send him back to his own. Each morning he woke to a clatter of plates and cups as a laden trolley, pushed by a stout woman in a flowered overall, rattled past his door, and to voices calling and doors banging as the children were woken.

And now he had been given this eiderdown and this warm bed, with its two pillows in ironed white pillowcases. And there was nothing to hear but quietness. He lay and looked. His bedroom—would he be allowed to stay here for more nights, for many nights?—was low and square, with dark wooden beams in the ceiling. Not too different from his bedroom at home. No books. No music. Of course no violin. A chest of drawers. A little table against the wall. Three hooks, for clothes

17

he didn't have, on the unpainted wooden door. In Prague someone had taken off him his torn and louse-infested sheepskin coat that had kept him from the worst of the cold through two freezing winters after its owner had been shot in the forest. As he stood in a line with other boys, they had taken all his clothes and shaved his head and puffed white powder all over him. DDT, they said, to kill the lice. They had given him some old clothes that didn't fit him and a thick greatcoat that had belonged to some soldier in some army, but he didn't feel that it was his as the sheepskin had been. The greatcoat was beside his bundle, on the floor—a wooden floor stained almost black, with a rag rug next to the bed.

This much he could see in the daylight, not yet sunshine, from a small window opposite his bed. The curtains, cotton, printed with small flowers quite different from the patterned eiderdown, were closed. He got out of bed and drew the curtains back.

Because it was dark the night before when he arrived, he had no idea what was outside his window. The kind woman had put a lit candle on the chest of drawers by his bed when she left him, and he was so tired that he blew it out and went to sleep almost at once, noticing only the deep quiet, the soothing weight of the covers on his bed, and an owl hooting not far away.

Now he saw that outside was a paddock with dry stone walls, at its far end a wide opening in the wall, with no gate. Beyond were another grassy field and more walls, and a small stone barn without a door or with its door open. There were sheep with black faces in the further field, and a stocky, strong black horse with feathered heels. Then a hillside with small, old oak trees, their leaves papery fawn, and above them on a long upward slope bracken turning tawny—it was the middle of October—then a line of young pines, dark green, almost black against a larch plantation high towards the flat moor, lit to pinkish gold at the very top, where the fading needles of the trees were catching the early sun. So his window faced west.

He opened the window, with some difficulty because it took him a few minutes to work out that half the window frame, with its small square panes, slid sideways across the other half, sticking a bit as it slid. He had never seen a window like it. He breathed in the fresh, chilly air, smelling of wet grass and faintly of smoke. There might have been a light frost. He could hear but not see water running over stones—was a small stream somewhere nearby? He liked what he saw, because behind him was the eiderdown someone had thought to put on his bed, and because the larches near the top of the hill—how they had changed colour in the autumn cold, while the pines had not—reminded him of the country beyond the city at home, and family picnics because his mother loved to be in the country. At home there would have been birch trees instead of oaks, no stone walls, and in every valley a lake, big or small. He liked what he saw from the window also because, although he could see no people and no houses, the fields and the woods were cared for, the walls were mended, the animals were healthy. He shivered. He was wearing one of the three shirts they had given him when he queued for his bundle of new clothes that first day by the lake.

The bell on the alarm clock rang, making him jump. He picked the clock up and shook it, but it rang on until he saw a little lever on the bell to stop it. The time was seven thirty. Late. They got them up at the lake every day at seven.

He dressed, put on the new working boots that were his only shoes, and opened his door, which had no handle but a latch, like doors at home. As he clicked the latch, he hoped it would be his door, his own, for a long time. A narrow passage lay straight ahead, with more doors. On his left, dimly lit by a skylight, one straight flight of wooden stairs led down. It was impossible not to make a noise, treading with his boots on the bare wood, but did it matter, here? He had no idea whether it mattered, but he was so used to making as little noise as possible that he tried to tread gently. At the bottom of the stairs he listened. Nothing. Two doors. What had the kind woman told him the night before that he should do in the morning? He had only partly understood. He opened the door to his right. A long, high, dark stable. On his left the top half of a door was open to the early sunlight. He breathed in a good smell of horses, hay, dung, soaked straw, and the warmth of horses' breath. The flagstone stable floor was crossed by sloping sunken channels with drains set in them. He looked for a tap. There it was, on the wall, with a hose coiled beneath it. On his right was a row of loose boxes, one with an open door, straw on the flags, three with half doors closed, horses inside: a big bay gelding, which turned its head to look at him calmly in the shadows; a smaller grey mare, sharing her box with a tabby cat, the latter curled up asleep on a heap of dry straw in a corner; and a young chestnut gelding with a fine head, startled by him and pawing the straw, whinnying. This was why he was here. But there was no time to get to know the horses. At least ten minutes had gone by since the alarm rang. He went back, closed the door, opened the other, which was straight ahead at the bottom of the stairs, and went outside into the morning.

Where to go? There was no one about. He walked to his right across the stable yard, a wide cobbled yard with flagstone paths, a stone mounting block, brown hens jerking their heads as they pecked about, half a dozen pigeons. The long back of a large stone house faced him— windows, a couple of closed doors, and yes, one open door. He hesitated. Then she appeared in the doorway, the kind woman, a tea cloth in her hand.

"Come in, lad. You'll be wanting your breakfast."

By the door a chained sheepdog lying on the flags growled as he approached. He held out his hand gently, palm upwards, as the woman said, "Don't mind Jess. She won't bite." The dog, still without getting up, wagged its tail. The woman led him through an untidy passage that had boots on the floor and work clothes hanging on pegs, then past a pantry with shelves, then by a scullery with a big rectangular stone sink and a wooden draining board, and finally into a wide, warm kitchen with a scrubbed table at which four men were sitting. One was the man who had fetched him from the station. They stopped eating. Another of the men put down a cup. They looked at him.

"Well, if it isn't the DP boy from Cumberland. A dab hand with horses, so we're told. Sit down, lad. What do they call you? Sit down, here. Cat got your tongue?"

He didn't understand, except that he was being told, not harshly, where to sit. He sat.

"What is your name?"

A German voice. How was this possible? He grasped the edge of the table in front of him with both hands to stop himself jumping to his feet and running from the kitchen, back to the horses. He made himself look at the man who had spoken: a young, fair-haired German, but his eyes, his expression, were friendly. He made himself speak.

"My name is Josef Halpern." At the lake they had told him to pronounce his name in English, "Joseph" with a *J* instead of "Yosef", but now, he realized, he had forgotten to.

"That's all right, lad. We'll call you Joe. That's a good Yorkshire name, like mine. I'm Ted. Eat your breakfast."

The woman had put a plate in front of him: bacon, a slice of bread fried brown, two halves of a fried tomato. When the children had arrived in their bus at the lake, kind women in cardigans behind trestle tables had given them tomato sandwiches, slices of tomato in white bread, and lemonade. He had never eaten anything so good.

He looked down at his breakfast. He was both hungry and too frightened to eat.

"No bacon for him. He is a Jew."

Another German voice, less friendly. Was this still real, or a dream? Would he wake up? How could this farm kitchen in England be full of Germans? It took him longer to make himself look at this man. He was a little older than the other, though still young, with rimless glasses, a thin face, a disapproving expression.

He pushed his plate away, not because of the bacon.

"Nay, what's the difference? The lad wants his breakfast if he's to get any work done in this weather. Eat up, Joe. Do you good, it will." This was Ted again.

He understood the tone of voice, not the words, and after a few seconds of forcing himself to decide, moved the plate back, picked up his knife and fork, and cut a bit of fried bread, then a bit of bacon. Both were very good. There had been too many years of hunger, too many years of eating anything that anyone could beg for or dig up or steal, for him to turn down food someone had given him.

"Where do you come from, then?"

He looked at Ted, who had asked the question. He thought he understood it, but there were too many answers.

"What is your country?"

The friendly German, translating. The question was simple. The answer was not, so he pretended to be still chewing a mouthful.

"Leave him be", the woman said, putting a cup of tea beside his plate. "Plenty of time for questions when he's made himself at home. You eat your breakfast, Joe. Keep you warm, it will. Put some sugar in that tea."

"Thank you", he said, adding a spoonful of sugar to his tea and picking up his cup. At the lake he had got used to tea with milk in it, which to begin with had made him feel sick.

Two or three weeks later, having prepared the question carefully, he asked Ted, who was showing him how to clean saddles and bridles in the tack room at the far end of the stable, "What is the reason Germans are here, on the farm?"

Ted looked up from the bucket of soapy water in which he was washing bits and stirrup irons.

"Fritz and Werner?" Ted pronounced the latter with an English *w*, as in "winter". "They're prisoners. Been here nearly a year, they have. To begin with they were in the camp. They were sent to work on the farm—we were shorthanded, see, on account of the war—and it was a lot easier to put them up here than to have them fetched and carried every day, what with the army lorry, guards, and whatnot."

Ted put the bit he was holding onto his lap. "They frighten you, don't they? Not surprising, where you've come from. You don't need to worry. They can't hurt you here, and Fritz—he's got some fancy German name, but we call him Fritz—is a right softie. Nothing about him to frighten anybody. A farmer's boy like I was, used to hard work, used to cattle, sheep, and suchlike. The other lad—well, he's different, I grant you. Reads books and that, does our Werner. Take no notice. As I say, he has to do as he's told here, and he does, I'll say that for him."

He understood more now, not all the words, but roughly what Ted was saying. He dried the stirrups Ted handed him.

"That's the polish there. And this is called a shammy, to get a shine on them."

"I do not understand how they are prisoners here."

"You mean why they're still here, with the war over and all? I daresay nobody's got round to sending them home. Not much home to go to, by all accounts."

"No. This is not prison. Good food. Warm. Good people. Not prison."

"They're prisoners of war. That's different. Soldiers, they were. Have to be treated right, as long as they do what they're told—which these two do—and as long as they don't run away, which there's not much chance of here. The rules say they have to wear those patches on their clothes. But there's no need in a place like this. Stick out like a sore thumb, they would, anywhere round here, patches or no patches. Understand?"

He understood enough of this to think of Vanya. In the forest one of the dogs had found Vanya one day, under a pile of branches, soaking wet, shivering, terror in his eyes as the dog barked and two of the partisans pulled him out. He remembered the man's toes, bleeding and blue with cold, sticking out of his shredded felt boots. "He's a Russian. Let the Russians take care of him." Vanya collapsed to his knees and pressed his forehead, creased with dirt, into the snow and sobbed. He had no gun—anyone hiding in the forest was welcome if he had a gun—but the decision was made to take him back to the camp, just for a day or two, to give him some food, even to find him some boots. Later, in one of the dugouts, when they stripped the rags off him, someone said, "But he's a Jew!" He looked from face to face, more terrified than ever. Someone else asked him a question in Yiddish. He didn't understand, or didn't want to show that he understood. They let him stay on after all, not only because he was a Jew—although he was a Jew who knew no Yiddish and nothing at all about Jewish religion or Jewish life—but also because he turned out to be a good craftsman, a blacksmith who could mend or put together something useful from any scrap of iron, any metal object, however broken or rusty, that anyone came across. He stayed almost till the end, but when they all knew the Red Army was not far away, he disappeared one night. Probably he was dead.

Vanya had been a prisoner of war.

That first night, in the Russian most of them could understand, he told them, holding a bowl of hot soup in his torn hands for the warmth before he drank it, that he was a soldier from a village near Smolensk. The Germans had taken him prisoner the summer before in Belorussia, with hundreds, thousands, of others. The Germans had left them to die, herded into a harvested rye field, nothing left in it to eat after the first day, barbed wire round the field. There was no water except what a few peasant women from the nearby village brought in cans at night and pushed through the wire. Some of them brought milk. Milk can keep you alive. Three of the women had been caught and shot. The next night the Germans set fire to the village the women had come from; the peasants were burned in their houses or in the church, or were shot as they ran away. The prisoners could see the blaze from the field. The night after, with some of them beginning to die of thirst, Vanya and two others crawled under the wire and ran. Shots rapped behind them, but it was dark and none of them was hit. He had lost the others in a marsh in the forest. They might be still alive, but probably they had drowned. He had been hiding in the forest, hiding and running, for months. If Germans or Russians or any partisans loyal to Moscow had found him, he would have been shot. Stalin had said all Russian prisoners of the Germans were deserters.

23

"Prisoners of war. Do you understand, Joe?"

He shook his head to banish the memory of Vanya, who became his friend and who was most likely dead now, to return to the tack room and the hot coals shifting in the little black range. "No. Yes. I think it is England. England is different."

"Very likely it is. Now look. In this tin, saddle soap. It's for leather. You put it on with this, and take it off with this. Try putting it on. That's right. How you came to be so canny with a horse when you haven't the first principles of tack, I'll never know. England is different from what?"

He couldn't answer.

"Joe?"

"Yes?"

"Where is it you come from? Which country? You can tell Ted."

"I don't know."

"What do you mean, you don't know? There's nobody doesn't know where they was born."

"I was born in Vilna."

"Where's that? That's not a country. You're putting too much soap on them reins. Give it here. Look. That's all you need. Countries are places like England, France, Germany. What country's this Vilna in?"

He concentrated and said, "Vilna was in Poland. Before, Vilna was in Russia. Now not in Poland. Now is in Litva, Letuva. Also it is again in Russia."

When he looked up to see if Ted understood, he saw only that Ted realized it had been an effort for him to get his answer put together.

"Oh, never mind for now, lad. I can't follow all that. We'll find a school atlas one of these days, and you can show it to us on a map. Like that." Ted pointed to a large estate map pinned to the inside of the tack room door. "Map. You see?"

"I understand 'map'. But ..." He gave up. There probably wasn't a map in England that had the frontiers of Kresy, the borderlands, drawn as they were now—if anyone, which would be the Russians, had agreed with anyone else where they were to go. Which most likely they hadn't.

That night, though he was very sleepy, he sat on his bed, his candle alight still on his chest of drawers, and tried to think through what he had learned so far of this new place. He was wearing flannel pyjamas too big for him, an old pair Ted had given him, and he had had a bath. He was becoming used to feeling clean. For years he had been sure he would never again feel properly clean, as he had felt every night at home, so he still enjoyed the sensation.

He usually went up to his room after supper, after he had dried the dishes for Mrs Thwaites, the kind woman whose name he couldn't pronounce, and when the news on the wireless was over. He had taken to drying the dishes because it allowed him to leave the table, where the two Germans and the man who had fetched him from the station, whose name was Bill, talked to each other and laughed. Ted, who lived alone in a cottage beyond the vegetable garden—"My wife died three years back, and our boy's still in the forces. Somewhere in Germany"—went home straight after supper every day. "Have to get my fire going in time for the news." Mrs Thwaites made sure the supper things were washed, dried, and put away before nine o'clock, when she would switch on the big wireless in its polished wooden box, which sat on a table covered with a plush cloth, in a corner of the kitchen. She and Werner listened to the news with great attention, Werner sometimes taking out a tiny notebook he always had in his back pocket and scribbling something down with a pencil stub. Joe at first understood very little, but he thought it was good for his English to try hard to gather some of what was said. The voice from the wireless spoke very differently from Ted and Mrs Thwaites. Night after night the ritual of the news in the peaceful kitchen, with the kettle on for Mrs Thwaites' last cup of tea, took him back to the forest, to the frantic struggle in the icy dark of a dugout to find the crackly wavelength of the BBC while outside extra lookouts crouched in the snowy undergrowth watching and listening for Germans or a single Russian partisan with a gun.

Bill and Fritz seemed not to be interested in the news and usually played a silent game of draughts while it was on.

Bill was the cowman. There were a dozen little golden cows in the big field to the east of the farm. When the sun was shining, Joe liked to lean over the gate and look at this field because it was so beautiful: a long gentle slope, grass like silk, and three old oak trees for shade, the pretty, gentle cows quietly munching. By the gate was a water trough for the cattle which filled a little as if by magic when a device he had never seen before, a floating ball held by a metal arm, sank to a certain level. Vanya would have loved this.

25

Bill brought the cows in to the byre twice a day, milked them, fed each of them a few handfuls of something called calf nuts—so good to eat that Joe knew he could have lived on nothing but them in the forest—and sent them back to their field through the muddy gateway, slapping their rumps if they dawdled—"Gid on with ye"—and fastening the gate with twine. Every morning he loaded the wagon with three tall milk cans, hitched up the black horse, whose name was Robin—which sounded to Joe vaguely Russian—and disappeared down the white farm road, returning a couple of hours later with empty cans. Once a week he took Mrs Thwaites with him, to market. She came back with a heavy shopping basket, complaining about rationing and the price of everything. "And me with four working men to feed, five now with you, Joe. It's all right, love; it's not your fault. Not your problem neither. It's just as well Ted's such a dab hand with the veg, or I don't know how we'd keep body and soul together." Ted grew potatoes, onions, carrots, leeks, beetroot, and other things Joe didn't recognize in the vegetable garden to the side of the house. It had a high stone wall at its back, facing south, with plum trees growing against it. There had still been plums to eat when Joe first came, and on the pear trees trained neatly with their horizontal branches tied to wires, fat juicy pears were still ripening. They had eaten all of them now, except the plums and pears Mrs Thwaites had bottled in tall glass jars with glass lids screwed on with metal rings.

"No," Joe said to Mrs Thwaites, "we have good, good food."

"You look the better for it, my lad, in the few weeks you've been here, I will say that. You didn't half need a bit of building up when you got here. But it's not like it was prewar, this kitchen, and I daresay it never will be again. Once upon a time I had a kitchen maid in here, and a dairy maid to do the butter and that."

On another day of the week, in the round dairy with cool slate shelves at the end of the yard, Mrs Thwaites made butter. "Come on, Joe. Your arms are younger than mine. You can turn this handle till you hear the butter coming." Later she would shape the butter between wooden bats, the top one carved with a pattern that came out on the butter. "Lovely, isn't it? Shame we have to part with so much of it."

He could usually grasp more or less what Mrs Thwaites was saying. What Bill said he could scarcely understand at all. The cowman, perhaps a year or two younger than Ted, had an odd, hoarse voice, spoke very indistinctly, and sometimes stopped whatever he was doing, even eating, and sat or stood staring with his eyes fixed as if he had seen something no one else could see. Ted must have noticed that Bill made Joe uneasy—Joe thought the cowman might suddenly lash out at him—because he said one day, "Joe, don't you worry about Bill. He was gassed on the Somme, mustard gas, in the Great War, poison, you understand?" Ted illustrated with an imitation of someone choking. "He's not been a well man since, but he'd never hurt you, or anyone."

Bill and the Germans had a bedroom each in the attic of the stable, as Joe did. At the far end of the passage, over the tack room, was a room with a sink and a tin bath. There was a cold tap. If he got to the stable soon after supper and the news, he could boil the big black kettle on the tack room range before it lost too much heat and, before the others left the kitchen, have a quick bath that was at least warm. He liked very much the tarry smell of the bar of red, nearly transparent soap on the sink in the bathroom. There was another on the sink in the scullery where Mrs Thwaites washed the dishes and scrubbed the pans.

"What is this soap?" He had looked up the word in his dictionary. "It is very good."

"Bless you, Joe, that's carbolic. It's only soap, you know."

On Mondays she did the washing, sheets and towels and tea cloths and all their shirts and underwear, in the washhouse in the yard, lighting the fire for the big copper before breakfast. On Tuesdays she ironed their shirts.

On Sundays Ted and Mrs Thwaites set off in the trap for chapel after tea, Ted in a dark blue suit and tie under his warm coat and Mrs Thwaites in a heavy brown coat that never appeared on any other day of the week, and a very peculiar hat that she fixed to her head—it must have been only to her hair—with a terrifying long pin as she frowned into the little mirror on the wall by the scullery sink. On market days she wore a scarf tied under her chin. Joe's mother, going shopping, always wore a scarf, but she tied it at the back of her neck. "To tell you the truth, Joe," Mrs Thwaites said to him one Sunday as she put on her hat, "I'm church, not chapel—always have been since a child—but Ted is old chapel and wouldn't miss it. And how could I get to Sunday morning service with no one here I'd trust to mind the dinner?" Of this he understood not a word except that the Sunday dinner needed her.

On his bed, warm, dry, and clean, he sat and thought. He was beginning not to be afraid that he would soon, one day, any day, be sent

away. Ted needed him to look after the horses, and no one had said anything about him being sent anywhere else. He reached for his dictionary,
thinking as he always did when he picked it up of the kindness of the
old woman at the lake who had brought it for him from Manchester. He
kept it by his bed and tried to look up new words he had heard during
the day before he went to sleep. Often he couldn't find them; English
spelling was very mysterious. He also set himself every night to learn,
from the list of phrases on pink paper in the middle of the dictionary, a
new set of words that might be useful. Most of them were about travelling on trains and shopping, so not at present useful at all. He kept himself awake with his dictionary as long as he could because he was afraid of
sleep. Nearly every night he was back in the forest, or back in the hayloft
with the rats in the dark where the peasant's wife had hidden him, or
back listening for German voices, Russian voices, commands, shots, and
cries, or back in the frozen fields last winter, not daring to go near the
roads, stumbling over ruts, looking for something, anything, to eat.

Tonight he found "mustard" and "gas", to make sure they were, as
he guessed, the same as in Polish. They were. So, after Bill had been
poisoned by Germans and would suffer the effects for the rest of his life,
how could he make friends with the German prisoners? Because they
were so much younger? Or perhaps because they were soldiers, as he
had been? Or just because it was impossible not to like Fritz?

Would Fritz have stood at attention at the killing pits and over and
over again shouted the command to the Lithuanians to shoot? Would
he have laughed as the lines of people crumpled and fell into the pits?
How would Fritz have behaved in Belorussia, in the forest? With the
Jews, with the wretched peasants? Would he have been one of those
who, in their tidy uniforms, had ordered all the women and children
and old people in a village into the church, locked the door, and burned
the church to ash?

He thought that once his English was better he might try to talk to
Fritz, to see if he could discover a little about how, why, it had been as
it had been. He wasn't going to let Fritz, still less Werner, find out that
he could speak German. That would be too complicated. Nor did he
want even Ted to know. "My mother was German. The Russians took
her away. If she had been there when the Germans came, the Germans
would have killed her." He suspected that if Werner, though perhaps
not Fritz, found out that his mother was German, Werner would dislike

him more, not less. And all of it was certainly too complicated for Ted. If Joe's mother was German, shouldn't Joe too be a prisoner of war? And weren't the Russians friends of the English because of how the war had gone? He had heard Ted talk about "Uncle Joe"—he had looked up "uncle" in his dictionary—as if Stalin were a kind relation and perhaps a bit of a joke.

He liked the work he was here to do.

"Anyone know how to look after horses?" The question had been called out, in the big room that was like a classroom, by a man in uniform who had arrived at the lake after they had been there about three weeks. The man had in his left hand sheets of paper with lists typed on them, in his right hand a pen. He stood behind the table at which the Jewish grandmother—so, now, they all thought of her—sat to teach them English. He was there to match the children in front of him to homes or jobs or schools that had offered to take one or two of them. The serious girl with spectacles who had been the chief interpreter since the night they arrived translated the question into Yiddish.

He put his hand up and looked round. No one else had responded except a boy of eleven or twelve who, in a row behind him, had stood up.

"You're too young", said the man, waving to the boy to sit down. "School for you, my boy." The serious girl translated the response, but into less blunt Yiddish.

"And you. How old are you?"

"Sixteen, sir." He didn't need a translator for this.

"How's your English?"

"I have a little English, sir."

"Good, good. Looks like we've got you sorted out, then. A fellow in Yorkshire wants a stable lad. What's your name?"

"Halpern, sir."

"What's your Christian name?"

"I am not—Josef, sir."

He saw the man scribble something on one piece of paper, cross out a line on another. And that was that. A few days later the bus; a railway station in a town whose name he did not know; another train, another station; and then, in the dark, Bill—"You the lad from Windermere?" in his hoarse voice—and the wagon taking him and his bundle of clothes to the farm, without another word.

His work wasn't difficult, and mostly he enjoyed it. Every day he mucked out, fed, and watered the three horses in the stable and took out each of them in turn for exercise. He had got used to the heavy saddles and the complicated double bridles. The big bay horse and the mare, whose name was Grey Dawn, were easy to ride, easy to hold. He liked the mare best of the three because she was the most like Renia, the little mare he had ridden away into the forest the night the Germans came, as the farmer's wife who had hidden him had told him he must if the Germans arrived to search the farm. "They always come at night, so they all say. You can jump from the loft. You'll be away in the dark before they've worked out how to find the ladder. They'll never catch you. They'll see I've been hiding someone, but if I say it's my son dodging being called up, they can't shoot me for hiding a Jew. They don't want more boys fighting for the Russians, do they? You'll be off in the forest by then, so quick that pony is. Jan always said he'd not had a quicker. And I could never manage her after Jan went." Little Renia. In the years since the shooting pits, he had loved her most.

The chestnut gelding, four years old, Ted said, was trickier. "Flighty, he is. Not been ridden enough since the summer. You come with me to the far paddock and we'll see how you do. We don't want you breaking your neck when you've come all this way for a bit of peace and quiet." Three times the young horse bucked him off in the paddock that morning, but after that he came off only once, when a pheasant clattered up in front of them as they were cantering along a track through the larch wood and the horse reared up and threw him onto his back. That was only two days ago. The horse by now was used to him, and so, after cantering off into the trees with the empty stirrups flying, the gelding simply stopped and was grazing quietly when Joe caught up with him.

The farrier had come one day, in an old van, to replace a shoe Robin had cast. While the man was there he checked the shoes on the three riding horses. Joe couldn't understand the few words he grunted in a thick accent, but because of Vanya, and because the horses trusted him, he helped. Even the young gelding stood quietly while Joe held its halter, his other hand on its neck. Ted watched. "Bye, will you look at that? Bloody marvellous, what he's done with that rapscallion."

"The lad can ride. I will say that for him", he heard Ted tell Mrs Thwaites when she asked him how Joe was doing. "And he's got a way with horses. When they come for the hunting, the colonel'll be fair capped with him."

Joe gathered this was praise and was pleased. But who was coming? He didn't want anyone to come. And who was the colonel? He couldn't find this word in his dictionary. When he asked Fritz, and Fritz said, "Colonel. That is *Oberst* in German. It means an important soldier. He is a good man, I think", he liked the prospect even less. He had hoped he was done with soldiers.

A few days later, on the first really cold morning of the winter, the young horse, whose name was Tiger Rag—"They call him Tiger for short"—reared and threw Joe on the icy cobbles of the yard as soon as he was in the saddle. He kept hold of the reins, calmed the horse, remounted though his right arm and his right side were bruised, and walked him round the far paddock until he stopped prancing and sweating in the frost. Joe rode back to the yard. Ted, who had been watching from the other side of the stable, helped him dismount.

"Champion. That's the style, Joe. Let him know who's in charge. When you've got his tack off you'll be wanting a cup of tea, with plenty of sugar. That was a bit of a bump on the cobbles. You'll know about it tomorrow."

"Ted?" he said later, over the tin mugs of tea.

"What is it, lad?"

"Who is the colonel?"

"Lord's sakes, don't you know that? Well, why would you if nobody's thought to tell you. The colonel's the boss, the master. This is his house, his farm, his land, as far as the eye can see. Who did you think the big house was for? Not for the likes of us. They're mostly in London, of course. The colonel's been in the War Office all through the war. But they come up here Christmas, Easter, and summer, and for the shooting. They'll be here more next year, I wouldn't be surprised, now that the war's over, though madam isn't what I'd call a country person. Happier in London, she's always been. It was the colonel told us we was to have a DP for stable lad, told us when to fetch you from the station and that. We didn't know what to expect, I don't mind telling you, with the POWs here already." Ted laughed. "All this talking in letters these days—POWs, DPs—when what you get is Fritz and Werner and young Joe. A mixed bag, I grant you, but definitely not letters."

31

"He will—" He corrected himself. "Will he come alone, the colonel?" He wanted to find out about the "they".

"What? Nay, why would he come by himself? They all come when it's holidays. The colonel, you'll like him. A real gentleman. Mrs Robertson, that's his wife. A bit hoity-toity, she is, stuck-up like—the Honourable Mrs Robertson, and don't you forget it. Then there's the younger son, James, but he's still in the forces like my lad. James is in the Canal Zone, last I heard. The older boy, Philip, was killed last summer in Normandy—that's in France—a week or two after D-day. His mother took it very hard. Then there's the daughter, Sarah—Sally, they call her—a pretty girl, about your age. Loves her riding, so you'll be seeing a bit of her. She's at boarding school somewhere in the south, so she won't be here till the Christmas holidays."

He understood some of this. He had no idea what was meant by "D-day", but he knew that the English and the Americans had fought the Germans in France. So the colonel's son was killed where Fritz and Werner had been taken prisoner. How must it be to have enemy soldiers in your house when their friends had killed your son? But there was Bill and the gas. Then he saw that battles were different from what had happened to his father, his mother, his sister, his aunt Anna, and the little boys. Soldiers fighting soldiers. That was different. He knew the difference was important. Perhaps one day he would be able to sort out why.

Later, remembering carefully, as he tried to every day, what Ted had told him, he was struck by the oddness of an English gentry family—a family like a prosperous *szlachta* family at home, as far as he could make out, with its manor house and much land—having a daughter called Sarah. He would never understand England. He remembered his mother telling him that Hitler had ordered every Jewess in Germany to be called Sarah, to abolish them as people along with their names.

"Have some more tea, Joe. Plenty in the pot." Ted put milk, then very strong tea, then sugar in Joe's mug and stirred it with the tack room's only spoon.

"Then there's Mr Ward, the chauffeur. He drives them up in the car. He's only a local fellow in actual fact, but he was the colonel's batman in the war, the first war, when he was a slip of a lad, and he's learned about motors and engines since and got himself into a fancy uniform. He valets the colonel too, looks after his hunting clothes and that. Waits at table if there's company. He can be a bit high and mighty. Wouldn't eat in the kitchen with the POWs when the family came in the summer. We had to open up the old servants' hall for him and Miss March. She's Mrs Robertson's maid, and she's a perisher: hasn't a good word to say for anything round here. Comes from London. But don't you fret. You won't have to be bothered with either of them. They don't lower themselves to come in the back."

When the family arrived, everything was immediately different, so that Joe looked back at the weeks he had spent on the farm before they came as a time of peace and safety that he might never again be allowed.

There was more work to do. That he liked, and it made him so tired at the end of the day that sometimes he slept all through the night with not a single dream waking him in terror. When he slept this soundly, he woke gently, feeling above all lucky—lucky to be alive, to be here, to be warm, to have breakfast ahead across the yard in the kitchen, to have his horses waiting for him. So he lay in bed for an extra minute or two, his arms in Ted's pyjama top lying straight at his sides outside the covers so that he could stretch his palms and his fingers on the smooth cotton of his eiderdown. He even prayed. Blessed be God. He thought of his father. On those happy mornings he dashed in bare feet down the freezing passage with its wooden floor to the sink and the carbolic soap to wash his hands under the cold tap before breakfast because that was a Jewish thing to do.

Mrs Thwaites was much busier because she had to cook for the house as well as for the farm. A girl called Mary now came early every day on a bicycle to help in the kitchen and with the washing. Her friend, whose name was Doris, bicycled up the farm road with her but then disappeared into the front part of the house, where she made fires and then cleaned and polished all day. She came into the kitchen for a cup of tea at ten o'clock; for lunch; and for another cup of tea in the afternoon. At the kitchen table the two girls talked to each other, too frightened of the Germans and of Joe even to look at them.

Mrs Thwaites gave Joe the chickens to look after. In the morning and the evening he scattered corn for them in the yard; at night he shut them in the henhouse to keep them safe from foxes. After a few days he had learned the different places where they laid their eggs. Collecting the brown eggs, often still warm, and putting them carefully into the shallow basket in the larder cheered him every day—with the hens laying and the larder cool and safe, there would always be something to eat, although most of the eggs had to go to the village with most of the butter and milk. This was because of rationing, which he didn't understand and couldn't find in his dictionary but which Mrs Thwaites grumbled about every day. "Now that the war's over, you'd think they could get things organized so we could eat what the good Lord sends. They even want most of Ted's honey." Ted had three hives at the edge of the cow pasture, which he occasionally did mysterious things to in a wide hat with a veil. The honey that sometimes appeared on the kitchen table to spread on slices of bread was delicious. "Feeding the ruddy Germans, that's what it is. If they are hungry in Germany, let them get on with it, I say. It was them that wanted the war in the first place. Both wars."

His work with the horses had changed. Twice a week, on Wednesdays and Saturdays, he had to get the big bay ready for the colonel to go out hunting. He had little idea what this meant. By nine or ten in the morning, depending on how far the colonel, in red hunting coat, white breeches, had to ride to the meet, the horse had to be gleaming, saddled and bridled in equally gleaming tack. The horse's mane had to be plaited in neat knots along his neck; this was really difficult to do, and Ted had had to give him several lessons. "It's a lot easier with white of egg instead of just water, but we can't waste eggs while rationing's on."

While the colonel was out hunting, Joe was left to exercise the mare and then Tiger, to take hay out to the barn for Robin now that the weather was cold and the grass not growing, to do odd jobs for Mrs Thwaites and Ted, and to wait for the colonel to come back, usually towards dark, with the horse muddy and tired, needing rubbing down, water, and corn. And the tack was to be cleaned again next morning.

On a Wednesday morning when there was no hunting because the ground was frozen hard, the colonel came to the yard and called him out of the loose box he was mucking out.

"Joe—I wanted a word."

"Sir?"

Out in the icy sunshine on the cobbles, the colonel looked at him carefully for the first time. On hunting mornings he had taken the reins from Joe as if from someone he had always known, had ridden away, and had thrown the reins back after stiffly dismounting at the end of the day.

The colonel was a tall, thin man with sparse grey hair, a moustache, a keen glance, an air of authority.

"Ted tells me you're doing well here. He says you're an obedient and sensible boy and very good with horses. Wonders you've done, apparently, with Tiger Rag. You know we're keeping him for when our son James gets home from the war. James rides well. He'll be grateful for your hard work." Then he said, carefully to be sure Joe understood the question, "I hope you're happy here?"

"Very good, sir." He had heard Ted say this often to the colonel. Perhaps it wasn't quite right as an answer. He tried again. "Thank you, sir. Yes, it is good here."

"Good. Capital. Now, I wanted to ask you a few questions. Nothing to be alarmed about, but your answers might be helpful to us—in London, you know—and to you. Come to my study after tea, will you? About five thirty. You'd better get out of those clothes first. I'll get Hebbel to come along. He can interpret. I hear you understand German."

"Yes, sir."

He bitterly regretted that they had discovered he could speak German.

One night a week ago, after he and the Germans and Bill and some other men and boys he didn't know had spent the day beating with sticks through brushwood and bracken to send a few pheasants towards the colonel and five of his friends, who were waiting with shotguns in a succession of places on the edge of the woods, he had woken sobbing and damp with sweat to find Fritz sitting on his bed with an arm round him. "It's all right now. You are awake. There is nothing wrong. You were shouting here. So I would come to see you are OK."

Through his sobs he said, "The guns and the line of men—to go through the forest towards them when what you must do is run, run. I have to go forward, forward, when I know I must run. The shots and all the shouting. And the pile of bodies higher and higher ..." He said all this in German.

Fritz, sitting on the side of his bed, moved away from him a little, took hold of Joe's shoulders in his hands, shook him gently, and looked into his eyes as Joe woke up properly.

"What is this?" Fritz said in German. "So you are a German after all? Why didn't you tell us?"

Joe pulled away, hid his face in his hands, and wept. Because of his nightmare, he had betrayed his secret. He had nothing but his secret that

35

was his own. He didn't want any of them to find out that his mother was German. He couldn't remember why it was so important that nobody discovered this—not the Germans, not Mrs Thwaites or Ted—but he knew it was. He wept bitterly for his lost secret.

"No", he said, after enough time for him to stop crying and pull himself together, as Fritz sat, not touching him anymore, waiting for him to answer. "No. I am a Jew. You know that."

"It's OK, Joe. It doesn't matter. Go back to sleep now. The shooting, it was only a game, sport, for fun, as they say. These English gentlemen, they enjoy killing foxes, pheasants, all sorts of creatures. Like the Junkers, you know. Like Göring. He loved his hunting. I expect that's all finished in Germany now." Fritz said all this in German, and it was good to hear.

"They're practising for killing people. Practising for killing us."

"No, Joe. War is fighting. War is not the same."

"But ..." Somewhere here was the difference between fighting and killing that he had recognized weeks ago after a conversation with Ted. But he couldn't explain it to Fritz even in German, certainly not in English.

Completely awake now, Joe took his handkerchief from beside his dictionary and blew his nose. He looked into Fritz's candid eyes.

"Where did you fight, Fritz?"

Fritz laughed. "Everywhere. First in Africa, in the desert. The Afrika Korps—you've heard of it?"

Joe shook his head.

"The English beat us in the end, but only just. There are a lot of our prisoners still there, but I was lucky. Then I fought in Italy. Then in France, where they took us prisoner."

"Not in Poland? In Russia?"

"No. My Panzer division—"

"Then you know nothing."

Fritz looked puzzled. "Nothing? I was in many battles, in my tank in Africa, in the heat and the cold, in the sand and the mud. Italy was horrible. And in France twice the nearest tank to ours was blown up. Everybody killed. That isn't nothing, I can tell you. Pieces of your friends—no, sorry, Joe. That's enough about fighting."

"You know nothing. In the east there was fighting, of course, which I didn't see much of. But there was also killing, which, as you just said yourself, is not the same as fighting. Hundreds and hundreds, probably thousands, of people, ordered out of the city, pushed and bullied, lined up by the pits in the forest and shot. Piles of bodies like the birds heaped up from hunting today. And I know there were other places, places called camps but they were not camps. They were places where thousands of people were taken to be killed, just to be killed."

"I don't believe there were such places. How do you know? What people do you think were taken there? Bolsheviks? Jews? Enemies of the Reich?"

"Just people. The ones I saw being shot by the pits in the forest were all sorts of people—old people, children with their mothers, babies. Yes, they were Jews. Harmless people, chased and shot like the birds. Later the few that were left, hiding in the forest like the birds, were chased by lines of men to be shot. I was one of them."

"Don't cry again, Joe. You are safe here. Nobody is shooting any people here."

He sniffed, blew his nose again.

"But did you know, Fritz? Did you know what the Germans were doing in the east? What they persuaded the people of the east to do to each other? The Lithuanians who wanted to stay on the right side of the Germans and who had always lived in Vilna, or in the country round about, and had always known the Jews and were used to them—they discovered when the Germans came that they, the Lithuanians, had always hated the Jews too, so they stood and shot them, hundreds of them in a day. Did you know this?"

"I was never in the east. Before the war, I heard the Führer on the wireless, going on and on about the Jews, the filthy Jews, vermin, like rats. Also how powerful they were, wanting to take over the whole world. My grandmother loved to listen to him. But I didn't understand, didn't take much notice. I didn't know any Jews. There were no Jews in my school, no Jews at all in our village in Swabia, except the good old doctor, and he left when I was a child. They went to America, I think, he and his wife. He certainly wasn't filthy or like a rat, or wanting to be powerful either. He was a kind gentleman, and he looked after the poor people for no money. My grandmother loved him. She cried when he left."

"Where is Swabia?"

"Swabia is in the south. The southwest. It is part of Bavaria."

"Are your parents still alive?"

"Yes. They are well. They write to me every week." Joe had noticed that Fritz got regular letters, on the kitchen table by his plate when they had their tea at ten o'clock, and that Werner got none. "My father was ordered to fight, at the very end of the war, though he is a farmer and he is lame because he was wounded in the other war. They put him in uniform and gave him a gun, but there was no fighting—only surrender to the Americans. He was a prisoner, but after three weeks he was allowed to go home. My grandmother is well too."

"You are lucky. What is this luck?"

"Perhaps you are lucky also. You are alive, Joe. That's good. Now lie down and go back to sleep. It's two o'clock in the morning, and there's work to be done tomorrow."

Fritz took his candle, waved from the door, and left him in the dark.

He lay quiet, warm, safe. There was too much he didn't understand. He didn't understand anything. Very soon he fell asleep, and was woken by his alarm clock. No more nightmares, that night.

That evening at supper, Werner put down his knife and fork in the middle of eating and said in German: "Well, Joe, how is it that you speak German and you never told us?"

Joe answered in English. "In my city many people speak two or perhaps three languages."

"Hark at him", said Ted. "His talking's coming on a treat. And we won't have any German in this kitchen, Werner, if you don't mind. It's not considered manners hereabouts to talk so as not everybody can understand."

Werner questioned him again the next morning when he was scattering corn for the hens and Werner was on his way to feed the pigs, a bucket of kitchen scraps in each hand. Joe shook his head and said nothing.

And now he had to go to see the colonel. He had put on a clean shirt, clean trousers, and a dark blue sweater belonging to Ted's absent son. "It's a bit big for you", Ted had said. "Never mind. Best to be neat and tidy like, when you go in their side of the house. And you don't want to look like a run-of-the-mill stable lad, which you're not, are you, Joe?"

"Come along, Joe. It is almost the correct time", said Werner, in a jacket, a clean shirt, and a tie. No encouragement in his cold eyes. Joe was suddenly very afraid.

38

"What are the colonel's questions for?"

"I don't know."

Joe and Werner left the kitchen by a door Joe had never been through. A cold passage with a red carpet on the flagstones. An open, panelled door on the left, a sunny room with two tall windows, a long polished table, chairs with tapestry seats. A hall with a wide staircase and more sunshine. Another open door, a beautiful room with more tall windows, a piano, sofas, paintings on the walls, a big fireplace with a log fire burning. Werner, looking at his watch, let him take all this in for a moment. Then Werner nodded him towards a closed door at the back of the hall, opposite the door into the dining room. Werner looked at his watch again and knocked on the door.

"Come in."

Werner clicked his heels, stood at attention. "Josef Halpern, sir. Five thirty."

"Yes. Good. Thank you, Hebbel. Sit there, would you. And Joe, sit in this chair so I can see you properly."

The colonel was sitting behind a large old desk with his back to the window. Outside were the familiar fields, stone walls, and sheep that Joe could see from his bedroom. They helped calm him a bit. On the desk were untidy piles of paper, mostly typewritten as far as Joe could see, and some framed photographs. He could see only the backs of the frames.

The colonel took a sheet of paper with some typed lines on it from one of the piles and then a fountain pen from an inside pocket of his tweed coat. He snapped open a small case on the desk, took out a pair of spectacles, and put them on. He wasn't wearing a tie like Werner's but a silk cravat of a kind Joe had never seen before. Joe knew he was noticing all these things in order to become a little less afraid. The colonel unscrewed the top of his pen, fixed it to the other end, and then, ready to write, looked across the desk at Joe.

"Now, Joe, there's no need to worry. I have some questions to ask you. If you don't understand anything, Hebbel there will translate into German and translate your answers for me. All right?"

"Yes, sir."

"Splendid. Let's start with the easy stuff. Your name is Josef Halpern." The colonel pronounced this as if in Polish, or German.

"Yes, sir."

39

"It says here you were born on the fourteenth of September 1929. Is that right?" Joe nodded. "So you are sixteen now." Across the desk, the colonel—his pen, with which he had not yet written anything, poised in his hand—fixed Joe with a stare. "I must say, you look quite a bit older. Are you sure you didn't chop off a year or two to get on that plane?"

Joe looked at Werner, who was looking back at him with expressionless eyes. Werner translated.

Joe said in English, "No, sir. I am sixteen since September only." He saw the colonel put a question mark on the paper.

"Yes. Well, I daresay you've been through a good deal. Don't let's worry about that for the moment. Now, this is important. Of which country are you a citizen?"

Werner translated, with a cold smile.

"I don't know, sir."

"How do you mean, you don't know? Everyone knows the country he belongs to. Let's start again. Where were you born"—he looked down at the paper—"on the fourteenth of September 1929, if it was 1929?"

"In Vilna, sir."

The colonel looked at Werner.

"Vilnius, sir. The capital city of Lithuania."

"Ah, now we're getting somewhere." The colonel shuffled some papers, pulled out what looked like a list, and for a couple of minutes studied it. "Lithuania is a Soviet Socialist Republic, is it not?"

Joe said nothing. Werner translated, and added, "It is, sir."

"I see. So you're a Soviet citizen. That means that in due course you'll be returned to your own country. According to the agreement that has been made between the Allied powers, citizens of the Soviet Union are to be returned to the Soviet Union. And now that you are sixteen, you no longer—"

"Please, sir . . ."

"Translate what I just said, would you, Hebbel?"

He did.

"I was born in Poland, sir", Joe said in English.

"I thought you said you were born in Vilnius."

"Yes. I tell the truth. May I speak in German?"

"Of course. That's what we've got Hebbel here for. Go ahead."

"When I was born, and until after the Red Army defeated the Polish army in 1939, Vilna was in Poland. Vilna is a Polish city, Wilno, nearly the same name. For hundreds of years Poland and Lithuania were not separate countries. They were called the Commonwealth. Later, for a long time, most of the Commonwealth was in the Russian empire—until the end of the Great War. So my father and my grandfather were born in Russia. But Vilna, when I was born, was in the new Poland."

"Hold on a minute, Joe. Let Hebbel translate all that."

When Werner, Joe could tell, had summarized rather than translated his explanation, the colonel said, "I'm sure all this is very interesting. But what we need to know"—he looked down at the paper in front of him—"is the nationality to which you belong."

Werner translated, giving Joe a peremptory look which meant "Don't waste the colonel's time."

"I am sorry, sir. I was born in Vilna. My father was a Polish citizen. I am a Jew. Vilna was a Polish city and always also a Jewish city. Now it is a Lithuanian city."

"Well, there you are, then. Vilnius is your home. You are a Lithuanian."

"No, sir. I am a Jew."

"We don't want to pick the Jews out and call them different, do we? That's exactly what the Nazis did."

He pronounced the word "Narzi" as Mr Churchill did. During the short time when they had had a wireless set in the forest, he had once or twice heard Mr Churchill's voice when they had managed to tune the set to the BBC. The wireless had got soaked in a marsh when there was a manhunt in the forest and everyone had had to move quickly, and the set never worked again.

Joe came back to trying to understand what the colonel was saying.

"Lots of German Jews thought they were German. Then the Nazis told them they were only Jews and chucked them out—or worse. We don't want to do anything like that. We—that's to say, the Allies, and specially the British—have decided that we are not going to deal with Jews as a special category."

While Werner translated, with approval obvious to Joe, the colonel found a document among the papers on his desk. He held it in both hands and read:

"'All Jewish displaced persons are to be treated as citizens of their countries of origin.' That's a government ruling. We have to do what we're told, you know."

41

In the silence that followed Werner's translation of this statement, Joe thought, and remembered. Then he said in English:

"Please, may I say another thing, sir?"

"Of course you may. If it's difficult, say it in German."

Frightened both by the colonel's expectant attention and by Werner's cold eyes, he looked from one to the other, swallowed, thought again, and managed to say:

"When I was for a short time outside Prague with other Jews from the east, before they took us to the aeroplane, the Jews were saying we should all go to Palestine, where there will be a home for the Jews. They said the English have promised."

The colonel's expression changed. A coldness appeared in his eyes too, and he bent his head and gathered his papers together, picking them up, shaking them, tapping them on the desk into a uniform pile, and putting them down again as if he were about to end the conversation. Then, not looking at Joe, he said:

"Yes. Well. That's as may be. There are more than enough Jews in Palestine already. Other people live there, you know, and they have to be considered too."

"Sir, I do not want to go to Palestine. My uncle, a rabbi in Vilna—he is dead of course—told me that if the Jews made Zion a country of this world, they would lose Zion as a belief, a memory, a hope. They would instead have guns and kill people to defend their land, as Jews have never done."

Scorn was back in Werner's voice as he translated this.

"Did he? Did he indeed? Did you say this to the Jews you met in Prague?"

"No. I was afraid of them."

"Well, there you are, then. You don't want to go to Palestine. And we would agree, I'm sure, that we must never concede that the Nazis were right to deny Jews their place in Europe. So you must go home to begin to build a new Europe after the terrible destruction of the war. You're young, and you're fit. You've been properly fed here, and you're working in the fresh air. When things have settled down a bit over there, you must go back to your own country and start a new life, a new Jewish life in an old Jewish place. Makes sense, wouldn't you say? A challenge that ought to appeal to a bright boy like you. Translate, please, Hebbel."

He did.

42

"No."

"How do you mean, no?"

"Jewish Vilna is dead. The Russians and the Germans have killed it. First the Russians—they took many people away, many, many people." He stopped, looked at the grass and the stone walls and the sheep beyond the window, and was grateful that Werner had to translate what he had just said.

He remembered what he had meant to say. "The Russians ordered the Jews not to be Jews anymore. The synagogues were closed. The Jewish schools were closed. A few rabbis taught children in secret. My uncle did. It was very dangerous. The Russians took my uncle away. Then the Germans came. They killed Jews. They wanted all of them to be dead, and there were very many in Vilna. They killed them in the streets, in the pits at Ponary, in the ghetto, later wherever they took them. The Lithuanians killed Jews for the Germans. They were ordered to, or allowed to. All this I know myself. I saw it. I cannot be a Lithuanian."

As Werner translated this into English that Joe could understand most of, he watched Werner's face for any reaction of any kind to what he was having to say about the Germans. There was none. Then he noticed that the colonel had taken another sheet of paper from his pile, had picked up his pen, and was writing fast.

"When was all this, Joe?"

He could answer this in English.

"In the summer of 1941, when the Germans came. I was almost twelve years old."

"Which months?" The colonel's pen was waiting to write down Joe's answer. He struggled to remember the English words.

"July, August. In August they killed . . . in August I ran away. Then . . ." He looked at Werner and went on in German. "They went on killing until there were no Jews left. All the months—1941, 1942, 1943."

The colonel was writing as Werner translated. He underlined some words and said, to himself, so that Werner didn't translate, "Yes. It's a pity he's too young to be a witness." He stopped writing and looked up at Joe, more kindly again.

"Did you say how you managed to run away?"

"I was in the last row at the pits. They missed me with the bullets. They had been shooting all day. They were drunk—the Germans gave them vodka every time they stopped shooting. I pretended to be shot. I fell in the pit on top of the bodies and lay still. When it was dark, I ran away."

Werner translated this, no less calmly. The colonel's expression had changed again. He looked shocked, perhaps a little impressed as well.

After a short silence, he said, "Joe, you must understand that all of that—the shootings, and everything—it's all over now. Finished and done with. The Nazis have been thoroughly beaten. Hitler is dead, and the most powerful Nazis are being tried, now, as I'm telling you this, by the Allies in a court of law. They will be properly punished. There is no need to be frightened anymore. Latvia, I'm sorry ..." He looked down at his list. "Lithuania. Lithuania will be a peaceful country again, and you, a bright boy like you—and brave with it, I must say—should be making your contribution to its future."

Werner translated this, his version shorter than what the colonel had said. Joe had picked up the colonel's tone, if not the meaning of every word. Before he answered he thought carefully what he would try to get the colonel to understand.

"Vilna as it is now I do not know because I am in England, but I know the Russians will decide everything there, and they shot everyone hiding in the forest who did not obey orders from Moscow."

Werner translated. At the end of the sentence he nodded, in what looked like approval. Approval of what Joe had said? Of his own cleverness at translating? Of the Russians shooting the partisans in the forest? There was no telling. The colonel, who was looking at Joe, had probably not seen the nod.

"Now listen to me, Joe. Isn't it time for Jews to live in their countries as ordinary citizens of those countries? They do in England, you know. If you were in a big city, in London, say, or in York—well, perhaps not York, let's say Leeds—you would find English Jews living quite happily, free to go to their synagogue or whatever they want, just as anyone is free to go to church or chapel here." He paused for Werner's translation. "I'm sure it will be the same in your own country, in Lithuania, once they have got themselves back on their feet. It takes time, you know, after a war. It's taking time even in England, with rationing and so on, and plenty of soldiers not home yet."

"No."

"You must learn to stop saying no, Joe. You know nothing about England yet."

This was not said unkindly, and Joe, after looking at Werner, whose expression remained blank, nevertheless felt safe enough to try to explain.

"It is not about England I say no. It is about what you call—excuse me, what you think to be—my own country. Lithuanians are the people who speak Lithuanian, a language I don't know, although I know Polish and some Russian as well as German, and Yiddish of course. Lithuanians care only not to be Polish. Lithuania must be a nation. Lithuania must have Vilna, however Polish and also Jewish it has always been."

He stopped and, while Werner translated, wondered if he should go on. He very much wanted to—the colonel seemed to be listening with interest and had written something else on one of his papers—so he did.

"I have heard, in my family, all this talked about, with fear, even before 1939, when I was only a child. My father was always afraid that Poland would disappear again if there were another war, that it would be divided as it used to be between Germany and Russia. The Lithuanians were happy when the Russians came because the Russians said Vilna was not any longer to be in Poland. They were not happy for long when they found they were to be in the Russian empire again, only now it was the Bolshevik empire, and of course they thought the Bolsheviks were all Jews. So they were even happier when the Germans came. They gave the soldiers flowers, eggs, butter, all the good things. The Lithuanians had always resented the Jews, and now they were told it was good to hate the Jews. It was Lithuanians who shot us at Ponary. The Germans gave the orders, gave the permission, but it was the Lithuanians who shot, and shot, and shot, all day."

Still expressionless, as if he were a machine, Werner translated, giving Joe time to pull a clean handkerchief, ironed by Mrs Thwaites, from his pocket and blow his nose.

"Don't upset yourself, my boy", the colonel said, glancing at Werner. "Nobody's going to hurt you here."

The colonel took the cap from the end of his fountain pen and screwed it over the nib. Then he put the pen down on the paper in front of him, took off his spectacles, and laid them on the desk.

"There are a few more questions I would like to ask you. Are you all right to go on, or shall we try another day?"

Werner opened his mouth to translate. Before he said anything, Joe answered in English, in a phrase the grandmother at the lake had taught the class, "I am very well, thank you. Ask the questions, please, sir."

"As you wish. You have plenty of spirit, I'll say that for you. Now ..."

He fiddled for a moment with his pen and then put it down again.

"Was it at that place—Ponary, did you call it?—that they shot ... that you lost your parents?"

Joe looked to Werner to translate. He wanted to be sure exactly what he was being asked.

"No. It was at Ponary that I lost my aunt and my cousins. I was with them when they were shot, in the same line, the last line. Hundreds and hundreds of other people were shot—the lines in front of us were all shot—that same day. I fell with them, but I was not even injured. It was there that I was supposed to die."

"And that was in August 1941?"

"Yes. Early in August. It was very hot. There were many, many flies. The Red Army had dug the pits before the Germans came, to store oil, I think. The Germans used the pits for the bodies of Jews to fall into. But they didn't cover them with enough earth."

The pen unscrewed, the spectacles put on again. A sentence written on a new sheet of paper.

"If that was not how your parents died, when did the Germans find them?"

"My parents and my sister died before. More than a year before. We—that is, my aunt and I—were never told that they had died. But they are dead. I am sure."

"But that would have been 1940. Surely the Germans were nowhere near in 1940?"

"The Russians killed my father. I do not know, but I am sure. The Russians took away my mother and my sister. They would have taken me if I had been at home when they came. My mother and my sister also are dead. I do not know, but I am sure."

"Hold on a minute, Joe. Did you say the Russians? That can't be right. Why would the Russians kill your parents? The Russians have nothing against the Jews now, surely? Haven't the Bolsheviks—the Soviet government, that is—always been pro-Jewish? I thought a lot of them were Jews themselves."

Werner translated this into German and then said, in English, to the colonel, "This is not true, sir. Or let us say it is no longer true."

"All the same, I see no reason why the Russians should be killing Joe's family. Do you have any idea why they should, Hebbel?"

"No, sir."

"Is it possible, Joe, that in what we call the fog of war, you may be wrong about this? Perhaps one or both of your parents may yet turn out to be alive. We're told many families are being reunited in the countries the Germans occupied, families who had quite given up hope. Let's see. What is your father's name?"

"Jacob Halpern. In Russian, Yakov Halperin."

The colonel pulled out several sheets of paper clipped together, turned the pages till he found the right one, and studied it. He shook his head and looked up at Joe.

"Nothing on your father here. What does he do? What is his job?"

"My father was a doctor, a surgeon. He would have been the next professor of surgery at the Jewish hospital in Vilna. He was trained in Germany, in Breslau at the university hospital. That is where he met my mother. She was a nurse."

"So your mother is German."

"My mother was also Jewish."

"Of course. But I still don't understand why you think the Russians are to blame for your parents' disappearance. Surely doctors and nurses are valuable people everywhere?"

Werner translated this with an odd expression, the suggestion of a scornful smile.

"My father was also a soldier."

"A soldier? Was he? Why didn't you say so before? How very odd. I would have thought that a Jew of a certain age, and a senior doctor, would have been well able to stay out of the war. A soldier fighting for whom, may I ask?"

"He was a reserve officer in the Polish Army Medical Corps. He always said ... I'm sorry, sir." Joe took out his handkerchief and blew his nose.

"No. Go on, go on by all means. This is most interesting. Take your time."

Joe blew his nose again. He shook his head and straightened his back.

"He always said that although many Polish people disliked Jews, Poland had long ago given a home to the Jews and had for hundreds of years allowed them to live as Jews, and that if there were a war—he thought Hitler was sure to attack and that there was sure to be a war—anyone who could help the Polish army defend Poland must do that.

47

The Germans did attack, and then, when the Russians attacked two weeks later, he told us ... he told us ..."

He saw his father, in his uniform—he had never before seen him in uniform—standing on that last morning in the sitting room of their narrow house in Vilna, holding his little sister, Rivka, in his arms, and saying to him and his mother, "This is right. I know it's right. I have to go to help Polish soldiers. That's why I joined the reserve. Poland must defend itself against Russia as it did twenty years ago, or we shall all find ourselves in the Russian empire again. The Soviets are more cruel than the tsars. Thousands of people the Soviets killed in the famine. Thousands more they have executed. Many of all these were Poles. So it is right for me to go, to do what I can, to patch up the wounded and help the dying. Every army needs doctors. Be a good boy and look after your mother, Josef. I will be back as soon as the fighting is over. Don't forget to practise your violin every day. These things matter most of all when there is a war."

He saw his father and listened again to what he said as he sat at the colonel's desk. So he couldn't go on.

"Hebbel," the colonel said, "fetch a glass of water, would you?" Werner stood up and bent his head briefly. "Thank you."

While they heard Werner's steps cross the hall and then vanish into the carpeted passage, the colonel laid down his pen, took off his spectacles, and leaned forward over the desk.

"I'm sorry to put you through all this, old chap. We need to know as much as we can about the behaviour of the Nazis in the east."

Joe nodded his head, without raising his eyes from the worn green leather on the desktop, to show he was willing to answer more questions, or because there was more to describe than what the Nazis had done. He wasn't sure which. Maybe both.

After a couple of minutes, Werner came back with a glass of water. Joe didn't think he wanted it, but he drank some. It made him feel a good deal better. "Thank you, sir."

"All right to go on? Splendid. Now, what happened to your father as a medic in the Polish army?"

Expressionless, Werner translated.

"The Polish army was quickly defeated. My father, with very many others, was taken prisoner by the Red Army. They were sent to Russia. The ordinary soldiers were soon set free. Many came back to Vilna, so we knew; the officers were kept in prison in Russia."

"That's perfectly normal, you know, in war. Prisoners of war on farms, like Hebbel here, and Boblingen, are lucky. Plenty of prisoners are in camps still, all over the place."

"My father was in a prison called Kozelsk, with many other officers. We knew because letters came, one every month, and to some other families in Vilna too. My mother sent parcels to Kozelsk, and from a letter of my father's we knew that at least one parcel reached him. We had five letters, one every month from November to March. He said the prison was very cold and the prisoners had no winter clothes. My mother sent my father's fur hat and warm boots. We never heard that he got them. Five letters. Then on the thirteenth of April, NKVD soldiers came to our house and took my mother and sister away to a train. They also took the families of two other officers in prison in Russia. I have not seen my mother or my sister since then. I know they are dead."

"What makes you think that? If they were taken to Siberia, they may well still be there, alive and well. They may soon be allowed to come back to your country. You should be there, you know, in case they come back."

"They will not come back. Some letters came, quite soon, from other mothers. Nothing for me. My mother and my sister are dead. Like my grandmother and my uncle when he was a baby. They died on a Russian train in the first war."

"How did you manage not to be taken with your mother and your sister to the train? Let's see. April 1940. You were only eleven."

"I was ten. I was staying with my aunt Anna and my uncle the rabbi. Before my father went away, he said he wanted me to learn enough about being a Jew never to forget, no matter what happened to any of us in the future. We went to my uncle's house for Passover. And I loved my aunt, so I stayed longer. She helped me with my violin practice. My mother did not play and my teacher had gone, I don't know where. Also I loved my cousins, three boys, all younger than me, three naughty boys, clever and funny."

"And where are they now?"

"Dead. They are all dead. I told you—"

"This was the shooting, when the Germans came?"

"Yes."

"I am very sorry to be asking you to remember all these things. It must be extremely painful for you."

Now Joe looked straight across the desk at the colonel, meeting his eyes.

"No", he said in English. "I remember every day, everything, every day. It is good to say ... to speak ..."

He drank the rest of the water in the glass.

"You are a brave young man." The colonel looked down, and then again looked across at him.

"And your father. Did any more letters come from your father—after they took your mother and sister?"

"No. Because by then they had shot him."

"Who had shot him?"

"The NKVD. The Russians. They shot all the officers in the prison at Kozelsk."

Werner translated this and at once added, in a harsh voice, "This is not true. Excuse me, sir. What he has just said, it is not true. When the Nazis invaded Russia, all the detained Polish soldiers were permitted to join the army of General Anders to fight against the Nazis elsewhere."

In English Joe said, "No. What I have said I know. The prisoners at Kozelsk were shot at the same time as they took their families from Vilna—in the spring of 1940. The Russians shot them. We knew, in the forest. Much later. But we knew."

"It is not true", Werner said.

"Hebbel"—the colonel put both his hands flat on the desk and leaned forward towards Werner—"what do you mean, it's not true?"

"This is a Nazi lie."

"Wait a minute, the pair of you. Hebbel, is this by any chance what's called"—the colonel put on his spectacles and spent some time going through his papers until he found the right one—"the Katyn massacre?"

"Yes, sir. The Nazis killed the Polish officers and later pretended that the Russians had killed them, to discredit the Soviet system."

The colonel was reading the typewritten paper in his hand. He put it down on the desk.

"Hebbel, according to the information I have here—prepared for the trial I was telling you about, Joe—you seem to be right. But surely you would prefer ... after all, aren't you a Nazi yourself?"

"I am a German, sir. Hitler is dead. The Nazis have failed, totally failed. There are no more Nazis."

"But what has that to do with what happened to Polish prisoners in—what was the name of the prison, Joe?"

They were speaking English, and Joe was understanding all of it.

"Kozelsk, sir."

"Kozelsk. That's right. That's not Katyn, is it? Perhaps we aren't talking about the same thing. Can you explain, Hebbel? What do you think happened to these prisoners, and how do you know?"

"On the eastern front, everybody knew. The Wehrmacht found mass graves in the forest near Smolensk in the spring of 1943. They dug up bodies. The bodies were Polish officers in their uniforms with their papers. Germany was by now losing the war. To blacken the Soviet government in all of Europe, Goebbels announced to the world that the massacre was a Soviet crime—and not only that but a Jewish crime, another Jewish crime. But this was a lie; it was Nazi propaganda. No one believed it. This was Nazi murder, committed in 1941 when the German army was successful, invading Russia with great speed and much death. They came to prisons full of Polish officers and shot them. One of the prisons was Kozelsk."

"Why would they do that? I don't understand. These were Polish officers. Not Jews."

Joe said, "Some of them were Jews."

Neither the colonel nor Werner looked at him.

Werner said, "Hitler had been ruling most of Poland since 1939. Now he had conquered the rest and was conquering as much of Russia as he could. After the war he would want to rule a Poland in which no officer class would make trouble for him. The Poles were *Untermenschen*, Slavs, second-class people. They could not be officers in the greater Reich. So they had to die."

"That sounds like Hitler, doesn't it, Joe?"

Joe shook his head. He hadn't understood everything Werner had said, but he knew it was wrong.

"Then, later in the war," Werner went on, paying no attention to Joe, "it was useful to the Nazis, who were committing great crimes everywhere in the east, to pretend to the world that this one crime was a Soviet crime."

"I see", the colonel said. "Thank you, Hebbel, you've explained that very clearly." He scribbled a sentence on the piece of paper he had found, and shuffled all the papers together again. Then he turned to face Werner at the end of the desk.

"Tell me, Hebbel, what do you intend doing when you are allowed to go back to Germany?"

"I shall return home. My home is in the east of Germany. Near to Frankfurt on the Oder."

"I thought Frankfurt was further west."

"That is Frankfurt am Main, a different city."

"I'm sorry. Go on."

"I shall work to restore the freedom and the prosperity of my people."

"I think you'll find that the east of Germany will be under Russian control."

"Exactly so."

The colonel looked hard at Werner for a few seconds.

"Ah, yes, I see", he said, while Joe stared at Werner with a new understanding. "Well, in any case, thank you, Hebbel, for your help with this interview. I think we've got as far as we can today. You'd better go back to the farm now, both of you."

Werner stood up, clicked his heels with a little bow of his head, and left the study. Joe also stood up but leaned towards the colonel with both hands on the desk.

"Sir?" he said.

"What is it, Joe?"

"You will not send me to Lithuania?"

"Not my decision, I'm afraid. I'll do what I can, but we'll have to see."

"And sir—"

"Now, Joe, no more questions. Isn't it time for your tea?"

But he had prepared some sentences.

"I listened to Werner. I understood his words. It is not true. The Russians also did not want the officer class in Poland. So they shot the officers who were prisoners at Kozelsk. In Poland, everyone knows."

"Well, we may never be sure what happened—the fog of war, as I said before. But it sounds like the sort of thing the Nazis went in for. Now, run along, Joe, there's a good fellow. I've got other things to do."

Joe got up to go. At the door he turned and said, "Sir, one day I may be an English Jew, as you said?"

"I can't make any promises, Joe. Now, off you go."

That night, sitting on his bed, he looked up one word, "witness", in his English–Polish dictionary. When he found the word, he wondered what the colonel had meant by saying he was too young to be a witness. He had seen what he had seen. So had plenty of children younger than he. But they were dead.

As soon as he got into bed, he went to sleep.

He dreamed he was searching for mushrooms in the forest. The air was warm and damp. His head was bent down as he pushed branches and leaves and ferns aside, but there were no mushrooms. The ground was spongy under his feet. Then he stood up. The colonel, in his silk cravat, was facing him across a few yards of brushwood, his head bent sideways, one eye shut behind his spectacles as he aimed his shotgun at Joe. Werner Hebbel, in Einsatzkommando uniform, was standing beside the colonel with one finger raised, about to give the order to shoot.

Sally came home from her school in the south on the day the first snow fell.

He didn't see her arrive. Mr Ward, who fetched her from the station, drove to the front of the house as he always did. But Joe knew she was coming because Mrs Thwaites had saved eggs to make a chocolate cake for Sally's tea. "There'll be a slice or two left for us in the kitchen, don't you fret."

It was getting dark, and the snow outside was thickening when Mr Ward appeared at the kitchen door that led into the house.

"Ted here? I need some help with Miss Sally's school trunk."

"They're out foddering the beasts", Mrs Thwaites said. "Joe's done the horses. He'll give you a hand. Jump to it, Joe. And leave them boots in the kitchen—you can't go tramping upstairs in boots."

"I suppose he'll have to do, then", Mr Ward said.

So Joe, in his socks, took the other end of the heavy trunk, which had "S. L. Robertson 76" in white paint on the top, and he and the chauffeur carried it up the wide, red-carpeted stairs, along the red-carpeted passage, and into a white bedroom with long chintz curtains drawn over the windows and a fire crackling in the grate. A pretty girl in a dark blue tunic and a white shirt was kneeling by the fire unpacking a small suitcase. She looked up.

"Could you put it over there, by the window? Thanks awfully. Hello. Who are you?"

Joe opened his mouth, but Mr Ward answered.

"He's the stable lad, miss. DP from God knows where."

"You must be Joe. Daddy wrote to say how well you've been looking after Dawn. She's lovely, isn't she?"

"Yes. She is very good." A look from Mr Ward. "Miss."

"Bother the snow. I was hoping to ride tomorrow."

"Come along," said Mr Ward, "back to the kitchen with you, my lad."

Later he thought that the arrival on the same day of Sally and the quiet snow which reminded him of home, because not since home had he been warm in a house with the snow outside, was a gift from God.

Chapter 2

That winter he was baffled by the English weather, and by more than the weather.

Two days after the snow fell it had all melted away, so that a damp, muddy morning, still dark as midnight at half past seven, was pronounced by Ted to be "Just the ticket" for hunting.

"Eat up quick, Joe", he said at breakfast. "There'll be two horses to fettle up today. Miss Sally'll be happy as Larry to be out with her dad. Lucky the meet's not far. Gives us a bit more time."

That meant he would help with the plaiting.

"Good morning, Ted. Hallo, Joe. Doesn't Dawnie look beautiful—you must have been up for ages."

Sally, dressed in a black hunting coat, white breeches, and shiny black leather boots, with her hair in a net and wearing a severe bowler hat, seemed quite different from the girl he had seen kneeling by her bedroom fire unpacking a suitcase.

The mare was excited, sweating and prancing on the cobbles. He held her head and calmed her while Ted, with a gesture he had never seen before, cupped his hands for Sally's booted foot and swung her easily into the saddle. Joe wished he were older, and stronger, and knew the trick.

"Tighten that girth a bit, Joe. We don't want the saddle slipping round." Ted took the mare's head. Joe carefully rebuckled the leather straps exactly right, not too loose, not too tight for the mare.

Ten minutes later Ted and Joe watched as Sally and her father trotted side by side out of the stable yard.

"Isn't she a picture, Miss Sally on that little grey. She's a natural. I can see her now on her first pony, when she was two or three years old. Never frightened. Never fussed. When she came off she was back on again in no time. Showing the pony who's boss. Like you, Joe.

"Mind you," Ted went on as he put the kettle on the tack room fire, "you bother on for a good hour to get them off spick-and-span on a morning, and when it's a mucky day like this, before you can turn round they come back filthy dirty. Horses filthy, tack filthy, coats, breeches, boots all covered in mud—at least we don't have to do all that out here. Only the horses and the tack. And it was more work before the war. The colonel had a change of horses in them days. And so did Master James. The groom we had then was to ride out with the second horses, meet the hunt, and bring the first horses back. William, his name was. He was one of them that didn't get back from Dunkirk. He was good with horses, William was, no doubt about it, but I don't say he was better than you, Joe. You've got a knack for them, somehow, that he didn't have. Now, we'd better be on with this tea. There's work to do."

The next morning, as Joe was saddling up Tiger Rag for his usual ride—the young horse needed regular exercise or he became nearly unmanageable—Sally appeared at the stable door, in an old pair of jodphurs, a thick sweater, and a scarf over her hair tied under her chin like Mrs Thwaites', looking as pretty as she had by the fire in her bedroom.

"Are you taking Tiger out for a ride, Joe? Why don't Dawnie and I come with you? No, don't stop what you're doing. I'll get Dawnie's tack."

They walked the horses quietly through the paddocks behind the stable, Tiger Rag pulling and sidestepping, agitating for the canter Joe didn't allow him.

"You know," Sally said, "I like an ordinary ride better than hunting, really—all that standing about while you wait for something to happen, and when it does you're tearing over the country not knowing if you're going to be able to stop. Let's go through the woods and up to the moor, just a gentle ride." She looked at Joe and laughed. "Well done, getting him to walk properly. He's a terror, isn't he? I tried to ride him in the summer, but he kept bucking me off. Ted could manage him, but Daddy thought Ted was too old to risk falling off. That's why he found you to come."

He understood most of this.

"He is a good horse. Only he is young."

"How old are you, Joe?"

He thought of saying seventeen, even eighteen.

"Sixteen—miss."

"Oh, never mind the 'miss', Joe. We're practically the same age. I'll be sixteen in January."

They trotted up the long hill to the edge of the larch plantation. Joe leaned down and opened the gate.

"When did you leave school, Joe?"

School. The word was almost the same, in Polish, in German. He saw himself, when he was nine or ten, walking through the bitter cold winter city, not yet light, the frozen snow scuffed and stained, the narrow streets and courtyards, through which he knew all the shortcuts, full of the sounds of poor people getting up, mothers shouting at children, babies crying, dogs barking, the icy air cut with the warm smells of bread, smoke, coffee, paraffin, steam from dirty warm water that had washed a whole family poured into the gutter. All this he loved because it was home. He remembered a discussion between his parents about whether to move to a new, light house in a clean street nearer the country. His mother thought it would be good for him and his sister—healthier, with more fresh air. His father said he would never move out of old Jewish Vilna because he could afford to. These were his people. This was his place. "I like to see the Great Synagogue on my way to work." His aunt Anna and the rabbi and their boys lived two alleys and a courtyard away.

He would emerge from these crowded streets and meet his friend Stefan, also the son of a doctor, who walked with him through the last few streets to school, a Polish school, with only a few Jewish boys, but, his father said, a very good school. "You are lucky, Josef, to be able to begin a fine education in mathematics and Latin, so work hard and do well. You will need, whatever the future brings, a trained mind, and you have a mind worth training." But when Vilna was given to Lithuania by Stalin—Joe's father had already gone to fight the Russians—there were riots in his school. The older boys refused to have lessons in Lithuanian, which they didn't understand, instead of in Polish. So his mother told him he shouldn't go to school anymore. For a few months he went to the cheder, the Jewish school attended by the oldest of his little cousins. He learned some Hebrew there, but the other lessons were too easy for him to learn anything new. Then the Russians came and ordered the cheder to be closed down. The mothers of the small boys cried at the padlocked gate to the courtyard where the cheder had been for hundreds of years. After that his uncle the rabbi, until the Russians took him away, taught him mathematics and some more Hebrew in the evenings, and his aunt Anna helped him with his violin practice. At home with his mother he had read German stories and poems. Until—

"Joe?"

The horses were walking side by side on the forestry track through the larches, a soft carpet of russet needles on the ground. He realized he had not answered her question.

"I was ten years old."

"*Ten?* What happened? Were you ill?"

"No. I was not ill."

After a minute or two he said, "I am sorry."

"Sorry? Why? Don't be sorry."

He said nothing. Then he pulled up Tiger. When she realized she was leaving him behind, she looked round, turned the mare's head, walked her back towards him along the quiet path, and stopped. She looked at him.

"What is it, Joe? I think it's me who should be sorry. I've upset you, haven't I?"

"No. It is my fault. It is too difficult to explain. I have not the English."

She smiled at him and shook her head.

"Never mind. No more questions. Let's get up to the moor and give them a canter. They've been very good."

She turned her horse again and trotted ahead of him along the floor of larch needles until she reached the gate in the stone wall.

"I'll do this one."

When the gate was shut, she looked at Joe with her eyes bright and happy. "Stick to the grass. The heather's full of rabbit holes and ditches you can't see."

Off she went, Grey Dawn cantering on the moorland turf that had more or less covered an old road. Joe and Tiger followed her, Tiger pulling to overtake Dawn but restrained by Joe. A few sheep got clumsily to their feet and bounded away from the track with surprising speed. A rabbit disappeared with a flash of white tail. A little further away five grouse rose from the old black tangle of the moor and flew away, low over heather.

At the very top of the hill, at an ancient crossroads marked by a single standing stone with nothing on it but yellow lichen, Sally stopped, standing in her stirrups and laughing as Joe caught her up.

"That was awfully nice, wasn't it? So much better than hunting, just coming up here with no one to shout at you for being in the wrong place. Look."

She pointed down at a farm below them in the next dale, wider and deeper than the one behind them. A stone farmhouse, stone farm buildings, faded red pantiled roofs; cattle and two horses in its stone-walled fields; and sheep—all looking small, peaceful, a long way down.

"The smoke from the chimney—absolutely straight. There's no wind at all. No wind down there anyway. There's always a bit of a wind up here. Doesn't it smell delicious? I do miss it when I have to go to London or silly old school."

She took a deep breath and raised her face to the sky. "Wonderful", she said to the damp grey morning.

Joe, sitting still on Tiger, whose head was down cropping the turf, breathed in the faint taste of peat and spent heather that came on the flickers of wind, a smell he had noticed every time he had ridden up here alone, a different smell from any he had ever met before. It was new to him, fresh, strange, English, like Sally.

That night he washed himself particularly carefully in his tepid bath and thanked God for his day as he went to sleep. But he dreamed he was trying to get home from school. His street was full of people, crowding him, laughing at him, holding him back, pulling at his clothes, telling him not to go home, in Yiddish, in Polish. Then ahead of him were tall, heavy soldiers barring his way and shouting—in Russian or German, he couldn't tell which. He had to get back in time, he had to warn them at home, to save them. He was struggling through the crowd, hitting people who were in his way, shaking them off his arms, his back, but the soldiers were too tall, too close together. He couldn't push through them, between them—why was he so small?—and there were more and more of them, laughing instead of shouting. It was too late; he knew it was too late. He woke sobbing. Quietly, so that Fritz wouldn't hear.

He went to his window and opened it, to see if he could smell the moor wind. Just, he could. He sniffed. He breathed more deeply and listened, because the sounds of the night helped, because they were real and now: the rustle of the beck, louder than usual after the snow; once, in the damp, ticking silence, the squawk of an unsettled pheasant quite near; further away the high, thin scream of a small animal, perhaps a rabbit, caught by a fox or in a snare; the shaking cry of an owl in the distant woods, repeated twice, after a while a fourth time.

When he had first opened the window, he could see nothing in the black darkness. Now he realized that he could see, dimly, the paddocks, the stone walls, the line of the moor against the sky. There must have been a full or nearly full moon above the clouds, giving a grey, even light to everything. He remembered nights like this in the forest—moonlight from an invisible moon, fear because if you could see, then you could be seen. He breathed deeply again—the faint scent of the moor wind instead of the marsh smell of the forest, growing and rotting vegetation, reeds and moss and grasses and whole rotting trees, always the smell of growth and decay except in the frozen winter. But here in the night he was safe. He listened to the clean water of the beck rattling over stones.

He thought to himself, Sally loves this place because it is her home. Although it is not my home, I love it also.

When he got back into bed and lay down, the shouting and laughing of his dream came back at once. He sat up, lit his candle, and tried to learn some new phrases in his little green dictionary. He didn't fall asleep again for a long time.

Two days later, on the morning of Christmas Eve, the weather was sunny, clear, colder. Mrs Thwaites had gone to the market with Bill and the milk churns when Ted came from the big house, in his socks, into the kitchen, where Joe and the Germans were having their ten o'clock mugs of tea.

"Now then, lads. We've extra to do today on account of it's Christmas tomorrow. There's a pile of logs at back o' t' cow byre that want splitting for the house. And we've to fetch a spruce from the plantation yon side of the larch. Pick one out—twelve foot the colonel says he wants for the hall, and a nice even shape—cut it down tidy like, and fetch it back here on t' wagon when Bill's home from market."

Fritz's face lit with a broad grin.

Joe said, "What is a spruce?"

"It's only a fir tree, Joe", Ted said. "For a Christmas tree. We bring it inside, and they put candles and that on. Lovely, it looks, when it's done. They don't have Christmas trees where you come from, maybe. We never had one all through the war—the colonel thought it wasn't right to do Christmas to much of a tune, what with our soldiers fighting and the bombs killing people. So this'll be the first tree in six years." He looked round the table. "Who wants to help me get it in?"

"I will split the logs", said Werner, scraping back his chair from the table and grabbing his coat from the peg as he went out to the yard.

"What's the matter with him?" Ted said. "Got out of bed on the wrong side, has he? Well, he's welcome to the logs. So, Fritz, you, me, and Joe can go for the tree. Fetch the big saw, there's a good lad. We'll have it down while dinnertime if we look sharp."

Not long after three o'clock that afternoon, the blazing winter sun with no heat in it had set behind the moor at their backs as they brought the tree they had felled in the morning down to the house. There was a mysterious golden quality in the eastern sky beyond and above the farm, all the way to the distant high skyline; the sun had disappeared, but from somewhere that they could not see, it was still shining into the air, thickening it with a kind of density that looked as if you could touch it, though it must have been only light.

As the wagon bumped down the slope towards the paddocks, Joe realized they would be taking it to the front of the house so that they could carry the tree into the hall. Would Sally be there? To admire the tree? To help?

Ted was driving Robin; Joe and Fritz were walking beside the cart, one on each side of the tree. It was beginning to freeze, but Joe—his arms across his chest, his hands, in a pair of woollen mittens Mrs Thwaites had knitted for him, gripping his shoulders—was warm, remembering the day-before-yesterday's ride, watching the fade of the strange glamour in the eastern sky.

As they rounded the end of the house, Fritz began to sing:

"O Tannenbaum, O Tannenbaum,
wie treu sind deine Blätter—"

"That's enough, Fritz", Ted said quietly but, for him, fiercely. "They don't want to be hearing German songs, do they? First Christmas after the war. They lost their boy only last year, remember."

"I am sorry, Ted."

Joe remembered his mother singing this song at picnics by lakes in the summer. "Wie treu sind deine Blätter"—how could leaves be true? Because they were always green? They were needles anyway, not leaves.

"Right. Here we are. Now, you lads get the tree down from the wagon. Carefully, mind. We don't want to be spoiling the look of it, breaking branches. When you're ready I'll open the doors. There's double doors, and the inside ones is glass, so watch out. We've not to let more cold air in than we're forced to, or we'll hear about it from madam."

In the hall a fire was blazing, a great basket of newly sawn and split logs beside it. The colonel was waiting for the men, standing with his back to the fire, his hands behind his back.

"Splendid, splendid. That's a very fine tree you've got there. Well done, Ted. Now see if you boys can get it upright and steady. Into that barrel, that's right. Careful now. We need a few more stones. Or logs would do. That's it, Joe. Just a couple to wedge the trunk. Thank you, all. Mrs Robertson will be delighted. Just one more thing, Ted. We'll need the big double-sided ladder, for decorating the tree, you know. Perhaps you could get Boblingen here and Joe to bring it? After tea would do."

"Very good, sir."

There was no sign of Sally.

But a couple of hours later, when he and Fritz had carried the ladder—a heavy, awkward thing twice as wide as an ordinary ladder and about ten feet long—from the back of the garage and round the outside of the house to the double doors, there she was.

"Oh, good. Thanks awfully for carrying it round. I know it's a monster, but you can't reach the top of the tree without it. Before the war I was too little to climb up. I always wanted to, and now I can."

She was wearing a red skirt and a white jersey. She looked wonderful, like the girls Joe and his friends used to watch skating happily in white boots on winter afternoons in Vilna. He and his friends mostly sat on a bench by the frozen lake and watched because they had only a couple of pairs of skates, with old black boots, between five or six boys. Not paying attention as he and Fritz set up the ladder close to the tree, Joe pinched the fingers of one hand quite badly. No one noticed. He squeezed his hurt hand with the other one but didn't look at it. There would be bruises. For her.

He and Fritz were going, not through the house to the kitchen but back outside, when Sally said, "Joe, would you like to stay and help with the tree? There's a lot to do, and it's rather fun."

A woman's voice from the top of the stairs: "I don't think that's a good idea, darling. I'm sure he's got work to do. Ward will help you."

Joe looked up, and then quickly down again. Mrs Robertson. He hadn't seen her before. He hadn't seen anyone like her ever: a smart, thin woman, with lipstick and arranged hair and a haughty look. He had an idea that some of the Polish boys at his school had mothers who looked a bit like this. He wasn't sure; tutors and governesses had usually fetched those boys from school.

"But Mummy, it's dark. He'll have done the horses by now. Haven't you, Joe?"

Joe nodded, and stood, looking at Sally. But only for a moment.

"Oh, let the boy help if Sally wants him to." This was the colonel, emerging from his study. "But shut those doors, or we'll all freeze to death. Thank you, Boblingen."

With a grin at Joe, Fritz disappeared into the night.

"Well, tell him to take those boots off, at least."

Mrs Robertson did not come down. A minute or two later a door was firmly shut somewhere upstairs.

Joe took off his boots and left them between the inner and the outer doors.

"We'll start with the candles. They're the most important thing. Look, in this box. I hope they'll still work. They must be awfully old. Oh good, here's some that've never been opened. They should light all right."

Sally had opened a cardboard box that had "Christmas Tree Candles" written in chalk on the lid. There were several packets of small twisted candles inside, and a jumble of brass gadgets, each with a clip. "You put a candle in each of these little holders. You see, like this. That's it. I'll go up the ladder, and you give them to me and I'll fix them to the tree. The trick is to get them upright, or they'll set fire to the tree. The whole thing used to frighten Nanny to death. She used to stand guard with a mop and a bucket in case the house burned down. Poor Nanny."

Joe understood almost none of this. But he could see what she wanted him to do.

It wasn't difficult. He twisted five candles into holders and climbed three or four steps of the ladder to give them to Sally, who was at the top carefully placing them on the needled branches of the tree. He put his candles in her left hand with his left hand; the fingers of his right hand, holding the ladder, were beginning to redden and swell, and he didn't want her to see the marks. He didn't want her to notice how much the casual touching of their hands over the candles meant to him; he could tell it meant nothing at all to her. Twice they had to move the ladder so that she could put candles on all sides of the top part of the tree— "Goodness, it weighs a ton, this ladder"—and then they put the ladder out of the way, Joe taking the heavy end, laying it on its side against the double doors, so that both of them could clip candles here and there to the spreading bottom branches. There was no reason now to touch her hand, and they couldn't even see each other for the dark green depths of the tree. He breathed in the resinous spicy scent of the pine needles. In the forest it had been a good scent. His best nights for sleep, when they had no proper shelter, had been on a bed of fresh-cut pine branches, soft if your coat was thick enough, long enough, caked with enough mud for the needles not to prick you. Better if you had some kind of mat or rug, or an old coat someone had taken off a corpse in the forest, on top of your own coat. Then you could even be warm, breathing in the resinous scent that no human or animal had spoiled.

"Look out", Sally said. "The candles have to be at the very edge, or they'll set light to the branch above them." She had been watching behind him as he clipped on the last few candles, and now she came forward, reached up to his shoulders—he was only a little taller—and moved him gently to one side so that she could reposition some of his candles at the tips of the spruce branches.

"That's perfect. You wait till you see it lit up tomorrow. Now we've just got the tinsel to do."

She opened another cardboard box. "I wonder if it's all got tarnished and horrid. No, it hasn't—look. Black tissue paper—Nanny again. The tinsel's as good as ever after years and years of the rotten war." She was taking out of the soft black tissue line after line of magical stuff, long silver threads with masses and masses of silver needles, glittering, supple silver copies of the fingers of the fir tree.

"There should be a star in here somewhere, to go on the top. Can you see it?"

He picked up one piece of the strange stuff. Very quietly it rustled out of its black wrapping and sparkled in his hand as he held it. It was so light that it was like holding nothing.

"What is it?"

She laughed. "It's called tinsel. It's meant to look like snow, snow glittering in the frost like it does. You put it on the branches of the tree. I suppose you've never seen all this before. You're Jewish, aren't you?"

He looked at her across the box of tinsel. Her eyes were friendly, interested. "Yes. I am a Jew." He didn't try to explain that he had seen Christmas trees in Vilna, specially a fine tall one outside the Lutheran church.

"Never mind. I don't think Christmas trees are very religious anyway. They just look pretty and cheer us up, specially this year. And after all, you're here, and not somewhere—well—somewhere with no horses to look after."

He shook his head to get rid of possible tears.

"Yes. Of course. Thank you."

She looked at him again, and smiled.

"Come on. Cheer up. Let's do the tinsel. Here's the star. Good. We'll have to put that brute of a ladder up again."

They had almost finished the tree when the colonel appeared from his study.

"Well, I must say, between the pair of you, you've made a very good job of that tree. I think perhaps Joe had better get back to the kitchen before your mother comes down. I'll give you a hand with the ladder, Joe. We'll just put it outside for now. You and Boblingen can take it back to the garage in the morning."

A little later in the kitchen, over their macaroni cheese and cabbage, Ted said, "Well, Miss Sally's taken a shine to Joe. And why not? Poor little lass needs a bit of company, without her brothers over Christmas."

"That's enough of that, Ted", Mrs Thwaites said, sharply for her. "Miss Sally needed some help with decorating the tree. She couldn't have done a tree that size all by herself, could she? But Mrs Robertson won't have liked it, so the less said about it the better."

But when they had finished supper she said, kindly as ever, "You've had a long day, Joe. You must be tired out. Just clear the table and do the dishes for me, there's a good boy. Fritz can dry up for you, can't you, Fritz? I've got the bird to stuff for tomorrow."

When Joe got back that night to his room, he sat on his bed, his two hands, one painful from the ladder, spread each side of him on his eider-down, and thought. There were things to worry about. The colonel had said nothing serious to him since the interview in his study, but the tone of his voice was always kind. Surely this powerful man—but how powerful was he? Impossible to guess—wouldn't have him sent back, to those burned-out villages, those freezing fields where every last rotten potato among the weeds had been found and eaten by someone else, to Vilna, where there was no longer a single Jew. Would he? It seemed as if Mrs Robertson wished he would.

He sat still. He understood that he should be worrying. But he wasn't. He felt happier than he had felt since before—before his father in his uniform had left to look after Polish soldiers, before his mother and his sister had been taken away by the Russians, before the Germans came. It was so long ago that he could remember only bits and pieces of a life that had been not frightening, that had been warm, and full of music and books and good food and his father and mother and his watchful little sister, every day.

Blessed be God.

On Christmas morning Joe and Werner Hebbel, with detailed instructions from Mrs Thwaites, were left in charge of the dinner. Ted and Bill and Fritz had set off, with Ted driving the wagon, for chapel. Fritz had on a jacket Joe hadn't seen before, with a prisoner-of-war patch on the front and another on the back, like the yellow stars of David the Germans had ordered all the Jews in Vilna to fix to their clothes, so that they could be pushed off pavements, out of shops, and into the gutters and be spat at. Fritz, who knew about none of this, Joe was now sure, was unbothered by his patches. "At home I am a Catholic," was all he had said at breakfast, "but it is kind of Ted to take me to his church for Christmas."

Mrs Thwaites, in her Sunday hat and coat, had gone, for once, to the parish church. "Mrs Robertson always likes me to go in the car with the family on Christmas Day. You two lads can be perfectly sensible when you put your minds to it, clever boys, the pair of you. If you do just what I tell you, the dinner'll cook itself—I've done all the work ahead. I'll do them sprouts myself when I get back."

She made Werner responsible for the goose, an enormous bird stuffed with the peculiar mixture she had prepared after supper the night before. It had looked magical to Joe because, that evening, everything did. The goose had been in the oven since breakfast, and Werner and Joe every so often were to pour the fat into a bowl while not letting the goose slip out of its tin. This was a two-man operation, which they did very carefully. Meanwhile, Joe was to keep an eye on the potatoes, roasting in fat from the goose in another oven—Mrs Thwaites' stove, stoked with precious coke every morning and evening by Ted from a rattling black hod, had four ovens—and also on the pudding. He hadn't seen this pudding, in a big basin wrapped in a cloth and steaming in a wide pan with a lid. His job was to make sure there was enough water in the pan. This was easy, and the goose and the potatoes smelled wonderful every time they opened an oven door.

The potato peelings went to the pigs in Werner's pail of scraps. Joe thought of his friends in the forest, where no piece of peel had ever not been eaten by a man, a woman, or a child, because there was never enough food. He thought of the thin mothers who gave everything eatable they could find to their children. Where were they now? Could they be about to eat delicious food, somehow, somewhere, as he was? He hoped, prayed, that they were. Had some of them been as lucky as he had been?

He was enjoying all this work in the kitchen, and he thought Werner was too until he said, in his cold German, "You should take care", as he shut the oven door on the sizzling, browning goose.

"What do you mean?" Joe answered, without thinking, in German.

"You get too close to them, you are too useful to them, and they will keep you here. Unpaid labour, which suits them very well."

Joe took the heavy kettle from the hob and poured a little more water into the pan where the pudding was steaming.

"I am safe here. I hope I am safe here. For a long time I have not been safe."

"Safe like the peasants on the old estates in Prussia, in Pomerania, where my family came from. You work, and they enjoy themselves. They spend the money that you have earned. They hunt and shoot, and you brush the mud off the horses and beat the trees to make the boar run or the pheasants fly. This is not safety. This is injustice. It is over, finished. There will be a new, a better, world. But not in England for a long time. They have won the war, these colonels and their proud wives, and so the people will not rise up against them in this generation. The people will be afraid of destruction. But destruction must come."

67

Werner was now sitting at the kitchen table in his usual place, serious and frightening, looking straight at Joe, as he almost never did. Joe wanted to go, to cross the yard, check the horses, go up to his room, touch his eiderdown. But he knew this would be cowardly, and in any case, he couldn't leave the potatoes and the pudding. He wasn't going to let Mrs Thwaites down because he disliked being alone with this German soldier. So he sat, in his own place, opposite Werner.

"Hasn't there been enough destruction for you, everywhere?"

"There is not enough destruction until the revolution is complete. Stalin knows that."

"Stalin is more cruel than the tsars."

"Cruel? What is cruel? What must be, must be. We do not decide. It is history that decides."

"Did history decide to murder the Jews in Vilna? In all of Poland? The peasants and the Jews in Belorussia? Was it history that made them kill each other after they had lived in the same villages for hundreds of years? Wasn't it Hitler who made all that happen?"

"Of course. But history was flowing then for the Nazis. Now it is not."

"So you think history is on the side of whoever wins. Does that make whoever wins right or good? Because history is good? I don't think so. Some things happen because bad, powerful men decide they will happen, and persuade millions of others that bad is good. There was a terrible famine in Russia when I was very young. In Vilna people talked about it because it was more terrible than the Great War had been. Thousands and thousands of people, whole villages, died because Stalin took all their corn away. Perhaps in Germany you never heard about it."

"I heard about it. Propaganda spread by enemies of the revolution."

"But ..." He realized he couldn't answer this. It was possible that Werner was right. He remembered his father talking about the famine, years afterwards. His father was sure it had happened. But how did he know? How does anyone know what he has not seen for himself?

For some reason he remembered the woman who had hidden him in her hayloft.

"But some things happen by chance, by luck, or because someone is kind to someone else. That has nothing to do with history or armies."

Werner looked across the table at Joe and smiled, but his eyes were cold. His eyes were always cold.

"You mean that you are alive instead of dead?"

"Yes. Why not? It is an example only. I was meant to be dead. The Russians meant me to be dead because my father was a Polish officer. The Nazis meant me to be dead because I am a Jew. So, according to you, history meant me to be dead."

"That is probably so. But a few Jews should be left. Always a few Jews have been left. For their intelligence, which is useful to the future."

Joe's eyes and throat filled with tears for his aunt and his three little cousins, dead in the pits at Ponary. And tears for his uncle, the quiet rabbi, taken away and killed by the NKVD. He swallowed his tears, sniffed, and said, "I would rather have died too than be useful to Stalin if he is the future."

"There is much you do not understand."

"My father told me", Joe said, "that the Russians don't like it that Marx was a German Jew, so they say Lenin invented Communism. He also told me that the cleverest of the Bolsheviks at the beginning were Jews, though they changed their names because Russians hate Jews. Later Stalin killed them anyway."

"Intellectuals are unreliable, unstable. They have their own ideas. They become spies and saboteurs. Stalin killed only enemies of the revolution, enemies of the people. He knew what he was doing, as you can see. He has won the war. And the Nazis were the means of enough destruction for the revolution to be victorious, in time and especially in Germany, where all that was old is broken and gone. The Nazis called themselves socialist, but truly socialist they were not. They depended altogether on the big banks and the big industrialists, on I. G. Farben and Krupp and the Ruhr. And the big landowners liked them because the Nazis were never going to take away land from people who supported them. 'Blood and soil'; the Junkers loved it all. Now everything will change. Real socialism will come. There will be no more ownership. Ownership of land means ownership of people. Ownership of factories, mines, railways, shipyards means ownership of people. Do you understand that? Peasants slaving on the land, workers slaving in the factories—slaves, the lot of them. Once Germany has achieved revolution—as it failed to do for Napoleon, as it failed to do in 1848, as it failed to do after the Great War, as it will not fail to do now—everything will belong to the people. The class war will be won. Things will be better than they have ever been before."

Joe was watching Werner as he talked. He was looking past Joe, at nothing, perhaps at the future. Perhaps at the past?

"What does your father do?" Joe said.

Werner looked at him with narrowed eyes. After a silence, in which Joe dropped his glance to a dark knot in the scrubbed wood of the kitchen table, Werner said, "You are not a stupid boy." He lit a cigarette, and went on, a little less coldly, as if he thought Joe deserved an explanation.

"That is exactly the point. My father worked in a factory in Frankfurt on the Oder. The factory made machinery parts for other factories, which made lorries. The workers were badly paid. There were many accidents. People lost fingers, even arms. When the war came the machines in the factory were changed to make parts for factories that made tanks. The changes were made too fast. There was a small explosion in the factory and my father and two others were killed."

"I am sorry."

"Why be sorry? They died for the war, for the Führer, as if they had been soldiers. My father was a good Nazi. So was I of course. But all the time the man who owned the factory became richer and richer and never got his hands dirty, was never in danger. All through the war his son worked in an office in Berlin. In a uniform, yes, no doubt, in a clean white shirt every day, ironed by some servant girl he was probably sleeping with. But never getting his hands dirty, never in danger. My grandparents grew potatoes and looked after pigs in Pomerania. They were very poor. The Junker family that owned the land was very rich. My grandparents never saw them. They lived in a grand house, much grander than this"—he nodded his head disdainfully backwards towards the door into the house—"but most of the time they were in Berlin, as these Robertsons live in London. The same slavery of the proletariat, on the land, in the factories—don't you understand? And now, an end. The war has wiped the slate clean. We start again. Better."

"Why—"

He was going to say, "Why will things be better when they have been so much worse for everyone since the war began?" But this seemed a useless question. He needed to think. He wished he had learned to think properly, like his father. He wished he had been to school, all those years. He got up, took the thick oven cloth, and pulled the huge tin full of delicious-looking potatoes out of the oven, putting it carefully on the top of the stove. He turned each potato over with the big slotted spoon Mrs Thwaites had told him to use. This took several minutes. Then he put the potatoes back in the oven, shut the oven door, took the lid off the pan in which the pudding was steaming, and added a little more water. He sat down again.

"So?" Werner said.

"I am sixteen years old. When I was nearly ten, my father went to join the Polish army. You know this because I told the colonel when you were translating. My father said he was a reserve officer in the Polish army not because the Poles loved the Jews but because the Poles had always let the Jews live, and Poland was in danger—in danger from the Russians, who would kill Jews when they could, and from the Germans, who didn't want any Jew to live."

"It is not a Soviet policy to kill Jews."

"Perhaps not. Perhaps it was never tsarist policy. But you have not lived in Poland. No Jew of the Pale—I am a Jew of the Pale though my father was a doctor trained in Breslau and my mother was a German nurse—can ever forget the yells of the Cossacks on their little horses racketing through the shtetls, reins in one hand, a bunch of flaming torches in the other, throwing the torches one by one at the huts, setting fire to the thatch, smoking us out. The sound of them yelling, galloping, on the road, on the ice. I can't forget it though I never heard it."

Werner looked at him without any warmth in his eyes, waiting for him to finish.

"I'm sorry. After my father had gone, I saw the Russians come to Vilna. They took away my mother and my sister. Then I saw the Germans come. I did not see the Russians last year come again to Vilna because I have not been in Vilna since I ran from the killing pits into the forest more than four years ago. But in the forest we heard a great deal. People who had escaped from the ghettos came, not many. Peasants came from villages that had been destroyed, sometimes children. Russians came, trying to escape the Wehrmacht or the Red Army or the Polish Home Army or the partisans who obeyed Stalin. A Russian soldier came who had been taken prisoner by the Germans. Two Russian deserters came. They were trying to get home because they lived near Minsk; that was when the Germans had gone far into Russia, and these soldiers left themselves behind. All of these people were lucky to find us in the forest. Germans would have shot them. Russians would have shot them of course. They told us much." He stopped.

"Who was with you in the forest? Who fed you?"

Joe was suddenly afraid. Had he said too much already? Had he put anyone in danger? Had he given names? Dates? No. But he must be careful.

"People who had nowhere else to go. The forest is very big."

Silence between them, for a minute or two.

"So you had a bad time in the war", Werner said. "So did I. So did everyone who was not able to stay out of the cold and avoid the fear and the death. And?"

Joe, looking at the table, thought some more.

"I would like to say that I know—I know, I am sure, that what you say about history, first making the Germans win and then making the Russians win so that now the Russians are good—it is not true. The Russians and the Germans are the same. Not exactly the same, but one is not better than the other. There are some good Russians, one by one. Of course there are some good Germans also. Fritz is good. But good people are afraid in Germany, afraid in Russia, often too afraid to be good. The Russian prisoner who had escaped from the Germans became my friend. He was before the war a village blacksmith. He had not been to school. But he was clever—perhaps because he was a Jew?" He looked up.

A faint smile from Werner, his eyes unchanged.

"My friend knew nothing about being a Jew."

"Of course. That is one of the great achievements of the revolution. Soon all the people will know nothing about being a Christian."

"Will that be good?"

"Of course. Christianity is finished. In this Hitler was correct, as Stalin is correct. All religion is finished. For centuries the capitalists, the nobility, the bourgeoisie, used religion to keep the people down. The rich, the powerful, made people believe those fairy stories of heaven and hell so that the rich and powerful would be obeyed. People wanted to go to heaven and were terrified of going to hell, so they obeyed their masters."

Werner leaned towards Joe, and said, "So. What did your Russian blacksmith tell you?"

"He told me that in his village you only had to say to the official who came that someone was a kulak—'He has three cows. He is a kulak'—and he would be shot or taken away and never seen again. And you could accuse someone for no other reason than that he was your old enemy in the village. My friend told me that in the Russian army every group of soldiers has a special official in a special uniform who is there to make sure that all the soldiers love Stalin and love the revolution. So if you don't like one of your comrades, you report to the official that he has made a joke about Stalin or has said that the revolution has done some terrible things, and again he will be shot or taken away."

"The Gestapo also asked for reports about Germans who made jokes about the Führer or said that Germany would lose the war. But Germany did lose the war, and the Gestapo has vanished. Ask in Germany now, and you will find no one who will admit to working in the Gestapo. There were hundreds of thousands of Nazis. Not all are dead. That is what defeat means. People are proud to belong only to the winning side. You wait and see."

Werner stood up, put both hands on the kitchen table, and leaned forward towards Joe as if he were addressing a crowd.

"All these things are necessary", he said, "for the inevitable to be achieved. Most people cannot think for themselves. Those who are capable of understanding the logic of history must ensure that others obey. It is necessary for great movements of ideas, of nations and classes, for those in power and their account of what is being achieved to be clear, to be consistent, to be supported by everyone. It is necessary for enemies of the people, for counter-revolutionaries and agents of imperialism, for those who are in the wrong place at the wrong time, to be eliminated."

Joe stood up too, and gripped the table. "No. There's something that doesn't ... I don't believe—"

The door from the house opened—both of them turned towards it—and Mrs Thwaites, taking off her coat as she came in and shutting the door behind her with her large backside, said:

"Now then. How have you two lads fared with my dinner? Hang up my coat in the back for now, Joe. That's right. And my hat"—pulling out the long pin—"here you are. Oh my goodness gracious"—a glance at the kitchen clock—"it's later than I thought. Let's be having those sprouts on at least." With two hands she brought a massive pan from the larder and put it on the hob. "My pudding's steaming nicely, that's one good thing. Well done, Joe. How've you managed with the potatoes?"

73

She pulled out the potatoes, then the goose. "Lovely, they look. You've done a good job, the pair of you, I will say that. You wait till you taste that goose once they've finished with it in the dining room and the servants' hall. There won't be that much left, so we'll be having a bit of boiled bacon with it."

Joe caught a quick look from Werner. You see? it said.

Joe knew there was something important that he had been about to say to Werner, something that Werner wouldn't have been able to knock aside, something that meant he didn't need to be afraid of Werner, today or tomorrow or ever. But now there wasn't time to think exactly what it would have been. He promised himself not to forget to sort it out properly later, even perhaps to write it down. Not because it would make any impression on Werner but because it was important. For him, for himself.

But the rest of the day was not for thinking.

At half past four, after a dinner every bit as good as Mrs Thwaites had promised, and a great deal of washing up which Ted and Joe did together, all of them except Bill, who was doing the milking, were sent off to their rooms to put on the most presentable clothes they had.

"We're to be in the hall at five o'clock, the colonel says. So look out whatever you've got in the way of Sunday best. It'll be like before the war, won't it, Ted? I never thought they'd be asking us into the house this year, with poor Master Philip gone and Master James not home yet. But the colonel said in the car this morning we were to come, and the POWs and Joe, so there you are. It's just as well I kept all last month's lard for the mince pies."

Werner said in German to Joe, "You are to put on your best clothes, and we are to go into the house at five o'clock."

Mrs Thwaites picked up the disdain in his voice.

"Don't you dare make that face, young Werner. It's very kind of the family to ask us in on Christmas Day. Think yourself lucky you're not in a camp, my lad, like most of the prisoners are."

Werner bowed his head briefly, as if Mrs Thwaites were his superior officer.

"You can wear your new shirt, Joe. Very smart, you'll look." She had given him for Christmas a checked flannel shirt that fitted him. "You're a lucky fellow, Joe", Ted had said. "She saved up her coupons for that shirt."

74

At five they trooped along the passage into the hall, Mrs Thwaites carrying a large dish of hot mince pies. Joe was last, in his clean trousers, his new shirt, the jersey he had worn to see the colonel, and, having left his boots in the kitchen, his socks. The hall was quite dark, but he had an impression that there were a lot of people there, a lot of people who stopped talking at the sight of them all appearing from the kitchen. Faces he could scarcely see turned towards them. Above all, over all, casting everything else into shadow, was the tree, tall and beautiful and black, with all its candles bright and flickering, up to the very top where the silvery star glittered. There was no other light but the sparking glow of the logs on the fire. He stood still to look at the tree, to be proud that he had helped. Piled under the tree were parcels of different shapes and sizes, wrapped in red paper, tied with ribbon. Kneeling with her back to Joe, looking at the little labels on the parcels, was Sally in a dark velvet dress that caught the candlelight here and there as she moved, stretched forward, picked up a parcel, read something on it, and put it down again.

"Well, here you all are." The colonel's voice. Joe saw him standing with his back to the fire. "Splendid. Splendid. And Mrs Thwaites' mince pies. Excellent. I don't know how you do it, Mrs Thwaites, with the rationing, but you always were a miracle worker. Let's have the port now, Ward, and we can all drink a Christmas toast."

Mr Ward in a neat black jacket moved through the guests carrying a tray of tiny glasses filled with what looked like dark red wine. He reached Joe last and, Joe could tell, reluctantly. There were two glasses left. Joe shook his head. But Ted, beside him, said, "Come on, lad. It won't bite you. It's only Christmas once a year." So he took a glass and watched Ted to see when he should drink the wine.

"Everyone got a glass? Splendid. Now, before Sally distributes our little gifts, I should like to say one thing. There are a number of different reasons why we all happen to be here for the first Christmas since the end of the war. We needn't go into that. But I should like you all to know that we appreciate the contribution you have made, the work you have done—some of you over many years, some of you in the last few months—and that you are all welcome here this Christmas. And I should like to give everyone, those in their home, those near to home, and those very far from home, the same toast: to peace, and safe journeys home!"

From the shadows round the tree and near the fire, they all raised their glasses and murmured in a blur of voices, "To peace and safe journeys home!" Then they drank. So did Joe. The wine was strong, sweet, warming. So was the mince pie he took from the dish Mrs Thwaites had put Fritz in charge of offering to the guests.

People, accepting mince pies, accepting more port from Mr Ward circulating with a decanter, had started talking again. Sally, her arms full of parcels, was checking the labels and distributing the presents one by one, then going back to the tree for more. Two or three people kissed her as she gave them their presents. Joe watched. When there were only three parcels left under the tree, Sally picked them up, looked round, and came over to where Joe and Ted were standing at the very back of the hall, where the passage to the kitchen began.

"This is for you, Ted", she said. Her long-sleeved dress was made of dark blue velvet, with a white lace collar. Her hands holding the parcels, and her neck bent as she peered at the labels, were as white and delicate as the lace. Joe longed to touch the velvet of her sleeve. "And could you take this for Bill?"

"Thank you, miss. And a merry Christmas to you."

Then she turned towards Joe and smiled into his eyes. "And this very last one is yours, Joe. Daddy thought you should have something useful, but I thought perhaps when you go home you would like—anyway, you'll see. And I found something for you which isn't any good to me."

Joe's throat was constricted. Very quietly he said, "Thank you."

She smiled again and turned back towards the tree and the other people.

Joe stood looking down at his odd-shaped parcel, holding it in both hands.

"Hold these a minute for me, Joe, will you?" Ted put his and Bill's presents, both heavy wrapped bottles, into Joe's arms on top of his own parcel. Joe heard and felt a faint crack and looked down, but neither bottle was broken. He saw Ted edge his way politely through the guests as far as the colonel, who was still standing with his back to the fire, and say something Joe couldn't hear. They shook hands, the colonel with his left hand on Ted's shoulder, and then Ted came back, took the two wrapped bottles from Joe, and said to Mrs Thwaites, who was halfway through one of the last mince pies, "Time for us to make ourselves scarce, I reckon."

Then Sally appeared in front of Joe. For a moment she rested her hand on his arm. "There's someone who wants to meet you, Joe. Don't be frightened—it's only the vicar."

Behind him Ted and Mrs Thwaites and Fritz and Werner—where had he been in the hall?—were going back to the kitchen. Awkwardly holding his parcel, Joe followed Sally to near the tree, where a white-haired man turned towards them when Sally touched his arm too.

"This is Joe", Sally said.

"How do you do, Joe?" To shake hands Joe had to hold his present in only his left hand and was afraid of dropping it. He hoped the bruised fingers of his right hand weren't noticeable when he shook hands.

"Sir", he managed to say. "I am well, thank you."

The old man looked at him attentively, kindly.

"I hear you lost your parents in the war. I am so sorry."

Joe felt tears rising. No one had spoken to him like this, in England, in Czechoslovakia, in Poland, in Belorussia.

"You are a brave boy. Your father and mother would be proud of you. You have a long life ahead of you, and a good life, I have no doubt. God bless you, Joe."

Joe nodded. "Thank you", he whispered, and turned to walk back to the kitchen. As he left the hall he heard among the people in the shadows behind him a woman's voice say, "I wouldn't have thought it necessary to give the Jew-boy a Christmas present, would you, Mr Ward?"

He knew the voice, didn't understand all the words, realized the question was about him, caught the insult and the contemptuous tone. Miss March, Mrs Robertson's maid. He had seen her two or three times, but she had never spoken to him. He didn't turn his head and didn't hear Mr Ward's answer.

In the kitchen Ted said, "Right you are, lads. Leave them presents on the table and get outside with you. Beasts still want foddering, Christmas Day or no Christmas Day."

Werner and Fritz and Joe put on their boots and thick jackets. In the yard, in the darkness, there was a thin, cold drizzle falling. A small half-circle of rain was lit by the lamp at the back door.

"That was so good of them, the party and the presents", Fritz said in German.

Werner spat on the cobbles.

They separated to feed the animals.

When at last Joe was alone in his room with his candle beside his bed, he undid the ribbon of his parcel, with some difficulty because his pinched fingers were swollen. Two presents. One was wrapped in newspaper: a pair of shoes, plain black shoes with laces, not new but not much worn. The laces were new, black, plaited stuff with hard shiny ends threaded through the holes. He turned the shoes over. Smooth, unmarked leather soles, new, with the bright heads of little nails all round the edges. Beautiful new soles. He tried the shoes on. They fitted. How did anyone know the right size? Had Mrs Thwaites looked at his working boots? And told Ted? Or told the colonel? Certainly she wouldn't have said anything to Mrs Robertson. But someone, perhaps two of them, had taken the trouble, and the colonel had spent the money on the new soles.

He thought of the old shoemaker he used to watch in Vilna on his way home from school, hammering little nails into the sole of a leather boot held upside down between his knees. Old Yitzhak, everyone called him. He had a long white beard, a crinkled face, a skullcap on top of his ragged white hair, and half-moon spectacles on the very end of his nose. After a bit he would raise his head, smile at Joe over the top of his spectacles, and say, "Are you being a good scholar, Josef? You must work hard and make your mother proud. Give my respects to your father"—much as the old man under the Christmas tree had said. Then he bent his head and went on hammering. Had he died before the Germans came? Joe, his own head bent, looking at his new shoes on his feet but not seeing them, for a long moment prayed that he had.

Home. Home was where old Yitzhak sat outside his tiny shop, for the daylight, and hammered nails into the sole of an expensive boot for a Polish officer, and knew Joe's name, and knew his parents. Today only the kind old man under the Christmas tree had not talked about him going home. Even Sally had. Perhaps the kind old man knew there was no home to go to, no family, no house, no street, no Vilna, no Poland. The colonel had got them all raising and clinking their little glasses to "safe journeys home". Where would he, where might he, send Joe, and call where he sent him home?

As he sat on his bed, he put both hands flat on his eiderdown. If he had a home, this was it.

Then he remembered the other present, wrapped in white tissue paper, with more ribbon, beside him on his eiderdown. A small photograph in a frame, the glass cracked—because Ted dumped the bottles on top of his parcel—and in the frame a picture. He moved his candle to see better. A picture of Sally on Grey Dawn, in the summer, in shirtsleeves and her old jodhpurs, smiling at him, leaves on the oak tree in the paddock, then the stone wall, far away the moor. She was smiling at him in the summer, this last summer, when he was hiding behind burned-out jeeps in the warehouse on the edge of Prague, afraid that soldiers, any soldiers, would find him, only thankful that it was warm.

Very carefully he took the frame to pieces, took out the cracked glass, put back the picture, and stood the frame on the little table by his bed. She looked better, clearer, happier without the glass.

And with the photograph was a book, not new, a small green-grey book, on the spine in gold letters "A Book of German Verse", then "Fiedler", and at the bottom of the spine a coat of arms and beneath it "AC. OX". He opened it. A name and a date in pencil: "Moritz Goldschmidt 1916". Two essays in German. Then 250 German poems by everyone from Luther to some poets he had never heard of, all the poems printed in Gothic Schrift. His mother had had books of poems that looked like this, by these poets. He shut the book, held it up shut in front of his face, and opened it at random, roughly in the middle. His mother, asking for help with the day, she said, used to do this with certain books, but not when his father was there. On the pages he had opened were short poems by Heinrich Heine, his mother's favourite poet. He read a little poem that began:

Du bist wie eine Blume,
So hold und schön und rein;
Ich schau' dich an, und Wehmut
Schleicht mir in's Herz hinein.

He read the lines through twice, the second time, quietly, aloud, and then closed the book. Sally. So kind and beautiful and—and what? *Rein*. So unscathed, unsullied, undirtied by the war, by everything. She had never seen a Russian, or a Nazi, except for Werner, and she had no idea that Werner had been frightening once, that he would be again, though not in Yorkshire, not in England. She knew nothing of any of it.

Two lines about Sally, and then two lines about him: watching Sally, looking at her, sadness creeping over him. So close together they had been, riding, decorating the tree. So far apart, really, they were. He thought of her mother and of what Miss March had said to Mr Ward.

The book was no good to her, she had said—of course, because she couldn't understand German. Where had she found it? Who was Moritz Goldschmidt, writing his name before either Joe or Sally was born? And only in pencil. She could have rubbed out his name. Why had she chosen not to? Could he ask her all this?

With his head so full of questions and thankfulness and anxiety and love and sadness that he couldn't think clearly, couldn't think at all, he took off his new shoes, then his clothes, and put on his pyjamas. He blew out his candle. As he opened his window, as he always did, to listen to the night before going to sleep, he remembered that he had promised himself to sort out something really important that he would have said to Werner if he could have got it clear in time, if Mrs Thwaites hadn't come back from church just when she did.

But now, as then, it was somewhere beyond him, out of his reach. He slid until it was very nearly shut, the half of the window that moved. It stuck a bit, and he always tried to do it as quietly as he could. He left a thin gap for fresh air in his room, closed the curtains, and got into bed.

The next morning he woke just before six o'clock, half an hour earlier than his alarm clock would have woken him; he could tell the time because the hands of the clock and a dot outside each number shone in the dark. The alarm was set for six thirty because today was a hunting day. There was something called the Boxing Day meet, which Ted thought demanded an extra effort. "Both horses spick-and-span by nine thirty, mind, Joe. It's a way to ride over."

As he lay in bed, warm and still, he realized what he had wanted to say to Werner Hebbel as the kitchen door opened and Mrs Thwaites came back. Is it possible to think while fast asleep?

It was to do with death, all the deaths that Werner had told him were necessary and, because necessary, unimportant. Joe could tell that Werner really believed this from how he talked about his own father: he died in an accident that needn't have happened, but that was all right— "Why be sorry?" Werner had said—because he died "for the Führer". That was when, according to Werner, history and the Führer were the same thing. Remembering this made him shiver. Then it made him angry; there had been a man, a worker in a dangerous factory, the son of Prussian peasants, the father of clever Werner. "He died for the Führer." Was that a good reason that this man, or anyone—any of all the dead soldiers, any of all the people the soldiers had killed "for the Führer"—should not be mourned? Herr Hebbel. At least he had a name.

There had been so many deaths that no one would ever be able even to count them, never mind name the dead. Where were the names of all those people, mothers, fathers, children, babies, old men and women? Their names were lost, with their bones in the pits, with their ashes in the furnaces Joe and the others had heard about in the forest. And where were they, one by one? Altogether lost along with their names? Blown out one by one, a million candles? But every single one of them was different from every other one, born on a certain day in a certain place to a certain mother, given a certain name, perceiving the strangeness of the world each in his own way—even the babies. Where were all these people? Not lost like their names, surely not altogether lost, flame by flame extinguished in the dark?

Now he remembered his father saying, when his grandfather died, that no one knows for certain anything about death except that the body stops, but that no Jew can believe that the meaning of a life stops with the body or that this meaning lives only in the memory of those who knew the dead person. Joe had no idea what this meant at the time—he was seven years old when his grandfather died—but sometimes in the forest, when they came across a dead body, he had remembered his father's words. If the dead man had no papers on him, as was usually the case, they had no way of finding out what his name was, where he came from, what language he spoke. Probably his family had no idea where he had got to, did not know whether he was still fighting as a soldier, had been captured, or had become a partisan or a deserter; whether he had been brave or a coward; whether he was alive or dead. Yet all these unknown things were known. Not by any person, but nevertheless known, because somewhere, somehow, they were the truth about this person. Were these things known by God? Is that what his father had meant?

And now he saw, although he didn't entirely understand why, that somewhere here was the right and sufficient answer to what Werner was saying. What did he say about religion? That it was finished. That the rich, the powerful, had used it, had told people lies about heaven and hell to keep them obedient. But then hadn't he practically admitted that this was exactly what Hitler had done, what Stalin was still doing? Telling people lies to keep them obedient, telling them that if they were good Nazis or good Communists, everything would be wonderful, and if they weren't, everything would be horrible—there would be punishment and darkness and death? And Hitler and Stalin both had enough power to make at least the hell part of the stories they told come true. As for the heaven part, the wonderful future, Werner now thought Hitler's promises empty and his stories lies—though it seemed he had for years believed them—because Hitler had lost the war. Did he really think that Stalin's promises would be delivered and that his stories were true because he had won the war? That was what he had said: history has shown that Hitler was wrong and Stalin was right. But he, Josef Halpern, hiding in the forest for three and a half years and afraid of all their soldiers all the time, knew that either of the armies could have won. He had seen enough to know that really it hadn't had much to do with the stories that either Hitler or Stalin told to keep people obedient. Both of them shot people to keep other people obedient. And the war wasn't about history and grand ideas; it was about how many soldiers and how many tanks and bombs and trains and guns and aeroplanes—

Without moving from the warmth of his bed, he shook his head on the pillow, to banish the noise of all that. Also he knew he was losing his hold on what he would have said to Werner.

Ah. He had it. He sat up in bed and wrapped his eiderdown round his shoulders.

What he had understood, the important thing he wished he had been able to say and now never would, even if there were an opportunity— because Werner would only laugh at him or produce an argument he wouldn't know how to counter—was something like this: Werner thought that the fact that Russia had won the war showed that history was on the side of Communism and not on the side of Nazism. So Communism must be true. To Werner, who had once believed Hitler's stories and now believed Stalin's stories, people one by one, their lives and their deaths, were of no account compared to the wonderful progress of history towards a heaven on earth. Could Werner see that stories of heaven and hell, happiness and punishment, used by powerful people to make others obey them—the description he had given of religion— really was a description of both Nazism and Communism? Apparently he couldn't, because now he thought Communism was not a story but true. Nor could he see that religion was an entirely different kind of thing, because it had to do with what was actually true. Joe couldn't sort out a way of describing to himself exactly how this was different, but he knew—he not only believed but knew—that it was. If what his father had said about death was true of one person, then it was true of everyone there had ever been, all the murdered, all the people who had died in the famine, all the people whose bodies had been thrown out of cattle trucks or burned in ovens and whose names no one knew anymore.

But how did this certainty deal with Werner's certainty that in order to have a golden future here, in this world, countless people had to be sacrificed and forgotten? For a moment he saw that what was wrong with this idea had some connexion to what his uncle the rabbi had told him was wrong with Zionism as a plan for the perfect life in the perfect place, here, in this world. It meant the loss, his uncle had said, of Zion as a belief, a memory, a hope. Joe saw the connexion, but the thought was too complicated for him, and quickly it dissolved like smoke into the air. He tried to track his way back to the understanding that he could deal with what Werner had been so sure of through what his father had told him about death. But how did this show that Werner was wrong? He knew that it did, but he couldn't see exactly how. There was a sequence of thought, somewhere here, a proper chain in which one thing led to another, that he couldn't think his way through. He wished he were able to talk to his father now, when he was so much older. His father would have been able to explain so that it would all make sense.

Then he remembered some phrases from a prayer his father used to say, as well as the Kaddish prayer, on every anniversary of his grandfather's death and on the anniversary of the death of his father's mother and little brother, who had died together, long before Joe was born, on a freezing train because the Russians had decided to move the Jews out of Vilna during the Great War.

O God, full of compassion, grant perfect peace under the wings of the Shechinah to the soul of your son, who has gone to his eternity. Conceal him in the secret of your wings forever and bind his soul in the bundle of life.

The prayer was longer than this, but this was all he could remember. He had said it by himself, quietly, but to God, for his father, his mother, and his sister, but he didn't know the dates of their deaths, so he said it when he thought of them. He had asked his father what the Shechinah was, and his father had said that it was a word for the presence of God, and the wings, like the wings of a hen protecting her chicks, were a picture to explain that in God was shelter and safety. When his father told him this, his mother said, "But you always say you aren't sure whether God exists", and his father answered, "I am a doctor, a rational being, so I know that God does not exist. I am a Jew, so I pray for my father on the day he died."

Was it possible to know one thing and at the same time do something which implied knowing the opposite of the first thing?

The question struck him as of great importance, more important than finding the right way to deal with Werner's faith in Stalin. Faith in Stalin? How could anyone—how could Werner, who was educated, who read books, who knew all sorts of things Joe didn't know—believe in cruel, pitiless Stalin as a saviour? In any case, Joe knew that if he tried to argue against this faith, he would certainly fail.

But what about his father and God? As he sat in his warm bed, wrapped in his eiderdown, he was too comfortable and too sleepy—though he knew that any minute now he would have to get up—even to begin to think his way through what his father had said about God.

He reached out for the little book of German poems. Perhaps they would teach him how to think better. In the dark, he didn't open the book. He held the book, his present from Sally, in both hands and listened to the silence of the farm, the fields, the dale. The cock crew. He realized he had been listening for him. He thought of the hens, letting them out after breakfast, scattering corn for them, looking for their eggs. And then the horses to be fed, watered, brushed, polished, plaited, tacked up. His alarm clock rang.

He smiled as he stopped the bell. He felt his father very close to him, saying something like, "You may be a Jew who has an obligation to the long past to think about the judgement of God." That's it, of course that's it. He'd reached what he had been struggling towards: "Blessed be the true judge." His uncle the rabbi had told him that a good Jew says these words when he hears of a death, any death. But—here was his father again—"Now you are a stable lad who plaits the manes of the horses and lets out the hens."

So, as Ted would say, "Jump to it."

Chapter 3

"Joe! Joe! Where's the fellow got to?"

The colonel's voice, echoing round the yard. Joe was in Ted's fruit cage, picking raspberries for Mrs Thwaites.

"Here, sir!" he shouted. He put down his bowl, half full of raspberries, left the fruit cage, carefully shutting the wood-and-chicken-wire door behind him because of the blackbirds, and came into the yard.

"Oh, there you are. Good. Now, Joe, I've got a friend from London who wants to meet you. It's all right; nothing to worry about. In fact, rather the reverse. Can you come to the study? Let's see—after lunch would probably be best. Shall we say about three?"

"Yes, sir. Three o'clock. I will be there."

"Good lad. Three o'clock it is."

The colonel walked away, round the corner of the house. Joe stood and watched him until he disappeared. He dreaded questions, strangers, anything to do with London. Above all he dreaded a decision which would send him away. "Rather the reverse"—what did the colonel mean?

"Joe!"

Mrs Thwaites was at the kitchen door, wiping her hands on a tea towel.

"Have you got my raspberries? I haven't got all day, you know. And can you find a few red currants to go with them?"

"I am sorry, Mrs Thwaites. Five minutes, I will bring them."

"Is something the matter, Joe?"

"No. No, nothing is the matter. I am sorry."

He picked more raspberries as quickly as he could, and then some red currants, pulling them gently off the little sprigs they grew on, cheered by their translucent brilliance. They shone like jewels among the raspberries in the bowl.

"Well done, Joe. That's lovely. I've a tart to make for their lunch, madam says. Posh guests from down south, apparently. I've kept some cream back from the butter—we're not supposed to with this rationing, but nobody'll notice, this once." She was making pastry as she talked, crumbling margarine she wished were their own butter into a bowl of flour with her fingers. Her voice was even more comforting than the red currants.

"Mrs Thwaites?"

"What is it, lad?"

He hesitated. "It is nothing. I will go and exercise the horses."

"Joe, there's something up with you, I can tell."

"No. Nothing is up."

"Well, get along with you, then. We've all got work to do. Just cut me a couple of Ted's lettuces, will you, before you do the horses?"

It was the middle of July, and the day was going to be fine again. This was his second summer on the farm, and it was more beautiful than the one before. More days were cloudless, blue and green days, the grass greener than any he had ever seen, the woods across the dale blue, the air hot but kind, always with a breath of breeze, scented sometimes with heather and peat from the moor, and never carrying the hovering clouds of biting insects there always were in the forest in summer.

Perhaps this summer was so very beautiful because the winter had been so fierce. Ted and Mrs Thwaites said they had never known a winter like it—snow piled high, everything frozen for weeks and weeks, sometimes new blizzards of snow overnight so that Bill couldn't take the milk to the village because the farm road had disappeared again. Day after day they were out looking for sheep in the drifts. They had brought them down off the moor when the bad weather began, but through the winter they lost dozens of them, mostly in drifts by the walls, finding the carcases only when the snow melted in April. Ted worried as much about hay and beets for the animals as about coke for Mrs Thwaites' stove. Food was rationed more strictly than ever. In the village even bread was rationed, which it had never been in the war, they said. Mrs Thwaites made them soda bread with buttermilk from the dairy; Joe thought it more delicious than ordinary bread. In the kitchen they ate mostly potatoes, carrots, parsnips, and beetroots Ted had dug up and stored, and apples from the apple store in the loft over the cow byre. In March they killed an extra pig.

The best of the cold winter had been moonlit nights when outside his window the white fields stretched across towards the woods looking like grey lace because of the snow under the trees. The shadows of the stone walls, the oak tree, and the barn were sharp and black on the snow. Everything he could see was black, white, grey, silent, and beautiful. In Vilna they hadn't left the city in winter; in the forest there had been many moonlit snowy nights but always danger because of the light, and never also a warm bed.

Ted's son Bob had come home from the army in the autumn, not long before Werner had gone back to Germany. There had been a difficult month when both Bob and Werner had sat in silence at every meal in the kitchen.

"I'm not talking to any bloody German. You haven't seen what I've seen. Animals they are, the lot of them. Worse than animals." Bob, a tank driver, had seen the piles of dead and dying prisoners at Belsen.

Fritz, who might have complicated Bob's opinion of Germans, had gone by that time, but only as far as the village. To Joe's amazement, Fritz had announced one day at breakfast in the early summer of 1946, "I have a big surprise. Doris and I will get married next week, on Saturday in the church. You will all come?" Mrs Thwaites got to her feet, rounded the table, and gave him a hug. "Well done, Fritz. I hope you'll both be very happy." It turned out that neither Ted nor Mrs Thwaites was surprised. Joe had noticed nothing and hadn't even wondered where Fritz had gone on Sunday afternoons and an occasional evening when he had been unaccountably not in the kitchen for supper.

Ted and Mrs Thwaites, in their Sunday best, drove Fritz, without his prisoner's patches, in the wagon to the wedding. Bill and Joe walked, in friendly silence, to the village and back. Werner, without a word of explanation, didn't come. Joe, who had never before been to any kind of Christian service and found most of the words impossible to understand, was impressed with the quietness of the little ceremony and the vicar's kind voice, which he remembered from the Christmas tree. He understood that Doris and Fritz, whose real name turned out to be Fritjof, were married when they had both said, "I will." Mrs Thwaites told him next day that Doris' mother, widowed in the war, liked Fritz and was glad to have a man about the house again, though it had been "no end of a game for the colonel to get the papers sorted out".

Later, when Joe started going sometimes to the village by himself, he found Fritz, cheerful and warmhearted as ever, at the counter of his mother-in-law's small, dark shop, selling all kinds of things: string, birthday cards, boot polish, nails and screws, paraffin, tins of corned beef, bags of potatoes, apples, and small white cards with hooks and eyes or some mysterious things for women's hair called Kirby grips, both of which he once had to buy for Mrs Thwaites. When Doris had a baby girl six months after the wedding, Mrs Thwaites was pleased and not shocked. "It's all right, Ted. No need to count. He's a decent boy, that Fritz, and a good worker. I'm glad for the pair of them." She knitted little coats for the baby and worried about whether Doris was keeping her warm enough in the freezing winter.

Bob was a big, strong young man who did all of Fritz's work and, after Werner had gone, most of Werner's too. Joe looked after the horses and the hens as always and did a good deal of shepherding, especially in the heavy snow. Jess, Ted's dog, who had taken easily to Fritz, worked better for Joe than for Bob. Joe could tell that Bob resented this, but he knew that Bob's unfriendliness, his set face when Joe talked, his refusal to meet his eye, let alone smile, was more deep-seated. Once when Joe was washing girths in the tack room with the window open, he heard Bob and Ted talking in the yard.

"When's he going, Dad?"

"I don't know, our Bob. The lad's got nowhere he can go. This is the only home he's got."

"I didn't think to find the farm full of bloody foreigners when I got home. I thought we won the war."

"We couldn't have managed without the prisoners, Bob, I'm telling you. And Joe's different. He's been through a lot, that boy, lost his family in the war, lost just about everything, the colonel told me. And he's marvellous with horses."

"I don't care if he is. He's a Jew—and clever, like they are. Have you heard him play that fiddle? He gives me the creeps. If it weren't for the Jews, there might never have been no war."

"I don't like that sort of talk, Bob. I'm fond of the lad, and so is Mrs Thwaites."

"Well, there you are. That's what I mean. Worming his way in here. It's time he went back to where he belongs, wherever that is."

Bob's hostility was bad enough. But probably the colonel hadn't noticed it, and, if he had, would pay no attention to it. After all, Mrs Robertson had given Joe, in all the twenty-one months he had lived at the farm, not one smile, not one friendly word. Had she ever even spoken to him directly? He didn't think so. And the colonel hadn't let his wife change his mind about having Joe on the farm. Had he?

James Robertson was different. The colonel was bound to be close to him, his only son now, safely back at last from the war. He loved him. Of course he did. So did Sally. And James also clearly wanted to get rid of him.

James came to the farm for the first time for the hunting in November, before the bitter weather began. Joe was looking forward to him coming; he was proud of how well Tiger Rag was looking and of how very much better behaved he was after a good year of his work on him. The horse was more obedient, was easier to ride, hardly ever bucked. "I can't get over what you've done with that horse, Joe", Ted said. "You wait till Master James has him out hunting. He'll be right capped with him, bound to be." But when Captain Robertson arrived in the yard on the first hunting morning, stiff in his black coat and black bowler hat, he looked at Joe with an expression of distaste, almost disgust, took the reins from him without a word, led Tiger to the mounting block himself, and trotted out of the yard without waiting for his father to join him. When they came back, with the horses muddy and tired in the darkening afternoon, James dismounted, threw the reins to Joe, and walked off to the front of the house without a word. The colonel said to Joe, "Tiger Rag went well all day. Really beautifully. Jumped like a bird. You should be proud of him."

"Thank you, sir."

When James went back to London, where, according to Ted, he was going to be "something in the city—don't ask me what", Joe felt as if he had come outside into the fresh air after being shut in a closed room in which he could hardly breathe. He said nothing to anyone; Ted and Mrs Thwaites were always loyal to the family, and he had the impression that even Ted, often in the yard with him when the horses left or returned, had noticed nothing.

When all the Robertsons arrived for Christmas, his second Christmas in England, he quickly had to accept that Sally had changed.

While she was at school—until last July, that was, soon after Fritz's wedding—he had heard nothing from her. But when she came to the farm in the spring for her school holidays, she had been pleased to be home, pleased to see Ted and Mrs Thwaites, pleased to see Grey Dawn, and pleased to see him. He didn't suppose she ever thought of him when she was away from the farm; how could she know how often, how much, he thought of her? Probably she was pleased to see him only because he was now a part of everything she was most attached to. But that was enough for him.

During the three weeks of her holiday, in April 1946, they rode together often. Mostly they rode without talking in a silence that Joe felt as the first happiness of his life since the day his father left for the army. "This way?" Sally might say, or, "Shall we go home through the plantation?" or, "Do you think the beck's too deep here?" and he would nod or shake his head.

One day, far from the farm, as the horses walked in single file along a rabbit-holed path in old woodland of oak and ash and holly, Sally, in front, stopped and waved a hand up the wood beside them. "Look— primroses. Aren't they lovely?" There were masses of small, creamy-yellow flowers under the trees and in sunlit, grassy spaces between them, and blue flowers too, delicate, smaller than the yellow flowers but on bigger plants. He remembered what they were called in German. He slid down from the saddle and, holding Tiger's reins, picked a few of each and held them up towards Sally.

"Which are the primroses?" he said.

"The yellow ones. The blue ones are called forget-me-nots."

The same as in German.

"Please, take them."

As he gave them to her, he bowed his head, just a little.

"They'll wilt before we get home, silly boy. But thank you." She put the little bunch in her belt.

As he remounted Tiger, she said, "Tell me, Joe—Daddy says you lived in a forest for years during the war. Was it a forest like this?"

He looked up the flowery hill through the gentle spring wood, no leaves yet on the trees, and down to the green floor of the dale below them: stone walls, some sheep, a hawthorn thicket, a wooded farm gate into a lane.

"No. Not like this. Very, very big, hundreds of kilometres every way. No hills like these. Wet, very wet—lakes everywhere, and bogs. In winter, very much ice and snow." That was the limit of his capacity to describe the forest.

What he wanted to say was how frightening it was compared with this English valley. Also how beautiful but in a quite different way, wild and dangerous, with its marshes and streams and thick, soft moss and small, bright bog flowers and black pools of water, and trees living and dead, birches and willows and pines, and the wolves you could sometimes hear or see tracks of in the snow. He wanted to tell her that if you had to hide in a pond in the forest you could breathe through a straw, a real straw—they all carried a few straws, in case—and stay completely underwater until the danger—Germans, Russians, a group of peasants collecting wood—had gone away.

"Goodness. It must have been difficult to keep warm."

"Yes."

They rode on.

Another day they were walking the horses quietly home from the village, where Sally had delivered a letter for her father. It had rained most of the morning and was now a mild afternoon, the sky clear and pale, the grass fresh beside the white farm road.

"It's going to be a lovely day tomorrow, but I can't come for a ride, I'm afraid. I have a Sunday lunch with guests. That'll take all the afternoon. And I have to go to church with Daddy in the morning."

"Is it good, to go to church?"

"It's quite boring. Daddy goes because he likes the vicar. Mummy never goes except at Christmas, for the look of the thing, she says."

"Do you say prayers for your brother who was killed?"

She stopped Grey Dawn and looked at him, surprised. "What a funny question. No, I don't. Perhaps I should. Poor Philip. You would have liked him."

They rode home.

Praying for the dead. He remembered a small church, ancient-looking brick with a little dome almost completely covered in green, creeping vegetation. He and a couple of fighters from the camp had come across it one day in what had been a clearing in the forest. The doorway was a rectangle of darkness; the door had been taken off, probably for firewood. Inside, in the dim light from the dome's overgrown windows, there was nothing except the broken supports of some kind of wooden screen and a block of stone like a table with a big black hammer and sickle painted on it. Outside, a few graves had almost disappeared under grass and brushwood. None of them said anything.

The third time he and Sally talked was on one of their last rides. They stopped by the beck to let the horses drink before walking them across the stony ford. He said, "Can I ask you something?"

"Of course you can, Joe. What is it?"

"Who is Moritz Goldschmidt?"

"What?" She laughed as she remembered. "Oh, the book. I'd forgotten all about it. Were you pleased with it?"

"Yes. I read it very often. I have no other German books. And my mother—yes, I was pleased with the book. Thank you."

"Well, Mr Goldschmidt was my piano teacher, in London before the war. I was quite little, seven, I think, when I started the piano. And I wasn't much good. But he was a dear old man, very patient and kind. The best thing was when he played for me at the end of the lesson. He'd do it only if he thought I'd practised enough in the week before. Lovely, lovely pieces he played. I've no idea what they were. Then when the war started, he had to go away. Internment, Daddy said. I didn't know what that meant. I still don't, to tell you the truth. But he never came back. He sent me the book then, with a card saying 'For Sally when she is older'. I've got the card somewhere. But the book—well, I don't know any German, and I thought you might like to have it."

He understood almost all of this.

"Are you playing piano now?"

"No. Not really. The teacher at school is hopeless, so I gave it up. Mummy doesn't think I'm musical anyway. Philip was. He played the violin really well. He played a violin concerto at Eton the summer before he left school. We all went to hear it. He was brilliant."

"I played violin at home. My father also. He played very well."

"Really? What a coincidence. You are a surprising boy." She looked at him across the necks of the drinking horses and smiled. "You know what? You ought to have Philip's violin. It would probably be good for it to be played, and nobody else knows how to. It's somewhere about, in his room, I expect. Would you like that? There's loads of his music too. I know where that is, in one of the cupboards in the drawing room."

The horses lifted their heads. They stood still on the short grass by the beck. Water rattled over stones. A pigeon flew past them, in and out of sunlight, blue and grey and white, and settled on a branch, folding its wings. Joe shut his eyes and opened them again.

"Do I understand? You would allow me to play your brother's violin?"

"Why not? It seems obvious, doesn't it, if you'd like to play it. I tell you what I'll do. When we get back, I'll ask Daddy if we can lend it to you. Mummy's very touchy about Philip's things."

"I would not wish—if she will be upset—"

"Oh, don't worry about Mummy. She needn't know anything about it. It'll be OK as long as she doesn't hear you playing. Isn't your room over the stable?"

"Yes, it is."

"Well, there you are. If you play up there and keep the window shut, she'll never know."

After supper that night, Sally appeared in the kitchen carrying a big pile of sheet music with a violin in its case on top. Ted had gone home. Mrs Thwaites, Bill, Fritz, and Joe stood up when she came in. Werner sat still.

"These are for Joe. Daddy thought it was a very good idea, Joe. So don't worry a bit."

"Thank you. Thank you, miss."

She looked across the kitchen table her understanding of the "miss", and that was the second-best thing that happened that day.

So every evening after that, he left the kitchen as soon as he could and practised for an hour or more in his room. He put together a makeshift music stand out of pieces of scrap wood. Ted found him an old paraffin lamp and taught him exactly how not to set the stables on fire. He found the familiar Ševčík exercises of his childhood in Philip's pile of music, as well as dozens of pieces by composers he already knew or had heard of. And he was doing what his father would most have wanted.

In the summer of 1946, the summer after the April day when Sally had found him the violin, the Robertsons came to the farm for more than two months. Guests stayed occasionally. Mrs Thwaites grumbled about producing what she called "dining room food" on the rations. Ted mowed the tennis court, and Joe helped him paint white lines on the grass, using a measuring tape to keep them straight, according to a plan in an old pamphlet Ted found in the tack room. But Sally never came.

One day Joe asked Ted, "Where is Miss Sally?"

Ted gave him a long look.

"Now, Joe, you don't want to be pining after Miss Sally. I know you've been good friends, with the riding and all, and Master Philip's fiddle she got hold of for you. But you mustn't expect anything to come of it, you know. She's a young lady, and now that she's left school, she'll be having, well, quite a different style of life from anything we see round here. I believe she's in Switzerland, Miss March said to Mrs Thwaites. At something they call a finishing school. Learning French and cooking and that. I don't think we'll see her here while Christmastime. And next spring she'll be what they call 'coming out'. That's curtseying to the king and going to dances with posh young men—a bit of a marriage market, from what I gather. It all stopped during the war of course, but they're gradually bringing these things back."

"I understand." He didn't, but he realized that Ted was warning him.

"Look, lad, these things are hard at your age. But she's growing up fast, and you'll just have to get used to it. Worse things happen at sea, and a lot worse you've had to cope with in your life already."

"Yes, Ted."

All he could do was to look after Grey Dawn with extra care, ride her where he and Sally had ridden together in the spring, make sure the horse would be in perfect order for Sally when she came home in the winter. But on a cold day in October a man in a tweed coat, breeches, and a bowler hat appeared with Ted in the stable yard and spent fifteen minutes in Dawn's box, examining closely her legs, hooves, mane, mouth, and tail. Then Ted said, "Saddle her up for the gentleman, Joe. He's going to give her a ride round."

"Very nice little mare, and in excellent condition", the man said when he brought her back. "I'll settle a price with the colonel on the telephone and send a box for her on Tuesday."

"Very good, sir."

Joe couldn't speak. He waited until the man had gone round to the front of the house, got into his car, and disappeared down the farm road.

"Ted? Dawn is to go? You did not tell me!"

"I'm sorry, lad. I didn't know before this morning. The colonel telephoned to say the gentleman was coming to have a look at her. Miss Sally doesn't want to hunt anymore, apparently. If she just wants a ride out when she's here, she can always take the colonel's horse. He's quiet enough. And the colonel doesn't think it's worth keeping a hunter for her if she's not keen."

"But she loves the horse."

"Oh, girls like Miss Sally, they change, you know. Very often they grow out of horses. They're all over their ponies when they're children, and then they get a bit older and it's clothes, young men, parties and that, and they're not interested anymore."

94

Joe went into Dawn's box, put his arms round her neck, and sobbed—not for her but for little Renia, who had saved his life that night when he galloped from the peasant's hut into the forest, escaping from the Germans. During his first winter in the forest, with forty or fifty people in the camp and snow and ice making the finding of food almost impossible, a raiding party sent to steal a cow or two from a farm had been ambushed on the way back by Russian partisans. They had shot the raiders—one was wounded only in the arm and shammed dead so that he got back, bleeding, to the camp—and taken the stolen cattle. The next day the commander of the camp came to find him where he was washing half-frozen potatoes in melted snow for the cooks and said, "We need your pony, Josef."

"What for? I can ride her, anywhere you want."

"No. You don't understand. We need her for meat. There's no meat in the camp. We have had no meat for several weeks, and we've nothing to give the fighters to eat."

"No, no, no, you can't. She saved me. She is all—"

"Exactly, Josef. You brought nothing with you. You had no gun, not even a knife. We took you partly because you had a horse. Well, now she needs more fodder than what we have to give her, and the snow's too deep for her to graze. She's growing thin and will soon die from hunger. But there's still some meat on her. And horsehide is useful stuff."

"If you kill her, I will go away."

"No you won't. Where would you go?"

Crying, he stumbled into the forest through the snow so as not to hear the shot. But he heard it.

He ate nothing but potatoes, turnips, and a few crusts of black bread for two weeks.

By the time an old cattle lorry that was adapted to take a couple of horses drove into the yard that Tuesday, Joe could calmly get Grey Dawn ready to travel, groomed and in her halter and rug, with her saddle and bridle polished to go with her. She wasn't going to be shot. He knew she would go to another stable yard, with hay and clean straw and a tack room, and be properly treated. But he cried again when the lorry had rattled out of the yard, because he also knew that watching Dawn go away was watching the end of riding with Sally.

So, several times before and after that second Christmas, he prepared only two horses on hunting mornings, and James Robertson's dislike of him was clearer each time James appeared in the yard.

Sally never came into the yard that winter, though he knew she was back for Christmas. "Pretty as a picture, Miss Sally. Have you seen her, Ted?" This was Mrs Thwaites, when she came back into the kitchen one day after talking to Mrs Robertson about the meals. "So grown up she looks all of a sudden. We haven't seen her for six months, mind, and she's almost seventeen, isn't she? Quite the young lady. More like her mother now, very elegant. And clothes are coming back into the shops in London, the papers say. Such a nice frock she has on this morning."

Ted and Bob cut down and took to the house a Christmas tree from the spruce plantation. "They want a much smaller tree this year, the colonel says. I don't know why. Beautiful it was, last year."

On Christmas morning Mary came up from the village on her bicycle to help Joe keep an eye on the goose and the roast potatoes while Mrs Thwaites went to church. Mary said almost nothing. She was a shy girl and had always seemed frightened of Joe—or perhaps she thought he didn't know any English. When he smiled at her over the sizzling goose as they poured off the fat, she blushed and looked away.

After tea Ted said, "They've only asked Mrs Thwaites and me and Bob in this year. They've got a lot more guests this Christmas, the colonel says." Joe was certain this was not the reason.

Ted came back to the kitchen with a wrapped-up bottle for Bill and an envelope for Joe. He opened it later in his bedroom, leaving his candle lit and not lighting his lamp so that it would be the same as last year. The envelope had in it a five-pound note and a card. The writing on the card said, "With best wishes and many thanks for a good year's work", and then "G. J. R.", the colonel's initials.

Once, not long after Christmas, when Joe was exercising the colonel's horse on a morning too icy for hunting, walking him down the crisp grass beside the farm road, the family's car passed him slowly. Mr Ward was driving. Sally, in a beret and a red coat, was sitting in the back beside a young man wearing a soldier's uniform. He looked perhaps two or three years older than Sally. Joe had never seen him before. As the car passed, Sally waved. Joe took off the new tweed cap Mrs Thwaites and Ted had given him for Christmas and waved it until the car was out of sight.

That wave was six months ago, almost exactly, and he hadn't seen her since.

And now the colonel wanted him to come to the study at three o'clock to talk to someone from London.

Through the rest of the hot morning, as he did his usual jobs, and then took Tiger for a quiet ride through the oaks and then the larches up to the moor, he tried to think out what he knew that might be helpful when he had to speak to the colonel and a stranger.

He knew now that he shouldn't have to be sent back to Vilna, because Vilna was in Poland, not in Russia, not in the USSR, at the very beginning of the war. Could they send him back to Poland? He knew that Polish soldiers who had fought with England in the war were allowed to stay in England; Bob had grumbled several times that there were far too many of them and that girls liked them too much. But Joe wasn't a soldier. He had done what he could, what he was asked to do, to fight the Germans in Belorussia. He had crawled through snowy undergrowth and through the reeds and alders of summer marshes to meet people bringing news from the ghettos or to find out, from the occasional peasant brave enough to talk to a partisan, the time when a jeep carrying German officers might be passing along a certain road. The commander had never given him a gun, but he had often acted as a lookout for fighters, or taken messages, as quickly and quietly as possible, to and from the camp. These things he had been asked to do because they were easier for a child to manage. And he knew, from Werner, that to most people the very word "partisan" meant "Communist". Werner hadn't considered the fighters in Joe's camp in the forest to be partisans because they didn't take orders from Moscow and because they always knew that the Russians in the forest were as likely to shoot them as the Germans were. "A Jewish bandit", Werner had said. "That's all you were."

The colonel had never asked him about any of this. Would he today? If he told the colonel and his friend from London all he could—though the truth of how it had been would be impossible for him to explain in English—would they be more or less likely to say he had to go back? He didn't know and had no way of guessing.

And back where?

The only thing he knew for certain was that James Robertson wanted to get rid of him as much as Bob did. More than Bob did. Naturally the colonel would pay attention to what James wanted. And Joe had recently realized that James had better reasons, or at least more serious ones, than Bob's for disliking him. Of these reasons, until he started concentrating harder on the news on the wireless and the news in Mrs Thwaites' *Daily Express*, he had had no idea.

Joe had never known anything about the war in Africa. In the forest he hadn't heard it mentioned by anyone. When James Robertson came home, Joe gathered from Ted and Mrs Thwaites and Bill talking at the kitchen table that years ago the English Eighth Army, and a general they called "Monty", had defeated the Germans in the desert in Africa. The Afrika Korps—hadn't Fritz said he fought in that? Many German prisoners had been taken, and they were still in Africa, in Egypt near the Suez Canal, being guarded by British soldiers. This was what James Robertson had been doing. "Not a bad lot, Captain James says", relayed Ted. "More like Fritz than like Werner perhaps. They think a lot of Rommel. No reason why they shouldn't. A very fine soldier was Rommel. Most of them don't seem to have had much time for Hitler. But they would say that now, wouldn't they?"

So far he understood.

"But the real problem out there's the Jews, Captain James says. No offence, Joe. We know you've never been in those parts. Hate the British, they do. D'you remember Lord Moyne? Murdered—in Egypt I think that was, in the middle of the war. He was a friend of the colonel's, Lord Moyne. We didn't take a lot of notice at the time of who actually shot him. Germans, Italians, Arabs—could have been any one of them. Well, it was Jewish terrorists. That's what they call them, apparently, terrorists. And that's not the only thing they've done. Blew up the King David Hotel last summer, that I do remember—a lot about it on the wireless there was, killed I don't know how many people."

"Where was the King David Hotel?" Mrs Thwaites, only half listening to Ted, was sitting at the kitchen table, for the light, turning the heel of a sock. Joe watched her big, apparently clumsy, fingers neatly dealing with four small knitting needles all at the same time. He said nothing.

"I don't remember exactly", Ted said. "Somewhere out there— Egypt, Palestine, where all the trouble is."

Joe remembered. His English, by last summer, was good enough for him to understand the news on the wireless and in Mrs Thwaites' paper. The bombing was in Jerusalem. The newspaper called it "a Jewish atrocity". His dictionary didn't have the word, but he gathered it meant a very bad crime. For days he had eaten his way silently through meals, left the kitchen as soon as he could, wondered if Ted and Mrs Thwaites were going to be suspicious of him, stop trusting him, start hating him. But there was no change in how they treated him. Only Werner said to him, out in the yard the night the news of the bomb was on the wireless, "You see? The Jews in Palestine. Heroes of the revolution. You should be out there with them."

"Heroes? What are you talking about? What is the good of more bombs, more killing?"

"British imperialists are oppressing the people in places all over the world. The British won't give up power anywhere because of the profits it brings—capitalist profits, bourgeois profits. Only bombs will teach them that oppression will not pay. It's simple: Arab bombs before the war, and now Jewish bombs. The British have to get out of Palestine and leave the Jews and the Arabs to sort it out. They will fight each other, and the Jews will win. The Jews have learned some good lessons from the Russians—most of the Jews in Palestine come from Russia. They will set up a socialist state. Good. Soon perhaps there will be bombs in England too. Better."

"How can you say that when—"

But Werner had disappeared into the dark with the bucket of kitchen scraps for the pigs. It was in any case useless to argue with him.

So to Englishmen, now, the Jews in Palestine were enemies. The colonel wouldn't send him to Palestine to join these enemies, would he? As far as he could gather, the Jews in Palestine hated the English because they wouldn't allow more Jews to join them. So it wouldn't make sense for the colonel to send him there.

Riding Tiger slowly down the hill towards the farm in the midday heat, he couldn't believe that the colonel, who was an English gentleman—"We should think ourselves lucky the colonel's an old-fashioned English gentleman", Ted had once said, but about what, Joe couldn't remember—would begin to hate the Jews when he had taken Joe on at the farm all that time ago. Wasn't it the colonel himself who had told him about the English Jews who were allowed their synagogues, allowed to live their Jewish lives in peace? But he knew that had once been true of the German Jews. His mother's family, for instance, had lived peacefully in Breslau for a long time. They had gone to their synagogue and taught their children Jewish ways. His mother had been a nurse in a

German hospital. And then he remembered the look on James Robertson's face when James saw him in the stable yard, a look that you might give a rat or a snake or a cockroach. Perhaps James Robertson had a friend who was killed by the bomb in the King David Hotel? But he must know that Joe couldn't possibly have had anything to do with the bomb, or with the murder of Lord Moyne, or with anything else that had happened in Palestine. Mustn't he?

But if Jews were enemies now, might England decide to get rid of all of them? Not just from England but even perhaps from the face of the earth? As Hitler had, when Jews were no one's enemies?

"Nothing to worry about. In fact, rather the reverse." What did the colonel mean?

"What's the matter with you, Joe? Don't you want your dinner? I hope you're not sickening for something."

"I am sorry, Mrs Thwaites. I am not ill."

After lunch he set himself to clean the loose boxes in the stable, already clean, as if the stranger from London were going to inspect his work. He wished he were. He kept looking at his watch—he had an old wristwatch now, which Ted had given him when the colonel presented Ted with a fine fob watch for his sixtieth birthday—but the time passed slowly.

Then he washed, changed, looked at his watch again, and walked through the empty kitchen into the house.

He knocked on the study door.

"Come in, come in, Joe. Sit down there, would you? Capital. This gentleman, Mr Peters, would like to ask you a few questions."

Why did something in the colonel's voice make him think that "Mr Peters" wasn't the man's real name? The stranger was sitting next to the colonel, with Joe facing both of them on the other side of the desk. Joe couldn't see the man's face properly because of the sunlight outside the window. He had an impression of weight: the man was heavier and younger than the colonel, and had no moustache.

"Very good, sir", Joe said.

"Excellent", the man called Mr Peters said. "Now, you are Josef Halpern. You are nearly eighteen, and you have worked for Colonel Robertson since shortly after you arrived in England in"—he looked down at some papers he had in front of him—"September 1945. Is that correct?"

"Yes, sir."

"You are an exceptionally fortunate young man. I suppose you know that?"

"Yes, sir."

"You have been happy here?"

The past tense frightened him. He thought for a moment.

"Yes, sir. I am very happy here."

"Do you have any family alive—parents, grandparents, brothers, sisters, aunts, uncles?"

"No, sir."

"Are you certain of that?"

"Yes, sir."

"Now, young man, how do you see your own future?"

"I am sorry, sir?"

"Not a simple question, I know. Let's try again." Mr Peters repeated the question in perfect German.

Joe put his hands on the edge of the desk in front of him. To hold on to something. As he had gripped the kitchen table at his first breakfast on the farm. He looked at the colonel, who smiled.

"It's all right, Joe. You may answer in German. It's easier for you."

He didn't want to say anything the colonel couldn't understand.

"But sir ... I would like to stay here and look after the horses and do my other work", he said carefully, in English, and to the colonel.

"Now, Joe, I'm afraid that's not going to be possible. We have other plans for the horses, and for the farm in general."

This was clearly worse than he had feared. He hesitated. He wanted to say, "Captain James wants me to leave." Instead he said, "My work is not good? I am sorry, my work is not good enough?"

"No, Joe. That's not at all what I mean. Your work has been very good all along, much better than I could have hoped. But things have changed. We're at last really leaving the war behind us, and I've always promised—well, let's just say that there are other arrangements I need to make. In any case, a clever boy like you, with all your languages and so on, and your music too—I've heard you playing that fiddle up in your room, you know—shouldn't be stuck in the depths of the country as a stable lad. You have no friends of your own age, no one to talk to. You need more of a life of your own, more interesting work to do. That's why I wanted you to talk to Mr Peters here."

Joe bent his head. What could he say?

The colonel picked up his fountain pen and took the cap off, then put it on again, twice.

"You have some more questions to ask him, don't you, John?" he said.

"I do, yes. Josef, I shall speak in German so that I'm sure you understand. Or Russian if you prefer."

Who was this man?

"I prefer German, sir."

"That's good. Now listen carefully. You know that Vilnius, the city in which you were born, is now the capital city of the Soviet Socialist Republic of Lithuania. Colonel Robertson tells me that you have no wish to return there. Is that correct?"

"Yes, sir. That is correct. Jewish Vilna, my city, is gone. The Russians will rule there. The Russians killed my parents. And also I cannot speak Lithuanian."

"I understand. I understand that you have serious reasons to dislike, perhaps to hate, also to fear, the Soviets. You say you cannot speak Lithuanian, but I gather that as a child you spoke several languages. Can you tell me what languages you know, besides German, which you obviously speak well?"

"My mother was German. We always spoke German at home. In the city and at school I spoke Polish. We all knew some Russian. And in the street where we lived everyone spoke Yiddish. No one we knew spoke Lithuanian."

"Useful. Very useful", Mr Peters said in English to the colonel. "In England you're lucky if you can find a young man of this age who speaks halfway decent French, never mind German or Russian. We have to start from scratch with them." He turned to Joe.

"How old were you when you stopped going to school, Josef?" He had gone back to German.

"I was ten, sir." He thought of Sally, and his first ride with her.

"Exactly. So it would be good, wouldn't it, to learn more, to study again, in a school, a college, with other boys of your age or a little older?"

"I should like to study music, sir."

"That isn't quite what we have in mind, I'm afraid."

Joe looked down again. It seemed important not to show any reaction to anything Mr Peters said.

Mr Peters leaned forward, as if his next question were to be more serious.

"What experience have you had of Communism?"

Joe thought before answering this question.

"Take your time", Mr Peters said.

"In Vilna, after the Russians declared that the city was no longer Polish, the Jews were told they could not live anymore as Jews. Also the Poles could not live anymore as Poles. Lithuanian was to be the language of the schools. I left school. My uncle was a rabbi. He refused to obey the rules about Jews. The Russians took him away. He died. My father, a medical officer in the Polish army, was a prisoner of war who was killed at Katyn. My mother and sister were taken away from Vilna by train. They died. Whether these decisions were Communist or only Russian, I do not know. In the forest where I lived with Jewish partisans from the time the Vilna Jews were killed by the Germans until the Russians were winning the war, I knew a Russian blacksmith, a soldier the Germans had taken prisoner, who told me much about how Communism was ..." He hesitated, looking for the right word. "Was managed, was enforced, in the Red Army. What he told me was very frightening, and I thought it was wicked. So did he. Then ..."

He looked at the colonel. But the colonel was looking at the fountain pen he was holding in both hands, and Joe knew he couldn't understand what he was saying.

"Go on", said Mr Peters. "This is most interesting."

"Then one of the German prisoners who was here on the farm when I came tried to persuade me that Communism had been proved to be the truth by history because Stalin and not Hitler had won the war. I did not believe him. I knew he was wrong. I did not see why both Nazism and Communism should not be lies. But I did not know enough to argue well with him."

"Where is he now?"

"He has gone home, to the eastern part of Germany. He lived before he was a soldier in Frankfurt on the Oder. He will be happy to work for the Russians there because now he is a Communist."

"Yes. I understand." Mr Peters turned towards the colonel sitting beside him. But the colonel was still looking down at his pen.

"Tell me, Josef," Mr Peters said, turning back to Joe, "did you discuss your father's death with this German prisoner?"

"He said that the Nazis killed the officers at Katyn and that the story that the Russians killed them was Nazi propaganda."

"Did you believe him?"

"I did not believe him. The truth about Katyn I know. So does everyone in Poland. In England I think this truth is not known."

"Why do you say that?"

"The first English person I met, a Red Cross official, or officer—I'm not sure of the right word—who was checking us before we were brought to England, asked me about my father. I told him. He said that the Russians had released all captured Polish officers to fight against Germany. The German prisoner here said the same thing. I said to the Red Cross officer that I knew this was not true, but he told me I was only a child who did not know what I was talking about."

"You are certainly not a child now. Tell me something else. What do you know about the Nuremberg trials?"

"I know from the news here, on the wireless, that some of the most powerful Nazis were tried and were executed. I think, although the BBC news did not say this, that no crime in the war that was committed by the Russians was referred to at the trials."

"Why do you think that was?"

"Because Stalin won the war. So there was a Russian judge with the British and the American judges at the trial. Is that correct?"

"Yes, Josef. That is correct. In fact, and this you may not know, the murder of the Polish officers was among the crimes the Nazis were charged with at the trial."

"But that is wrong. That is a lie."

"That's as may be. But you couldn't expect a court established to try the Nazis to wish to hear evidence exonerating them from a crime, could you? Even if such evidence exists, which I doubt."

"If no such evidence exists, it will be because the Russians have destroyed it."

Mr Peters said in English to the colonel, "He's no fool, this boy."

The colonel said, "What did I tell you?"

"So, Josef," Mr Peters went on in German, "tell me something about your father. Did your father and his friends talk about Communism at home?"

"Of course. They talked a great deal. In the evening after the sabbath was over—excuse me, on Saturday evenings—my father and his friends talked. I remember …" What should he choose to tell Mr Peters? "I remember my father saying that Communism had once filled the young with hope, especially young Jews. My father was sixteen at the time of the Bolshevik revolution. Perhaps the revolution would make everyone equal and everyone free, even Jews. But the revolution had been a terrible disappointment, a catastrophe, my father said, because it was Russian and because Lenin so quickly took all the power. If the revolution had been German, as Marx had expected, it might have turned out better. My father lived in Breslau, which is a German city, when he was a junior doctor. That was where he met my mother. He admired the German socialist party because it was separate from Bolshevism and not cruel. He said the socialist party was hated equally by the Nazis and the Communists, and that must be a good start."

Mr Peters laughed.

"What do you think your father meant by saying the revolution had been a catastrophe?"

"He said Lenin had destroyed the hope there was in Communism by taking everything bad from tsarism and making it worse. He said the tsars would never have killed the thousands of people who died in the famine, which was created by taking away the peasants who grew most of the corn and then taking away all the corn that was left. The Third Section, the Okhrana, the Cheka, OGPU, NKVD—they were all the same, he said, but each was worse than the one before. I remember the list. I didn't know what the letters and names meant, until I knew that the NKVD killed my father. They are all names for the Russian secret police, the Russian Gestapo. My father said that in Russia the secret police will always rule the people. The Russians have been slaves for a thousand years, he said. They will always be slaves. Also I remember him saying that the Poles believe that all Jews are Communists and that all Communists are Jews. So let us not be Communists, to prove them wrong."

Mr Peters laughed again.

"An interesting man, your father. You remember a great deal, Josef. Here is another question. Would you describe your family as religious?"

"No. Yes. It is complicated. They did some Jewish things but not all. Compared to my uncle the rabbi, who was married to my father's sister, my aunt Anna …" He stopped.

"You were fond of your aunt Anna?"

He looked at Mr Peters. His expression was now kind as well as attentive.

"She was shot the day I escaped. And her three little boys."

"I am so sorry." Mr Peters gave him a minute or two to pull himself together.

"Please go on if you can. You were saying—"

"I am sorry. Yes. Compared to my aunt's family, you would say my parents were not religious. I think my mother was religious when she was young, though my father said the German Jews had given up being Jewish in order to be German. He didn't say it unkindly. It was a sort of joke. If you had met them, you would think my father much more Jewish than my mother. I remember my father saying once that most people believed in something that would save the world, but he didn't. He said he was a doctor who didn't believe in science, a socialist who didn't believe in history, a Jew who didn't believe in God. I think that was a sort of joke also. He said prayers."

"I see. It was complicated, as you say. What did your father think of Zionism?"

"He thought it was un-Jewish. But that was before ..."

"Before?"

"Before Hitler decided to kill all the Jews. Of course that has given the Jews who are still alive a new case for Zionism. My friends in the forest were nearly all Zionists. But ..."

"But?"

"There were Zionists in Prague just before I was brought to England who frightened me."

"Were there indeed? That doesn't surprise me. Do you think that if your father had survived the war, he would have changed his mind?"

Joe hadn't thought about this. "I don't know." Then he said, "Yes, I do know. He would not have changed his mind. He would have thought the same, but his reasons would have been stronger."

"Can you explain?"

"He always said nationalism was a dangerous thing. He didn't like it when it was Polish, or German, or Lithuanian. Lithuanian was the worst. He thought Lithuanian nationalism would destroy Vilna—old Vilna, Polish and Jewish. He loved Vilna. So he thought nationalism would not be good for Jews. He said Jews should live anywhere anyone would let them live, because they always had. He said a definition of a Jew is a person in the wrong place, and that is good. Jews should not be nation-alists themselves. They should not fight; they should not have guns. It was bad that the empires had made the Jews fight for them, but it would be worse if the Jews began to fight for themselves. Now he would be sure that Zionism is a harmful thing. Now that there are murders and bombs in Palestine, he would be saying, 'You see, give Jews their own land and they will fight for it. Why does anyone expect Jews to behave better than everyone else?' And then my uncle the rabbi would say, 'Because, through the centuries of exile, of suffering in strange lands, they did.' I can almost hear them talking."

He stopped again. What he had said had surprised him. He hadn't thought of all this before. How could this stranger—Mr Peters, if that was his name—have got him to say all this, to go back to the talk that used to go on and on through winter evenings at home when he was supposed to be in bed but loved to listen, from his stool in the dark corner by the door to the stairs? How could he have imagined—not invented, which was different—what his father and his uncle would have said about Palestine now if they had still been alive?

Blessed be God.

But if they had still been alive, they would have known, as he did, what had happened to so many Jews, so might they by now have felt dif-ferently about Palestine? Was it, after all—as his father's friend the Zionist doctor had said when there were arguments about Palestine at home—the only place where Jews would not have to be afraid, because it could be their own? But Jews did not have to be afraid in England. Did they?

"So you know", Mr Peters said, "what is going on in Palestine?"

He shook his head to clear it, to return to the colonel's study, and the desk in front of him, and Mr Peters.

"I know very little. Only what I have heard on the wireless and read in the newspaper in the kitchen."

"But you can think about what you hear and read, and that is excellent."

Excellent for what?

"Will you allow me to ask you just a few more questions? First, you may or may not know that there are many thousands of Jews who managed, as you did, to survive the war and are now in camps for dis-placed persons in Germany. Where do you think these thousands of Jews should go to live?"

Now he was afraid. His answer might make all the difference to what the colonel was going to do with him.

"I don't know", he said, and looked across the desk at the colonel.

"Joe, what's the matter, my boy? John, what have you asked him? Whatever it is, it seems to have upset him, and he's managed to answer all your questions so far, hasn't he?"

"Indeed he has, and I must say I'm impressed. I just asked him what he thought about the thousands of Jews in the DP camps."

"Poor devils. Nobody wants them. The Americans want us to let them go to Palestine because they don't want them in America."

"They can't go to Palestine. You should hear the Colonial Office on the subject; I was at a meeting the other day. The Americans seem to think there's no one living in Palestine except a few Jews. It's like the Wild West to them. Red Indians didn't count as people. Arabs don't seem to count either. Americans haven't the faintest idea about the Arab world. Meanwhile, the mandate is costing us an arm and a leg. Just as well it hasn't got long to go."

"What do you think will happen when we leave?"

Had they forgotten he was there? Or did they think he couldn't understand? He wasn't understanding everything, but he was listening very carefully, his eyes on the desk in front of him.

"They'll have to fight it out between them, won't they?" Mr Peters said. This was what Werner had said about the Jews and Arabs. "Meanwhile, what are we going to do with the DPs? We can't expect the Germans to put up with them indefinitely. God knows, we need the Germans on our side now."

Joe was so surprised by these two sentences that he looked up. Neither of them noticed.

"Haven't we said all along that they should go back to their own countries? Poland is where most of them came from, I gather."

"At the end of the war the London Poles wanted to send all the Jews who had managed to survive to Odessa, as if the Russians hadn't been bullying Jews for centuries. And believe it or not, hundreds of Jews who went home to Poland after the war have come back to the DP camps in Germany because there is too much hostility at home."

"That's understandable, I suppose", the colonel said. "The wretched Poles are bound to be afraid that the Jews will want their houses, their property, back."

"To tell you the truth, I think everyone's been surprised at how many Jews are still with us. Of course, they've always made the most of their sufferings. But I don't believe any of us had any idea how many of them there were to start with. Anyway, they won't be our problem much longer. Lord knows we've got plenty of problems to be going on with."

"Well, it's no good asking Joe what he thinks, is it? He's been out of it all for a couple of years, looking after my horses."

"Yes, exactly. Now, Josef ..." Mr Peters turned towards him. Joe looked at Mr Peters.

"I am sure you will agree"—Mr Peters was speaking to him in Russian—"that you owe Great Britain a considerable debt of gratitude. No doubt you would like to do something to repay that debt." His Russian was stiff, somehow automatic, as if he had learned this speech and often recited it before.

"Yes, sir, I would. But I have nothing I can give to repay any debt." Joe answered in Russian.

"You have more than you think."

Mr Peters put both his forearms on the desk and leaned towards him.

"I'll go on in German, if you don't mind. That was a little experiment. My Russian is a bit rusty, and your German is excellent. Your mother tongue of course. Let me put something to you, Josef. You have heard Colonel Robertson say that it's not possible for you to stay here, and I do understand that you don't want to go back to Vilnius after all you have been through. How would you feel about coming down to the south of England to work for my department? We would offer you training for at least a year, for very important work for the government of this country, and then, if you completed the training satisfactorily, you would have a job with us, which would be an excellent way of returning the generosity of Great Britain and of Colonel Robertson in particular."

How frightening was this? He must try to discover.

"What kind of job, sir? What kind of work?"

"Work that needs young men who have a range of languages, as you have, and who have shown that they have the intelligence and the resourcefulness to cope with the unexpected in a variety of situations. Courage too. You clearly have plenty of that. Tell me, Josef, about your life in the forest with the partisans. What did you yourself do? You were only a child when you joined them, weren't you? When was that?"

"In the winter of 1942. I was twelve years old. A peasant let me live in her loft for some months—I'm not sure how long—after I ran away from the shooting. I looked after her horse and her geese and hens, and she told me to ride into the forest if the Germans came. So when they came, I did. The partisans let me stay with them because I was a Jew and because of my horse. I did errands for them, quickly because I rode. Then they shot her."

"Why?"

"For meat, for the real fighters."

"I'm sorry to ask you to remember all this. And then?"

"After that I still did errands, to get news from people who brought messages from the ghetto in Nowogródek, sometimes from the ghetto in Vilna. A few of them found ways to get out and get back in, mostly girls. Sometimes I was sent to meet peasants who would tell us when the Germans would be driving into the forest or along roads where they could be ambushed. I was useful because I was small and I moved quickly. I took messages from the camp to the fighters. Also I worked for the cooks in the camp and for the blacksmith. Our commander said that for us to stay alive was more important than to kill Germans."

"When did you leave the camp?"

"We moved often, the whole camp. There were many dangers in the forest. When we heard that the Russians were coming, not just partisans but the Red Army, our commander said we had to break up and scatter and move west in any way we could, so as not to be captured. The Red Army soldiers would have shot us. All partisans not obedient to Moscow were traitors. I was soon by myself. For a few weeks I joined some German farmers travelling west from East Prussia to get away from the Red Army. At first I thought they might kill me. But they didn't care that I was a Jew. I was useful to them because I spoke Polish. They thought I was a German Jew. I looked after their horse."

"It's a remarkable story. You are a remarkable young man. I think you will be very well suited to the kind of work we have in mind for you."

Joe looked at the colonel, who was staring down at the papers on his desk. Then he said to Mr Peters in English:

"What is the work you want me to do?"

The colonel looked up and exchanged a glance with Mr Peters, who answered in German:

"I can't tell you now precisely what your work will be. But if you do well in the training I was talking about—and I expect you to do very well—I can promise you that it will be interesting work, and very valuable to England, which has treated you well."

He thought of Mrs Robertson and James.

What did the colonel want? All this was surely his doing. Joe wanted to go back to English, to include him.

"Sir?" he said to the colonel.

"Joe, I promise you this is a great opportunity. Mr Peters can't tell you very much at present about the kind of work you might be doing. This is for good reasons which you will understand one day. But you are being given this chance because I have been most impressed with you while you have been here. Of course you are good with horses. But you are far too intelligent to spend the rest of your life looking after horses, however much you think at the moment that that's what you want to do. You are clever and brave, and you're able to speak all these languages—English as well now. I'm sure you will contribute to some very valuable work that needs to be done for us, for England."

He listened to the colonel. He understood that the colonel did not just want to get rid of him but wanted to find him something useful to do. He looked at Mr Peters. Both of them were looking at him with attention, waiting to see what he would say.

There was a silence. He wasn't sure of the right English words.

"You want me to be a secret policeman."

Both of them looked away. There was annoyance in Mr Peters' expression. Neither of them spoke.

"Like the NKVD and the Gestapo. But I am in England."

The colonel laughed. An embarrassed laugh.

"My dear boy, every country needs ... needs to keep an eye on ... on what's going on in different places, for its own safety."

He thought of everything he had said to Mr Peters.

After another silence Joe said, "You will send me to the east of Germany, where the Russians are."

"No flies on this boy, damn him", Mr Peters said. Joe didn't understand the words but did understand that his deduction was correct.

"I've no idea", the colonel said, "what work you might be given to do, Joe. But you can be sure it will be important. I should have thought you would have plenty of reasons, family reasons and other reasons, for wanting to do your bit in the cause of freedom."

He looked at Mr Peters, who translated this into German.

"No", Joe said to Mr Peters in German. "For four years I was afraid all the time. I am not afraid in England. I do not want to be given important work which will mean going back to Germany, to Poland, to Kresy. I never want to go there again. I will do any work here, any work with horses, sheep, hens, on a farm, anywhere in England. This is not important work, I know, but if I am allowed to choose, I choose not to go back there."

Mr Peters translated.

The colonel said, "Where is Kresy?"

Mr Peters knew. "It's Polish for the borderlands between Poland and Russia. A lot of it very backward. Frontiers disputed of course. Where Josef's partisans lived in the forest, I imagine."

"Yes, sir. Belorussia. Where the Germans burned the villages and the Russians have always kept the people poor." The English for this sentence came from he knew not where.

"Now, listen to me, Joe", the colonel said, in a firmer, colder voice. "If you don't understand, ask Mr Peters to translate. Nobody's suggesting that you go back to Europe now, or probably for years. Things change. The terrible effects of the war will wear off. People will rebuild. We all hope that there will be peace in Europe for a long, long time. In fact, the work Mr Peters thinks you may be able to do would be part of making that peace more likely."

Mr Peters translated.

Joe said in German, "The effects of the war will last until after I am dead."

The colonel didn't wait for a translation.

"What I'm trying to say, Joe, is that I think you will be making a serious mistake if you decide against taking up Mr Peters' offer. This is an extraordinary opportunity for you to achieve something really worthwhile after—well, after such a difficult start—and I think you will regret it for the rest of your life if you turn your back on it. Thank you, John."

Mr Peters translated, and the colonel stood up before Joe said anything in reply.

"And in any case, if you don't agree to this plan, what do you propose to do? I've already explained that I can't keep you here."

"I don't know. I will find some work."

"It's not so easy now that most of our boys have come home. And the unions aren't happy about foreign workers—not that you'd know about them."

Mr Peters stood too, beside the colonel across the desk. So Joe had to stand. The interview was clearly over.

"I will give you twenty-four hours to consider what I have put to you, Josef", Mr Peters said in German. "Colonel Robertson and I both think that you would be very foolish, very foolish indeed, to turn your back on an opportunity that very few young men in your position will ever be offered. So think very carefully about what we have said, and come back here at the same time tomorrow, three o'clock, to let us hear your decision. Remember that if you accept the offer I have made, you will be looked after. You will have somewhere to live. You will have friends engaged in the same kind of work. You will be paid. If you decide not to accept my offer, I have no idea what will become of you. Certainly you will be on your own. Again."

"Sir."

He bent his head in acknowledgement, not as smartly as Werner would have done, and left the study.

The next day, at three o'clock, he went back to the study and, without sitting down, told them both that he could not accept Mr Peters' offer.

Mr Peters said, "You will regret this, young man."

The colonel said, "It's all right, Joe. I think I understand. And this is, after all, a free country. Long may it remain so. I shall do what I can for you. For the moment, carry on with your ordinary work, and if you don't mind, say nothing to the others for the time being."

"Sir."

As Joe left the study, Mr Peters said, "Well, if that's the way it is, he wouldn't have been much use to us anyway."

He did as the colonel had told him. Not for a moment did he wonder whether he had made the wrong decision. He was surprised to find that, although he was now certain that he was going to have to leave the farm, the horses, his room, and Ted and Mrs Thwaites, he felt more carefree, lighter at heart, than he had for months. Was it because Mr Peters had made him remember and describe so much? Or because

Mr Peters had made him decide something for himself? Probably both.

The fine weather went on, day after beautiful sunny day. Every afternoon he took Tiger Rag on a long ride and galloped him home across the floor of the valley. When he dismounted in the yard and took off the saddle and bridle, he thought Tiger looked at him gratefully as he put on his head-collar to lead him back to the paddock. Poor Tiger.

Two weeks after Mr Peters and his wife left the house—he watched the car in its cloud of summer dust rattle down the farm road as Mr Ward drove them to the station—Ted said at dinnertime in the kitchen, "Colonel wants to see you after tea, Joe. Five o'clock in the study. Serious, he looked, this morning."

"Thank you, Ted."

"Joe? You've gone quite white. Not in trouble, are we?"

"No. Not in trouble."

The weather broke that day, and a thunderstorm had crashed about the sky in the morning. By the late afternoon the rain had stopped, and the air was fresh and cool, the dale rinsed of dust and heat.

"Come in", the colonel said when Joe knocked on the study door, and then, as Joe shut the door behind him, more gently, "Come in, Joe. Sit yourself down. That's right. Cigarette?"

He pushed a shagreen and silver box towards Joe.

"No, thank you, sir."

"Now look, Joe, I'm sorry that my idea of you working for Mr Peters' outfit came to nothing, but don't let's worry about that anymore. Water under the bridge. And you won't say anything about it in the future to anyone at all, will you?"

"No, sir."

"Good. I'm sure you understand why not. Now then ..."

The colonel looked through a pile of papers on his desk, found the paper he wanted, and smoothed it out. Ted often said "Now then". It had a friendly sound, and did in the colonel's study too.

"I've been in touch with a Jewish committee in London which helps young Jewish people who have come here without any family to support them. They've answered my letter, very promptly I must say, and they say they can find you somewhere to live in London, a room in a Jewish hostel, and also that they will do what they can to help you find some suitable work. A lady from the committee will meet you off the train in London on Tuesday and take you to where you're going to stay, so there's no need to worry. Ted will get you your ticket when he takes you to the station. He'll tell you how to change trains in York. I'll give you a bit of money to get you started. How does that sound?"

"Thank you, sir."

"What is it, Joe? Something you want to ask me?"

"The violin, sir. Your son's violin."

"Oh, the violin. Have it, my dear boy, have it. Take it with you. It's no use to anyone here. You play it remarkably well, I must say. You must have had a fine teacher when you were a little boy."

"Yes, sir. Also my father played violin very well."

"Ah."

The colonel looked at him across the desk.

"You have lost a great deal in your short life, haven't you, Joe? Well . . . I hope you feel that your time here has been a gain, something that you will look back on as good."

"Yes, sir. The horses of course. And Ted and Mrs Thwaites have been very kind."

"Good, good. I'm afraid that you may not find everyone you meet in London so kind, particularly at the moment. Keep your head down is my advice. Don't get into arguments with people. If in doubt, pretend you don't speak English. Do you understand?"

"Yes, sir."

"Splendid. Right you are, Joe. You get back to work, now. Come and say good-bye on Monday, about this time."

Joe got up.

"Thank you, sir."

"Oh, and Joe," the colonel said as he left the study, "take the music with you too—Philip's music. Nice for you to have it, and it'll only clutter up a cupboard here. I'm sure Ted or Mrs Thwaites will find you an old suitcase to put your things in."

"Thank you, sir."

It was Thursday, the last day of July. That evening Ted, Mrs Thwaites, Bob, and Bill were still at the kitchen table finishing cups of tea, and Joe was washing up, when Mrs Thwaites got up to switch on the nine o'clock news.

"The two British sergeants kidnapped in Palestine by Jewish terrorists nearly three weeks ago have been found hanged in an orchard. The site of the outrage was mined, and a British captain attempting to retrieve the bodies was seriously injured in an explosion. These murders are thought to be in reprisal for the execution of three convicted Irgun terrorists on Tuesday. Serious disturbances in various places in the mandate territory have been reported, and this evening we have learned that five Jews have been killed by soldiers or police in the streets of Jerusalem."

"Serves them bloody right", Bob said. "I hope we kill plenty more of them for this. God almighty. Makes you think Hitler had a point, doesn't it, Dad?"

Joe, out of sight in the scullery, went on drying the supper dishes.

"Two wrongs don't make a right, Bob."

There was a brief silence. Ted had probably nodded in Joe's direction, to stop Bob. But Bob was not to be stopped.

"I wonder if Captain James knew those sergeants. He'll be livid, more than livid, if he did. He'll wish he could get back out there and deal with some Jews himself. Pity he's been demobbed. I'm sorry I've been demobbed myself when this sort of thing's going on."

Joe tidied the sink, folded his tea cloth, and left the house by the back door without going into the kitchen.

On Friday Mrs Thwaites' *Daily Express* had a horrible photograph of the dead sergeants and a big black headline: HANGED BRITONS: PICTURE THAT WILL SHOCK THE WORLD.

"What do you think of this, then?" Bob, at dinnertime, was holding up the paper at Joe and jabbing at the picture with his finger. Ted was out somewhere with the colonel.

"I think it is very horrible. I have seen many such horrible things in my country."

"Oh. That makes it all right, then, does it?"

"No. All such things are very bad, very cruel."

"That's right, Joe. You stick up for yourself", Mrs Thwaites said. "None of this has got owt to do with Joe, Bob. You know that quite well. You should be ashamed of yourself, taking it out on a lad who wouldn't hurt a fly."

"That's what you think. I wouldn't trust any Jew further than I could throw him, however good he is with horses."

"That's quite enough, Bob. I won't have you getting at Joe in my kitchen."

"He's off on Tuesday, anyway. Dad told me. Good riddance, I say."

"Bob! I'm not telling you again."

Then Joe saw her realize what Bob had said.

"Joe?"

"Yes, Mrs Thwaites. I have to go to London. A committee will give me a room." The word was the same in Polish, almost the same in German. "They will help me to find some work."

"But Joe, that's dreadful! London, of all places—and you a country boy. I've never been to London, but I've never liked the sound of it. Too many people, too much traffic—a nasty, dirty place from what I hear."

"I was not a country boy before the war. My home was in the city."

"But your horses, Joe—you'll miss them. And they'll miss you. We all will. And what's the colonel thinking of, sending you to London all of a sudden?"

"Colonel always promised Albert Lumley groom's job, didn't he?" Bob said. "Promised he could have it when he was demobbed. And now he's back here. Fair's fair."

This took a moment or two to sink in while she looked at Bob.

"Ah. Well, I suppose that makes it different. Albert's dad was in the colonel's regiment, wasn't he? Killed just before the armistice, he was. Blood'll always be thicker than water, you've got to admit that."

Bob said nothing.

"But it's hard on Joe, I do think. Very hard. When he's made such a good go of it on the farm. What does Ted reckon?"

"Just one of those things, he says."

They helped him leave.

The colonel had given him four five-pound notes the evening before, in an envelope with a letter addressed "To whom it may concern" describing Joe.

The colonel had said, "If you're asked for a reference, give them this. But get it back when they've read it."

He hadn't asked Joe to sit down.

"Be careful with the money. It should last you till you're being paid."

The colonel stood up and shook Joe's hand across the desk.

"Good-bye, my boy. You've done very well here. I'm grateful. And good luck."

"Thank you, sir."

Mrs Thwaites came up to his room to make sure his few clothes were clean, mended, and folded properly on top of the music, his dictionary, and his book of German poems, in the old suitcase Ted had produced. When she had gone, he took the glassless photograph of Sally from his now empty drawer, and put the photograph in the folds of his respectable jumper.

On Tuesday morning he got up very early and went out to say good-bye to the horses. Tiger trotted up to him in the paddock and Joe sent him off, after stroking his nose and telling him in German, "No ride today, old fellow." The colonel's horse looked up from the far end of the paddock and then went on grazing. Joe realized he was fonder than he had noticed of black Robin, the big, stocky Dales pony with feathered heels who pulled the wagon. Robin had never been coddled in a loose box like the riding horses. He had stayed out all through the cold winter, needing only his hay in the open barn and someone to break the ice on the water trough every day. He had given no one any trouble through all the time Joe had been at the farm. But Joe could say good-bye to him at the station.

He went up to his room, picked up the suitcase and the violin, and looked back as he left. At the door he put down the case and the violin, went back to the bed, and ran his hand over his eiderdown.

A hug from Mrs Thwaites, a handshake from Bill, and he climbed into the wagon beside Ted. Bob wasn't there.

At the station Ted bought his ticket and stood beside him on the platform until the train appeared. Then he too shook his hand.

"Good-bye, Joe. Don't forget us, will you? You're a grand lad, and don't you let anyone down south tell you different."

In the train he cried.

At King's Cross a German woman, appraising and efficient, not very friendly, met him, checked his name against a list, and carried his violin on the underground train. He hoped she didn't notice that he was frightened by the underground train. They got out at a station called Hampstead and walked for ten minutes. They stopped at a large oldish house with a flight of steps down to the pavement from the front door. On the door was a large poster fixed with two drawing pins. In red letters painted to look like flames it said, HANG ALL JEWS.

The German lady pulled it off the door, leaving the torn corners attached to the drawing pins.

"Pay no attention, Mr Halpern. This will pass."

Chapter 4

In London he was alone. To be alone and safe was new, unfamiliar, not easy.

After the murders in Palestine and Mrs Thwaites' *Daily Express* and the poster on the door in Hampstead, he was expecting London to be something like Vilna after the Germans arrived. Although he had seen them in the streets for only a few weeks before the killings at Ponary, he could not forget their marching, their uniforms, their pushing of Jews— even the old and frail—into the gutter, or the fear it was so easy for them to spread, as if they had brought it with them like a plague.

But there was no marching in the London streets. He saw people in uniform but always one by one: the man on the bus who sold the tickets; the occasional soldier; a policeman, in the peculiar helmet London policemen wore, walking mildly past houses and shops, clearly frightening no one. He had been told on his first day to ask a policeman for help if he got lost; he had his address written on a piece of paper so that the policeman could tell him how he should get home. That this was a safe thing to do he could hardly believe. But it turned out to be the case.

One beautiful day he decided to get off the bus halfway home and walk back to Hampstead. He did get lost. He looked up and down a shopping street he didn't recognize. When he saw a policeman he made sure he had in his pocket his Nansen passport, the document for a stateless person each of the children on the aeroplane had been given when they arrived in England. He walked up to the policeman, afraid, his heart beating hard, and asked the way to the address he produced on his piece of paper. The policeman looked at him for just long enough, he could tell, to see that he was young and a foreigner and then took him to a corner where more streets were visible, and patiently explained which turnings he should take. That the policeman hadn't asked his name, or wanted to see his papers, he thought almost a miracle as he found his way back to the house.

Above all, people in London didn't seem to look at each other suspiciously. In those early weeks he caught only in the eyes of a single man at work what he had seen in James Robertson's: disgusted recognition of the Jew.

His bus took him downhill—the whole journey seemed downhill, though perhaps it wasn't—through poorer and poorer streets more and more scarred by the ragged spaces where houses had been bombed. These spaces, bombed sites, were his work. An older Jewish woman from the committee had come to see him in his room on the day after he arrived in London. She spoke to him in Yiddish, and then in Polish when she found he knew the language. She apologized for not being able to find a way of allowing him to study.

"We should like you to continue your education, but these things are very difficult at present. The best we can do is to find you, for the time being, some work that needs to be done and will earn you a little money. You are young and strong. I see you have worked in the country, on a farm. That is good. This Colonel"—she was looking at the reference the colonel had given him—"Robertson, he speaks well of your work. With his horses. Indeed? That is remarkable for a boy from Vilna. And I see that you arrived in England on one of those RAF aeroplanes in the summer of '45. You were very lucky. But I expect you know that.

"There is another young man from Poland, not in this house but living nearby. He will collect you outside at eight o'clock tomorrow morning and show you how to catch the bus and where your first job will be. It's only clearing rubble, I'm afraid, from the destruction the Germans inflicted on London. Wear the roughest clothes you have. After a while perhaps we may be able to find you something better."

The other young man, taller, stronger, and several years older than Joe, was silent and unfriendly. He must have been Jewish, or the committee wouldn't have known about him, but he didn't look Jewish and he showed little interest in Joe. He asked him, in Polish, on the bus, "From a camp? In the east?"

"No", Joe said and thought it best not to add anything.

"I was a soldier", the young man said. "In General Anders' army."

"I thought—" Joe began and then stopped. Someone at the farm, probably Bob, had said that the Jews in the Polish army, which had been training in Palestine to fight with the English in Italy, had deserted to join the Jews already in Palestine. Now they were the terrorists bombing hotels and hanging sergeants in orchards. Well, clearly not all of them had stayed in Palestine.

When they got off the bus, the young man waved Joe over to a group of workmen, some as young as Joe, some much older, who were being given heavy gloves, picks, and shovels beside a deep, jagged hole littered with broken brick and stone and charred chunks of timber, under dirty flakes of white plaster. Here and there at the bottom of the pit were clumps of a tall crimson-purple flower with soft, dark green leaves that Joe had seen at the edges of the larch wood above the farm. It used to appear, as brittle, juicy, fast-growing shoots, in Ted's vegetable garden. "Fetch it out, lad. That's right. Along with the buttercup and the creeping thistle." In the bomb crater on patches of earth among the bits of old buildings, the plant was alive and bright and in the wrong place. Joe wished he felt as brave as it looked.

When he turned round, the Polish soldier had gone. He never saw him again.

The work, obviously, was to clear the debris and load it into the battered barrows at the bottom among the piles of rubble and the willow herb and then into wide, dirty buckets that were swung up on chains and emptied into trucks by the side of the road. Every day for six or seven weeks he did this work, moving from site to site as each was cleared, shouted at in a general way, along with a dozen others, by a foreman who, at street level by the trucks, worked as hard as any of them. It was dull, noisy, not difficult, and left Joe's back aching at the end of the day. Nobody talked much. When they did, over their thermos flasks of tea and chunks of bread and dripping, or sometimes Spam or even jam, he could understand very little of what the Londoners said. Their English wasn't like Ted's and Mrs Thwaites', or like the colonel's.

He soon bought himself a thermos at Woolworth's and found out how to light the gas under the kettle in the house kitchen, make tea with a very little of his ration, and fill his flask before he left for work.

There were two other foreigners in the group. Like him, they kept quiet and worked hard. It was on the face of one of them that he caught from time to time the look he had feared to meet everywhere in London.

Apart from this look—which could be met occasionally in the streets of Vilna even before the Germans came—London and Vilna, although they were the only two cities in which he had ever lived, were as different from each other as the Belorussian forest was different from the woods above the farm in the Yorkshire dale.

He thought that the buildings of Vilna: the university; the Great Synagogue and its courts; the elaborate churches with their white towers; the river and the sunny squares; the old, narrow streets, dirty, crowded, and noisy, were much more beautiful than the buildings of London. He knew that on his bus journeys and at his work he hadn't seen the important, perhaps the great, buildings of London. His group was clearing rubble north of two big railway stations—poor streets, poor people, harassed women shouting at children, a bad smell which did remind him of Vilna. Hampstead, on the other hand, at least the part of it where he was living, seemed to be all sky and trees. Every street was wide and quiet. It was summer, and mostly warm and sunny, but no one who wasn't walking or bicycling to somewhere else was in the streets. No one sat outside a house to work, to watch, to talk, to greet people passing by. People didn't look at each other suspiciously, but perhaps that was because people didn't look at each other at all.

At first there hadn't been time to do more than find out from strangers, the other people in the house, who answered questions but seemed set to remain strangers, how to eat as cheaply as possible, where to wash his shirts and socks and underwear, how to dry them in his room. He discovered by listening, by observing their comings and goings, how to find an hour here and there when no one who lived in neighbouring rooms was in, so that he could practise his violin without annoying anyone.

The other people in the house were wary, as he knew he was himself. They spoke only English to each other, some better, some worse than he did. They said as little as possible, rarely smiled, never asked each other how they came to be in London or what had happened to them during the war. All of them kept food in their rooms, as he did, very carefully, and brought to the little kitchen perhaps an egg or a quarter of a cabbage or a couple of potatoes to cook. One youngish woman, perhaps thirty years old, once a week collected a few coins from each of the others, and one or two precious meat coupons, to buy a cheap boiling chicken. She made chicken soup on a Thursday evening and gave everyone some on the next evening in the mug each of them brought to the kitchen. This seemed to him both very Jewish and very un-Jewish because there was nowhere in the house for them all to eat together. As far as he could tell, no one in the house said prayers. But perhaps some did when they were alone, as he did when he remembered his family.

There were eight rooms, eight people, in the house, but the people changed. Someone would leave, without saying he was going, or where to, and then someone else would arrive.

After a few weeks an old man came, an old man who liked to talk, in good English with a heavy German accent.

"And who are you?" he said to Joe, coming into the kitchen one evening as Joe was washing his mug and his plate.

"I am Josef Halpern, sir."

"Are you indeed? That is a good Jewish name, and not too difficult for these English to say. My name is Aharon Leschnitzer. Imagine an Englishman trying to say this name. So now I am Albert Carver—they like Albert, because of the prince, a good German, by the way—and Carver is a good English name, no?"

"Yes. Of course."

"So, Josef, where were you born?"

"In Vilna."

"Ah, Vilna, mother Vilna. I never was there. So you are a good Litvak. What was your father?"

He was grateful to the old man for assuming that his father was dead.

"My father was a doctor."

"He was? Good. Very good. So how are you alive and in London, Josef?"

"It's a long story." This was what Ted had told him to say if anyone in London asked him how he came to be in England.

"For sure it is. And for sure it is a sad story also. There is no Jewish story now which is not sad. When has there ever been a Jewish story which is not sad? A Jewish story that is not sad must be funny, no? Or sad and funny at the same time, maybe."

He wasn't sure he understood this. He smiled uncertainly.

"Now come, Josef, you are young. Tomorrow is another day, as the English say. What work have they given you? You have dirty clothes and rough hands, I see."

"I am clearing bombed sites."

"A doctor's son clearing bombed sites? This is not so good. Do you have your *Abitur*?"

"I haven't been in school since I was ten years old."

"Ah, of course, of course. The war. Poor Josef. We shall see what might be done. Unfortunately I am staying here only a short time. Hitler bombed my house in 1940. He killed my wife. My wife's family was from the east. But she was not a Litvak. Her parents came from Czernowitz. You have not heard of it? No. Why should you? Czernowitz, in the Bukovina. Who knows where it is now. In Russia, I suppose. All the same, she was English. She was born in London, and when she was young she was beautiful. My family did not want me to marry a Romanian Jew. They were German, you understand. To them Jews from the east were not—it was not good that my family thought as they did. But there you are, as the English say. I married her, whatever they thought. And she died so, in the blitz." He bent his head for a moment. "Since Hitler bombed us, I have been living with my good neighbours. But now they say our whole street is to be destroyed. Pulled down, that's what they say. It must be pulled down because the houses are rickety—is not that a fine word?—too rickety to be safe. There are great cracks, you know, because of the bombs. So they sent me here. Not for long, they say. They promise to give me a new flat to live in. A flat—can you imagine? Soon. Where I may work also. I am an upholsterer. Do you know what that is?"

"I'm sorry. No."

The old man laughed.

"Of course no. It is I who should be sorry. An upholsterer—what a word. It took me weeks to learn to say it when I came to London, and more weeks to learn to spell it. I came a long time ago, in 1928, from Hamburg. My sister and her husband were in London already. My brother-in-law tuned and mended pianos. My sister was older than I, her husband much older. They died before the war, first he, then she, quietly, in their beds. They were fortunate."

He paused, a melancholy look on his face. Then he raised his head and smiled. "An upholsterer makes curtains, chair covers, cushions. He stuffs sofas. Horsehair he loves. And he sews. Always he sews. I learned how to do all these things from my father a long, long time ago. *Ein Tapezierer*. Do you know German?"

"Yes, I know German", he said in German. "My mother was German."

"Ah! Good. Better. Wonderful", the old man said in German, and clapped Joe on the shoulder with a firm hand. "So your mother was not born in Vilna?"

"She was born in Breslau. She was a nurse in the hospital where my father was a doctor when he was young."

"Ah, Breslau, another great city. I have not been there, so far east. Now, you know, it is a Polish city, very much destroyed but Polish. It is not Breslau now but Wrocław. All the Germans were moved out to the west. Of course no Jews were left, though many used to live there, quite happily I think, your mother's family among them no doubt. But Hitler would have the city made Jew free, like all of Germany, like all of the world. What a plan! How would the world get on without the Jews to remind it of God? But there, Breslau, another story of sadness. Too many, too many sad stories."

"Breslau is no longer a German city? I didn't know. But Vilna, my own city, is used to change. Vilna was in Russia when my father was a child, and then it was in Poland, and now it is in Lithuania and again in the Russian empire, as it was when my father was born. The tsars are not called tsars since the revolution, but tsars they are, my friends used to say. But my mother's city, I think, is not used to change—a whole city to be in Germany and now to be in Poland—"

"And therefore also in the Russian empire. Because the unhappy Poles are back in the Russian empire, as when your father was born. The English are fortunate of course. Their cities are not suddenly in another country. They do not know about such things."

Again the melancholy look. Was the old man perhaps saying a prayer when he bent his head? Again he looked up and smiled.

"And you are in London—which on the whole is good, whatever it is, and it is much, that the English do not know. Tell me, where have you been since the war was over, Josef?"

"For nearly two years I was in Yorkshire, working on a farm."

"On a farm? Wonderful! The good fresh air. All my long life I have lived in cities. First Hamburg, then London. Big, dirty cities with smoke and soot and ships coming and going."

Ships. Joe had never seen the sea. Many, many lakes but not the sea. The aeroplane that brought him to England must have flown over the sea, but there were few windows and he was sitting among the other children in the roar of the aeroplane's engines too far from the small windows to see out. He had forgotten, or he had never known, that London was a port. He knew that Hamburg was a port because leaving from Hamburg for America, paying for your steerage passage with the money you had buried under the floor where the Cossacks wouldn't find it, was one of the stories of the Pale that everyone knew.

The old man, while they were talking, had put the kettle on the gas stove, and now it whistled. Holding it with a cloth because the handle was hot, he took it off the flame and made some tea in a brown teapot. He opened a cupboard and then a drawer and found a glass, a teaspoon, and some sugar in a bowl.

"Here, Josef, some tea. Not quite the tea of Russian Poland but as near as we can get in London."

With the other tea towel Joe took the very hot glass. He was close to crying. "Thank you. No one in England has—"

"Ach, England! Always milk in the tea. Most of the English are good people, you will find, but they know nothing about us. Some of them of course think they dislike Jews, especially now because of the horrible things in Palestine—it is most unfortunate to give people good reasons to dislike Jews—but most of the dislikers have never met a Jew. Tell me, Josef, did you read the newspapers on your farm?"

"Recently, yes, I tried to. I had little English when I came. But every night we listened to the news on the wireless. And I learned more English."

"Of course. So you will know about the fighters in Palestine. They are very angry—naturally they are very angry—that the English will not allow more Jews to live in Palestine. There are Jews whom the war has left with nothing, no homes, no money, no country, nothing at all, and the truth is, as usual, that nobody wants them. Nobody ever wants the Jews, though when they come, people find them quite useful after all. They will pay them when they want their chairs stuffed or their pianos mended. They will pay them a great deal when they want their money to become more money, and they give it to the Rothschilds to look after."

The old man laughed and sipped his tea.

"But the fighters in Palestine should be more careful, or the whole world will want to kill the Jews as Hitler did. The newspapers tell us about Palestine because British soldiers are there. But now that the war is finished, about Europe they do not tell us. The English newspapers, and even the BBC, are not very much interested in anything that is happening east of the Elbe, although what is happening east of the Elbe is no doubt bad, very bad. But even during the war they would tell us only what the English soldiers were doing. Of course; it was natural. People listening had sons and husbands and brothers fighting. So I myself know very little of what happened, really, in the rest of Europe. I know that Hamburg, my city, the city of my parents and grandparents, was four years ago most terribly destroyed by bombing and fire. If there were people there I knew as a child—we knew Christians, of course, as well as Jews—they were burned to death perhaps."

The downward look. The prayer.

"I do know also that there has been a great silence in the east. Jews in London—Jews from Poland, from Russia, from Romania—have written letters for years to their families in these places, and for years they have heard nothing from this silence. One day perhaps we shall discover what has become of all these Jews. It is not possible that they are in Palestine, because we know the English have not allowed them to go there. So where are they? Did Hitler chase them all into Russia? Did the Russians chase them all into Siberia? Who knows?"

Then the old man noticed.

"Josef?"

Joe had put down his glass of tea because it was too hot to drink. Also because now he was crying. He took out his handkerchief, dirty from wiping dust off his face in bombed sites, and sobbed into it.

"Josef, I am sorry, so sorry. I am a silly old man who talks too much. Forgive me, my child."

"They are dead", Joe said. "The Jews of Poland and Russia are dead. They cannot write letters because they are dead."

He picked up his plate and his mug and left the kitchen. Back in his room he threw himself on his bed, with its grey blankets, and cried. He was crying with fury as well as with grief. An idiot of an old Jew who knew nothing. Was there no one in England who knew anything?

He cried until he was too tired to cry anymore and there were no more tears. He lay still. Yet the old Jew was kind. And people in England had been kind to the old Jew. Could he tell him what had happened in Vilna, at Ponary, in the ghettos in Belorussia, in the places he had heard about in the forest, places where people were taken only to be killed? Treblinka. Majdanek. Was it important that the old man should know? If he knew, he would pray for all the dead. Was that important? Perhaps it was.

He slept, not for long because when he woke up it was still light. He looked at his watch. Nearly half past eight. As he got to his feet he saw that a piece of paper had been slipped under his door. Written on it, in German, in old-fashioned, hard-to-read German writing, were the words:

"What great nation is there that has a God so close at hand as is the Lord our God whenever we call upon him?"

The Torah. He thought of his uncle the rabbi and his aunt Anna. He took his violin from its case, tuned it, and began to play, a quiet piece by Bach that he knew by heart.

By this time in the evening the others who lived in the house would be back in their rooms. But nobody banged on his door or shouted at him to stop playing. So after this day he played for an hour every evening, when he had got back from work, washed, had his supper, and tidied his room, and it seemed to be all right.

Not long after this, however, work became frightening.

He was always a few minutes early for work because he was afraid of being late. One morning while they were all collecting their gloves and tools, he saw the foreman looking at his watch and then at the list, clipped to a board, on which every day he ticked off their names. Someone was late. After a few more minutes the foreman looked at his watch again, shook his head, and put his list down under the stained old canvas bag that held his thermos and his lunch.

Three hours later they had stopped work for half an hour and were sitting on broken masonry eating their lunch when a new worker arrived, with a small man in a suit who explained something to the foreman, perhaps apologizing for being late, and then walked away. Joe, a few yards away, looked at the new man, who was big and strong, taller than the foreman, with very fair, almost white, hair and pale blue eyes. Something about him was vaguely familiar and made Joe shrink back into concentrating on the apple he was eating, not wanting to be seen by the stranger.

There was a shout, a cheerful shout of recognition, "Mikolaj!", from the foreigner who had several times shot at Joe the familiar look of disgusted recognition of a Jew.

"Viktoras!" the new worker shouted back. Both were on their feet and in a moment hugging each other while the others watched, the Englishmen mostly looking dubious or embarrassed, though one or two smiled. The other foreigner, who had been there all along and who had never exchanged a glance, let alone a word, with Joe before, now caught his eye with what Joe was puzzled to interpret as some kind of sympathy.

As soon as the reunited friends started talking to each other, rapidly and enthusiastically, both still standing, Joe realized why he had been suddenly afraid. They were Lithuanians.

Even before the foreman had called everyone to get back to work, the one Joe now knew was called Viktoras had nodded in Joe's direction so that his friend registered Joe's existence, raised his eyes to heaven, and apparently asked Viktoras a question which was answered only with a shrug.

The following week there were a few days of really hot weather which the Englishmen grumbled about. "It's all wrong for the middle of September unless you're on a beach." On the hottest morning most of the workmen in a particularly deep and shattered crater had taken off their shirts before it was time for lunch. Five of them, in a chain, were passing from one to the other some heavy charred planks too long for the barrows. Joe found himself taking the pieces of timber one by one from the man behind him, upending each one which was then taken, easily because he was so strong, by Mikolaj, the new Lithuanian, standing above Joe on a broken but solid wall of brick. He then passed the plank upwards again to the next man in the chain. As Mikolaj raised his arms to do this, over and over again, Joe, looking upwards, saw a small tattoo, a letter, a number, on the underside of Mikolaj's left arm. While he remembered what this tattoo was, what it meant, where he had seen it before, he made himself keep the rhythm of taking a plank from the man behind him and passing it up to Mikolaj. He mustn't let the Lithuanian see he had noticed the mark on his arm. It was strenuous work in any case, which was good, and, better, the rhythm had to be sustained for the sake of the men below him in the plank-shifting chain. Turning and lifting, and turning and lifting again, he kept going.

He knew about German tattoos. The Nazis were keen on marking people forever, or for however long they might be allowed to live.

On the crowded roads west in the winter of 1945 there had been thin, ragged, desperate people of all ages, speaking all the languages Joe could understand and more he could not. All of them needed food. Most of them needed shoes, a warm coat, anything clean to put on. All of them were using whatever strength they had left to get further away from the Red Army, nearer to the Americans. The Germans on the roads were frightened not only of the Russians but of the freed prisoners and labourers, starving and raging, who might appear at any moment from the woods and kill anyone they thought was German.

A young Jew from Budapest, a year or two older than Joe, so thin that the bones in his arms and legs showed sharp, told him in German, very quietly as they sat beside a spring in a destroyed village, that many prisoners had already been made to walk west in starving crowds from the German work camps in Poland. Nazi guards had shouted and bullied them along bombed roads, shooting those who fell exhausted to the ground, until the guards realized that because they had had enough food to move faster than their prisoners they should abandon them and get as far ahead of the advancing Russians as they could. Some of the prisoners who managed to survive had numbers tattooed on their arms, camp numbers. "Like this", the Hungarian said, showing Joe the inside of his arm. The numbers meant that the prisoners had been in the labour camp at Auschwitz, which was separate from the death camp. The Hungarian boy's mother, grandmother, younger brothers, and sister had all been killed in the death camp.

But there was another kind of Nazi tattoo, for another purpose.

In the forest one winter evening someone had come across a dead German soldier in the snow. He had killed himself. His pistol was by his hand. He had shot himself in the mouth. No other human tracks were in the snow near him. Carrion crows had pecked at his eyes and his bloody face, but he had not been dead long, for no wolves had got to the body. Whoever had found him took three others from the camp to carry him in, so they could take his good greatcoat, his gauntlets, his precious boots, and all his clothes, besides of course the submachine gun across his back and the useful knives, pouches, and other bits of kit on his belt. They covered the ruined face with an old cloth while they undressed the body. Joe watched. When they took off the man's greatcoat they saw from the lightning flashes on the collar of his tunic that he was an SS soldier, with one pip on his shoulder, a junior warrant officer. They pulled off the flashes and the pip and muddied the tunic and breeches so that a partisan could wear them. Several men wanted his flannel shirt; they drew lots for it. They left the underwear on the body. No one said anything, but Joe knew they were treating the man with some respect because he had killed himself. They would never know what he had done, what he had seen. But if he had been unable to live with whatever it was, that was perhaps good.

They buried him in a shallow grave, which it took picks to cut from the frozen forest earth. While the body was lying in the snow, Joe saw a small tattoo, two letters and a number, black on the white left arm. One of the partisans knew what it was. "All the Waffen-SS have that tattoo. It's his blood group. In case he's wounded. Someone else's blood can't save him now."

Mikolaj had been in the Waffen-SS.

That morning on the way to work Joe had bought himself for his lunch a corned beef pie at the Lyon's Corner House by his bus stop. This was a treat that rationing allowed him only once a week. When they all sat down for their break among the rubble, each trying to find a bit of shade to sit in, he got it out of his bag but couldn't eat it. He sat with it, wrapped in a greasy paper bag, on his knee, and tried not to look at the Lithuanians, who were some way off talking to each other as they ate. Was he imagining that they were talking about him? That they knew he came from Vilna? That they wondered why he was alive?

An old man, not as old as Mr Carver but perhaps about sixty, who would smile at him from time to time at work and had weeks ago asked him his name—"Joe", he had answered, and left it at that—was sitting near him.

"What's up, Joe? Lost your appetite?"

Joe jumped at being spoken to, as if he had been almost asleep.

"No. Yes. I am too hot."

"That's a nice pie you've got there."

"Would you like it?" Joe held it out to him.

"No, son. It's your pie. You eat it. It'll do you good. My wife puts me up a nice sandwich."

"I can't."

The old man looked at him more carefully.

"Is it those foreigners upsetting you? It is, isn't it? You Jewish, by any chance?"

Joe nodded.

"I thought so. You people have had a lot to put up with in recent times. A lot too much, in my opinion. Plenty of Jews where I come from. If you don't bother them, they won't bother you, I always say. Stepney, that's where I live. Cockney born and bred, I am. Ever heard of Stepney?"

Joe shook his head.

"No, you wouldn't have. Cable Street?"

Joe shook his head.

"A right old schemozzle, that was."

Joe was astonished at the Yiddish word.

"The battle of Cable Street. Before the war. I was there—Mosley's Blackshirts, marching, Hitler salutes and all. 'Down with the Jews.' The East End wouldn't stand for it. We let 'em 'ave it, we did. They didn't 'ang around long, I can tell you. London can't be doing with that type of thing. The war put paid to Mosley and all that, and a good thing too. There's been a bit of 'Down with the Jews' lately, on account of them two British sergeants getting hanged. Shocking business, that. But 'Down with the Jews' won't wash in London. It'll die down, you'll see."

Joe glanced over at the Lithuanians. They had stopped eating, stopped talking, and were lying on their backs in the sun on a piece of cleared ground waiting to be called back to work.

"Don't you worry yourself about them", the old man said. "They can't hurt you here. The gaffer wouldn't stand for it."

So Joe hadn't imagined the hostility.

"Lord knows where they're from, them two. Funny lingo and all."

"Are they prisoners?"

"Prisoners? POWs, you mean? Not them. They've only just arrived. EVWs, they're called—European something workers. More and more of them arriving every day. We need the labour, see. Don't suppose there's much in the way of prospects where they come from. Lord knows there's plenty of work to be done here, clearing up after the war. There's always mining and that. Been clearing up after Hitler for years, I have. I'm a builder by trade, a bricklayer, but I was an air raid warden all through the war. Some terrible sights I've seen. I was on the Somme when I was your age. Just as well I'd seen plenty of terrible sights before the blitz. Not put off my stroke by much, me. I've been lucky, you could say, all my life. Jerry never got me first time round but for a scratch that had me sent back to civvy street for a bit, and Jerry never got me second time round neither, though he tried hard enough. There was one night. A shocker it was—"

The foreman shouted. They all got to their feet, picked up their gloves and shovels.

The old man had been talking to cheer him, Joe could tell. He'd understood only a little of what he'd been saying, but that didn't matter. "All right, son? Back to it. Chin up!"

"Thank you", Joe said.

He worked on through the afternoon, but he couldn't get the tattoo out of his mind. He tried to guess how old the Lithuanian was. Twenty-three? Twenty-four? Was that too young to have been shooting the Jews at Ponary? Impossible to tell. Did the English know about the Waffen-SS? If they did, why were they letting them come to work in London? If they didn't, what else didn't they know?

That night he played difficult exercises on his violin for longer than usual to make himself concentrate, to tire himself out so that he would sleep.

A chaos of dreams kept waking him. In the larch wood above the farm, at the back of his bus to work, in a snowy clearing in the forest, on a train where he was sitting beside the old Londoner who was talking and talking but Joe couldn't hear him for the rattle of the train, everywhere, the Lithuanian, in uniform now with his shiny boots ready to kick, his gun in his hands ready to shoot, appeared, fixing Joe—who couldn't run for trees, for snow, for people crowding the bus, the train—with his pale blue eyes. As he woke in the dark, he realized that the rattle of the train was the rattle of pouring rain on the kitchen's flat roof under his window, but he couldn't banish the dreams.

He was asleep when his alarm clock rang. He lay in bed for a few minutes, too tired to get up. But the day had to be faced—the mud there would be in the bomb crater after the rain, the two Lithuanians he must learn to ignore.

He got up, washed, dressed, made the tea for his thermos, drank some tea from his mug, and immediately had to go to the lavatory to be sick. He had eaten nothing the day before except the corned beef pie he had forced himself to eat for his supper. Being sick almost made him cry.

He washed again, put on his coat because it was a much cooler morning, and went to wait for his bus with two apples for his lunch.

When he got back to his room that evening, having hung his sopping coat on a hook in the hall, having got through the day by not once looking at the Lithuanians, by working as hard as he could through the rain and mud, by eating his apples and drinking his tea far away from the old Londoner, another piece of paper had been slipped under his door.

"Josef, I have some good news for you. Come to my room, which is on the top of your room, at eight o'clock and I will give it to you. Albert C."

How could there be any news for him? From whom? From where?

He took off his boots, the old working boots they had given him at the lake. He had worn them every day on the farm. Ted had shown him how to look after them, how to stuff them with newspaper to dry them properly, how to dubbin them so as to keep out the wet. He still had the tin of dubbin Ted had given him. His socks were dry, even today.

He looked at his watch. A quarter to seven. What could he do for an hour and a quarter? He wasn't hungry. He couldn't play his violin. What was this news? Could there possibly, after all these years, be some news of his mother? His sister? He shook his head fiercely. Of course there could not.

Sally? No.

He went to the window. It had stopped raining. The sky was clear. He put his boots on again and went out to walk the quiet streets for an hour, without his coat. He was stiff and tired but he walked briskly, saw almost no one, avoided the glance of anyone he passed, and as it got dark began to enjoy the cool emptiness of the evening.

At eight he knocked on Mr Carver's door.

"Come, Josef."

The room was very like his own, except that there was a lamp with a cream-tasselled shade on a table with a red cloth by the window, and a sewing machine beside it. The bare bulb hanging from the ceiling—the only light in his own room—was switched off. So it was darker and warmer, more welcoming. There was cigarette smoke in the air, which reminded him of Mrs Thwaites' kitchen after supper.

"Sit down, Josef. Sit on my bed, since we have only one chair and I am old. Good."

At once all his hopes, gradually but not entirely banished by his walk, came back.

"Is it ...? Have you heard ... something, from—"

"Oh, my poor Josef. No. I am so sorry. Not news of your family. I am an old fool. I should not have raised your hope. Forgive me."

Joe shook his head.

"No", Mr Carver said. "My news is not of the past, alas. It is for the future. You are very young. The future is most important for you."

Was it? He realized that from the time that he had understood he wasn't going to be allowed to stay at the farm, he hadn't thought once of the future. Getting through each day in London had been enough to deal with.

"Now, Josef, you are the son of a doctor. You have excellent German, of course, and good Polish, Mrs Levitsky tells me. Your English is not bad, and from Vilna you will have also Yiddish and some Russian. Am I right?"

Joe nodded.

"And better than all this, you play the fiddle well, very well, I would say. I was brought up with music, long ago in Hamburg. I know what is playing well."

What could the old man be going to tell him?

"I have been speaking to Mrs Levitsky. She agrees with me that you should not be clearing bombed sites. She promised me to present your case to the committee. Now, this morning, I received a letter from her. The committee has had its meeting, and they have found something for you. What it is, I don't know. But it surely will be better than clearing bombed sites. Tomorrow morning you do not go to work as usual. You stay here in the house, and at eleven o'clock Mrs Levitsky will come to see you, and she will tell you what the committee has done. Is not this good news?"

Suddenly, although he had no idea what the news might turn out to be, he saw that he might never again have to face the Lithuanians.

"Yes. It is very good. Thank you, Mr Carver, for helping me."

"Oh, don't thank me, Josef. There is not much good I can do for anyone anymore. I do not know many people now. It was good of Mrs Levitsky to listen to me. Who listens to a silly old upholsterer from Hamburg whose house was bombed by Hitler? But she did. As you see. Now ..."

He stood up, with some difficulty, and held out his hand. Joe got up and shook hands. The handshake turned into a warm hug. Mr Carver patted Joe's back.

"You go downstairs and play something for me. And then you must sleep. You look very tired tonight, Josef. It will be good when you are perhaps using your head more than your back and your arms and your legs. Clearing bombed sites—indeed not right for a boy like you. Good night. I shall soon be gone."

What did he mean?

The old man laughed. "No, Josef! Not yet to my fathers. I hope not quite yet, though one never knows. All is in God. I am leaving only this house. They say my flat is almost ready for me. That is good, is it not?"

"Yes. I hope you will be happy in your flat. Good night, Mr Carver. And thank you."

"Good night, Josef."

The next morning Mrs Levitsky, sitting at the small table in his room which had on it only piles of music, his two books, and his photograph of Sally in its glassless frame, said:

"Mr Halpern, I hear you have done well with the clearance people, arrived for work regularly and punctually, and worked hard. This is good. Mr Carver is of course quite right. This is not suitable work for you. The committee would like you to be able to study, to study violin, which I hear you play well, as no doubt you would be doing at home in ..." As the colonel had, she looked down at the papers in front of her. "Ah, in Vilnius. Poor Wilno. Yes. And Mr Carver says your father was a doctor?"

Was she saying he might be able to study violin? Properly? In London?

"Yes. Also he played violin. He would have liked—"

"He would have liked you to study music? I'm sure he would have. I'm afraid that is not possible at present."

Of course. Too much to hope for. She talked on.

"There are too many who wish to study. And many Englishmen who could not begin or could not finish their studies because of the war have now come back. However—"

For the first time Mrs Levitsky smiled at him.

"By a fortunate chance, the committee has been asked to find a young man familiar with German and other languages, and with musical knowledge, to work for a small firm dealing in books, music, and manuscripts—letters, memoirs, notebooks, and so forth. A large amount of such material brought to London by people seeking refuge from the Nazis has reached this firm, which has recently lost its founder, an elderly Jew from Vienna, who has died. The business is now in the hands of his daughter's husband, an Englishman. He requires the help of a junior assistant in the work of sorting and classifying this material, describing items accurately for sale catalogues, and so forth. You would be paid, not a great deal at first, but of course considerably more than the few shillings you have been earning clearing rubble. If you were to learn to do this kind of work satisfactorily, your wages would naturally increase in due time. You should even at the start be able to find yourself somewhere to live perhaps a little better than in our hostel here. And we of course have others badly needing a room."

He had listened carefully to Mrs Levitsky's rather formal Polish. He imagined himself working among books and music instead of in the wreckage of broken buildings. He looked at his little Polish dictionary and his book of German poems, on the corner of the table at which Mrs Levitsky was sitting.

"I do not read Russian so easily as German or Polish", he said.

"Mr Halpern"—she actually laughed—"you must learn to say to people what you can do, not what you cannot do. Now, would you like me to recommend you to Mr Gray—that is the name of the owner of the business—for a month's trial? You will work for a month, and then Mr Gray will decide whether he wishes to give you permanent employment. Do you understand?"

"Of course. Yes. Please. I should very much like to try. I will do as good a job as I possibly can."

"That's better. I'm sure you will. I shall telephone Mr Gray when I return to the office. He would like whomever we recommend to begin as soon as possible." She pulled a small card from the paper clip holding her papers in one sheaf and wrote some numbers and a couple of lines on it. "This is the address of Mr Gray's shop, and I have written the number of the bus—the stop here you know—and where you should get off. Charing Cross. It is only two or three minutes' walk from there. Can you begin tomorrow?"

"Yes. Of course."

"Leave here at eight fifteen. That will give you plenty of time to arrive by nine o'clock. Your clothes." She looked down at his boots. "Have you a pair of shoes?"

"Yes, I have."

"Wear them tomorrow. And have you a decent jacket and a tie?"

"No, only my work coat. I have some good shirts."

"We shall go out now and buy you a jacket and a tie. They will not be new, of course, because of the coupons, but we shall find something suitable. I have a little money from the committee for such things."

"Thank you. Thank you so much."

"You should perhaps write to the committee to thank them. Here is the address." She unfixed another card and gave it to him. "We do our best to look after our own. And, as you will have noticed, we do not ask unnecessary questions." She smiled again.

After their shopping expedition, when Mrs Levitsky had gone, he tried on his jacket. It was dark blue and a bit too big for him, but it was smart, he thought. It took him a long time to find out, by much trial and much error, how to tie his new tie. He had never worn one before.

In his jacket and tie he went upstairs to find Mr Carver. A woman's voice answered his knock. "Come in." He opened the door. No red tablecloth, no sewing machine. A middle-aged woman was unpacking clothes from a suitcase. He apologized and went back downstairs to his room.

Next morning he made tea as usual. After some thought he decided not to take his workman's thermos, and he left earlier than Mrs Levitsky had said in case he got lost.

Five weeks later, he knew that, for the first time since he was eleven years old in the summer of 1941, he had stopped escaping.

Above the shop, which was in a narrow street off the Charing Cross Road, were three floors of dusty rooms full of piles of books, music, pamphlets, old periodicals, dictionaries, other kinds of reference books and maps. Sometimes there were old letters tucked into books or scores. Almost everything was in German. He soon understood that for several years people who had managed to bring out of smashed and ruined Europe their libraries, their music, some of what they or others had collected in the past, had delivered boxes and trunks of material to the shop. Someone in the shop had quickly looked for anything obviously remarkable, and everything else had been taken upstairs and dumped in heaps. His job was to sort, list, tidy, stack, properly describe, and store all this, so that things could be found again. The prospect was both daunting and—as he saw after even his first morning—exhilarating.

In his lunch hour he went out and bought two tomato sandwiches and a cup of tea in the Lyons Corner House in Trafalgar Square. The square was the grandest London sight he had yet seen. He stood, turning slowly, as he looked at the mixture of grey, impressive buildings untidily placed on the square, which wasn't square. Pigeons flew low in little groups or poked about on the wide, paved spaces. He looked up, wondering who was on top of the tall column. What was Trafalgar? He had never heard the word. He looked at Ted's watch. He was supposed to be back at the shop in ten minutes. At the bottom of the Charing Cross Road he found a stationer's shop in which he bought himself a thick school exercise book, two pencils, and a rubber. He felt he was investing two of the few shillings he had saved up from what he was paid for clearing rubble, in an intellectual future of which his father would approve.

That afternoon he asked Mr Gray, a friendly, untidy, middle-aged Englishman with thick spectacles, if he could clean the windows on the upper floors of the building. Mr Gray was delighted.

"Good idea. Excellent idea, in fact. Tap, bucket, cloths, brushes, and all that in the basement. Good luck. I don't suppose anyone's cleaned those windows since before the war. And Halpern ..."

"Sir?"

"You needn't wear a tie for work, you know."

"Thank you, sir."

At the end of Joe's first month, Mr Gray called him down to the shop after it was closed for the day. Joe was still working, because he enjoyed what he was doing too much to stop before Mr Gray left, usually at about six o'clock.

"Well, Joe, you've only been here four weeks, and I can see how fast you're learning. You're doing so well up there that I should very much like you to stay on—if you want to, of course."

"I should like to, very much."

"Good. I hoped you'd say that. I'll be paying you a bit more, naturally. Now, you really need to move out of that hostel. They want the room, I know."

Joe had worried about what Mrs Levitsky had said about others needing a room. He had no idea how to begin to find himself somewhere else to live in London.

Mr Gray smiled. "It's all right. No one could expect you, by yourself, to find somewhere to live when you've only been in London five minutes. We've got an empty attic in our house. It's by no means *haut luxe*, but it's a nice room and it's quiet. Right at the top of the house so you can play your fiddle—I gather you're quite a violinist—without being afraid of bothering anyone. It used to be our daughter's room, but a few months ago she went and got married. God knows why, but there you are. She always said it was a nice room. You can have it for as long as you like, and then you needn't worry about renting somewhere. And it's a good deal nearer here than Hampstead is. What do you say?"

"Thank you, sir. Thank you very much."

"Come back with me this evening, and I'll show you the room. I'll show you the way too. London must be difficult for you to find your way round. Then, if you like the room, you can move in at the weekend."

"That is very kind, Mr Gray. Thank you."

"Well, we'll see how we go. There must be a good six months' work for you to do up there at the very least. We'll give the whole arrangement six months to begin with, shall we?"

On his first evening in Mr and Mrs Gray's house, he unpacked his few clothes, his two books, Philip Robertson's music, and Sally's photograph. Then he sat on his bed, which had an eiderdown, flatter and more faded than his eiderdown at the farm, and looked at the room. It was square, larger than his room at the farm, or his room in the hostel, or his room at home; but as in his room at home, part of the ceiling sloped because it was under the roof of the house. There were two windows, wider than they were tall, and outside, a long way down, was the quiet street. The floor of the room was wooden boards, painted white a long time ago, with a big, beautiful rug, a little threadbare, dark red and gold and brown. There were a chest of drawers and a cupboard, both painted white; a table with a lamp and a mirror; two small chairs; an old armchair with a freestanding lamp beside it; and best of all a bookcase between the windows, full of books.

The whole house was full of books. It was a big, comfortable house in a part of London that, from his new bus route, he had discovered was called Maida Vale. Everything about the house looked as if the Gray family had lived in it for a long time.

Everything about it he liked.

They had asked him to have dinner with them, soon after he arrived. Mr Gray did most of the talking at the meal. He asked Joe about his time in Yorkshire, about how cold the winter had been so far north, about whether he liked being in London. Mr Gray said nothing at all, asked not a single question, about the war or where Joe had come from. Mrs Gray was beautiful, dark eyed, dark haired, with a slight German accent.

She was much tidier than her husband, even elegant, and cooler to Joe, more appraising. Mr Gray asked whether he liked to be called Josef or Joe and then called him Joe several times. Mrs Gray listened more, talked less, and called him by neither name. Their sons, two schoolboys of about twelve and fourteen, shook hands with him and took no further notice of him.

A woman a little like Mrs Thwaites, not so large but with the same kind of apron, had brought the food to the table and left it for Mrs Gray to serve. He understood that he was now on the other side of things, not at the kitchen table but in the dining room.

How? Why? He couldn't understand England. Perhaps one day he would.

That night, too tired to think, he said, "Blessed be God" before he fell asleep. But a dream of the Vilna streets, of standing outside the locked door of his family's house and beating and beating on the door and no one coming, woke him to a flood of tears. His father and his mother and his sister would never know how lucky he had been. It wasn't fair. It wasn't right that he had lived to find himself here, safe, with a whole bookcase of books to explore and a low, soft armchair to read them in. And they had died, all of them, in what fear and cold and illness and hunger he tried not to imagine.

For them, and for all the people who had rescued him from hunger and cold, and most of all from fear, he must do his very best to repay . . . to repay what? The goodness of his parents, the goodness of the Belorussian peasant woman who had hidden him and told him to ride away with Renia, the goodness of the partisans in the forest and of Ted and Mrs Thwaites and Mr Carver and the old Londoner in the rubble and Mr Gray. The goodness of God.

Before he went back to sleep, some phrases came into his mind.

On an evil day he will grant me the protection of his tent. I was sure I would see the goodness of the Lord in the land of the living.

Chapter 5

One day at the beginning of December 1955, Joe was alone in the shop. Early in the afternoon a customer came in. Joe stubbed out his cigarette and put his half-empty mug of coffee on the low bookshelf beside him so that it wouldn't look unprofessional on the old desk where the person in charge of the shop always sat. Usually he went out to lunch. Today because no one else would be about at lunchtime he had brought sandwiches to work and made himself coffee in the little kitchen in the basement. Instant coffee, cheap and good, was one of the pleasures of his life in the last couple of years since rationing in England had finally ended. He drank four or five mugs a day. He was wearing a corduroy jacket and a tie, as he now always did for work.

The customer took off his hat, a black Anthony Eden hat, as he shut the street door behind him. He came up to the desk.

"Good afternoon, young man."

Not an Englishman. Evidently a German. Upright and thickset. Many of the customers were foreigners. This one Joe had never seen before.

"Good afternoon, sir."

"Is Mr Gray here today?"

"I am afraid Mr Gray is away for a few days."

"Ah, away. I see. He is taking for himself a holiday at this time of year?"

"Mr Gray is in Scotland for a family funeral."

"I am sorry. But it is good to be out of London when the fog comes, is it not?"

"Yes, sir."

"Smog. Smoke and fog together. That is why it makes everything so black and smells so unpleasant. I very much dislike London at this time of the year. However, this is not to be helped. I live in London and that is that. Now ..."

The customer sat down in the chair on the other side of the desk, his hat in his hand.

"I am here to find a present for a pupil of mine who is leaving the school where I teach violin."

Joe looked at his customer more carefully. This must have been obvious, because the man said, "You play violin yourself?"

"I do. As much as I can."

"But not as much as you would wish?"

Joe wasn't used to anyone paying him this much attention. He guessed the German was about fifty. He had grey hair that had once been fair, and blue eyes—not blank, pale blue eyes like the Lithuanian on the bombed site whom he had never seen again, but sharp, deep blue eyes, small and intelligent. And he was wearing a bow tie. Mr Gray often wore a bow tie, but Joe had seen few others in London. Schoolteachers sometimes came into the shop. This man didn't look like a schoolteacher.

Joe didn't answer the man's question about whether he played violin much but said, "Are you looking for some violin music for your present?"

"No. Not at all. To tell you the truth, she doesn't play well. She is a good pianist, a very musical girl, but she began violin too late—only two years or so she has played, and she does not practise because she plays piano instead. Also she sings—very nicely although no one has trained her voice. Or possibly because no one has trained her voice. She is a talented child. So I will give her some songs for her to take into the world as she leaves school, and she may learn them as time goes by. For how long have you worked here for Mr Gray?"

Joe had the impression that this violin teacher who looked like a soldier was thinking and observing all the time he was talking.

"Eight years I have worked here."

"Since 1947? Why is it I have not before now seen you in the shop?"

"Because my work is almost always upstairs, sorting and cataloguing the stock, dealing with boxes people bring."

"You are a scholar, then? What the English call a backroom boy? We do not see you, but you do the really important work."

Joe blushed, and shook his head to disguise the blush.

The German looked closely at him for a moment and then shook his own head.

"What do you think I should give my pupil for her leaving present?"

Joe thought.

"Does she understand German?"

"Not well. I have taught her a little. But some good songs, if she cares to learn them, will teach her more—and perhaps in the best way, with music."

"Some Schubert songs, then? *Die schöne Müllerin?*"

"Exactly so. My own thought. With perhaps *Winterreise* also, for when she is older and real sadness has come, as it does to us all."

Joe, nervous, and surprised to be nervous because he was always calm at work, stood up. "If you will wait a moment here, sir, I will bring you some of what we have."

He went upstairs to where he knew the Schubert lieder, in old and new editions, fat and thin scores—some bound, most not—and many sheets of single songs, occupied a long shelf. He took out separate paper scores, sewn but not bound, of the two song cycles, and a thicker volume with both song cycles as well as the fourteen songs of *Schwanengesang* and twenty-two other single songs, published in Leipzig in 1884 and nicely bound in blue-grey boards with leather corners and spine. *Schubert-Album* was in gold letters on the spine. The paper scores, *Die schöne Müllerin* and *Winterreise*, new and in the most recent German edition, were seven shillings and sixpence each. The bound collection was two pounds and ten shillings—at least he had himself written "£2/10" in pencil on the flyleaf, because of the binding. This now seemed too expensive. He rubbed out the price and took all three scores back to the shop.

"Ah, a fine binding you have here. Allow me to look."

The German put his hat on the desk, took the score, and opened it on his knee. He took a spectacle case from his pocket, snapped it open, put on a pair of spectacles, and left the case beside his hat. He had thick, strong fingers, a wedding ring on his left hand.

Joe sat at his own side of the desk and watched. Marbled endpapers; the flyleaf, slightly flecked with age, with a signature, Leopold Kirchner, in faded ink; a good-quality print of Schubert with his curly hair, his wire spectacles, a confident look—particularly in the firm mouth—a high white collar, and a black floppy tie. Joe knew this portrait well. It appeared in a number of other scores and books.

"The poor fellow", the customer said, as if he had known Schubert. Then: "This is the same album that lay always on my mother's piano.

Not of course this copy, but this edition." He pointed at the ornate title page facing the portrait of Schubert, with its faint, reddish engraving of muses, lyres, and a scroll framing the text.

" 'Kritisch revidirt von Max Friedlaender' ", the German man read. "A Jewish scholar editing Schubert. So it was, once upon the time. My mother played these songs to me now and then, if I had practised well my violin. She sang sweetly, perfectly in tune as not all singers do, but she did not have a strong voice, so she sang only at home. But she played piano, Schubert overall, most beautifully.

"I am sorry", he said as he looked across the desk and smiled. "All this was long, very long ago, in another world."

Joe bent his head.

"Now, let us see."

The German closed the book and opened it again, at random, as Joe in his room above the stable used to open his little book of poems.

"Ah. Good." He read very quietly:

"Ich stand in dunkeln Träumen
Und starrt ihr Bildnis an."
I stood in dark dreams and gazed at her picture.

Joe went on, as quietly:

"Und das geliebte Antlitz
Heimlich zu leben began."
And the beloved face secretly came to life.

Sally. When he found this poem, years ago now, in the book of Heine's poems that was in his attic in the Grays' house, he would say it to the photograph in its glassless frame, to her, Sally herself, grown up by now, probably married to someone like the man in the car that day, in any case altogether lost to him.

"Ach. So", the German said, "Heine you know. You are German?"

"My mother was German", Joe said in German.

"Long ago, in another world?"

Joe couldn't answer.

The German closed the book of songs and laid it gently on the desk. He took off his spectacles and put them on the book. He looked at Joe with an intentness that was almost frightening.

"And your father?" He was now speaking German.

Should he tell him anything more? He was of an age, and of a kind, to have been an officer in the Wehrmacht, perhaps in the SS.

"I have lived in England for more than twenty years", the German said. "I am now an Englishman. During the war I was a soldier in a part of the British army."

Joe couldn't decide whether to be more, or less, afraid of this stranger because he seemed to know all the time what Joe was thinking. He looked across the desk into the deep-set eyes. Then he did decide—to trust him, to be less, much less, afraid. Why? He couldn't have said.

"My father was a surgeon in Vilna. He died at Katyn. He was a medical officer in the Polish army. A prisoner of the Russians."

"At Katyn? Where is that?"

"Katyn is in Russia."

"Katyn—I think I have heard the name. Is Katyn where many thousands of Polish officers were killed?"

"Yes."

"Who killed them? Do you know?"

"The Germans said that the Russians killed them. They called it a Jewish crime. The Russians said that the Germans killed them. No one wanted to believe the Germans, so it was easy for the Russians to pretend that the Germans were lying. But the Russians killed the Polish officers."

"You know?"

"I know."

The German, one hand resting on the album of songs, took off his spectacles with the other and put them on the desk. He said nothing for what seemed a long minute.

"Turn your head, young man. Look a moment over there." The German pointed to the stairs at the back of the shop.

Joe obeyed.

"Thank you. A surgeon in Vilna ..."

Another silence.

Then the German said, "May I ask you, what is your name?"

"My name is Josef Halpern."

The German jumped to his feet.

"I knew it. I knew it as soon as I saw you. I did not dare to believe it. Your father was Jacob Halpern. No?"

"Yes."

147

"Was he a young doctor in Breslau? Did he play violin extremely well?"

Joe also got to his feet.

"Yes, he was in Breslau. Yes, he played violin."

The German sat down, both hands on the desk, as if he needed a solid barrier between himself and Joe, who also sat again.

"Your father was my friend. And also my enemy. We played quartets in Breslau. I was a student. Your aunt Anna played viola in our quartet. Is she . . . ?"

"She is dead. And her three little boys. Lithuanians shot them under the orders of the Einsatzgruppen who came to Vilna in the summer of 1941. They were shot into pits in the forest of Ponary. I was there. I was supposed to die too."

The German hid his face in his hands. Joe knew that the man was seeing in his mind the picture, so familiar to Joe, that he had just described.

When the German looked up at last, his face was older, more lined, sunken.

"I am sorry", Joe said.

The German's grief-stricken eyes came back to focus on Joe.

"No, no, my poor boy. It is not you who is to be sorry. It is I. My country . . . my people . . . I cannot . . ."

He took out a handkerchief and blew his nose fiercely. Looking past Joe, not at him, he said: "All these years I have imagined her, far away in Vilna, with her husband the rabbi, and no doubt children growing up. Naturally I did not expect to hear from her ever again. But I have always thought of her alive. I have known nothing of what took place in Vilna during the war. The English papers, the BBC news—I doubt if they have mentioned Vilna twice since 1939."

He blew his nose again.

"I have not seen her since the spring of 1928, more than a quarter of a century ago, when her brother, your father, sent her home to Vilna because I had been stupid. So stupid. Then he was my enemy, because I loved Anna and he sent her away. But the fault was mine."

He looked at Joe.

"No. Not in the way you are thinking. We were very correct. Innocent children. But it is a complicated story and one I should not load on to your memory of your father. Also it will be difficult for you to understand, now, so much later. Were you close to your aunt Anna?"

He seemed to be able to think in two ways, on two levels, at the same time.

"I was. I loved her. She helped me with my playing. And she made me laugh. Her boys were very funny—clever and funny."

"You resemble her very much, you know. I think you are more like her than you are like your father. Do you wear spectacles?"

"No. My eyesight is good."

"She wore spectacles to play. They made her look even younger."

Suddenly he shut his eyes and winced, remembering, Joe could tell, that she was dead.

The man shook his head again.

"Why does it make so much difference to hear that she is not anymore in the world?" Then, looking over Joe's head, his eyes changed, almost to a smile.

"Is it possible that the dead may be closer to us than the living if the living had been a thousand miles away? It depends, does it not, on whether there is God, to care for the souls of the dead? In his love. In our love." His eyes turned back to Joe. "What do you think, Josef?"

The door to the street opened, and a stout elderly man whom Joe knew, an important dealer in musical memorabilia, came into the shop, coughing.

"Filthy weather out there. Can't see your hand in front of your face. Christopher not here?"

Joe was on his feet.

"I am sorry, Mr Harris. Mr Gray is away."

"Oh well, I suppose you'll have to do, then. I hear that a Liszt autograph has come your way. If so, I'd like to give it the once-over. Plenty of dodgy Liszt autographs knocking about."

Amazed, as he often was, by the bad manners of the English, Joe said, "Excuse me, sir", in a correct, impersonal voice, to his father's friend, or enemy, as if he were talking to a stranger. But the man was a stranger still.

"You are busy. I shall go now", the German said, in English of course. "Will you be good enough to reserve the Schubert songs for me? I shall return in a few days. I shall leave my name for you."

He took a small piece of scrap paper from the pile kept on the desk, and the pencil beside the pile, and scribbled a name. He gathered up his spectacles and their case and put the piece of paper inside the Schubert album.

"Good day to you."

"Good day, sir."

He took his hat, gave Mr Harris a polite nod as if to rub in his lack of manners, and left the shop.

"Now, Halpern, can we take a shufti at this so-called Liszt autograph? By the way, who's the Kraut? Haven't seen him in here before."

His name was Max Hofmann.

Joe made out a proper slip, named and dated, reserving the Schubert album so that no one would sell it to anyone else. Then he waited, through the days that followed, for him to come back.

Mr Gray returned from Scotland. Mr Harris, who was an authority on nineteenth-century composers' handwriting, decided that the Liszt autograph, a note to a pupil changing the time of a lesson, was genuine, and bought it, for a sum Joe was sure was too small.

"I know, Joe", Mr Gray said, not just about the price. "But he matters in this little world. We have to put up with him, and he's almost always right."

Joe asked Mr Gray what the price of the Schubert album should be. "Two pounds would be fair enough, I think. It's nice, but it's not in the least rare."

The fog lifted. There was a day of rain, which washed some of the black deposit of the smog, flakes of soot like black snow, from the pavements and steps, the railings and the grass, and then the weather became brighter and much colder.

Days in the shop were ordinary again, and long. Joe was never bored at work, because there was always something that needed sorting, identifying, placing, listing, setting on one side to be repaired. But now he could settle to nothing and kept looking at his watch, still Ted's old watch, to see how the slow hours were going. Perhaps Mr Hofmann wouldn't come back. Perhaps finding Joe in the shop had upset him more than he wished to be upset. Perhaps he would find a different present in a different shop for his pupil who played the piano and sang.

He found himself wishing he could meet this girl, because perhaps she knew Mr Hofmann better than he did.

He was used to being alone. Three years ago he had left the Grays' house, where, though Christopher Gray had always been kind to him, Mrs Gray had seemed only to tolerate his presence. Unlike Mrs

Robertson, Mrs Gray never made him feel that she was actually hostile or wished him gone; however, although he ate countless meals with the family in the dining room—when they had dinner parties they sometimes invited him and sometimes didn't—and although she occasionally asked him to play his violin with friends of hers who came to play chamber music in her drawing room, he always felt uncertain of where he belonged in the household. Not, clearly, in the kitchen with Mrs Tibbs, the cook, and Mrs Hunt, the charwoman, cheerful, foul-mouthed, and to Joe almost incomprehensible, who came every day from somewhere north of King's Cross, from the ruined streets he had helped to clear. He seldom saw her, because he left for work in the morning before she had emerged from the basement. Yet he was equally clearly no one's friend. An employee. A lodger. Someone who could help the younger son of the house with his German homework. Someone who could reliably play second violin in a domestic performance of a Mozart quartet. He had met, one way or another, a number of people in the house, even from time to time girls of more or less his own age, daughters of the Grays' friends, but no one had ever asked him anything about himself beyond what he was doing in London—"I work in Mr Gray's shop"— and he was too shy to think of something new to say to a strange English girl who evidently had no interest in him.

One evening a woman Mr Gray had told him was a journalist was sitting next to him at dinner and said, "I gather you're a refugee. Christopher says how lucky he was to find you. You're a terrific help in his shop, apparently. Well done, you. Tell me, were you in a concentration camp in the war?"

"No, I wasn't."

"Oh, what a shame. I'm writing a piece about people who survived concentration camps; they're really hard to find in London. I hoped you might be just the chap to tell me all about it."

She turned to help herself to the pudding, which a parlourmaid, brought in for the dinner party and in a black dress and white apron, was handing to each guest at the table.

"Chocolate mousse! I haven't seen one since the war." She turned back towards Joe. "Marianne, sorry, Mrs Gray, is wonderful, isn't she? I don't know how she manages this kind of thing with chocolate only just off the ration. And proper cream! Viennese magic, that's what it is." She looked at him over her spoon. "Well, if you weren't in a concentration camp, you can't have had too bad a time. Not much good for my article." She ate some more chocolate mousse. "So what do you think of England?"

Three years before the Grays' older son, by then an undergraduate at Oxford, wanted to take over the attic, bigger than his old bedroom and further from the rest of the family. An elderly couple the Grays had known for years, their house a few streets away towards Saint John's Wood, had a basement flat they let for a low rent on condition that the tenant mowed the lawn, took the dustbins up to the street, and when they were away looked after their cat and kept an eye on the house.

The arrangement suited Joe perfectly. He liked the old couple. He liked having his own front door, which he had to go down the area steps to reach. He liked the cat except when it killed a bird. He loved the long London garden with its dirty brick walls and grass, its roses and viburnums, its one magnolia tree with magical white flowers in the spring, and its population of squirrels, robins, blackbirds, pigeons, sometimes a song thrush, and once, only once, on a hot June night when his bedroom window was wide open, a nightingale. He did much more in the garden than mow. Ted had taught him how to prune roses, which he did with the knife he had had since the forest. At the back of the house his flat was on the same level as the garden, and a door led into it. His bedroom and his sitting room both had windows looking onto the garden. Best of all, in his sitting room, where he could keep on three shelves fixed to the wall all the books and music that were by now his own, there was an old upright piano, made in London but by a maker with a German name, and very nearly in tune. His violin in its case lived on top of the piano, and he had a music stand made of carved wood which had arrived in pieces at the shop in a trunk full of sheet music and scores, and which Mr Gray said he could have. "Just about worth mending. You're good at that sort of thing, Joe. Not worth selling anyway."

Occasionally, now, Mr Gray sent him on an expedition to look at a collection of books or music that someone wanted to sell, usually because an old musician or scholar had died and a house was to be cleared. He enjoyed these trips. He enjoyed looking out of a train window at England and tried to learn a little more of the country by looking at a map before he set off and when he came back. The people in the houses he was sent to were usually friendly, allowed him enough time to look carefully at what they had and make proper lists, and brought him cups of tea. One or two of the people were doubtful. "You look awfully young to be doing this kind of work." Once someone said, "I wasn't expecting a foreigner", meaning a Jew.

About six months ago, in the summer, Mr Gray had sent him to Edinburgh. Amazed by the high dark drama of the city, of which he knew nothing, he found his way to a flat in a tall house where, in a cluttered study, there was a shelf of Russian opera scores from before the revolution. The unmarried middle-aged daughter of the dead man who had brought the scores from Russia in a suitcase through difficulties Joe could only imagine was delighted to find he spoke some Russian. She fussed over him, gave him strong tea in a glass with lumps of sugar and jam in a saucer, and when he left, telling her Mr Gray would write to her about the scores, kissed him on both cheeks and once more, as Russians do.

On the journey back to London he found himself facing an oldish man. There was no one else in their third-class smoking compartment. The man was dressed as an English country gentleman, in beige trousers, not new, a tweed coat with leather patches on the elbows, and a striped tie, but something about him made Joe sure he was not English. He was smoking a pipe and reading a journal with close-printed lines and no pictures. Joe looked out of the window at the sea, close to the railway line, surprisingly blue in the cloudless summer evening. Christopher Gray had told him to make sure not to miss Durham Cathedral—"It's the best building in England you can see from a train, except perhaps Ely"—and he had seen it, wonderfully old and grand and plain, on the way north. He knew he would not see it again for nearly an hour. He looked more carefully at the man opposite, who was relighting his pipe. Joe saw that the journal, now shut on the man's knee, was Polish.

Half an hour later, with the train slowing to its stop at Newcastle and Joe waiting to see, after the station, the bridges over the Tyne, the man said, "Excuse me, young man. Would you have a pencil or a pen you might lend me for a moment?"

Joe had several pencils in the inside pocket of the blue blazer he wore for summer trips. He chose a reasonably sharp one and handed it to the man, who scribbled a few lines at the bottom of a page in his journal, and handed back the pencil.

"I am obliged. Thank you."

"Thank you, sir", Joe said, in Polish.

The man looked up sharply and studied Joe for a long moment before he spoke, in Polish.

"You are Polish?"

"I was born in Vilna."

"Ah, poor Wilno. Lost. Lwów and Wilno, our lost cities. But you ... how did you come to be in England? You are too young to have been a soldier, no?"

"Yes, sir. I escaped. I was very fortunate."

"You are a Jew, I see, yet you escaped. How did you escape? A Polish family hid you, perhaps?"

"A Belorussian peasant hid me until the Gestapo came. Then I was with partisans in the forest."

"Were you? Were you indeed? Stalin's partisans, I suppose."

"No, sir. Jewish partisans."

"Under orders from Moscow, no doubt."

"No, sir. In danger from the partisans who took orders from Moscow. If they found us, they might kill us, for our guns and our food. They despised us because we were wasting bread and potatoes keeping alive women and children and old people. Not many, but we tried. Of course the Nazis also hunted us, just to kill us. Often. We hid."

The Pole looked at him, searchingly. He puffed on his pipe. Joe wondered if he believed him.

"Hard, very hard, it must have been", eventually he said. "Where was all this exactly? This forest?"

"It is not possible to say exactly. We had to move, many times. But the forest was large. The Nalibocka forest. In Kresy. South of Vilna. West of Minsk."

"Ah, Kresy. I too am a man of Kresy, although I have never been so far north as your forest. All of Kresy was Poland once, you know. All of Ukraine, all of Belorussia, all of Lithuania. In the days of the Commonwealth, all was Poland."

Joe wondered where this man came from. A *szlachta* family, clearly. An estate no doubt. The man answered the question Joe hadn't asked.

"I am a Habsburg Pole. My family lived in Galicia for hundreds of years, not far from Lwów. Most of Galicia is lost now, including Lwów itself, to the Ukrainian Soviet Socialist Republic." He said the words through his teeth. He tapped the cinders out of his pipe into the ashtray beside him as if he were hitting someone, refilled his pipe, lit it, puffed a couple of times, and then said, looking out of the window, in a calmer voice, "I was born a subject of the emperor Franz Josef. We considered ourselves fortunate, after the tragedy of Poland's partition, for more than a hundred years to belong to a Catholic empire where Poles were not bullied merely for being Poles, as the tsars had always bullied them, or despised, as the Prussians had despised them. Then after the '14–'18 war there was Poland reborn, the Poland that defeated the Russians and the Ukrainians and the Lithuanians, Piłsudski's Poland. Piłsudski was born in Lithuania, like you. Did you know that? Many of the heroes of Poland were born in Lithuania. Mickiewicz of course. Kościuszko. But poor Poland, a country again, did not know which way to turn. Enemies on either side, Hitler to the west, Stalin to the east."

He has made this speech before, Joe thought. Is he going to stand up? No. Not quite.

"Their agreement to share Poland between them was the most iniquitous treaty of European history. And the most iniquitous betrayal of European history was the gift by the Americans and the English of nearly half the country to Stalin. Iniquity upon iniquity. Galicians who were made to leave for Silesia after the war, my peasants for example, are still waiting with a suitcase packed, ten years later, in case they may be able to go back to their farms. Did you know that?"

He looked at Joe, almost accusingly. Joe shook his head.

"No. Few people in England do." But his speech was not finished. He straightened his back and went on:

"Observe the irony of history. In the '14–'18 war Poles had to fight for Austria, for Russia, for the Kaiser's Germany. All of them lost. Poland was restored. In the '39–'45 war Poles fought with England and France and America, from the first day of the war to the last. All of them won. Poland, however, was lost."

He laughed, bitterly.

"And the English would not allow us to march in the victory parades. And would not give our soldiers pensions."

"But Poles have been allowed to stay here. I was allowed to stay here because I was born in Poland."

A sharp look.

"That is true", the Pole conceded. "Indeed. And naturally we are grateful. As you are, I imagine, even more grateful."

He filled his pipe carefully, relit it, resumed his speech.

"Not that the loss of Poland in 1945 should have been a surprise. In 1830, in 1863, Poland rose against Russia. England and France said how sad and did not help. Naturally Poland was beaten. And in the same way in 1945 we lost two of our great cities. Mr Churchill and Mr Eden did not even say how sad. They were only irritated when we pleaded for Lwów and Wilno. I know; I was there. I think they had little idea of where Lwów and Wilno are on a map, let alone of what they have always meant to Polish people. Would Mr Churchill and Mr Eden have agreed to lose Oxford and York when they had won the war? And Mr Roosevelt lied to our prime minister. He promised that Poland would keep Lwów when he knew full well Lwów had already been given to Stalin. They were afraid of Stalin of course. They had no wish to fight the next war when the last one was scarcely finished. Alas!"

But then the Pole turned his head and looked straight at Joe.

"Your parents—they are dead, I imagine?"

"They are dead."

"Killed by the Nazis, no doubt."

"They were killed by the NKVD."

"Really? How strange. I've always understood there are a lot of Jews in the NKVD. And I thought the Jews in Wilno welcomed the Russians in 1939."

"Some did. But many remembered how the Russians had treated the Vilna Jews in the '14–'18 war. They also remembered that the Germans had treated them much better. They were more afraid of the Russians than of the Germans. My father—"

"Your father—what was your father?"

"My father was a doctor, a surgeon. He had lived in Germany for several years, before Hitler was in power but not long before. And so for the Jews in Vilna he was equally afraid, of the Germans and of the Russians."

"A Jewish doctor. Our doctor at home was always Jewish. They are excellent doctors of course. And you say it was the Russians who killed your father? Are you sure of that?"

"He was a reserve officer, as a doctor, in the Polish army. He was taken prisoner by the Russians in 1939. In 1940 he was killed at Katyn."

The Pole took his pipe out of his mouth and bent his head for a long minute. The train rattled over some points. Rattled on.

"My dear boy, I apologize."

For what? Joe knew for what.

"The Russians will never admit it. Never. As they will never admit that they killed General Sikorski. That aeroplane crash at Gibraltar was no accident. The Russians had tried to kill the general twice before. No. They will never admit it. They do not care for the truth. Why should atheists care for the truth?"

Joe shook his head, to remind himself to remember later to think about this question. The Pole must have thought he was simply agreeing.

"Friends of mine were among the officers killed in 1940, at Katyn and no doubt elsewhere, for there are thousands more unaccounted for. Of course the Russians killed them. It was easy for them to blame the Nazis in 1943, and even easier at the end of the war. It was less easy to falsify all the evidence, but they did it, in their usual way. We knew the truth in London, although we have never been able to persuade the British government to admit it. I work for the Polish government in London, as you may have guessed. I was an officer in General Anders' army. I was deported to northern Siberia late in 1938. I was fortunate to survive the cold and the typhus. Many of us died. Nearly three years I was there. It was not easy, you may imagine, to reach the army General Anders was allowed to form after Hitler invaded Russia, but I was fortunate again. We expected all the officers from Russian prisons to join us. They never came, thousands more of them than those we knew had died. They never came. Where were they? General Sikorski asked Stalin himself. Naturally there was no reply. Later we heard that the letters had stopped, at the same time, from all the prisons. Where was your father held?"

"At Kozelsk."

"Then no doubt Katyn was where he died. At least you know the truth about his death. So many don't. And your mother?"

"The NKVD took the families that spring. To trains. My mother and my sister. I'm sure they never reached the place they were being taken to. No letters came. I wasn't at home when the Russians took them."

The Pole leaned forward.

"I am very sorry to hear this, my young friend. There are so many stories we do not know. Thousands and thousands, no doubt, that no one will ever know."

He leaned back in his seat, puffed at his pipe.

"You didn't think, after the war, of going home?"

Joe looked out of the window at green hills. He had missed Durham Cathedral.

"No. I was extremely lucky. I had work in England, somewhere to live, safety. I was luckier still to be allowed to stay."

"Because you were born in Poland."

"Exactly. After the war I had no home to go to. No people. No place either. Where would I have gone? To Vilna, in the Lithuanian Soviet Socialist Republic? Or to somewhere in the People's Republic of Poland, because Vilna had been Polish? I don't think so. The Soviets killed my family. Also I knew there were plenty of Lithuanians who joined in the killing of the Jews. I saw them. And I knew there were plenty of Poles who were glad it was happening."

The Pole winced.

He took his pipe out of his mouth, put it on the ledge by the window, leaned forward again, and clasped his hands. "There were difficulties of course, for years, perhaps for centuries. Peasants in the countryside did resent the shtetl Jews, because they were better traders, because they could read and write and were clever with money so they had power over the peasants, more power very often than the *szlachta* families who owned the villages. But in the cities, most of all I would have thought in Vilna, it was different. Jewish political parties, Jews in the Sejm—I can see them now, in the parliament chamber, honoured figures, in their fur hats—and of course Jewish scholars and professors. There was a professor of Jewish history at the University of Warsaw, I remember. As for doctors, like your father, they were much respected everywhere. Poland gave the Jews a home for hundreds of years. It wasn't easy, but we never tried to kill them."

This was becoming another speech he had made before. He shook his head, as if to return himself to the railway carriage and to Joe.

"I apologize. You. We never tried to kill you. The pogrom was a Russian invention. The Protocols of the Elders of Zion, the deliberate blackening of the reputation of the Jews, the wicked propaganda Hitler picked up—all a Russian invention. Not Polish. I know for a fact that there were many Poles, very many, who were appalled at what the Nazis were doing when they came in 1941 on their way to Russia. I also know that the Nazis shot many Poles because they had helped Jews."

He sat back and picked up his pipe, which he had put down to make his speech, and searched his pocket for matches, as if what he had said settled something satisfactorily. He added, however:

"But perhaps, People's Republic or no People's Republic, you may have a point. It may be that now that things have settled down a little, Jews would not be . . . welcome, in Poland. Their houses, their property, now—"

"Belong to Poles. It is easy to imagine. The Jews have gone. Who would want them back? And have they been welcome anywhere, ever?"

The Pole looked out of the window.

"The Germans welcomed them once, for their brains and their hard work. Then they resented them, for their brains and their hard work. Then they humiliated them. I was in Vienna in 1938. Then they killed them. It is a crime that will not be forgotten. There have been so many crimes in our terrible time. So many committed by Hitler, so many committed by Stalin. One of the worst was Stalin's famine in Ukraine, not far from my home, when millions were starved to death because of Stalin's theories. We saw the wretched Ukrainians in the streets of Lwów—peasants like skeletons, on their hands and knees. Many died in Lwów because it was too late for them to eat. No doubt you were too young, and too far away, to know about that. Then there was the purging of Poles from Kresy, especially the *szlachta*—class enemies, they were called—with thousands upon thousands sent to Siberia, Kazakhstan, deepest Asia, before the war. Many died. Another crime forgotten. And Katyn has been a crime transferred. We who know that Stalin committed it must never cease our efforts to bring the truth to light. At present it does not suit the English to help us. One day it may."

Another speech. But Joe was impressed. The Pole turned back from the window to face Joe.

"Tell me, young man, how do you make your living in England?"

"I work for a music bookseller in London. We buy and sell second-hand scores, sheet music, books about music."

"A Jewish enterprise?"

"Originally, yes. The owner of the business now is an Englishman."

"As you are, now?"

Joe laughed. "He is a real Englishman. I try. I do not always succeed."

The Pole smiled. "Does one ever?"

The train was slowing again.

"Ah, York. This is where I leave the train. My son is at school near York."

He got up, took a small case from the rack above his head, put his journal in it, and snapped it shut.

"We very much admired the courage of the Jews in the Warsaw ghetto in '43. Good-bye, my friend. It has been a pleasure to meet you. I wish you well in your English life. Do not forget Poland."

Joe saw him hesitate for an instant as to whether to shake Joe's hand. Then he decided that he would, or should, and Joe got up.

"Good-bye, sir."

Joe knew it was Katyn that had made the decision.

He was more alone than he had been at the Grays' house, and that was good. Or he had thought it was good.

On the evening of the fourth day after Mr Hofmann's visit to the shop, he came home in the frosty dark, switched on the lights, closed the curtains, and stood in the middle of his sitting room, looking at the things in it as if he had never seen them before and wondering who it was who had lived here, reasonably content, for three years. Max Hofmann, who had known his father and loved his aunt Anna, had broken the connexion between him, as he stood here now, a stranger even to his violin and his books, and the Joe Halpern of the carefully assembled London life, who until four days ago had been pleased to come home to this flat, with something for supper in the string bag he mostly kept in the briefcase the Grays had years ago given him for Christmas, and with a book to read or a score to repair. Last year Mr Gray had sent him on a course to learn elementary bookbinding, and he had a screw frame and various tools and papers on the square table in the middle of his sitting room where he could mend scores and books that weren't too valuable for his basic skills.

He looked at the table now and was close to tears. It was all pointless, all stupid, all no more than a collection of devices to protect him from remembering who he was and what had happened to everyone he loved.

Why was he more alone than he had ever been because he had met someone who knew them?

He went into his bedroom to look at his photograph of Sally, beside his bed. But wasn't she another device, another mere consolation? Had he really known her? Hardly. Had she known him? Not at all.

He shivered. He turned off his bedroom light, went out into the chill basement passage and then into the narrow bathroom between his bedroom and the big, warm boiler room full of pipes, meters, and racks for drying clothes, and looked at his face in the mirror over the sink. Did he look like his father? No, because he had no beard and no spectacles. Did he look like Anna? He shut his eyes, trying to remember her face, small, alive, always about to smile. He opened his eyes and could see nothing of her in the face in the mirror. Yet he, now, here, in London in December 1955, was all that there was of them, and of his mother and his sister, and his little cousins, and the life there had been.

Unless ... what exactly had Mr Hofmann said about the dead living in God?

Since Mr Carver years ago in the hostel in Hampstead, he hadn't met a single person to whom the idea of God appeared to mean anything whatever. The old couple in whose house he now lived seemed to have no religion of any kind. They certainly didn't go to church on Sundays or synagogue on Saturdays. He knew them scarcely at all. They had told him he was just the tenant for them. He was young and polite and did what he had said he would do in return for his low rent, and that was that. Occasionally the wife would thank him for his work in the garden. They were kind to him as the policeman had been when he got lost on his way back to Hampstead. He detected in the way they treated him no sense of recognition that he was a Jew, and no sense that they would have treated him differently if they had known.

Christopher Gray, he supposed, was a Christian, but neither he nor his children ever went to a church except for the occasional wedding or funeral. Mrs Gray was, he knew, a Jewess. She was born in Vienna, where her father's famous collection of books and music had been the beginning of the business of buying and selling in London that became the shop. She seemed to have nothing of the past or the present binding her to Jewish life, no memory of the festivals through the year, not even of the High Holy Days or Passover, no sense of anything that bound her to other Jews. When, as occasionally she did, she talked about Vienna, which she had left with her family as a fifteen-year-old girl, she looked back to a city of enchantment, prosperous and civilized, where her parents had moved in a world of painters and playwrights, musicians and intellectuals, and people as rich as themselves. "You should have seen the houses on the Ringstrasse, the beautiful things inside them, the wonderful parties. I was allowed to watch from the landing. But I was old enough before we left to come down to dinner on special occasions. The deliciousness of the food, you wouldn't believe. God knows what's become of all that. Vienna has had so much to suffer." Some of the people her parents knew were famous. Some of them were Jews. None of them, as far as he could make out from the way she talked, lived in a way that anyone he had ever known in Jewish Vilna would have recognized.

Once, only once, when he was helping her set out chairs, music stands, and parts for a performance of the Schubert octet in her drawing room, she asked him a question about his childhood.

"Where did you learn to play the violin?"

"In Vilna, where I was born."

"Vilna? That's a city, isn't it? I thought you were a shtetl Jew. Where is Vilna exactly?"

"When I was born, it was in Poland. It's not far from Minsk."

"Minsk? I don't know where that is either. I haven't even heard of it. It sounds Russian. So, Russian Poland, obviously. Then how did you come to know German?"

"My mother was German."

"Really? I had no idea. And were there German violin teachers in Vilna?"

He saw that she was imagining Jewish fiddlers at shtetl weddings, and wild Hasidic dancing. He was suddenly furious.

"My father, who was a much better violinist than I am, had the same teacher in Vilna as Jascha Heifetz. Heifetz and my father were the same age and as boys had lessons on the same days."

"Really? How extraordinary. I thought all the great Russian violinists came from Odessa."

She was rearranging a vase of flowers on the piano, not looking at him. He wanted to make her stop, make her look at him. He wanted to tell her that for hundreds of years the Jews of Vilna were the most learned in Europe, that the Great Synagogue and its schools and courts and libraries had never been put to shame by the Catholic university in the city, which the Russians in any case had closed for nearly a century. He wanted to tell her that the Vilna Gaon, the famous eighteenth-century rabbi, was the wisest, the most scholarly, the most levelheaded Jewish figure of modern times. "Remember, Josef," he could hear his father saying, "that the Litvak tradition is calm, rational, neither unbalanced nor embittered by emotion." But how could he even begin? And he knew by now that nothing he could say would breach her imperviousness to any Jewish story that was different from her own.

She never again asked him anything about his life before he arrived in her house.

And wasn't he as bad a Jew as Marianne Gray? Since he was eleven he had never been inside a synagogue. In the forest the old men—three of them when he first saw them, afterwards two when one died, then three or four later—had prayed, standing and swaying in the snow or the insect-heavy evening sunshine. The fighters didn't seem to pray. Joe thought they looked after the old men, found them food, kept them as warm as possible, so that they could pray for everyone else. Did they give their fear and their sorrow to the old men so that the old men could give them to God? Had he not always given his own grief for his father, his mother, his sister, Anna, and the little boys to God? What else was there to do with it? Had not Mr Hofmann been doing just the same when he said what he said about Anna?

He longed suddenly, with new, concentrated longing, for Mr Hofmann to come back to the shop so that he could ask him about his father. Mr Hofmann had known his father well, as a young man, as an equal, who talked no doubt a great deal. Joe had known his father only when he himself was a child. He wanted to know who his father had been in the eyes of someone who was not his son. He wanted to know how his father would have faced death. But would Mr Hofmann ever come back?

Chapter 6

The next day, he did.

"Joe!" Mr Gray's voice, shouting from the shop, from the bottom of the stairs. This happened several times a day. Joe would clatter down the stairs, to be sent to find something for a customer, to look at something someone had brought in, to compare it with something else. Not this time.

"Someone to see you, Joe."

"Good morning", Mr Hofmann said, formal, correct, his hat in his hand.

"Good morning, sir."

"I have come to collect the Schubert album. You have it for me?"

"Yes, sir, I have reserved it, as you asked."

Joe took it from the shelf in the shop where books and scores reserved for customers were kept. He took out the slip he had filled in and went to wrap the book in brown paper at the table at the back of the shop. His hands were shaking so that it was difficult to tie the string.

"And what is the price? I forgot to ask you when I was before in the shop, I think."

"Two pounds, sir."

"Two pounds. That is good."

Mr Hofmann gave two pounds to Christopher Gray, who was sitting at the desk. Mr Gray opened the drawer, put the notes in the cashbox, closed the drawer. "Thank you."

Then Mr Hofmann said, "I was impressed last week, Mr Gray, by your young assistant. May I ask him something?"

"By all means", Mr Gray said. "Of course."

Still talking to Mr Gray, Mr Hofmann said, "When we were looking at some songs of Schubert, we discovered a shared interest in the poems of Heine. I have an old book of Heine I should like your assistant to see. It may even be of some value. I do not wish to take up his time at his work, since this is not a book concerning music." He turned towards

Joe. "So would it be convenient for you, young man, to meet me after your work one day, so that I could show you the book of Heine? At what time do you finish your work?"

Christopher Gray laughed.

"Nobody knows what time this fellow finishes work. He's always here when the rest of us go home—the shop shuts at five, but he never seems to have got to the end of what he's doing by five. So he locks up whenever it suits him."

"In this case, would you have any objection if I brought my book of Heine here to your shop to show Mr Halpern at, let us say, five thirty today?"

"None whatsoever. Joe's time is his own after five, Mr Hofmann."

"Ah, you remember my name, Mr Gray."

"Of course."

"Forgive me, sir. I have never introduced myself properly. I am Max Hofmann and I am the teacher of violin at Saint Peter's High School for girls."

Christopher Gray got to his feet and they shook hands. Mr Hofmann's formality was clearly infectious.

"Delighted to see you again, Mr Hofmann", Christopher Gray said. "You will find Joe a highly intelligent young man."

"I am sure. Thank you, Mr Gray."

He took his parcel from Joe, turned back to Christopher Gray, and with a stiff little bow of the head, put on his hat and left the shop.

Mr Gray looked at Joe and laughed again.

"Well! A Prussian friend!" He looked more carefully. "What's the matter, Joe? You're as white as a sheet."

"Nothing. Nothing at all. I thought he would not come back for the Schubert."

He fled upstairs.

For the rest of the day he found it almost impossible to concentrate. At lunchtime he went out. He was too nervous to eat anything. He walked down to Trafalgar Square in crisp winter sunshine and stopped among the pigeons and the homeless beggars, by one of the stone lions, deciding to make himself think about something else.

Not long after he started working in the shop, he had read about Nelson and the battle of Trafalgar. He was astonished. He had always understood that first the Russians and then the Germans had defeated Napoleon. He looked across to the fine, long front of the National Gallery with its colonnaded portico. It had struck him as a neat contrast that a beautiful open space in Vilna, not as big as this but impressive to the child he had been, with the Bishop's Palace on one side, was called Napoleon Square.

At his Polish school when he was ten years old, he had learned, he thought, all about Napoleon; the boys were told that Vilna had twice been at the very centre of European history, all on account of Napoleon.

On the day Napoleon's army invaded Russia, Tsar Alexander was at a magnificent summer ball in Vilna, dancing with Polish ladies. Napoleon and his soldiers marched into Vilna to a tremendous welcome from the people, who hoped he would liberate them from the Russian empire. The Jews of Vilna, thinking Napoleon not a liberator but a man who scorned all religion, were noncommittal, cautious. More than a century later, when Joe retold this story at home, his father said that the Jews of Vilna were still proud of this pious Litvak response to the great conqueror—"They thought an atheist emperor might be even worse than a Christian one. Who's to say they were wrong?" Six months after Napoleon's invasion, ragged, starving remnants of his army reappeared in the city, where thousands of them died. Vilna was back in the Russian empire, and the Russians built the new Bishop's Palace with a long, handsome front, colonnaded and pedimented like the National Gallery in Trafalgar Square. After 1918, Polish Vilna, with Bolshevik Russia menacing and not far away, chose Napoleon's name for the grand square as a statement of defiance. Now that the Red Army and the Wehrmacht and the Red Army again had marched into Vilna between 1939 and 1945, and gone again—if the Red Army had gone—Joe had no idea what they had decided to call the square in Lithuanian Vilnius.

By now he was walking in Saint James's Park, briskly, to keep warm. When he realized, as perhaps he hadn't before, that he would almost certainly never see Vilna again, he stood still with a groan, so that a woman coming towards him with two heavy shopping bags stopped, looked on the point of asking if he was all right, saw that he was, and walked on.

How could he not see Vilna again? How could he see it?

He was standing almost at the edge of the lake. There was a thin film of forming ice on the shallow water by the bank. Ducks of different colours, different kinds, were swimming beyond the ice, and a small boy taking bits of stale bread from a paper bag was failing to throw them far enough to reach the ducks.

And Vilna was not what he could ask Mr Hofmann about. Most likely Mr Hofmann had never been there. Joe's own memory was all there was for him, and all there would be, of the Vilna he had known and loved because it was his home.

He looked at the lake and watched. The child with his bag of bread was dressed in a tweed coat with a velvet collar, a tweed cap matching his coat, buttoned leggings, and woollen gloves. Beside him stood a formidable nanny, with a hat like Mrs Thwaites' Sunday hat, her hand on an enormous, gleaming black pram with a baby in a white woollen hat sitting up in it. Children of a rich family. He looked across the lake to Buckingham Palace beyond the leafless trees. The British Empire. Here he was, a Polish Jew at the very core of the British Empire. How mild and without menace it seemed after the marching armies of the Russian, the French, the Nazi, the Soviet empires that had paraded and bullied and murdered and burned, and sometimes stumbled, their way into and out of Vilna.

Two years before, he had watched, among thousands and thousands of cheering people in Trafalgar Square, the coronation procession go by. Many people had arrived the night before and slept on the pavements under rugs in the rain to be sure of a good place. Too far back in the crowd to see the horses properly, he had watched the plumed helmets of the Horse Guards and the pioneer hats of the Royal Canadian Mounted Police bob up and down as the riders trotted by. Through the rain and the press of cheering people, he had just glimpsed some of the groups of marching soldiers from, apparently, all over the world. A band came into earshot, went by, faded as another came, and another, and another. The procession took almost an hour to pass. The crowds cheered and cheered, waved flags, cheered more, cheered most loudly for the queen herself, in a great, heavy coach made of gold. He saw the top of the coach pass by; only in pictures in the newspapers next morning had he seen the queen, young and beautiful. Warm, friendly, and unthreatening the whole day had been.

But he wasn't an Indian or an African or one of the West Indians, descendants of slaves on the sugar plantations, who had arrived in

London on a ship—he couldn't remember the ship's name—not long after he started work in the shop. They had come because they were promised work, and more had come since. He had seen them working on building sites, as street sweepers with barrows and brushes, as bus conductors, their wives and daughters as waitresses and cleaners. He had also seen people looking at them with the old, familiar contempt every Jew from the east knew well, and sometimes shouting insults or pushing them aside. In the windows of poorer streets where rooms or flats were to let, he had seen notices saying "No Blacks". A few weeks ago he had seen a black boy of about fifteen get off the bus in which Joe had been travelling late back from work. While the bus waited at a red light, the boy was surrounded by half a dozen white boys shouting, "I smell a nigger! I smell a nigger!" The boy ran; they jeered but left him to run. They might not have. Should he have jumped off the bus to shout at them? Would it have helped? Was he too afraid?

Perhaps it had not been only the end of British rule in Palestine and the creation of the state of Israel that had encouraged a sense, detectable in the newspapers, that the "Jewish problem", whatever that was, had been solved. Perhaps black people, visible in London as clearly few had been before the war, had simply replaced the Jews as the object of suspicion, disgust, even hatred. Was there always a given quantity of hatred in every society that had to be directed towards whichever group was at any time suspected of taking jobs, taking houses, taking girls, taking favours from the government, that the poor majority thought were due to them?

He looked at his watch and turned away from the freezing lake and the ducks to walk back to the shop. He even smiled as he realized that he had succeeded in overlaying his excitement, the nervousness that had made him feel sick in the hours before lunchtime, with some time spent in actual thought, however confused and inconclusive. It was a small victory, but he felt better.

At exactly half past five Joe was standing in the shop with the street door locked, when there was a knock on the door. He knew Mr Hofmann would be punctual.

He came in from the dark street. Joe shut the door and Mr Hofmann stood, without taking his hat off, and said, in German, "Good evening, Josef."

168

Joe couldn't speak.

"If this were a European city, we could go to a quiet café and sit at a table with a round marble top and have some coffee and perhaps some cake, and talk. But as this is London, there is Lyons Corner House or a pub. Both are noisy, and neither has good coffee. Shall we stay in your shop to talk?"

Too grateful to answer, Joe nodded, went to the chair behind the desk, and waved Mr Hofmann to the chair he had sat in when he came to ask about Schubert songs. When Mr Hofmann had taken off his hat and his coat and his scarf, both of them sat down.

"I could make some coffee", Joe said.

"No. No coffee."

Silence.

Mr Hofmann put his hand on a pile of books on the desk, tensed it so that all his strong fingers were straight and raised up from the books, and then relaxed his hand.

"Josef, I have had some days to become accustomed to these deaths. You have had many years without your family, and you lost all your family when you were a child." He said this as if summarizing what he had been thinking for the last few days.

Then he said, "Tell me about your mother."

"The Russians took my mother and my sister, who was younger than I, at about the time they killed my father and the other prisoners, in the spring of 1940. They took them away with other families of prisoners, mostly Poles, some Jews, on trains. The men who took them weren't ordinary Russian soldiers but the NKVD—as if my mother and my sister were counterrevolutionaries, or spies, or dangerous to anyone. I don't know where they were taking them, but I know they died soon because there were no letters. Letters came from some of the other wives who were taken. The Russians would have taken me too if I had been at home, but I was with ... I was with my aunt Anna and my uncle the rabbi. I stayed after Passover so that I could have lessons with my uncle, since my father had gone and my school was no longer—and so that Anna could help me practise violin."

"Josef, tell me about your mother."

"She was German. Her family had lived in Breslau for a long time."

"Ah, Breslau. Was she perhaps a nurse in the university hospital?"

"Yes, she was. How did you know?"

"I guessed. The university hospital was where your father was working, although I had no idea then that he ... Never mind."

Joe looked up for the first time, and met the acute blue eyes.

"Was your mother more German, or more Jewish?"

"She was more German. It is complicated to explain. She was proud to be a Jewess but more proud to be German. She read me German stories, German poems. She was not religious. She thought that my father ... she would accuse my father, not angrily, you understand ..."

"She would accuse your father of being religious when he said he was not religious. She thought he was too clever and too modern and too much of a doctor to be religious."

Joe was astonished.

"How do you know all this?"

"It is not difficult to guess. Remember that I knew your father quite well. Students in Germany in those days—they talked and talked."

He paused, clearly remembering a time Joe knew almost nothing about.

"Also," he went on, "your father and the violin. He was a very good player, most unusually good for a man who was not a professional musician, a very much better player than I was. Your father, when he was young, when I knew him, denied that he was religious. He was, of course, a doctor, a scientist, a rationalist. But he played like a man who was sometimes near to God."

"So my mother was right?"

"Perhaps she was."

"But how could both of them be right?"

"Because they meant different things by the word 'religion'. People do, you know, mean a large number of different things by this word."

"But ... I don't understand how there is a connexion between music and religion."

"Not necessarily, and not precisely between music and religion, but in some people some of the time possibly between music and God. Music may open a soul that has otherwise decided to be closed. May it not?"

"I don't know. I ..."

"Go on, Josef."

"My father wanted me to learn from my uncle and Anna about being a good Jew. But it was too long ago. I remember only a few prayers, a little Hebrew. And the violin has been such a different thing."

"Has it? I wonder. The dedication to music, the practising, the hard work—is it not dedication to something outside the self, something which is good and beautiful, and even true? Consider the difference between playing a complicated passage both correctly and in tune and playing the same passage not quite correctly and not quite in tune. And then there is the difference between playing this passage musically, or merely correctly and in tune. Dedication is needed. Is this dedication not close to dedication to God?"

"Is it? I don't know. But perhaps I understand. Perhaps you are right."

"And there must be more than dedication to make a musician. Is not the musical player a gifted player, one touched by grace? And is not such a gift a gift of God?"

Joe looked into the compelling eyes.

Mr Hofmann was reminding Joe of his father, because Joe had met no one since his father's disappearance that morning in his Polish officer's uniform who had, in just this way, thought while he was talking, so that what he discovered or invented as he talked was like a lamp being lit.

"I don't understand this word, 'grace'."

"It is not a Jewish word. But if a soul is touched by God, as any soul may be, that is grace."

"In the secret of his wings", Joe said.

"That's it. You do understand. I knew you would."

"Mr Hofmann ... do you think any of this, the dedication to music, some kind of sense of God, might have helped my father when he knew he was going to be killed? I mean, you knew him as someone of his own age ... how do you imagine he died?"

"Bravely."

Mr Hofmann paused.

"You knew that. Also, I expect you would agree, angrily. The stupidity of all the killing, killing not even in battle, would have made him angry."

Both of them smiled. It was good that both of them knew he had been angry.

"But the answer to your real question, I can't give you. No one could. It is not possible to guess. The answer is between the soul and God. But I can tell you that I am certain that your father was a soul not far from God, not far from the secret of his wings."

Joe felt tears rising.

Mr Hofmann took out a packet of cigarettes, offered one to Joe, took one himself, and lit both with a petrol lighter.

"You are young still, Josef. And you have not had the opportunity to talk as we talked then, before Hitler. Was your uncle the rabbi a good man?"

Mr Hofmann's voice had changed. Clearly this was something he badly wanted to know.

"He was. I think he was a very good man. He was always quiet. I never heard him speak loudly. When his little boys were naughty, he spoke to them quietly. Sometimes just his quietness made them cry. But he was kind—wise and kind. He had his shul, where regular prayers were said, and he spent hours of every day with holy books, but if someone came to see him—a yeshiva student, or someone asking about Jewish law, or someone in trouble—he always asked them in to his library. It was called his library though it was a small room: lots of books, a desk, three chairs . . ."

Joe looked round, at the shop and its shadows, with one lamp lit on the desk. He had turned off the ceiling lights before Mr Hofmann arrived.

"A bit like this."

He smiled. The similarity hadn't struck him before. "And he talked to them, sometimes for hours. So the boys and I knew to be quiet in the house. My father said that he and my grandfather—my grandfather was also a doctor, though not a surgeon—had studied for years and years to learn their way out of old Jewish tradition and into the modern world of science. My grandfather was a medical student in Cracow, my father in Breslau of course, when you knew him. And then, in spite of the science and the medicine and the modern ideas and the shelves and shelves of Polish and German books, the whole nineteenth century"—Joe smiled again as he remembered his father using this phrase, which he hadn't understood at all—"his sister had married all of old Vilna wrapped up in Uncle Moshe, the perfect example of the Litvak rabbi. But my father looked pleased when he said this because he liked him. It was my father, not my mother, who wanted me to learn Hebrew with my uncle. My uncle was patient with me, and I liked him because he was kind to my aunt Anna. But I think she was a little afraid of him. And he did not like German music, which of course she loved."

"What happened to him? Did the Nazis . . . ?"

172

"Not the Nazis. My aunt Anna told me—and I now understand better than I did then what she told me—that the Russians, when they were ruling Vilna before the Nazis came, wanted to destroy all Jewish life. They decreed that rabbis were no longer to function as rabbis, that they could not teach, or decide Jewish questions in rabbinical courts, or be paid by their community. Each of them had to announce in the Yiddish press that he had ceased all rabbinical duties and that no one was to consult him about anything. This was to be the end of hundreds and hundreds of years of religious life. My uncle refused to put such a notice in the newspaper. He continued to work as a rabbi as he always had. His people continued to consult him, to depend on him. So the NKVD took him away, in the winter of 1941. They killed him. The Russians had many prisons near Vilna where they killed people, not because they were Jews, as the Nazis killed people, but because they disobeyed Soviet orders. The Russians called people who disobeyed Soviet orders saboteurs or enemies of the revolution or foreign spies. How could my uncle be a foreign spy? He had never left Vilna in his life."

The terrible injustice of his uncle's death struck him more forcibly than it ever had. He had not thought of the quiet rabbi for years. He swallowed.

"We had already lost my father, my mother, and my sister. My aunt Anna said that she would look after her three boys and me and that she would do whatever she was told to do by the Russians to keep us all alive. Then the Germans came."

"And then", Mr Hofmann said, "there was nothing she could do."

"Nothing."

A long silence. They stubbed out their cigarettes in Christopher Gray's French café ashtray, heavy green pottery with "Pastis Ricard" in raised white letters round the edge. Joe kept his eyes on it.

Mr Hofmann, who seemed to notice everything, said, "Is the ashtray yours?"

"It's Mr Gray's. He loves France."

"Have you been to France?"

"No. I haven't left England since I came."

"Don't go to France. I took my wife to Paris for a holiday last year. A bad mistake. I look—I am—too German. Also the French are confused, dangerously confused, I would say. The atmosphere reminded me a little of my part of Germany when I was young. We were all told we had lost

173

the war when we knew we had won it—in the east, you understand. The French are told they won the last war when they know they lost it. The effect is much the same, a kind of bitterness directed at everyone else—*ressentiment*, in fact, as Nietzsche described it. Not good."

Was he talking about France to help Joe to relax?

"But tell me, Joe, how did you manage to escape?"

Yes. Joe swallowed. He wanted to tell him.

"I was one of the last to be shot that day. The Lithuanians were all drunk, not aiming properly. I fell with the others onto the bodies. I realized I wasn't even wounded. I waited until it was dark, quiet. Then I ran into the forest."

"And so?"

"I went south because I knew the forest got wilder, deeper. It was summer. I ate berries; the wild apples were not yet ripe. After a few days a peasant woman whose husband was dead and whose son was in the Red Army took me in. She was finding it difficult to keep going. It wasn't a proper farm, more a clearing in the forest, with ducks, geese, hens, and a little horse to pull the cart. She grew potatoes and onions, and cabbages which the slugs made holes in. She used to take potatoes and eggs and sometimes bundles of sticks tied together for kindling in the cart to market, just a small market in the village. I couldn't understand everything she said. She cried a lot, and she spoke Belorussian with a strong accent, but she had a few words of Polish and I knew some Russian. I learned some Belorussian from trying to understand her. I was there for several months, through that winter to the early spring. I slept in a loft, very low, above the shed where she stalled the pony. She said if the Germans came, I should take the pony and ride into the forest. They came, and I did. I hope the Germans never found out she had hidden a Jew. She was going to pretend she was hiding her son so that he shouldn't have to fight in the Red Army. If they found out the truth, they would kill her."

He stopped. Remembering her after so long, he found he was praying that she was still alive and that her son had perhaps after all come home.

"And then?"

"Then I was even luckier. On my second day in the forest, as it was getting dark, my little horse was picking her way through thick, tangled undergrowth and over marshy ground. I was trying to find a dry place to sleep. The forest was wet, muddy with melted snow. Everywhere the sound of water, the streams that appear in the spring, dripping trees,

174

dripping rocks. Someone shouted at me to stop—I can't remember in what language, but not German—so I stopped. I jumped down. The ground was so wet my feet sank. I remember thinking that if I had to run, I couldn't. A man in rough clothes, not a soldier's uniform, with a gun across his back, took me by the shoulders and turned me towards what light was left in the sky. 'You are a Jew', he said, but in Yiddish. So I knew he wouldn't kill me. I stayed with them until the Red Army got close in the spring of 1944."

"Who was 'them'?"

"Jewish partisans. Belorussian Jews mostly, some Polish, some Russian—but what was the difference there in Kresy?"

"Kresy?"

"The borderlands. Between Poland and Russia. No one knew where the border was. In the forest it was impossible to tell. Probably it still is."

"Did they fight?"

"Yes, they fought. The fighters had guns, mostly stolen or found on men who had been killed in the forest. At the beginning the fighters tried to kill Germans, to ambush them on the road or shoot them when they were drunk in a village at night. But what the Germans did to a village if a German was killed nearby was so terrible that less and less the fighters set out to kill Germans. Our commander said it was always more important to save a Jew than to kill a German. So there were more and more of us, women and children and a few old people, who had managed to escape. It became very difficult to move the whole camp, but we had to, often. It was most difficult in the winter, in the snow, because we could be seen more easily, and smoke is impossible to hide."

"Were the leaders and the fighters Communists?"

"No. That was another problem always. There were Russian partisans, Communists of course, also in the forest. The Nalibocka forest is very big; it is hard in England to imagine how big. They hated us because we took no orders from Moscow. They were not as sure to kill us as the Germans were, but they despised us, stole our food, and stole our guns if they could. So we hid from them also."

"Who was your commander?"

Joe was still. He shut his eyes. How had he allowed himself to say so much? Then he shook his head.

"You can't tell me. Of course. Forgive me. That hidden life is above all to be secret. Also, for you, a German of my age ... I understand."

175

Mr Hofmann again produced his cigarettes, his lighter. Each of the men drew deeply on his cigarette.

"Do you know whether your commander is still alive?"

"I don't know. I don't know what happened to any of them. He told us that spring that now that Russia was defeating the Germans, the Red Army regarded all partisans not under Russian command as enemies. Every group of Russian partisans had its commissar belonging to the NKVD, who had taken my mother, my sister, my uncle, who had shot my father. So we were told to separate and find our way towards the west as carefully and as quickly as we could. Our store of food was shared out among us. There was no money. I kept going for some time, walking west, hungry and frightened, sometimes walking with people from camps or people who had been slave labourers and had escaped from factories, sometimes alone. Sometimes during the harvest I got a lift for a few miles on a wagon, on a pile of beets. I travelled for some weeks with a family of German peasants from East Prussia, mother, children, and the old grandfather, with a cart and everything they had been able to load on it. They needed help with their horse. When I first saw them the horse was bolting towards me on the road, the cart rocking behind it on the ruts. Something had frightened the horse. One of the children fell off the cart. I stopped the horse, quieted it. The little girl wasn't badly hurt. They had some food, a few potatoes, cabbages, sausage, also a little money for milk. They didn't mind that I was a Jew. Perhaps they didn't know. They had been told to leave everything and travel west to Germany. East Prussia was not Germany anymore. We saw ..."

Joe found himself laughing.

"What is it?"

"A memory. I had completely forgotten. Two or three times on the road with the German peasants, we saw Russians, by themselves, partisans lost or in the wrong place, with bicycles they had stolen. It was funny because they didn't know how to ride a bicycle. Of course if they had managed to get hold of any vodka, they were drunk as well. They made the children laugh. It doesn't seem funny now."

Joe was suddenly tired, so tired that for a moment he sat in his chair, his head and shoulders bent forward, his cigarette burning unnoticed between his fingers.

"Josef, what can I say? Compared to your young life ... how old are you now?"

He stubbed out his cigarette and looked up.

"I am twenty-six."

"Twenty-six. I was twenty-eight when I was so fortunately able to come to England, late in 1933. The time of terror in Germany had only just begun. I escaped. Compared to your life, my own has been easy—from time to time sad, but easy."

Joe looked across the desk at Mr Hofmann, met his eyes.

"Why did you come to England? What did you need to escape?"

"Ah." He in turn stubbed out his cigarette, and sat very straight in his chair.

"Since you have told me so much, let me try to explain. I am, as you see, a German. My father was a landowner, a Prussian count. A Junker. My real name is Max-Ernst von Hofmannswaldau. We lived at Waldau in Silesia, in the foothills of the Riesengebirge, close to a beautiful river."

He stopped. Joe watched him remembering.

"My father was killed in 1919 soon after the war was officially over, although in reality it was not. There was trouble between Germans and Poles in our village. My father went to calm things down. He was shot, no doubt by mistake, by Freikorps officers, wild young men with guns, out of anyone's control, left with nothing to do after the armistice but gallop about to deal with disorder and in fact to make it worse. I was fourteen, older than you were when they tried to kill you. In fact, per-haps the men who had your family murdered were those very boys grown up, colonels by then. After my father's death I went to school in Breslau and then to study at the university. It was there, on account of music, that I met your father and your aunt Anna. She ... yes, well, she was a lovely girl."

He paused, but only for a moment.

"Germany in those times, in the years before Hitler became chan-cellor, is difficult to describe now. The whole process of the country losing its mind—Germany, so celebrated for its mind, its intelligence, its learning—was slow. But if you were watching carefully, you could see it happening. Two of my friends, one a Polish count, a student of law as I was, and one a baron from East Prussia, a junior doctor at the same hospital where your father was a surgeon, were offered brilliant academic careers and excellent salaries if they would work to prove what amounted to Nazi racial theory, years before the Nazis were in power. The lawyer was to join an institute set up to show that the Aryan race had ancient rights to all the European lands populated by the Slav peoples. The doctor was to work on a scientific project to demonstrate the racial inferiority of the Jews."

"The lawyer was Polish?"

"Ah. He was a count, he had been educated in Germany, and his mother was a Viennese aristocrat. Also he was very clever. All good enough for the professors."

"Your friends refused?"

"They refused."

"What happened to them?"

"As the result of their refusal? Nothing. Just no academic posts in Breslau."

"What happened to them when … later?"

"My Polish friend went back to Poland. He had lived as a child in Galicia. He became a priest in Cracow. Then he went to work as a priest in Lemberg, in Lwów. He was imprisoned by the Russians when Poland was partitioned, again, between Germany and Russia. The Russians killed him when the Germans invaded in 1941. They cleared the prison in Lwów by killing the prisoners. My Prussian friend became a medical officer in the Wehrmacht. He was executed after the July Plot in 1944—Count von Stauffenberg's attempt to assassinate Hitler. You have heard of it?"

Joe nodded.

"How deeply my friend was implicated in the plot, I have no idea. But I am proud that he was thought by the Nazis to be part of it."

He paused again.

"It took me a long time to find out what had become of both of them. Now that I know that your father and Anna were also killed by these monstrous machines, the NKVD machine, the Nazi machine, it seems to me more than ever that all the good people died."

Joe bent his head.

"I know."

"Josef …" Mr Hofmann leaned forward over the desk and made Joe look at him.

"Listen to me. This is most important. You must not feel guilty that you are still alive while all those you loved are dead. You must not. I know this guilt. In my case perhaps there is some reason for it. I could have remained in Germany and protested perhaps, or refused some order, and probably I would have been killed. Would that have served any purpose or prevented one single injustice, one single act of cruelty? Almost certainly not. But would it have been the good, the honourable, path to take? Over all these years, as you may imagine, I have thought about this, and still I am not sure. But in your case there are none of these complications. You are alive by luck, by the grace of God, because strangers cared for you and because of your courage. There is here nothing, nothing whatever, of doubt, of shame, of guilt. In this, even if only in this, you are more blessed than I shall ever be."

Joe crossed his arms over his chest, his hands on his shoulders, warmed.

"But ... but what would have happened if you hadn't come to England?"

"Impossible to know. Impossible even to guess."

He leaned back in his chair.

"You see, I am not only the Prussian count, easy to identify, easy to place in an old German world that has gone. My mother was Jewish. But she was also baptized. That is to say, she belonged to a family that had lived in Breslau since early in the nineteenth century, when my great-grandparents had their children baptized into the Protestant Church—not because they were religious but because they were not. They thought religion belonged to the past, and baptism, to which they attached little significance, in those times made many things easier for Jews. It was not difficult, for example, for my grandfather to become a professor of medicine in Breslau. It was not difficult for my mother to marry a count. Happily for them, although very sadly for me at the time, both my mother and my grandfather died before the Nazis were in power.

"I was not, in any sense you or your father would recognize, a Jew. Hitler thought differently of course. When his government decreed that all Jews holding state posts were to be dismissed—university professors, museum curators, orchestral musicians, lawyers—I could perhaps have escaped dismissal if I had kept very quiet. I was then a lawyer, a junior judge in the old Prussian system which was respected throughout Europe. My name and my appearance might have preserved me in my career. My brother, eight years older than I, was already an officer in the SS, with the same name, the same Prussian appearance. And the same Jewish mother. But also he had married the rich daughter of a prominent Nazi factory owner."

He stopped.

"They had two daughters. What became of them, I don't know, and have never tried to discover. Perhaps they are all alive and well in South America."

He smiled at Joe.

"It is too late for me to worry about my brother. We were very different. And I would prefer not to know ... about his war."

"And you?" Joe said. "You didn't keep quiet enough?"

"I attracted attention. I thought at the time that what I did was required of me by honesty, by honour, by tradition. I was horrified that the judge for whom I was working and all the judges everywhere in Germany, as far as I could tell, were supporting the Nazis and their laws as if they were not clever enough to understand the concept of an unjust law. They were presiding over courts which sentenced Jews and Communists with unjust harshness, and Storm Troopers with unjust leniency. Have you heard of Storm Troopers, Brownshirts?"

Joe shook his head.

"Nazi thugs. They bullied people, put people in concentration camps without trial, killed people, all with complete impunity. The judges said nothing, did nothing. The judges did not object when their Jewish colleagues were sacked. It was because of all this that I began to write an essay. It was intended to be a serious, scholarly piece of writing, to be read only by my own superior, a judge for whom I had, before Hitler, the usual German respect for a senior figure in one's own profession. I wanted to prove to him that what was going on contravened not only the traditions of Prussian justice but the principle of equality before the law common to all civilized systems of jurisprudence. The work I was doing was noticed, and I was sacked and, by implication, told that since Hitler regarded me as a Jew and clearly I was not prepared to enforce his laws, I had better leave the country. I was fortunate enough to have an opportunity to do so, and I took it."

"But surely that was good and brave to try to defend what was right when you must have known it was dangerous to try?"

"Ah—this is exactly the point. My work in the law library of the university provoked their attention. I needn't have done it. It was certain to be useless. Later, much later, I understood that, unconsciously, I actually wanted to provoke their attention. I wanted the Nazis to make the decision for me. Or, more precisely, I wanted them to confirm the decision

I made on the day I saw a notice forbidding Jews to enter the park in Breslau—the beautiful park, my favourite place in the city, where I had taken your aunt Anna to walk, to skate in the winter, to sit in the summer sunshine. When I saw that notice, I decided that I was a Jew."

"But ..."

"But I am not a Jew."

He laughed—the first time Joe had seen him laugh.

"Of course. You are your father's son. You know perfectly well I am not a Jew. But then ... then, I suppose, though this was not clear to me at the time, I chose my mother's family, their history, over my father's. Partly because my brother, the good Prussian soldier, was now in the SS. Also, in a way, because of your aunt Anna, whom I had lost."

He lit another cigarette. Joe shook his head.

After a pause, Mr Hofmann added, "In England there is no one who knows all that I have told you. Nowhere is there anyone else who knows. God knows, perhaps." He smiled.

Joe understood that Mr Hofmann was—what? Happy? Relieved? Pleased, at least, to have shared something of the weight of memory he had carried alone for many years. Joe smiled back.

"In England, you will have realized, they do not want to know. Has anyone, since you reached England, asked you about what you lived through during the war?"

"A Polish gentleman I met on a train, not long ago. I don't know his name."

"What was his response to your story?"

"It was mixed. It wasn't easy for him, I could see. Poles ... you know. But he was a kind man, I think. Years ago I told my story to the colonel for whom I worked for two years as a stable lad in Yorkshire, and then also to a friend of his from London. They wanted to train me to be a spy. They wanted to send me to Poland, or Lithuania, or more likely Communist Germany."

"You refused?"

"I refused. I didn't have the courage to go back to Europe."

"It was brave to refuse. And by the way, England is in Europe. Or don't you think so?"

Joe laughed.

"No. It's too different. Europe is Europe. But England really doesn't understand about Europe, and in many ways that's good."

"You are a wise young man, Josef."

Another smile.

"And no one else, Josef? You have told your story to no one else?"

"No one else."

"One Pole and two intelligence officers. Exactly. For the English the war is a story of triumph—a quiet, deserved triumph naturally, so like them—a story of patience and resourcefulness at home, and brave young men in aeroplanes and ships and tanks fighting the monstrous Nazi machine. It was far more monstrous than they knew then or than they wish to know now. They do not feel remorse for abandoning Poland to Stalin—poor wretched Poland, even if Poland has been given my Silesia and, to make room for Poles, if the good German farmers of my childhood have all been moved to the west. And the English know almost nothing of how monstrous the Soviet machine has been. This is more serious, since the Soviets are still so powerful. Even at the end of the war the people in the English government had already decided not to know. They sent back to Stalin thousands of prisoners, thousands and thousands of wretched Russians and Cossacks taken prisoner by the Germans, slave labourers and so forth. Stalin killed them. Do you remember the English newspapers when Stalin died? The front pages with pictures of him, the most cruel man in Russia's cruel history, at his peaceful end, a hero. 'Uncle Joe is dead.' Of course, if it were not for Russia, England would not have won the war, but even so, the English know very little about the east. Victory they know. Defeat they do not know, except for the defeated Germans in the west whom they did their best to treat decently after the war, having learned from how the Nazis came to power the danger of inflicting humiliation. But loss, absolute loss—what do they know of this? The loss of so many and of so much in Poland; the loss of my Silesia, of your Vilna, to a future severed from the past. A different past will be invented of course and taught to the children in the schools in the hope that the truth will be so smothered in lies as to die. But as long as we are alive, you and I, the truth we know does not die. And in God the truth never dies. Do you believe this, Josef?"

"I don't know ... yes, I think I do. What can I do for my parents, my sister, my aunt Anna and her little boys, except to remember them? And more and more I know I can't remember them properly, accurately, let alone completely. I was too young. So if even I can't ... Are they nowhere now? Or are they perhaps ..."

"Of course. For you to believe that they are in the memory, in the safety and peace of God, is for you to pray for them. That is what you can do."

"Shechinah."

"What does that mean?"

"The presence of God."

"Yes, Josef. Yes—another thing the English, most of the English, do not understand. I have an English wife."

Joe looked up at him, surprised that it hadn't occurred to him even to wonder about Mr Hofmann's wife, though he had noticed his wedding ring and he had talked about taking his wife to Paris.

"Yes. She is a good and a kind person. During the war she was a nurse, like your mother. But she has never wanted to know about the Germany of my youth, my childhood. She is pleased that I escaped, certainly. But she thinks that what I escaped from does not concern her, or perhaps would frighten her if she were to understand it—as if a freezing wind would blow from the east and kill the flowers in her garden, or great trees would fall and crush her roof. So she prefers not to know. Why do you think we are sitting to talk in this shop instead of in my warm house? It is because I have never told her about our quartet in Breslau, about your father, about Anna. And now it is much too late."

Then his voice changed.

"It is cold, Josef, don't you think? Perhaps you might make us some coffee after all? Not Camp coffee, I hope?"

Joe laughed.

"Instant coffee. But it tastes like coffee."

"More or less. We have it in the school where I teach. But it will warm us a little."

It took Joe ten minutes to make two mugs of coffee in the basement. He brought them up on a tray with a plate of shortcake biscuits from the tin in the kitchen. Mr Hofmann was sitting exactly where Joe had left him, his clasped hands on the desk in front of him.

"Wonderful", he said, like old Mr Carver.

They sipped the hot coffee, warming their hands on the mugs.

Mr Hofmann took a few pieces of scrap paper from the pile on the desk, arranged them neatly, and put his mug down on them—as if Christopher Gray had not, over the years, left rings from mugs and glasses all over the desk. He lit yet another cigarette.

"Do you live alone, Josef?"

"Yes."

"Happily?"

Joe spread his hands wide above the desk for a moment, as if someone might put something into them.

"But that is your father, your father exactly", Mr Hofmann said, his face lit with pleasure.

Joe was glad. He tried to remember his father making the gesture but couldn't.

"And do you have friends?"

Joe shook his head. "Not really", he said. "But I don't mind. Mr Gray is very kind."

Then he said, "Last winter I went to some meetings. Mr Gray worries about me not meeting people of my own age, and he suggested I try this political club. Young Socialist Zionists, they're called. Their meetings aren't far from here. Well, I tried."

"So?"

Joe laughed. "It was terrible. Not because they didn't welcome me— they wanted me to be a member at the first meeting I went to, wanted me to sign a paper, pay a subscription. I said I would take the paper home and read it properly before I signed it. They were surprised at that. They're very young, younger than I. They were born here in England, or reached England with their parents when they were too young to remember living anywhere else. Two or three are teachers or learning to be teachers. Most of them seemed to be students. And also they work hard in what they call 'the cause', which seems to be a mixture of supporting Israel, with money they raise, and supporting what they call international socialism, by raising more money and distributing leaflets and putting up posters for meetings. There's a lot of discussion about who's going to make the tea, bring the beer, put out the chairs—that kind of thing. I soon saw that when they talk about 'the party', they don't mean the Labour Party but The Party, capital *T*, capital *P*."

"Are they actually Communists?"

"Some of them like to think they are, but I doubt if any of them has ever met a real Communist. I think they call themselves socialist because 'socialist' sounds harmless in England, while 'Communist' doesn't, and because the Labour Party is in favour of the state of Israel and against the Arabs. They don't ask if it's right for Jews to be bullying Arabs, fighting

Arabs, killing Arabs. That's the Zionist bit. At the same time, they think the Labour Party is too middle-of-the-road, too compromised by capitalism to qualify as properly socialist. Too bourgeois, they say, these bourgeois boys and girls, deliberately scruffy—you can imagine—as if they're too poor to have a clean shirt, which plainly they're not. Socialism is good; capitalism is bad. Therefore, America is bad and Russia is good. 'Russia is the future', someone said. A murmur of approval from everyone else. It's just a slogan. At the second meeting I went to, I said I couldn't sign their membership paper. One of them asked me to explain why: 'You're a Jew', he said. 'You have to be a Marxist.' 'That's what they thought in Poland', I said. But he just responded, 'What's Poland got to do with it?' We had quite an argument. He said only the future matters. We have to build a 'fairer and better' future. Israel is the future; Russia is the future. What is capitalism? According to him, it's freedom for the rich to grind down the poor—but of course he said freedom for the bourgeoisie to grind down the workers. So I asked him—all of them, since they were all listening by then—why they thought that freedom for the bourgeoisie to grind down the workers was so much worse than freedom for the powerful to grind down the powerless. After all, the Russians don't just grind the powerless down. They send them to camps in Siberia, kill them—call them enemies of the revolution and kill them—because of what? Because the Germans had taken them as prisoners of war, or because their father was a priest or a peasant who had worked a bit harder than his neighbours. The socialist said all this is just a phase; it will soon be over, and then Marx will be proved right to all the world. Surely you believe in Marx, he said. Then he leaned towards me and said in a serious voice something like, 'Unless you're ... you're not religious, are you?' When he said that, all the rest of them were very quiet—not threatening exactly but very quiet."

"How did you answer?"

"I said no, I didn't think I was. But I knew that religion was good—ancient and holy and good."

"That was brave of you."

Joe smiled and shook his head. "Not very brave. A bunch of English students who think they're Marxists is not very frightening. The fact is, they know nothing about anything. When I said what I said about religion, a girl laughed and said, 'Perhaps he's a Hasid, a crazy Hasid.' 'I am a Litvak', I said. Blank stares. Then I said, 'Have you heard of the NKVD?' More blank stares. 'The NKVD is the name of the Russian secret police. They killed my parents and my sister.' 'You must be wrong about that', someone else said. 'It was the Nazis who killed all the Jews.' So I told them the NKVD doesn't kill people because they're Jews but because they're in the way—in the way of the revolution. I told them they needed to know more about Russia before they called it a good model for anyone's future or, in particular, a good model for Israel."

"You must have confused the poor things. But it sounds as if a bit of healthy confusion might be what they need. Did they talk about the wonders of the kibbutz?"

"All the time. The kibbutz is socialism in practice, heaven on earth. But they're in London studying for bourgeois careers, not hoeing banana plantations on a kibbutz. Perhaps life on a kibbutz ... I don't know."

"Have you thought of going to Palestine, to Israel, yourself?"

"I have, of course. My father thought the Zionists set their faces against what it is to be a Jew. I remember him saying this during one of those long arguments with his friends. I didn't know what he meant, and this was before the war and all the killing. So now that there are so few Jews everywhere, it is perhaps different. But ..."

He looked round the dark shop, to the stairs up to the floors of tidy shelves, and thought of his filing cabinets of index cards and the years of work.

"England has been good to me. England is complicated. Often I know I don't understand it at all. But I like that. I didn't want to go back to Europe after the war, and I don't want to now. And Israel is Europe in a way that England is not. Do you know—" Joe leaned forward suddenly, both hands on the desk.

"What?"

"I think I could have gone further when I was talking to the Young Socialists. Perhaps I should have. Don't you think that Russia really is the model for Israel, not only because socialism is the model for the kibbutzim—which may be good places, for all I know—but also in a terrifying way? The Jews who murdered Arabs, that killing in Deir Yassin, and English soldiers and other people and—what was his name?—Count Bernadotte: didn't they learn how to do these things, learn about assassination and terror, in Russia, from the NKVD? Didn't they?"

"So did the Gestapo."

"Did they? Really? But—"

"Yes, Josef, they did. The Nazis always said they were fighting against Communism. And so they were. The Brownshirts were killing Communists in Germany before Hitler was chancellor. The courts were lenient with these murderers; as I told you just now, this was one of the reasons for which I left Germany. But also, always, the Nazis learned from Stalin."

"I remember now something I had completely forgotten. When the Nazis came to Vilna, that summer, a few weeks before ... before ..."

He cleared his throat and swallowed, so as to go on.

"Anna said to me that some people in the city were pleased to see German soldiers because in the 1914 war the Germans had treated the local people so much better than the Russians had. 'But now,' she said, 'the Germans have learned.' I didn't know what she meant. Now I see."

"Stalin's so-called trials, for instance—trials which convicted the tortured from whom pain and fear had exacted false confessions—were a model for the Nazis. Have you heard of a Nazi monster called Roland Freisler?"

Joe shook his head.

"The Russians took him prisoner late in the 1914 war. He was a commissar in Russia after the end of that war. He came back to Germany and was trained as a Prussian lawyer, as I was. He was the president of Hitler's People's Court, set up to convict enemies of Nazism along the lines of Stalin's show trials of twenty years ago. You were too young to know about the Russian trials. Thousands and thousands of obedient Communists in Russia were convicted and shot on the evidence of informers, rumour mongers, Stalin's paranoia. Stalin's chief prosecutor was a wicked man, very clever, called Vyshinsky. Freisler studied his methods, his rhetoric, his cruelty, and ran the People's Court accordingly. He sent to his death that friend I told you about, a friend also of your father, the young doctor who played quartets with us when we were students in Breslau."

"What was his name?"

"His name was Joachim von Treuburg. He was a real Prussian Junker, not half-Jewish like me. He played cello most beautifully."

"I don't think I ever heard his name from my father."

"Nor my name, as we know. Perhaps he thought we had become good Nazis."

Now Mr Hofmann laughed.

"Don't look so anxious, Josef. No. If I'm sure of one thing about your father, I'm sure he never thought we became good Nazis. He knew us better than that."

"I'm glad. I'm so glad he did."

For a long minute Mr Hofmann looked down at the desk. Then he wiped the back of his hand across his mouth, raised his head, and said:

"Do you have a girlfriend, Josef?"

"No, I don't."

Mr Hofmann said nothing. Joe met the piercing blue glance.

"Once …"

"Yes?"

"Years ago, nearly ten years ago, in Yorkshire, there was a girl … she was called Sally. She was … well, she was very young. So was I, of course."

"But you were carrying already very much, and she was not."

"Yes. There was that. And she was very English. She was the daughter of the colonel. She was kind, I think. But she was also the daughter of her mother."

"And?"

"Nothing happened. She grew up. Her mother did not like me. There was a great distance between us that could never be crossed. Then I was told that I had to leave. The colonel had given my work to a local man who had been a soldier and had come back from the war. I understood."

Mr Hofmann looked at Joe again.

"I think you did", he said.

He crushed his cigarette in the ashtray.

"So, nothing? Innocent children like Anna and me?"

"Yes. But …"

"But?" The blue eyes were searching him for something else, something Joe had managed not to remember for years.

"Someone before Sally? Someone in the forest?"

"How did you know?"

"Tell me."

What was this? How had this man, whom he had never seen or heard of until a few days ago, got him to remember something he had for years succeeded in replacing in his mind with the memory of Sally? Sally riding ahead of him through the larch wood. Sally with the candles and the little metal candleholders above him on the ladder to decorate the Christmas tree. Sally in her velvet dress. Sally disappearing down the farm road in the car beside the young officer.

"Please, could I have another cigarette?"

His hand shook as Mr Hofmann lit the cigarette. Joe looked down at the desk as he talked.

"I knew a girl, in the forest, older than I was, perhaps sixteen when I was thirteen or fourteen. She was a messenger between the ghetto in Lida and the partisans. She came with news, always bad news. If she could, she brought things we needed that were difficult to beg or steal from the peasants, things that could be hidden—salt, matches, needles I remember once. Three or four times she came and went back. It was very dangerous and became more and more dangerous because we had to move further into the forest, further away from Lida."

"Where is Lida?"

Joe looked up, found Mr Hofmann's eyes not meeting his but also fixed on the desk, and actually laughed. Mr Hofmann raised his head and smiled.

Joe said, "Of course. I'm sorry. No one has ever heard of Lida. It's a town—not an important one but quite large, forty or fifty miles south of Vilna. A lot of Jews always lived there."

"Which country is it in?"

Joe laughed again.

"That is a good question. It's so difficult for people in England to understand." He caught a sharp look. "Even for Germans, I think."

Mr Hofmann nodded acknowledgement, smiling.

"In Kresy—the borderlands between Poland and Russia—the country someone said a place was in made no difference, most of all during the war. Lida between the wars, like Vilna, was in Poland, which was good for the Jews, or bad but not so bad. Then the Russians came, then the Germans. Finally, after we left the forest, the Russians came again. Lida, like Vilna, was used to being in Russia. The Lida Jews preferred to be in Poland, but after the Germans had come and gone, there would have been no Jews. Now Lida is probably in Belorussia—so, inside the Russian empire again. There is forest all around Lida—deep forest, no roads that you would call roads but only marshes, lakes, deep, deep forest. That is why I am alive."

Silence in the shop. Joe put out his cigarette.

"The girl from the Lida ghetto?"

"Yes. She was a Jewess of course. But she knew almost nothing of being a Jew. Her name was Roza. She was named for Rosa Luxemburg, so you see her parents were keen Communists."

"I see."

"Her father was a teacher in a school in Minsk." He looked up to add, "Minsk is a big city beyond Kresy, beyond our forest."

"I do know where Minsk is. An old Jewish lady in Breslau gave your aunt Anna a beautiful coat from her youth in Minsk."

"Forgive me. So Roza's father was a faithful Communist and also a journalist. In 1936 or 1937—I'm not sure exactly when—he wrote an article which mentioned Trotsky. According to Roza, there was only a single mention of the name. The NKVD took her father away and said he had been shot trying to escape. You know what that means?"

"I know what that means."

"After that, Roza's mother brought Roza and Roza's sister, and her own old mother, Roza's grandmother, to Lida because Lida was safer. Then the Germans came. When Roza returned for the last time to the Lida ghetto from our camp, and crawled under the wire in the dark and went to the cellar where her family were living, the whole family had gone, had been taken away, so they were dead or very soon to be dead. She came back to us and stayed. She was strong. The fighters taught her how to use a gun. They put us on watch together, at night, because we were small. We could hide well. We could run fast. She wasn't frightened of much, but she was frightened of wolves. She had always lived in cities. The wolves howling scared her, so she liked to have someone with her at night. But ..."

He stopped. He thought he was going to cry.

"But?"

"I can't ... it isn't right to tell ... anyone ..."

"Josef, listen to me. There is something here which is not good. This is so, is it not?"

Joe nodded.

"It was not good for you then; it is not good for you now. But if you describe it, if you reach into your memory and fetch it out, you will be able to throw it away, into the past, to get rid of it. Give it words, wrap it up and throw it away, like a piece of rubbish wrapped up and thrown into the dustbin. No?"

"I don't know you."

"Not well. You don't know me well. But I was your father's friend. And in any case, that I am here is an accident, is by chance. I am not a policeman. I didn't come to find you. I didn't know you existed until last week. I can listen. And I can forget—entirely forget. As a priest is bound to do when a penitent makes his confession."

"A priest? A Catholic priest?"

Mr Hofmann laughed.

"It was an illustration only. Something I knew about once upon a time. Again, in another world."

"All right."

He swallowed the last of his cold coffee. He felt better. He had no idea why.

"It was perhaps not so bad a thing. But I didn't know—I was sickened and afraid and excited, all at once. On some nights, not every night, when we were watching in the forest, by the river, a good distance from the camp, everyone asleep—in the summer, this was—one of the fighters would come, very quietly from the camp. Roza would say, whisper, very quietly, 'Go away, Josef, along the riverbank. Wait till you hear me whistle. Unless there is danger. If there's danger, you must whistle and come quick to tell me.' So I would go, and I knew why. I thought I could hear them, though I crept away quite far. But probably I couldn't—there were many noises in the forest at night, especially in summer, and I had to listen for anyone coming. That was why we were there. At last she would whistle, a whistle almost like that of a bird. When I got back to our hiding place—like a cave it was, under a hollowed-out bank with branches for a roof and soft pine needles on the sandy floor—he had gone, and she was different. More alive. Also more lazy. Satisfied, I suppose. I hated it. He had a wife, a wife who worked hard all day looking after the little children, her own and others. We had in the camp one or two who had lost their parents. She was good, his wife. I hated it. Then ..."

It was difficult to go on. He looked hard at the desk, moved the ashtray further from them both.

"Then?" Mr Hofmann said, very gently.

"After the harvest—this was 1943, and we had more people in the camp to feed than the year before because the ghettos were being cleared and always a few managed to escape, like rats from a stack at threshing. So, after the harvest the fighter and two others took a horse and one of our carts to find food, potatoes, a sack of rye, beets, anything, whatever they could beg or steal from the poor peasants. They did not come back. Maybe the Germans shot them, or peasants killed them. Or Russian partisans might have killed them, for the food. After two weeks the commander told the camp to give them up, to give them to God. One of the old men taught the Kaddish prayer to Roza's fighter's son, who was six or seven years old, and all the men said Kaddish with the little boy, for the three fighters.

"A few nights later I was as usual keeping watch with Roza. She had said almost nothing to me, night after night, since the fighter had gone. It was cold, October I suppose, not yet any snow but cold, the forest and the river silent with the beginning of winter. She put her arm round my shoulder, I thought for warmth. Then she kissed me. Kissed me—as I had never even seen anyone kiss anyone. I hated it, but at the same time I ... so I ran away into the forest. I fell in water that was beginning to freeze, scratched my face on thorns, branches, I don't know. I ran on, back to the camp. Someone on watch stopped me. 'What happened? Where is Roza?' I couldn't answer. They sent a fighter with a gun to find Roza. Next day she said I had been scared by a noise. They decided I was too young, too unreliable, to keep watch. They found someone else. They said I should sleep at night and work with the women in the day instead, grinding rye, making bread. I didn't have to talk to Roza again, because there were enough of us in the camp."

Then he added, as he remembered, "Her hair was dirty, thick, dull. Her hands were dirty. How could they not be, in the forest? Mine were too."

He stopped. He could not look up.

After a long silence Mr Hofmann said: "So you did not kiss Sally?"

Then Joe looked up.

"You understand? Her hair ... her skin ... so clean ..."

"I understand."

Mr Hofmann stood up.

"I must go now."

Joe looked up at him.

"Please ..."

"No, Josef, I must go. And probably I shall not see you again. I am glad, more glad than I can tell you, to have found you, but it is not good that you should be too much in the past. I knew your father before you were born. He is and will always be your father, but I am part of a past not your own, which is entirely gone. You have your life—by the grace of God, I would say—and it is to be lived now in England, into a future that will, I have no doubt at all, be good."

Joe stood up. Mr Hofmann put on his coat, his scarf, took his hat. At the door of the shop he turned.

"One more thing", Mr Hofmann said. "Forgive them both. Do not forget them, but forgive them. And here ..." He put his hand in the pocket of his coat. "This is for you."

He gave Joe a small leather-bound book: Heine's *Buch der Lieder.*

"An old copy. I was not lying to Mr Gray. It is for you, from long before Germany became a terrible place. Love and intelligence—don't lose sight of either."

Joe took the book and could not speak.

They shook hands.

Mr Hofmann said, in English, "Good-bye, Josef. Good luck. All the good luck in the world."

And he went out into the cold night.

When Joe got home, he took the photograph of Sally on her pony out of the glassless frame, found the poem "Ich stand in dunkeln Träumen" in the *Buch der Lieder,* and slipped the photograph between the pages. Then he took the frame outside and threw it in the dustbin.

A few weeks later he saw her, once more.

Christopher Gray came into the shop one morning waving the *Times.*

"What was the name of your colonel, Joe? The one whose horses you looked after in Yorkshire?"

"He's called Robertson. Colonel Giles Robertson."

"I thought so. I remember the reference he gave you—sensible of him to say you spoke a lot of languages and played the fiddle, or you might not have ended up here. Anyway, he's died, I'm afraid."

Joe remembered the colonel, sitting at his desk beside the irritated Mr Peters and appearing to understand Joe's refusal of Mr Peters' offer. He remembered him trotting out of the yard on hunting mornings beside Sally, the horses as beautifully prepared as he and Ted could manage.

"I am sorry. He treated me well."

"I just happened to see it in the paper. Private funeral in Yorkshire, it says here. But there's a memorial service for him on Tuesday in Saint

Martin-in-the-Fields—you know, the big church at the bottom of Saint Martin's Lane, three minutes from here. Perhaps you'd like to go?"

"I don't think so. I'm not used to churches."

"No, of course you're not. No need to worry about that. It won't be very religious, I'm sure—more military, with the Last Post and all that, a soldier blowing a bugle for the end of the day, the end of a life. Quite moving, it can be. I'm sure they'd be having the service in the Guards' Chapel if it hadn't been smashed to smithereens in the war. Anyway, think about it. I'd be delighted, of course, to give you an hour off to go."

He went—in the suit Christopher Gray had told him he should wear—to see Sally.

He saw her, from the back of the church, sitting in a front pew between her mother and a tall man in uniform, clearly her husband, with James, in a morning suit, and a third woman who must have been James' wife beside them. All three women were elegantly dressed, and the family group looked united, belonging together. There were a lot of people in the church, many of the men in uniform, all the women in black coats and black hats of varying peculiar shapes. The service was indeed not very religious: several hymns; a few prayers; two scripture readings in a kind of English he found difficult to understand; a psalm sung by a choir; and a speech by a clergyman praising the colonel for his courage in the Great War, his invaluable service to the country since then, his sacrifice of his elder son in the second war, his devotion to his children and grandchildren, his kindness to many. The word "grandchildren" struck Joe. They must be too young to come to the service. Joe was so afraid of being noticed by James that he left the church before the end and waited on the pavement to one side of the church steps, where plenty of passersby were walking, to see Sally come out.

He heard the bugler play the Last Post inside the church. He had heard it before, when Mrs Thwaites had switched on the wireless in the kitchen for the Remembrance Day service, the two minutes' silence, the Last Post—"For all the soldiers, Joe, who were killed in both the wars". This was Ted, of course. So the Last Post was for Joe's father. Outside Saint Martin-in-the-Fields in the February drizzle he heard it again and prayed for his father and all the officers who were shot at Katyn.

Sally appeared, with her husband and her mother, and her brother and his wife, at the top of the steps behind the tall columns of the portico.

194

She was surrounded by people greeting her, shaking her hand, kissing her. She looked pale, sad, very grown up, very pretty. Every so often she smiled at someone she was pleased to see. Her smile.

After a few minutes of watching her, as if she were a tiny figure on the other bank of a wide and dangerous river, he joined the flow of people in Trafalgar Square and walked back to the shop.

In the following summer the Grays gave a party for the coming of age of their younger son. They invited Joe. By this time he had a dinner jacket, passed on from the same boy when he grew out of it three or four years earlier.

At dinner—which was for about thirty people, with an extra table in the dining room—he was placed between a clever elderly woman he had met before, who was a refugee from Vienna and once a pianist and liked speaking German, and a shy girl, a stranger, with long brown hair, a velvet hairband, and spectacles. On the girl's other side was a young man much taken with his other neighbour, a talkative blonde who laughed at everything the young man said. Joe by this time was accustomed enough to the Grays' dinner parties to know that, by the time they were finishing their second course, he should find a way of detaching himself politely from his undemanding conversation about music in old Vienna and think of something friendly to say to the shy girl eating in neglected silence. At the end of a story about Bruno Walter conducting Mahler in a half-empty concert hall shortly before the Anschluss—"Two Jews, you can imagine"—he gave the Viennese lady a little bow, at which she smiled, understanding, so that he could turn to the girl.

"Are you an old friend of Charlie?"

"I'm his cousin, actually", she said, looking at Joe for the first time, with thanks in her eyes. "But I don't know him very well. You see, I haven't lived in London very long."

This was easy.

"Where did you live before you lived in London?" He hoped, unreasonably, that she might say Yorkshire.

"Oh, in the country, in Hampshire, with my mother. My mother is Christopher's sister. She's quite a lot younger than Christopher. She's over there, in the blue dress, sitting next to the man with lots of white hair."

The girl's mother looked thin and tired, at least as old as Christopher Gray, and as shy as her daughter. She was listening without much life in her face to the white-haired man, whom Joe knew to be a Jewish publisher who never stopped talking.

"And your father?" he said.

"My father was killed in the war. I was just four, so I don't remember him very well."

This was clearly a little speech she had been making all her life.

"I'm so sorry", Joe said. "It is sad that your father died when you were so young."

She looked surprised. "That's kind of you." Then she smiled. "But perhaps it isn't all that sad. I might not have liked him. I don't think Mummy"—she hesitated, glancing across the room at her mother, and then went on—"found him very easy, though she's never said much about him. There are photographs of course—of him in his uniform, of him in hunting clothes on a horse. He looks nice in the photographs."

"Do you enjoy hunting?"

She laughed. "I've never done it. I used to ride when I was little. Lessons, you know. But Mummy couldn't afford a pony, so no, I never did the pony club or hunting or anything. Do you? Like hunting, I mean." She looked at him more carefully. "You don't look like a hunting person. And you're not English, are you?"

"I am not English. I should say I have not always been English. No, I have not hunted. But a long time ago . . ."

"A long time ago?"

"I think it is difficult to explain."

"Never mind. I'm sorry."

"No. You must not be sorry."

Their plates were taken away by one of the several maids in uniform imported for the party. When another offered to fill their glasses with more wine, both of them shook their heads. The Viennese lady and the girl's neighbour were both talking, the girl's neighbour, perhaps rather drunk, roaring with laughter. They were both safely turned away from Joe and the girl.

"What do—", she began. "Where do—", he said, simultaneously. "Sorry", they said, and smiled.

Joe spread his open hands towards her, to indicate that she should go first.

"I just wondered what you do in London—for a job, I mean."

"I work for your uncle in his shop."

"Oh, I see. That's why you're here, I suppose. Is it fun working in the shop? With all those dusty old books? Perhaps it's interesting."

"It is, yes. I like my work. Every day it is interesting."

"Lucky you. Actually, I shouldn't complain. Mummy sent me to London to do a secretarial course. She said I would never meet anyone miles from anywhere in the country, and she was sick of us being asked to things because people felt sorry for us. You see what she meant? Well, perhaps not. Never mind. Anyway, I came to London, and I'm staying with a friend from school, in her parents' house. I couldn't stick the secretarial course. I was hopeless at typing and even worse at shorthand. So I chucked it, which did save some money, and I got a job, a nice job actually, looking after the youngest children in a school. Five-year-olds."

"So you are a teacher?"

"Oh, no. I just help with the children—listen to them reading, teach them songs, help paint, clear up the mess they make, organize games when it's too wet to go to the park. There are two proper teachers who do the real work. I enjoy it, really, but ..."

She paused to take some chocolate profiteroles from the dish offered by one of the maids. Joe did the same.

"But?"

"Well, it's not doing the trick, is it? Not what Mummy wanted. I don't meet anyone, and people ask me to things because they feel sorry for me—like Aunt Marianne this evening. It's the same as at home."

"You have met me."

She looked down, blushed, looked up, and smiled, most beautifully.

"Of course. Yes, I have. I'm so sorry. I am so tactless."

"Tactless?"

"Clumsy. Thoughtless. Stupid."

"No. This is not true. You are not stupid."

"You don't know me. You don't know how stupid I am."

"I do not think you are stupid. You must allow me not to think you are stupid."

"You are sweet. You know, I've never met anyone like you before. I nearly didn't come tonight. Charlie's friends from Oxford ..."

She looked round the crowded dining room, which was becoming noisier and noisier.

197

"Too brainy for me, I thought. Some of them must be brainy, like Charlie, mustn't they? And too grand as well. And good at games—rugby, rowing, cricket, I don't know. What would I talk to them about? Just a dull girl from Hampshire, they would think. And I'm a bit older than their girlfriends. Debs, you know." She laughed. "Perhaps you don't, which would be nice. I'm actually twenty, which Mummy seems to think is practically middle-aged. Anyway, I'm glad I did come."

Another beautiful smile.

Joe couldn't answer.

"These chocolate things are wonderful, aren't they?" she said.

"Old Vienna", Joe said.

The woman on his other side turned her head.

"What are you saying about Vienna?" she said in German.

Joe smiled at the girl before he turned to answer. As he talked without thinking about chocolate and cream and Vienna, vaguely pirating conversations he had heard at other dinner parties at the Grays' house, he was aware that at last the man on the girl's other side had spoken to her.

"Are you up at Oxford?" he said, unnecessarily loudly.

"No, I'm afraid not."

"Oh. Shame. How did you meet Charlie, then?"

"He's my cousin."

"Your cousin, is he? You don't look like him at all. Oh well. Can't be helped, I suppose."

That was the end of the attention he was prepared to give her. Joe found himself wanting to put his hand on hers, which was on the table beside him. Of course he couldn't, and was so surprised at the very idea that he found he had altogether stopped listening to the Viennese lady.

"Forgive me", he said to her in German. "What were you saying?"

She looked at him with intelligent eyes.

"My dear boy, I am boring you. Talk to your friend again. She has an Englishman there with no manners, who will not be kind to her. Don't worry about me. The old are happy to watch the party."

Joe blushed, and was annoyed with himself for blushing. But he turned back to the girl.

"I do not know your name. My name is Joe."

She looked into his eyes.

"That sounds so English. What's your real name?"

"Josef Halpern."

"Josef." She copied his way of saying his name. "That's a nice name." She looked at him carefully. "Was your father killed in the war too?"

"Yes. He was killed in the war."

"And is your mother alive?"

"She also was killed in the war."

"How dreadful. In the bombing, I suppose."

"Not in the bombing."

"I know that Uncle Christopher thinks we bombed the Germans too much at the end of the war. Well ... it's a long time ago now, isn't it? Horrible war."

She finished her profiteroles.

"Goodness, that was delicious. I have lunch with the children at school. You can't imagine how nasty it is. My name's Polly. My name's actually Mary, but I've always been called Polly."

Like Sally.

"Polly is a good name. English and good."

"I think it's rather silly. It reminds me of Mother Goose: Polly put the kettle on. But never mind, I—"

Christopher Gray was on his feet tapping a glass with a spoon. He made a speech. Everyone drank to Charlie's health. Charlie, more or less sober, made a speech. A little later everyone got up and moved to the drawing room, some taking glasses or cups of coffee with them. The chairs and sofas had been rearranged so that there was a small space for dancing. Charlie's brother put records on the gramophone one after the other, a waltz at the beginning and then jazz music of different kinds, and most of the young people danced.

Polly and Joe stood and watched. He said, "I am sorry. I do not know how to dance."

Her smile. "Of course you don't. That's all right. My shoes hurt anyway."

It was easy not to talk.

When the party was getting still louder and more hectic, Polly's mother, with a coat over her arm, threaded her way between the dancers at the end of a record and, standing in front of Joe and Polly, said, "Introduce me to your new friend, darling."

"This is Josef Halpern." Polly looked at him to see if she had pronounced his name correctly. He nodded. "Josef, this is my mother."

"Good evening", he said, raising her hand to his lips as he knew foreigners were supposed to do.

"How do you do", she said, without warmth. Then: "Darling, it's time we were making tracks. There's school in the morning, remember, and I have an early train to catch."

"Of course. I'll just get my coat."

Polly's mother turned her back to Joe to watch the dancing and wait for her daughter, who soon reappeared with her coat.

"Good night, Joe", she said, giving him her hand. He gave it a very slight squeeze, unnoticeable he hoped to her mother, and she smiled again.

Six months later they were married. Her mother did come to the wedding, as did Christopher Gray, in Marylebone Register Office, on a bitterly cold December morning. The registrar was friendly. Polly looked pretty and very young, in a white dress with a full skirt but not long like a wedding dress, a fur jacket belonging to her mother, and a summer hat. Her mother cried, not because she was happy. The Grays gave them all lunch, with both the Gray sons, their daughter and her children, and the other two people who worked in the shop. Joe and Polly went to Devon for the weekend and walked hand in hand on empty beaches with sunlit waves crashing and the cries of seagulls.

For a while they lived in Joe's basement flat and Polly kept her job in the school, which she now said she enjoyed. Eighteen months after the wedding, Polly's mother became seriously ill with the kind of cancer that later would kill Polly. Although Polly was pregnant and being sick every morning, she spent much of the two months in which her mother was dying in Hampshire looking after her, for the last fortnight with the help of a nurse. When the funeral was over, Joe asked her if she had told her mother about the baby.

"Of course I didn't. If she'd been pleased, it would have been sad for her. And she wouldn't have been pleased, would she?"

The house in Hampshire, bought long before the war by Polly's father's parents, turned out to be worth a good deal of money. Joe and Polly bought a small, pretty house in a Bayswater mews—"Nearer the park, for the baby"—and there they lived, brought up their son, and were as happy as most married people are who care for each other and have a little more than enough money to live on. The birth had been difficult, and they were told after it that it would be dangerous for her to have another child. She was always thin, pale, and easily tired, but she looked after the little boy herself—which was thought very modern by her school friends, who all had nannies looking after their children—and Joe was deeply devoted to her and to their son.

Polly told Joe, the second time he took her out, to a film, and walked her back to the house where she was staying, that her father had died in a blazing tank during the retreat to Dunkirk, a few weeks after his own father was shot at Katyn. He knew that he was more haunted by the picture of this death than she was.

On the same walk, through Kensington streets on a warm September night, she said, "Was your father in a tank regiment?"

"I don't think so. My father was a doctor."

"Oh, I see. Much better than just being a soldier because everybody was being a soldier. So he must have been a bit older than my father. A doctor—what a waste."

They walked.

"Did you want to be a doctor like your father, when you were little?"

"Perhaps. Really I wanted to play violin as well as my father played."

She stopped walking and looked at him, under a street light.

"Did you? Well, I suppose it's different abroad. I know almost nothing about music. I had some piano lessons when I was nine, but I didn't like my teacher, and Mummy said I wasn't musical and there was no point going on. I was so pleased." This story was the same as Sally's, except that Sally had liked her old teacher, Mr Goldschmidt, who had been interned. But once Joe and Polly were married he took her to concerts, and after a while she much enjoyed big romantic symphonies and piano concertos, and the *Messiah* in the Albert Hall at Christmas. String quartets and Lieder she couldn't cope with, and opera she never thought anything but silly. "Ridiculous they look, singing away for such a long time when they could say whatever they're saying in a minute or two."

But for her honesty and generosity and the sweetness of her nature, he loved her. In the spare bedroom of their house in Bayswater, he kept his violin, his music stand, the piano which the old couple in Saint John's

Wood had given him when he and Polly left their flat, and all his music. He played for an hour most evenings before kissing his son good night, and every so often, while Polly, cheerfully, stayed at home, he played chamber music at the Grays' or in the houses of their friends.

They never talked about either of their fathers again, and she never asked him about where he was in the war or how he came to be in England. When other people asked her about her husband, she said, "He was born in Poland, but he's been in England since he was fifteen", which was all she knew. He understood from the beginning that she had loved and trusted Christopher Gray since she was a small child, and since Joe had been miraculously invented by her uncle, she needed no further explanation for his existence.

So he became an English bookseller with an English wife and an English son.

The shop never seemed wholly English, which was one of the reasons he was so attached to it. For years exiles on the tides of poverty, death, and hope, with their bags of books and music—occasionally just a single precious score—continued to float in and out of his working days. Often they were delighted to find someone they could talk to in a language that in London they were rarely able to use. When, in the months after his wedding, refugee Hungarians began to appear in the shop, he would apologize for not being able to speak their first language, but they always knew some German or Russian, though they were reluctant to admit to speaking Russian. Although he had been preoccupied with Polly and the wonder of returned love in the autumn of 1956, he read with anguish of the crushing of the crowds in Budapest by Soviet tanks and understood how cynically the Russians had assumed, rightly, that western politicians and newspapers would be too busy dealing with the disgrace that Britain and France were inflicting on themselves in the Middle East to pay much attention to Hungary. When he read, a little later, that the Russians had killed thousands of Hungarians and arrested tens of thousands more, he wondered what the Young Socialist Zionists in the Charing Cross Road were making of it. He was now too grown up, too English, and too much in love with Polly even to consider bothering to find out.

In January 1957 he wrote to Max Hofmann, care of Saint Peter's High School.

Dear Mr Hofmann,

Last month I married the niece of Christopher Gray. We are very happy. I would like to thank you for everything we said a year ago, and for the Heine.

With best wishes and my gratitude,
Josef

The next day the afternoon post brought to the shop an envelope addressed to Joe Halpern. Inside was a postcard with a picture of a Stradivarius violin on one side and on the other:

Josef,

This is wonderful news. I wish both of you everything good for the rest of your lives. Do not forget that God knows all our stories, much better than we know them ourselves.

M. H.

Prologue II

My dear,

You have worked wonderfully. The young man in your story is, I think, a better, a less untidy, person than I myself have been. But is it not always true that the writer makes a more orderly story than the untidiness of reality allows the living person to perceive? At the time, at any time, there is always more anxiety than order, is it not so?

Now, it is right that you should stop. It was more than fifty years ago that I met Max Hofmann. He helped me in ways you so well have understood. From then until now, in so very long a time, my life has not been interesting. To me, of course, it has been interesting enough. I married, quite happily, as you know, and I lived as if I had always been the almost-English young man who worked well for Christopher Gray and might in the long run, as the English say, take myself the management of the shop—as I did, for many years, until the good old building was bought to be developed, whatever that may mean (in this case it meant an expensive coffee shop, which sells nevertheless quite bad coffee, and some very expensive offices in the floors above). By now, actually three years before this, my wife had died. So I sold the stock, whatever remained of value, to another dealer and retired to where and how I now live, as you have seen. This does not make a story that is remarkable. And the story that is perhaps a little remarkable, in England in any case, although alas, as we know, not in eastern Europe, you have told. I could not have told it, although I have carried it for so long inside my everyday, inside my contented-on-the-whole, but not interesting, life. (You will notice how much your writing has improved my English.)

There is one more story, however, if I am bold enough to ask, that I should so very greatly like you to tell, so that I may possibly read it while, however old, I am alive. It is the story I do not know, and have wanted to know always. I have thought much of my father in all these years. I have heard his voice in dreams. I have so often seen him as he was in that day when he left us, wearing his uniform, telling me to look after my mother and my sister. (That I failed in this, we know.) The story I want you to tell is his, the story of the prison. The facts we know. The truth has to be imagined, as you are able to imagine. When I remember my father, I have the memory and the imagination only of a child. Will you attempt this for me?

Is it possible that I may see you once more? Perhaps if you are so patient and good as to try to write as I have just asked you to, I may see you when you have told this story. I know this story is also my story, and I know I am not sure of how it may have been. I have a belief that I need to know it to understand better the past and perhaps the present and possibly also the future. Most of all I think the future.

Unfortunately, or it may be fortunately, I am not now so well. My knee in these days is bad, but the doctor tells me that I must not have the operation that would make it good because my heart is not so strong.

You will understand, because understanding is what you do.

Tell me if you will try the story.

I am already more grateful to you than I can write, certainly in English. But that also you know.

J. H.

Chapter 7

All day he looked forward to the night, to lying on his bunk in the dark because that was when, at last, the noise stopped. Every night after he had climbed up to his plank bed—the badly put-together wooden structure shaking under his weight unless the man who slept in the bunk below was already lying down—he remembered again that it was impossible now, in December, not to be too cold to go to sleep except eventually from shivering exhaustion. Most of the windows in the church were broken; in some, whole panes were missing; in many, the glass was cracked. On stormy nights snow blew in, and didn't melt, on prisoners sleeping close to broken windows.

The noise, the false cheerfulness of political speeches and the lists of what were meant to be inspiring production figures, in Polish and sometimes in Russian, interrupted by military marches, newly invented boisterous folk songs, Bolshevik anthems, and occasional prison announcements from the hut that was the control room, stopped at ten o'clock. Loudspeakers all over the camp blared and crackled most of the day, early each morning, at all meals, and all the evening in all the buildings where the prisoners slept. The church was only one of eight of these buildings; the others were smaller and more like barracks, some old and built of plastered brick or stone, some long, wooden huts, set at odd angles to each other inside the perimeter wall of the prison, an old, peeling, plastered wall perhaps eight feet high with coils of barbed wire along its top.

Dr Jacob Halperin hated the noise more than the cold, more than the mocking grins of the young NKVD guards who enjoyed having Polish lords to push into lines and shout at, more than the sour potato soup with bits of cabbage and pork rind ladled into tin plates for them to eat. They were given just enough food to keep them alive, a chunk of black bread every day with the soup, onions sometimes, pieces of turnip and beet. But all of them were hungry all the time.

It was of course too much to hope that the night which followed the turning off of the loudspeakers, the long night in the huge, cold wreck of a church, would be actually quiet. Several hundred men stacked on shelves with one thin blanket each and whatever they had brought or managed to get hold of in the way of a greatcoat on top of the blanket were not going to sleep peacefully through the freezing hours until a siren from the loudspeakers woke them at six in the morning. Several times every night he would lie awake, listening to snores, groans, muttering, coughing, creaking planks as restless sleepers turned, occasional shouts from the depths of nightmare, sometimes suppressed sobbing that seemed to spread from one to another, the thump of someone jumping down from a top bunk to go to one of the half-barrels that four prisoners would have to empty in the morning. But these sounds at least represented warmth, the animal warmth in the icy building of hundreds of bodies, however cold and undernourished each of them was, huddled under his blanket, untidy and not very clean—they did their best, but there was no way of heating water, and there was no soap. He was glad he had had a beard for twenty years. Every single prisoner was tormented by lice. A beard made the torment a bit worse, but he kept his beard because of the difficulty of shaving every day.

The haphazard sounds of the night inside the church were companionable, even consoling, after the hours of propaganda from the loudspeakers, propaganda pretending to be logical argument, pretending to be reliable history, pretending to be mathematically tested statistics. Pretending to be true. Only human beings lie, he thought. And not when they are asleep.

What was more, his hundreds of fellow prisoners could achieve real silence. He knew they could because they had, every night for the last three weeks. For a few minutes, just after the loudspeakers were switched off and before, presumably, anyone was asleep, no one spoke, no one moved, no one struck a match or even coughed. It was so quiet that he even thought he could hear the few candles flickering in jars here and there against the high walls of the church. These few minutes had a quality that nothing else in the prison day came anywhere near.

This regular silence had begun one night soon after more than half the prisoners in the camp had suddenly been released.

This had happened on the morning of a day in November; he didn't remember the date, or hadn't paid attention to it. Outside each of the buildings where prisoners slept, the NKVD officer taking the roll call, after checking that all prisoners were present or accounted for, read out a shorter list of names. "These prisoners are to assemble at the main gate at eight o'clock with their possessions." Afraid—because they thought they were going to be moved even further from their homes, most likely to Siberia—the prisoners on the shorter lists had gathered in their hundreds at the gate. He had stood with a few others at the door of the church and watched, across the wide space of unmown, trampled grass, white with hoarfrost, that had once perhaps been a garden. Then a ripple of excitement travelled quickly through the crowd, heads turning. Broad smiles. Some prisoners hugged each other; a few crossed themselves. They were being freed. One guard must have told one prisoner; in less than a minute all of them knew. They might have cheered, but no doubt every one of them was afraid to attract attention in case it might provoke a change in the decision. They crowded near the gate. After a delay of almost half an hour—they waited patiently, prisoners being accustomed to unexplained waiting—the commandant himself appeared with a megaphone on the steps of the building from which the prison was run. This building, the least dilapidated in the camp, was to one side of the empty space. The crowd turned to hear him.

"Comrade Stalin and the politburo of the Union of Soviet Socialist Republics have selected you for the privilege of release, workers of Ukraine, of Belorussia, of Poland. You will return to your homes and make your contribution to the socialist future which the revolution promises to you all. There will be no more ownership of land and property and the means of production. There will be no more abuse of power, no more exploitation. The Polish lords, your officers, from whose age-old oppression you are freed as you walk free from here today, will remain detained. As you all know, they still have much to learn."

A scattered and doubtful cheer greeted this speech, which had probably been inaudible to most of the crowd. The commandant waved his megaphone before returning indoors, followed by his sergeant. Two guards opened the double doors of the gate. The prisoners turned again, picked up their bundles, crowded together, and poured through the opening like sand through the funnel of an hourglass. In a very short time they had disappeared. The guards shut the double doors and, having shot the huge bolts that fastened them, stood with their backs to the gate as if nothing had happened.

The four thousand released prisoners were ordinary soldiers of the Polish army, most of them young lads, peasants from eastern Poland, many no doubt from Kresy families who had preferred their sons to fight for Poland rather than for Russia. Their fathers and uncles had fought for Russia in the last war. Many had not returned. He imagined these boys now, struggling to find their way back to their villages, returning perhaps to widowed mothers who needed their help, younger brothers and sisters, old grandparents huddled in shawls by the stove. He thought of them trudging through the snow in the short days, hitching lifts on carts, scrounging a few potatoes, a crust of bread, a night in a barn. Young and without guns, in now-scruffy Polish uniforms, they would probably not be regarded as enemies by Russian peasants. But it wouldn't be easy.

The prison was far inside Russia, how far he had no means of telling. The Polish army in the east, heading for Romania after the swift shock of the German invasion, had been rounded up by the Russians in the few days that followed the appearance of the Red Army on Polish soil. The numbers of Russian soldiers made resistance clearly futile. Some of the older officers who had once fought in the tsar's army thought that the Russians had arrived to help Poland fight against the Germans, a hope as quickly disappointed as the hope they had all had, two weeks earlier, that France and England would, as they had promised, come to Poland's aid. Within a few days their Red Army captors were replaced by NKVD guards; the possibility of any help from anywhere had vanished.

But why were they prisoners when there was no state of war between Russia and Poland? This was much discussed among the officers. Had they been prisoners of war, there were various international rules that should apply to their detention; if there were no war, they couldn't be prisoners of war, so was there any point in demanding that these rules be observed? Three senior officers, one of them a lawyer from the reserve, had, after several meetings with the commandant, extracted permission for the prisoners to write and receive letters, one a month; and some time after each of them had sent a first letter home, parcels from their families and letters—bland letters because of the censors but real letters— had begun to arrive. But questions as to why they were imprisoned had not been answered. With what offence could eight thousand—now four thousand—Polish soldiers be charged? And they knew there were other camps to which more of the Polish army had been sent; in the rapid sorting done by the NKVD before the end of September, friends had tried and failed to stay together.

Officers and men bound for this camp had been assembled after straggling marches from north, west, and south and had been herded into old tsarist prison trains, forty or fifty to an empty, filthy carriage like a cattle wagon, with two buckets of water and a bucket for a lavatory and nothing else but some loaves of black bread thrown in once at a stop on the slow journey from the Belorussian border to Smolensk. Jacob Halperin had been in a train like this before, when, in 1915, the Russians had moved thousands of Jews to Warsaw from Vilna because they decided that the Jews were helping the Germans. On that train his mother and his two-year-old brother had died.

At Smolensk they had been put on another train, not so humiliating because it was built at least for people, which rattled, not fast, through forest to a small station he never saw the name of. They walked, in the dark, along a rough road to the prison.

When they arrived, the officers were separated from the other ranks so that the ordinary soldiers could be given the better quarters. The rest of the old buildings in the camp were less damaged than the church—presumably not deliberately stripped and mutilated, as the church had obviously been at the revolution—and the huts were quite new. So, in accordance with Soviet priorities, the peasants had a little more space for their bunks, in smaller rooms than the huge church where officers were crammed together, with many, to begin with, sleeping on the floor.

After the release, with the population of the prison halved, nearly everything improved for the officers. The camp authorities—the commandant Major Korolev and his NKVD staff—allowed the prisoners to sort out for themselves who was going to sleep where, now that there was twice the space and everyone who remained was, according to the Russians, a "lord". The Poles behaved towards each other with what Halperin thought was, in the circumstances, remarkable courtesy and consideration. The older prisoners, mostly reservists like himself and including dozens of doctors, lawyers, engineers, university teachers, and senior officers who had once served in the tsar's army or navy, were given beds in the smaller buildings, where they had a little more room for their possessions and less-uncomfortable nights. He chose to stay in the church, though he couldn't have said why. With the floor cleared of sleepers and a third tier of dangerously rickety bunks taken apart, it had become a more possible place to sleep. Like many others lucky enough to sleep beside a wall, he had taken a few nails from the dismantled layer of bunks and, using a boot, hammered them into the crumbling plaster above his bed. There he hung a few spare clothes from his kit bag and his violin in its case. Except when inspected by uninterested guards, his violin had been in his kit bag since he left home, and he had not played it. And, on a nail of their own, he hung his spectacles, which he was very afraid of breaking or losing and took off only to sleep. One night near the beginning of the imprisonment he dreamed that he had lost his temper with a guard and shouted. Instead of shouting back, the guard had grabbed his spectacles from his face, thrown them to the ground, and stamped on them. Tiny pieces of glass on the stone floor. He had never been able to think or speak competently without his spectacles, though he knew this was absurd. Now that he knew they were safe on their nail above his bunk, he could use his kit bag as a pillow with only soft things inside it.

In the three months that they had been in the prison, he had heard not a single complaint that anything had been stolen from one prisoner by another. The guards of course stole, levying their share from anything prisoners bought from the local pedlars and which was allowed, under the eyes of the guards, into the camp—cigarettes, vodka, apples, matches—and also took what they fancied from the parcels that had begun to arrive from the officers' homes in the last two or three weeks. But they didn't come into the church, leaving to the officers themselves their own organization and discipline.

The silence after the noise from the loudspeakers was switched off was new, one result of the changed times in the prison after the release. It had begun some days later. In the sudden quiet, someone called out a single word.

"Oremus."

He knew what the word meant, but whoever called it out couldn't have been a priest.

There had been, at the beginning, a number of priests in the prison, army chaplains. He had seen but not spoken to three or four priests. He had never heard that there was a rabbi in the camp, though rabbis had been army chaplains as well. The priests had all gone, presumably taken somewhere else, soon after the release of the ordinary soldiers. He had been surprised to find that he was sorry they were no longer there. One of the priests, he had heard, had asked the senior officers who presented prisoners' requests to the commandant to demand that Jews be moved from the church to sleep elsewhere in the camp. He was proud of Poland when he heard that the senior officers had refused to pass on this request.

That was only one of the priests. He didn't know which. He didn't know them. He didn't know even their names. But he was sorry they had gone.

Religious services were not permitted in the camp, but, in a dark corner of the church, blanket and clothes pushed to one side of someone's plank bed, he had several times, earlier in the morning than the siren, seen one or another of the priests holding a quiet service among the stacked bunks and kit bags, a number of prisoners kneeling close together behind the priest. Watching from his bunk, a short way back in the church full of sleeping men, he could hear nothing. Perhaps there was nothing to hear. Perhaps the stillness of the kneeling prisoners collected in itself a kind of laden silence, a silence heavy with unspoken words that they knew and he did not, and this silence held them in twenty minutes of memory and hope that he found himself almost envying. He could see the dark figure of the priest, standing, kneeling, standing again, bowing, in the fitful light of two candles on the boards of the cleared bunk. The priest was holding something in his hands. Behind him the group of prisoners knelt motionless, except when they bent their heads and crossed themselves.

Of course he had never been to a service in a church, in Vilna or in Breslau, though in Vilna he had often heard organ music playing as people in their best clothes came out onto a square on a Sunday morning at the end of Mass. In Breslau he was almost always working in the hospital on Sundays, with other Jewish doctors, allowing Christians the day off.

He watched, and found himself, the first time he saw this so quietly taking place, confused, and irritated at his confusion. This Christian ritual, whatever it was, should have made him angry or afraid—these were Catholic Poles. They had been taught by their Church down the centuries that the Jews killed Christ and that however mild and inoffensive a Jew might be, however useful to Christians as a doctor or a lawyer or a shopkeeper or a village innkeeper, he could never rid himself of the taint of this ancestral guilt. In the last few years he had seen the ancient hatred of the murderers of Christ become, in Poland, even more noxious, since it was encouraged by the government since Pilsudski's death, and mixed with two different sets of ideas from the last century—poisonous nationalism and poisonous racial theory—which had spread like contagious diseases among all kinds of people, constantly gaining both stupidity and destructiveness as more people were infected.

The breaking into pieces of the empires which had started, and lost, the last war had encouraged in restored Poland, as even in small, weak Lithuania, an angry nationalism that wanted to shut out—from education, from work, from politics, from "good" places to live—as many people as possible who were not "real" Poles, "real" Lithuanians, whatever that might mean. The Poland of the long past, before the partitions, had never been only Polish. Even the noble families were often partly German, partly Lithuanian, partly Russian—even, however much this was denied, partly Jewish. If it was seldom possible to describe an individual as purely Polish, it was obviously even less possible to imagine a Poland that was purely Polish. There were and always had been in Poland Belorussian and Ruthenian and Lithuanian peasants in their villages, speaking their own languages, mostly illiterate and barely able to understand Polish. In Vilna, since 1919 said to be the rightful capital of the new country of Lithuania, and to have been stolen from the Lithuanians by Pilsudski's Poland, he had in all his life met very few people who spoke Lithuanian. And Jews were everywhere—in Vilna, in the towns and villages nearby, in the whole of Poland, speaking Yiddish, Polish, Russian, and German as necessary—as they had been for hundreds of years. There they still were, in universities, in schools—like Josef in his Polish school in Vilna—in hospitals and offices and businesses, in political parties, in the Sejm. And they were in the army—here in the prison, among the officers. But increasingly, in the years before the German invasion in September, you saw in the Vilna streets in the eyes of some Poles the burning wish that you were not there, not anywhere in Poland, anymore. This nationalism had behind it, beneath it, lies—lies about the past, lies about the present, lies encouraged by the victorious French, British, and Americans at the end of the war. President Wilson, meaning well and knowing nothing, had talked in Paris at the Peace Conference about self-determination, Poland for the Poles, Lithuania for the Lithuanians, and so on through the collapsed empires, and the result had been the chaos he remembered well during the years after he and his father and his sister Anna had got back from Warsaw, years in which he had finished his school examinations, still in Russian, and become a young medical student. "Now you will all speak Polish in the hospital, Polish in the university." Vilna, poor Vilna, his home and his beloved city, had been ruled by the Russians at the beginning of the Great War, by the Germans during the war, and, after the European though not the local war was over, by the Bolsheviks and then the Poles and then the Bolsheviks again and finally the Poles. Finally? Of course not. The Russians were already back. And had the French and the British, having promised to protect the Poland they had so generously returned to the Poles after 1918, kept their word? When had they ever? There was a lack of knowledge, a lack of common sense, a lack of truth, in France, in England, in Russia, but also in Poland itself. Pilsudski had done his best. He had understood at least what kind of Poland deserved to be restored. But he had not in the end succeeded. And he had died, and the narrow, cruel ideas of Dmowski had prevailed.

Dmowski and those like him had mixed with untruthful nationalism the second set of ideas, even more damagingly untruthful because of their cheap, baseless claim to be intellectually respectable. In Germany, a mishmash of scientific theory deliberately distorted to "prove" racial superiority, and combined with the Nietzschean seduction of the will to power, had been fed by charlatans into the minds of the people for more than a generation. The disease thus produced had been caught by others, caught in Poland by Dmowski and his National Democratic Party; and at the bottom of the hierarchy of supposed racial merit were, always and everywhere, the Jews. The National Democrats, known to everyone as Endeks, prided themselves on being both modern and truly traditional, truly Polish. What they were was fascist.

Dmowski had never held high office and had died at the beginning of the year, before the Germans and the Russians invaded Poland. But he had passionate supporters among the imprisoned officers—"The best leader Poland never had", an angry colonel had said one evening, glaring at Halperin across the table at which they were eating their wretched soup and black bread, slowly so as to nurse the illusion that they were getting enough to eat. Halperin looked down at his plate.

"He was not. He was a menace", the colonel's neighbour said. This man was a surgeon, like Halperin, but not a Jew. The two of them, the day before, had worked together to amputate the gangrenous foot of an old prisoner who had trodden on a rusty nail in the church. They had a few surgical instruments that the other doctor had managed to persuade various guards on the way to the prison to let him keep, and they also had a small stock of ether, a little of which they mixed with vodka, bought from a guard with someone's cufflinks, to keep the patient more or less unconscious. Boiling water to sterilize instruments they had to beg from a different guard, who fetched it from the kitchens.

"Dmowski and the Endeks", the other surgeon went on, "did Poland a great deal more harm than good. Spreading the idea that we would be better off without what they called 'minorities'—where was the good in that? Dmowski had the loudest Polish voice in Paris after the war, so the Peace Conference drew these nationalist lines on the map which left people hopelessly divided—Ukrainians, Belorussians, Lithuanians, some inside Poland, some outside—and that was a recipe for hatred and bloodshed. Our peasants in the east always preferred us to the Russians until idiots told them they should be Ukrainian patriots, Belorussian patriots, Lithuanian patriots. And now some of them have been persuaded by Bolshevik propaganda that they'll live like lords in Stalin's Russia—where, if they have one cow, one horse, and a spark of ambition, they'll be called blood-sucking kulaks and killed. 'Make soap out of the kulaks!'—that was the cry of the Bolsheviks in Ukraine in 1933. And who encouraged our peasants to think that Poland didn't care for them anymore? Dmowski. As for the Jews, Dmowski wanted to deport the Jews from Poland— three million people. Where would they go? Three million people to be torn from the homes where their families have lived for hundreds of years. Most of them are no more than poor, good people who work in our villages, make our shoes, and mill our corn, or toil in our cities keeping our factories going. They're Poles. Dmowski or no Dmowski, the Jews of Poland are Poles. Look at the lawyers we have here in this prison, reservists willing to die for Poland and perhaps also for the rule of law. Half of Poland's lawyers are Jews. As for my profession, we would be weakened beyond recognition without our Jewish doctors." He looked across at Jacob in his turn. "Halperin over there is a better surgeon than I will ever be. He's a very clever fellow, and he did his specialist training in Breslau, one of the best medical universities in the world."

The colonel spluttered furiously and put down his spoon with a bang. "There you are. Proves my point. Riddled with Jews, Germany is. Powerful Jews, trying to take over the world. They've made a very good start in Russia. That's what we're doing here, as prisoners of Bolshevik Jews—they're keeping us out of Poland. Get rid of the lot of them, as

Dmowski said. Send them to Germany. Send them to Russia. Let them go where they belong."

"Jews belong nowhere", Halperin said, too quietly for the colonel to hear through the crackling march from the loudspeakers which was going on throughout this conversation.

"They belong in Poland as much as we do," said his colleague, "after so many centuries. And we should be ashamed of how we've treated them—some of us, some of the time."

In the quietness of the church, remembering all this with his usual sense of outrage, Halperin turned over, on his bunk, to see whether, now that anger had warmed him, he might get a little more sleep before the siren.

But he was thoroughly awake. And he knew that those quiet figures he had watched, kneeling behind the priest in the dark church, had not been contemptuous, not been threatening, not, at those moments, hating him or anyone, not even the Russians who, for no reason, given or imagined, had put them all in prison. How did he know? He knew. He had watched them often, surprised to find himself not feeling excluded from their silence, and heard, although there were the usual restless sounds all round him, the stillness of the praying prisoners as the stillness of a kind of attention that he almost recognized. It had reminded him of something. What? Not the synagogue.

His grandfather was a rabbi, but his grandfather had died before he was born. His father, a doctor who always said he believed in science and not in God, had taken him as a small boy several times to the synagogue on the High Holy Days. "We in our family have left all this in the past, where it belongs. A new day of enlightenment has come to rescue people from the fears and the false promises of religion. But the tradition of our ancestors for thousands of years is something I want you to know you belong to. It still beats in the hearts of so many in this city, and it has a value of its own for those not fortunate enough to have received a modern education." Jacob was five or six at the time. He remembered what his father had said, though he couldn't have understood it at the time. Probably his father had said all this later too; probably he had said it several times. His mother, who so much admired his father that she took all he said on trust as good and right because he said it, nevertheless made a little ceremony of the sabbath eve meal on Fridays, bought the challah plaited loaf from the baker on the corner, blessed and lit the candles, and waited for her husband to bless the wine, which he did cheerfully enough. Jacob remembered the knocks on their door on those Friday evenings: pious women collecting challah and fish from the more prosperous to distribute among the poor for the sabbath. After his mother's death these customs were sustained by his father's sister, widowed in the Great War, who was a devout Jewess and kept a kosher kitchen in their house.

The crowds of men in the synagogue, the strange music of the cantor's singing, and worst of all, the eerie sound of the shofar, the ram's horn blown for Rosh Hashanah, had terrified Jacob. The first time he heard the ram's horn, he cried. His father took him home. Nine days later they returned for the lamentations of Yom Kippur. He didn't understand the Hebrew words, but he did understand that if God was being addressed, prayed to, remembered by all these men in the synagogue—and he knew that that was what was happening—then God was a god to be feared for his tremendous power. The Days of Awe, the High Holy Days were also called. When he was a little older, perhaps nine or ten, his father asked him if he would like to go, as usual, to the synagogue on the High Holy Days, and after looking carefully into his father's face to see if his father would be disappointed if he chose not go, and understanding that he would not, he shook his head.

"That's all right, Jascha. It's strong stuff for a child, and the services are long. You must make up your own mind about all this when you grow up."

His mother had nodded, and smiled at him. "Your father is quite right. It will be for you to decide, for yourself."

Had he decided, ever? He had not, except by neglect of the question. What, indeed, was the question?

His mother and his little brother had died in that Russian train because the Russians had decided that the Jews were helping the Germans. Exactly, he almost said aloud. The Russians in 1915 thought all Jews were Germans at heart; now the Germans think all Jews are Bolsheviks. Dmowski managed to think both things at the same time. More stupidity, on a grand scale. More terrifying stupidity. As if all Jews had ever been anything.

After his mother's death his father—who had looked after him and his sister Anna in the train and in Warsaw and, with his aunt's help, when they got back to Vilna after the war—had never, as far as he knew, returned to the synagogue, although several of his friends were faithful

Jews. A learned and very intelligent rabbi, probably his father's closest friend, came often to the house. They would argue, sometimes only with each other, sometimes with four or five more friends, all men, some on one side, some on the other of whatever the issue happened to be, through long evenings of tea and vodka and bread and pickled herring and cucumbers. His sister Anna flitted about, filled glasses, emptied ashtrays—they all smoked black Russian cigarettes—until their father sent her to bed. Jascha, as he grew up, listened carefully.

The conversations were about all kinds of things: the Russian Revolution and where, particularly after Lenin's death, it was likely to lead; the Bund and whether a political party that was socialist and Jewish but not Marxist, and had been founded in Vilna, could gain enough non-Jewish support to improve the lives of the poor in Poland; Zionism and whether it had been supported by England and Germany only as a way of getting rid of the Jews, and whether the rabbis were right or wrong to suspect it of threatening the true Jewish tradition of exile from which only the Messiah could rescue the people. As he more and more enjoyed listening to these discussions, and gained the confidence sometimes to make a contribution of his own, he found that he changed his own mind about the issues from one week to the next according to whether his father or one of his father's friends talked more persuasively. Should he join the Bund? Should he join the Communist Party, as some of his cleverest school friends had? Should he join the Vilna Zionists? Should he set himself to read what Marx had actually written? Should he talk by himself to his father's friend the rabbi to discover more about living as a good Jew? He had inspected all these possibilities except the last, of which he was, for some reason, afraid. He went to meetings of various groups. He read pamphlets. He heard speeches. He joined nothing before he went to Breslau and became a German-trained surgeon, highly respected and very busy after his return to Vilna. In Breslau, in Hofmannswaldau's flat, he had talked to the others after they'd played a quartet, to Zapolski and Hofmannswaldau and Treuburg, about all these unanswerable questions. After he was married and living with Else in their own house—he winced at the thought of her, of the children, of the house, as, here, he always did: was she bravely managing everything at home? Of course. How was Josef? Was he practising his violin? No, he wouldn't be practising now; they would all be asleep. He could see Else in their bed, probably with little Rivka beside her, in his place, for comfort. Josef, who was brave, was certainly sleeping alone upstairs in his attic.

He forced himself to stop thinking about his family, to return to memories of the time before his marriage, of his father and his father's friends, talking and talking.

He remembered that, listening to the long evenings of argument in his father's study, he had also found that more and more he was trying to place his father and his father's friend the rabbi side by side rather than in confrontation. They didn't disagree about everything; far from it. But sometimes they arrived at what Jacob felt to be an impenetrable wall of incomprehension on either side of which one was saying something that the other simply could not hear. He found himself baffled, even upset, by listening to two thoughtful middle-aged men, devoted to each other since boyhood, both good, both passionately concerned to make Vilna and Poland and the world better, freer from prejudice and injustice, kinder, healthier, and more prosperous, yet finding that at the deepest level they could not understand each other. Eventually he realized that the true reason for the impermeable quality of the wall that separated them—although every such evening ended with smiles, a hug, pats on the back—was not the simple and evident fact that one of them was religious and one was not. "I am a rationalist", his father would say. "My heroes are Descartes and Voltaire." The true reason for the wall was not the difference between their contrasting ways of looking at the world but the difference between the degrees to which each of them thought the disagreement mattered. His father, Jascha noticed often, didn't think it was of much importance whether a person of goodwill and good intentions had any sense at all of God as Creator of everything, God as loved and honoured and feared by the people of Israel, God as the judge of all that human beings do. "I'm a doctor, a practical man. I'm here on this earth to apply scientific knowledge assembled for us all by men of medical genius which I know will help my patients, help them to live, or, if there is nothing science can do to keep them alive, allow them to die with as little suffering as possible. If being a good Jew would make me a better doctor, I would be a good Jew. But I see no reason to think it would." "I am not concerned", Jascha had heard the rabbi reply, "with your work. I am concerned with you." "I and my work are not separable." "The time will come when you will stop working. Then perhaps you will discover that you need to remember your Creator in the days of your age." "Perhaps; perhaps not. I rather think I will be just an old doctor dealing with death as best I can."

When the time came, four years ago, his father had done exactly that, dying bravely of an inoperable cancer, having, in the presence of Jacob—now himself a senior surgeon in the Jewish hospital in Vilna—said good-bye to his friend the rabbi with a smile that meant, "You see? This can be done."

So which of them had been right? Was it his father, who seemed to him at the time to have demonstrated by his life and the manner of his death that whether a person was or was not a religious Jew made no necessary difference to the quality of his life or to the calm with which he was able to accept the deaths of others and, when the time came, his own? Or was it the rabbi, to whom the difference between faith in God and faith in the secular world was as great as the difference between light and darkness, between blindness and sight? Still he didn't know.

Did Anna? Perhaps she did. As a young girl, after their mother's death, she had sometimes gone to synagogue with their aunt and come home happy, her eyes shining. In Breslau she had disliked the grand German synagogue; she had been half in love with Count Zapolski, who disappeared to Poland to be a priest; she had been more than half in love with Count von Hofmannswaldau, whose mother was a Jewess baptized a Protestant but who became a Catholic under Zapolski's influence. Music, he knew, had been an important part of all this. He and Anna had played chamber music with these noblemen in the flat Hofmannswaldau and Zapolski shared, Anna playing viola, frowning as she concentrated on keeping up, on not making mistakes with players better than she was. The playing, the keeping up, the beauty of the music, she loved. Also Zapolski's beautiful playing of the clarinet in Mozart, in Brahms. Dangerous beauty. Hofmannswaldau, who played second violin in the quartet he himself led, had taken Anna to a Catholic church. When Jacob discovered that Anna had gone to a Catholic church by herself while Hofmannswaldau was away, he had sent her home to Vilna to prevent any of it going any further. And, not long after, she had married her rabbi, good Moshe Heschel, a younger version of their father's friend, quieter, not so clever, but a serious Litvak scholar. Perhaps Anna had listened more carefully than he realized to those long evening conversations in their father's house. Or perhaps not. Arguments were not important to her, except insofar as they revealed feeling, in and between the people arguing. When their father and his friend disagreed, she would have noticed that the rabbi felt the more strongly of the two. If Jascha had tried to explain to her how she had made the important decisions in her life, she would have objected, or more likely laughed. But about this he knew he was right. And, after all, her decisions in the end had been good ones. She was now the model rebbetzin, with her three naughty, talkative little boys and her warm, welcoming, correct kitchen, but still with her laugh and her music.

As he thought about her, he envied the certainty he knew she had, about God, about doing things right, about not worrying about how much sense the reasons for doing them made. If she had married Hofmannswaldau and become a Catholic, he now saw, she would probably have been equally certain and equally happy. But in Germany? With Hitler bullying the Jews? Thank God, or prejudice, or sound ancient instinct, or whatever it had been that had made him send her home that day, so that she was safe in Vilna.

Meanwhile in the prison, in the cold night, he remembered watching the end of the early morning services held by one priest or another before the Russians took them all away. Far down the church, between the two candle flames, the priest would turn to face the kneeling Poles. With a raised hand he made the sign of the cross over them. They bowed their heads and crossed themselves. After they got to their feet, the priest would read something to them, very quietly. At a certain point in the reading the priest and his little congregation of prisoners would all kneel briefly, stand again for a few moments, cross themselves again, and then quickly tidy up. One of the prisoners would take something off the plank between the candles and fasten it round his neck—a crucifix on a chain? Why had it been on the plank? Two others would be putting the clutter back on the cleared bunk when the siren from the loudspeakers would tear the quiet of the church with its raucous mechanical wail and all the prisoners would hurry to find their clothes, scrambling between the bunks and crowding to the doors at the back, wrapping scarves, if they had them, round their mouths for the bitterly cold roll call out in the snow.

This was why he was sorry that the Russians had taken the priests away. There were no more gentle services in front of two candles before the morning siren. But the silence in the church every night after the loudspeakers were switched off had the same quality. No one had needed to call for it to begin after that first "Oremus". It began. It lasted perhaps five minutes, no more than ten. Then, gradually, it disintegrated, unravelled, as people shifted, coughed, talked softly. But the silence could not have happened, and been repeated night after night, if all of them had not wanted it, needed it, at the very least respected it.

What was it that it reminded him of? Night after night, he recognized something, something past words, something in himself, in the silence. What? Or was it only the recurrence of the silence that, in the deprived, crowded, horribly noisy life of the prison, he had got used to? Then one very cold night, with snow blowing in the fierce wind outside, he understood: the silence was a longer, better, freer version of the kind of momentary silence in which he, the surgeon, paused to collect his concentration before making the first incision, or in which he, the violinist and the leader, paused, collecting the concentration of three others as well as his own, before, with a nod, bringing down his bow on the first note of a string quartet. That was it: the silence was the silence of attention, the silence of submission. But to what? Here there was no demanding enterprise to be begun. Unless ... was the mere requirement to keep calm and remain oneself, in this nowhere place under the contemptuous eyes of the NKVD, not in itself a demanding enterprise? And was the attention not only submission to the need to gather one's wits, pull together one's own resources, but submission to something outside oneself? Even to God, after all? Yes. No. Possibly. Possibly was as far as he could go.

What would his father's friend the rabbi think? Would he think that the silence was the silence of a lot of Catholics praying and that a despised Jew should shut his ears, his mind, his heart, to something the Catholics would not wish him to pollute? No. Somehow he knew this was not what the rabbi would think.

Perhaps his decision as to what it meant to depend on this silence mattered scarcely at all. He knew he would have been not just disappointed but actually saddened if they—all the prisoners in the church, however many hundreds there were—had failed to find, make, allow, remember, whichever it might be, their silence.

In the daytime there was too little to do. He found himself agreeing with one or two others who wished the Russians would give the prisoners some work, however rough. "They keep telling us we're lords and that the day of lords is over. So why not set us to felling trees and chopping wood for the fires that would warm us? They don't know that half of us wicked lords have worked in our woods and fields since we were children." There were more doctors than the few sick prisoners needed, and only once, for the old man with gangrene, had surgeons been sent for. Some of the prisoners had books in their kit bags, one book perhaps, two at most, and although after the first week or so they had pooled all the books and a bright young captain had organized a rudimentary lending library so that at least which person had borrowed which book was known, there were far too few to go round. There were newspapers, in Russian and in Polish, all of them full of Communist pride, Communist promises, Communist lies, insults to Poland. They appeared at supper. Prisoners took them, tore them up, used them for toilet paper.

He walked a lot, usually alone. When it struck him as a possibility—in the daylight as he paced, as fast as was reasonable, round the camp below the barbed wire whenever it wasn't snowing—that for some reason the silence might not happen, he found himself nearly in tears at just the idea. Was being in prison undermining something in his ordinarily strong, controlled character? He couldn't remember the last time he had wept before he was imprisoned. Was it when his father died? No. His mother and his little brother? No, not then. But now, yes. Often also, tears came when he remembered Josef, who needed him, and little Rivka, who might forget him. He shook his head fiercely. This was nonsense. A child of four years old, nearly five, doesn't forget an absent father. And he would be home soon no doubt, as soon as the Russians understood they were wasting money and men keeping all these Poles in prison for no reason.

Was there a reason? Could the Russians really be hoping to turn the prisoners into good Communists, with their elementary propaganda, their astonishingly bad newspapers, their empty broadcast descriptions of the wonders of the Soviet state, and their terrible films of hefty young men on tractors ploughing the steppe, hefty young men in overalls welding steel in showers of morale-raising sparks? How many converts to what was proclaimed several times every day to be "the only land of true freedom" was all this likely to make among four thousand Polish officers, nearly all of them Catholics?

Had they removed the priests from the camp to demoralize the Catholic officers, to weaken their resistance to Marxism-Leninism? If so, they were demonstrating only how little they understood Poland. He had been amazed at the scale of the quiet—and at times not-so-quiet—celebration of Poland's Independence Day on 11 November that had been managed, remarkably, until a line of guards had appeared among the trees and threatened to shoot at hundreds of tearful, hymn-singing prisoners.

Probably they had taken away the priests to kill them. There were bullet holes in the walls of the church. In places there were blood-stains. What had happened here, perhaps at the revolution, more likely during the civil war, was obvious. Priests had been murdered in their church because they stood in the path of the future, barring the way to the young destroyers who thought they were able to build a new, a better, Russia only on the ruins of the past. If he had been a young man in Petersburg, Petrograd, Leningrad—there was something hysterical about those changes of name—instead of in Vilna, would he have joined the young destroyers? He would have rejoiced, as he did in Vilna, to see the end of the tsar; the end of a cruel, superstitious church which had always encouraged hatred of Jews; the end of romantic Russian patriotism, which had painted ignorance and peasant poverty in the soft colours of nostalgia: autocracy, Orthodoxy, nationalism—the watchwords of Nicholas I and the Russian empire at its most oppressive. But what of the wrecking and the looting and the murder that the glorious future was said to be unattainable without? How soon would he have understood that the end does not, ever, justify the means? Perhaps not until the utter ruthlessness of Stalin had become evident. And by then, the ends that were justifying the means—justifying the deportation of thousands of Poles, the starvation of millions in Ukraine, the murders of countless docile Communists who were in Stalin's way—were, lo and behold, Stalin's autocracy, Marxist-Leninist orthodoxy, and a new Russian nationalism. What else but a restoration of all that was most brutally oppressive in old Russia could account for this imprisonment of four thousand Polish officers who had surrendered to hugely superior force in an undeclared war?

It was because he was a Pole as well as a Jew that he had mistrusted the revolution almost from the beginning. He was born in 1901. He had been too young to be conscripted into the tsar's army for the 1914 war. By the time he was old enough to be a soldier, there was no tsar and only Russians fighting Russians, and when he was eighteen he became a medical student in Vilna. Through most of the civil war he hoped the Red Army would win; when they did, and then attacked Poland because Poland had taken advantage of the civil war to attack Russia, he celebrated the Poles' extraordinary victory with almost as much enthusiasm as his Polish fellow students. When did a Polish army, by itself, last defeat a Russian army? But now, without even a battle, here they were in a prison for defeated soldiers with Russians keeping them alive—for what?

The prisoners discussed this all the time—speaking in rapid Polish that the guards had no hope of understanding—at meals and while walking among the buildings of the prison, first in grey autumn weather sometimes lit by golden, warmthless sunshine, then, since the third week of November, in the snow. Older men, who had been in tsarist prisons in the past, told the rest how lucky they were to be in a prison clearly not built to be a prison, and in the comparatively gentle Russian countryside, not in Siberia, not in Kazakhstan, not in Moscow or Petersburg in terrifying city buildings with miserable exercise yards the sun never reaches and dark basements from which the cries of the tortured echo at night.

There had been interrogations. Once every few nights an NKVD sergeant, a hefty fellow like a professional boxer, with a broken nose, banged open the small door at the back of the church at about eleven o'clock, when almost all the prisoners were asleep. With a powerful torch in his hand he would shout out three or four names from a list. "Get up! Get dressed! Come with me! Now!" The named prisoners fumbled for their clothes in the dark; were lent, if they didn't possess them, scarves, fur caps with earflaps, and gloves by those nearby who had them; and felt their way along the lines of bunks to the door. "Get on with it!"

By morning almost always those who had been summoned were back in their beds. The next day they said little about what had happened to them.

"Fools they've sent to deal with us", a younger doctor from Cracow told Halperin. "Peasant lads filled to the brim with Leninist slogans they don't understand. They have no education, and no idea about anything the Party hasn't poured into their empty heads. They've been taught to read and write and at the same time taught the revolution—slogans that they know by heart, labels and phrases from books they'll never read

226

and couldn't possibly understand. After this process of turning them into good Marxists terrified of putting a foot wrong, they've been called commissars and sent into the Red Army to keep an eye on the Party discipline of soldiers just like themselves but without the reading and writing. Now they've been taken out of the army and sent here to keep an eye on us and told to convert us to the Party. They know nothing, absolutely nothing, about us except that we're 'class enemies' who've been hoarding untold riches and oppressing workers since time began. I told my commissars I'm a doctor, trained to help sick people. 'But you are also a lord. You wouldn't be an officer in the Polish army if you weren't a lord.' One of them asked me if I'd ever travelled outside Poland. I told him I'd been to Paris in 1926 to visit my aunts. 'So you are a bourgeois-fascist spy', he said. 'What were you sent to Paris to find out?' I said I was sixteen in 1926 and that I stayed in Paris three weeks in the summer holidays looking at famous buildings and famous paintings which anyone can look at. 'Why?', he said. 'Who for?' Then he asked me if I knew French. When I said I knew some French, he looked at his colleague—they were both about twenty-three—as if he had achieved a victory. 'That is the language of former people. We do not allow it in Soviet Russia. Now you are in Soviet Russia, the land of socialist freedom. You will speak Russian at all times.' Arguing with them is clearly useless and possibly dangerous. They let me come back to the church, as you see. A completely ludicrous interview."

Five of those summoned in the night had never returned to the church. No one knew what had become of them. Had they been released? Transferred? Murdered? Punished in some other way? Were there cells for solitary confinement somewhere in the camp? What had those officers said to get themselves freed or killed or whatever had been done to them? There was no way of finding out. Questions to the commandant put by the senior officers had been met only with a shrug of the shoulders.

All the way through December and January Halperin half-dreaded and half-hoped to hear his name called out. He wanted something, anything, to happen that might mean the beginning of the end of these long, dark, dull, crowded days. He didn't mind, even welcomed, the prospect of a challenge. At the same time he was afraid—afraid of provoking some unpredictable response of unreason in the NKVD that might prevent him ever getting home.

Chapter 8

When his name, his name alone, was called, as the beam of the sergeant's torch swept through the icy dark of the church, it was almost the end of January, and life in the prison had become a little less uncomfortable. The weather was colder than ever—colder, they all thought, than any Polish winter any of them could remember. But at the end of December, proper winter clothes, by some uncharacteristically efficient effort of Soviet organization, had arrived for the prisoners—padded coats, thick trousers, felt boots that didn't slip on frozen snow, even woollen mittens and fur caps—though not quite enough to go round. Nothing was new; this bounty was presumably Red Army surplus from some warehouse at some barracks. The commandant was thanked. The prisoners rolled up and put in their kit bags their filthy, second-best summer uniforms—they had kept their best uniforms as clean as they could for the day of their release—and rejoiced to dress every day as Russian peasants.

Parcels from home now included things the prisoners had asked their families to send. This meant, above all, that their families were getting their letters—opened and read by the NKVD no doubt—so the prisoners were sure that their wives and children knew they were alive and where they were being held. Food, vodka, and tobacco were always stolen from these parcels, but many wives had the sense to send things the prisoners would value and the guards would not. Books arrived. Photographs arrived. Pencils and paper arrived; pens were usually stolen. A bottle of ink broke in someone's parcel and spoiled the shirt and underwear wrapping a book. Best of all, music arrived.

Halperin discovered in the middle of December that the captain who organized the book-sharing library for the prisoners played the flute and that he had brought his flute with him in his kit bag, as Halperin had brought his violin. He learned this because the captain had set himself to find out how many instruments there were in the camp. His enquiries revealed that the prisoners had managed to hold on to almost twenty violins, four violas, another flute, and one clarinet. Prompted by the captain, the three senior officers who regularly met the commandant had eventually got his permission to allow the owners of these instruments to meet on two afternoons a week—the evenings were all now taken up with propaganda lectures and films—in a large, bare room in one of the buildings near the church. When they all produced their instruments for the first time, they looked at each other and laughed. No one had any music; and in any case, what could be played, by any combination of any of them, without either a cello or a piano? Then a grey-haired major took his violin out of its case, tuned it, which took a few minutes, and in absolute silence like the silence of prayer each night, began to play the Bach Chaconne. None of them had heard a note of real music for three months. Halperin was soon in soundless tears. So were several others. About halfway through the long Chaconne, the major stopped playing, No one applauded. No one said anything. Four or five other prisoners, not Halperin, played, less well, pieces they knew by heart.

Three weeks later they had turned themselves into a rudimentary string orchestra. A few scores had arrived in parcels. Parts had been copied. The clarinettist, who turned out to be a resourceful musician, played cello parts as fully as could be managed. Halperin sat beside the grey-haired major, who led the playing, their part propped in front of them on one of the chairs they had to leave in neat rows for the Party lecture in the evening. Most of the prisoners who had bothered to pack their instruments were reasonable players, and the music they made, if eccentric, was lively and mostly in tune. For the first time since he left home there was something good to which he could contribute.

The Party lectures, on the other hand, of which there were now several in different rooms every evening and at which attendance was compulsory, were becoming more and more difficult to sit through. The themes were the glories of the workers' achievements in the Soviet utopia and the inevitable abolition of Poland, which no longer existed and had never deserved to exist. The historical logic of dialectical materialism—he doubted whether the lecturers had any idea of the meaning of any of these four words—proved that Poland would never exist again. Those who stood in the way of history and attempted to block its inevitable progress would become nonpersons, as the nobility in Russia already had. These harangues were so boring and so badly delivered—in a curious monotone shout while the speaker gazed with fixed eyes over the heads of the audience—that it was easy not to listen. Twice, however, he had been present when young officers, unable to bear the insults to Poland, had stood up and interrupted the speaker, one of them managing to deliver a brief, emotional speech about heroism and victory which produced a cheer from the other prisoners. Each heckler had been marched out of the room between two guards and not seen again.

And now, under a blaze of cold stars in the moonless dark, he was walking uphill on frozen snow between snow-flocked fir trees, the sergeant's huge hand gripping his elbow. Guards had opened the gate of the prison, banged it shut, and bolted it behind them. He had no idea where they were going, but his exhilaration as he walked—beyond the prison wall and the barbed wire, breathing deep into his lungs the clean, icy air of the night, absolutely silent beyond the creak of two pairs of boots on the snow—made it impossible to be afraid.

After a few minutes the beam of the sergeant's torch lit some long wooden steps. Above the steps he could see cracks of dim light from the shuttered windows of a house, not large. At the top of the steps they crossed a wide platform of wooden planks, without snow because sheltered from the weather by a projecting wooden roof, and with a railing that extended along the front of the house. He had a sudden vivid picture of this place in summer: long, warm evenings, basket chairs, gentle talk, bowls of wild strawberries from the forest. Was this some dacha that had once belonged to class enemies, nonpersons, now probably dead? The sergeant thumped the door at the top of the steps. A young commissar with a clever Jewish face, clearly drunk, opened the door.

"Come in, come in", he said, sweeping a mock bow. "The prisoner will have to wait in the anteroom until the tsar is ready to grant him an audience."

"Stop playing the fool, Milshtein." Then: "Over here!"

This was an order to Halperin. Sitting behind a rickety table, papers in front of him and an oil lamp placed so that his face was almost invisible, was another commissar, not much older. The sergeant released his grip on Halperin's arm, and he approached the table. He took off his woollen mittens and stuffed them in a pocket of his coat.

"Name?"

"Dr Jacob Halperin."

The commissar found his name on a list, marked it.

"Captain Halperin?"

"Yes."

"Jew?"

"Yes."

"And why not?" said Milshtein, thickly. "We are the chosen people, chosen to suffer, chosen to rule—"

"Shut up, Milshtein. Place of birth?"

"Vilna."

Milshtein laughed. Why?

"Date of birth?"

"The ninth of April 1901."

The young man at the table leaned forward and looked carefully at Halperin, as if surprised at his age.

"Reservist?"

"Yes."

"Profession?"

"I am a medical doctor, a surgeon."

As he said this a door, facing the door through which they had come in, opened in the wall on his left. Warmth, the resinous scent of pine logs burning, and more light came from the doorway. The door was being held open by someone out of sight. An old man, a prisoner he hadn't seen before, white haired, stumbled into the room. As the old man passed him, Halperin saw tears on the hollow cheeks. A figure appeared in the doorway and said, "Take the general back."

Milshtein bowed mockingly towards the prisoner, almost falling over. "No need for that", said the figure in the doorway. The sergeant stepped forward and took the old man roughly by the elbow. "Or that. You're to make sure the general doesn't fall on the path. That's all."

"Yes, comrade", the sergeant said, with insolence in his voice. The old man straightened his back, regained his balance, and left the house ahead of the sergeant. Icy air from the night was shut out again when the door closed.

"In a couple of minutes," the figure in the doorway said to the commissar at the table, "bring in the next prisoner."

"Yes, comrade", the young commissar said, without insolence, as the older officer went back into the inner room, closing the door behind him. The commissar wrote two or three words on the list in front of him and then on a card.

"Married?"

"Yes." Another mark.

"All right." The commissar looked at his watch. His drunk colleague was doing an imitation of the general's unsteady walk. Almost falling, he clutched at the table, which tipped but didn't quite overturn; the commissar saved the oil lamp from falling, but his pile of papers slid to the floor.

"For God's sake, Milshtein. Sit down, can't you?" The sober commissar picked up his papers, sorted them, and put them back on the table. He found the card on which he had been writing. Halperin saw, as the young man's face briefly caught the light from the lamp, how exhausted he looked. "I've had about enough of you this evening, Milshtein. Where did you get the vodka in any case?"

"I have my reasons. I beg your pardon, I'm sure. I mean I have my sources." But he sat on the floor by the wall and at once lay down, curled up with his thumb in his mouth like a two-year-old child.

The other commissar, now on his feet holding the card in his hand, looked at his watch again, then at Halperin, and nodded towards the inner door.

"Time for you to go in."

The inner room was quite large, lit by three oil lamps, two hanging low from chains fixed to wooden beams in the ceiling and one on a desk at which a man, evidently the one who had appeared in the doorway, was sitting. The room was warm, much warmer than any room Halperin had been in during his months in the prison. A huge old brick stove, the kind of stove on top of which Russian peasants sleep in winter, was alive with warmth, as logs and ashes gently shifted, behind the man at the desk. The commissar followed Halperin into the room, gave his card to the man at the desk, saluted, and left, shutting the door behind him.

Halperin's spectacles had misted over in the heat. He took them off, rubbed them clear with his thumbs and fingers, replaced them, and looked round the room while the man at the desk glanced at the card, shuffled some papers, and placed one typed sheet on top of the pile in front of him. Shadowy corners. Empty. There was no one else there; he had expected, from the reports of other prisoners, two interrogators.

"Sit down, Captain Halperin."

Without looking at him, the officer, writing something, gestured with his left hand towards an old rush-bottomed chair facing the desk. Halperin sat down. The officer raised his head and looked at him, across the desk, for a long moment, with shrewdness and something like sympathetic interest in his eyes. He was a few years older than Halperin. He had an intelligent face, thick-lensed spectacles, receding hair. He sat back in his chair and lit a cigarette.

"Why are you here?"

Halperin found himself looking round the warm, shadowed room as if he might have been somewhere else.

"I was sent for", he said.

"No. I know why you are in this room." He paused, his eyes meeting Halperin's look. "Why are you serving with the Polish army?"

"I am a Polish doctor, a medical officer in the army. I am a reservist, not a professional soldier."

"I know that. I also know that you were born in Vilna in 1901." He had not needed to look down at the card to check. "So you were born a subject of the tsar. As was I. We have seen a number of changes, you and I. Imperial Russia no longer exists. What is your feeling about this fact? Your personal feeling."

In spite of the warmth of the room, he was now alert. He remembered the excitement of 1917 in Vilna, he and his school friends eagerly reading the Russian papers, the Yiddish papers, trying and failing to make sense of what was going on in Moscow, in Petersburg. He was sixteen. He said only, "About the end of imperial Russia I have no regrets."

The commissar waited.

"At the time of the revolution I had personal reasons to ... to welcome the end of a cruel regime which had deprived me and my sister of our mother and our younger brother."

"I see", the commissar said. "Personal reasons are often a good beginning."

He flicked ash into an ashtray that contained only one cigarette butt.

"Did they die because they were Jews?"

"They did."

"Precisely", the commissar said.

He carefully crushed out his cigarette, pushed the ashtray further away, and again sat back in his chair.

Halperin was hot, a sensation so unfamiliar that he found it uncomfortable.

"You may take off your coat and cap", the commissar said.

He stood up, took off his fur cap and then his coat, stiffly, and put them on the floor beside his chair. Then he wished he hadn't. In his dirty summer uniform, pulled on when his name was called along the beam of the sergeant's torch, he felt defenceless, and too close to the commissar across the desk in his neat NKVD uniform. He sat down, pushing his chair a little further back.

The commissar, watching him, his voice unchanged, said, "We—that is, you and I—have also seen, after the war, the restoration of Poland—not a great success, as I expect you would agree—and in the last four months the assignment of Poland to what, for the time being, appears to be its natural place, partly in the German and partly in the Soviet ..." He paused. "Sphere of influence."

This unpleasant euphemism for empire was new to Halperin. He winced a little, regretted it, and said nothing.

"There was no realistic hope that the Polish army would be able to defend Poland on two fronts. Was there?"

"In 1920—"

"Nineteen twenty was the exception that proves the rule. The Red Army had beaten back Polish aggression in the middle of a civil war on several fronts. That it failed to take Warsaw was merely a temporary setback in a cycle of Polish insurrection and defeat that all realists should recognize to be now at an end. A fine, constructive future awaits at least the eastern half of Poland, a socialist future."

This time he allowed himself a question.

"At least?"

The commissar shrugged.

"Do you believe that Hitler and the so-called Third Reich can survive for long? We have, the Soviet Union has, for the moment a nonaggression pact with the Third Reich. It is necessary, for the moment, for us to promote the merits of National Socialism—the Nazi Party does have 'socialism' in its title. But you and I know that this fascist combination of brutal capitalism and brutal racism is surely doomed. Hitler will overreach himself. The man is scarcely sane, and the people round him are of low calibre. I lived in Germany for four years. Recently."

He paused. Halperin thought it better to say nothing.

Then, in good German, the commissar said, "So have you, I believe. And is it not the case that you have a German wife?"

Jacob Halperin swallowed. So the card delivered to this desk by the boy in the other room was what? The official, visible tip of an iceberg of information, collected how and when? What else was in the dark water? He had to say something.

In German he said, "Yes. I have lived in Germany. I was for four years—yes, I also lived there for four years—a junior doctor in the university hospital in Breslau. I left Germany in 1928. And yes, my wife is German. Also she is a Jewess."

"Indeed."

This was said with a note of satisfaction, almost of finality, as if the commissar had proved something. Halperin waited.

"You have attended meetings of the Polish Communist Party in Vilna." The commissar had reverted to Russian.

This was a statement, not a question.

"I did attend some meetings, yes. A number of years ago. I did not join the Party."

"I know."

"At much the same time, when I was a medical student, I also attended meetings of the Bund and of the Zionists. I did not join either of these groups."

"Why not?"

"I was not wholly convinced by the arguments I heard at any of these meetings. And I still thought ..."

He stopped. What was he being drawn into here? He looked across the desk. The commissar's expression was friendly, even slightly amused.

"You still thought?"

Well, what could be the harm? It was long ago.

"I still thought that the best hope for Poland was what Pilsudski wanted all along, a country something like the old Commonwealth—tolerant, sufficiently confident again perhaps to treat the Jews with the generosity of Casimir the Great, who, by the way, welcomed the Jews to save them from the Germans six hundred years ago. I hoped this might be possible in Vilna above all."

"If that is what you hoped for Poland, I'm surprised that you didn't see in a socialist future the promise of confidence and tolerance, and the treatment of Jews not just as recipients of generosity from the powerful but as equal contributors with all other workers to victory over capital-ism and fascism. I gather that the treatment of Jews in Poland has been deteriorating for years on account of fascist influences on your ruling class. After all, even your Pilsudski was only a military dictator, like General Franco. And you have to admit that the Commonwealth is now in the distant past. Try persuading the Lithuanians of its merits, and you will not get far."

The commissar smiled. He offered Halperin a cigarette. Halperin shook his head. The commissar did not light another cigarette for himself.

"Would you describe yourself as a romantic, Captain Halperin?"

"Certainly not. I am a scientist, a rationalist."

"If that is the case—and it must be the case since you have achieved a highly distinguished medical career—I'm surprised that you were not, as a student, struck by the logical and historical weight of the Marxist explanation of the world in which, as young men, we both found our-selves. You, however, having enjoyed a degree of bourgeois privilege and a protracted education not available to a Moscow errand boy who left school at twelve years old, might have been expected to grasp the principles of dialectical materialism rather more quickly than I did. Not that the Polish Communist Party in Vilna would necessarily have been well informed as to the philosophical foundations of their hopes for revolution."

Halperin gave himself permission to be irritated by this. "Some of the leaders of the Party in Vilna, including friends of mine, were invited to Moscow a few years ago to drink from the pure spring of Marxism-Leninism. They have not returned."

"Ah. It is possible that they deviated from the correct path. This has not, in recent years, been a prudent thing to do."

Was there here a suggestion of menace? But he went on, in a slightly altered voice, to ask, apparently interested in the answer, "Have you, Captain Halperin, read *Das Kapital?*"

"I have never had the time. Nor the inclination. Marx' ideas are nev-ertheless familiar to me."

Another smile.

"No doubt. Familiar—to whom are they not familiar nowadays?—but not properly known, not thoroughly understood. You didn't con-sider attending Party meetings after your return from Breslau to Vilna?"

"I did not."

Another pause.

"Are you a religious Jew?"

"No. That's to say ... no, I am not."

"So. Where is your difficulty with socialism? True socialism, I mean. Not, obviously, the capitalist socialism of the Nazis. And not the half-baked, half-hearted socialism of the Bund, or of the German so-called socialists before Hitler was chancellor. I would have thought that you, as a Jew who is not religious and who is a loyal, if romantic, Pole, would be perfectly placed to see the force of the case for a Polish future in which there will be no distinction between Jews and others, in which, once the class war is over, there will be no more exploitation, no more institutional injustice imposed by the owners of land and of the means of production, no more religion encouraging people to despise one another and to close their eyes to the possibility of the creation, here and now, of a better world. And no more of the fascist nationalism that has poisoned the Poland you believe Pilsudski dreamed of."

Had he already said too much? He knew he was being seduced by the warmth of the room and the commissar's evident intelligence, but he couldn't resist defending what he knew to be true.

"Fascist nationalism is indeed a poison, in Poland as elsewhere. But Poland, much to its credit, refused the offer of an alliance with Hitler last year. Soviet Russia did not."

A long silence. The commissar's eyes had hardened. Halperin looked down at his own hands, clasped in his lap. He was sitting on the rush-bottomed chair with his back straight, his knees together, his heels raised from the floor—wooden, with more rushes—as if ready for sudden flight. Where to?

Now he had certainly gone too far. At last the commissar spoke, more quietly:

"The survival of Poland as an independent country was a romantic project—as we see. History has not been on the side of this survival, and will not be. The priorities which govern the foreign policy of the Soviet Union are entirely different. They are founded not on romantic aspiration but on the logic of history. Therefore they will prevail."

So he was prepared to continue the discussion.

Halperin said, "Predicting accurately the course of events has never been possible."

"Until Marx."

237

"Even Marxists can't predict human mistakes. Who could have predicted in 1812 that the man who ruled over most of Europe would three years later be a solitary prisoner on a God-forsaken island in the middle of the ocean?"

"Do not forget the might of the Russian people. I presume you have read *War and Peace*. Leaving *War and Peace* aside, however—or not leaving it aside, since this was something that Tolstoy certainly understood—the history I am speaking of is a matter of the broad sweep of forces, of historically determined truths which will prevail. It is not a matter of individuals, whose lives and deaths are not important. Even if the individual is Napoleon."

"It's not possible for a European to say that Napoleon is not important."

"He was, perhaps. He is not now important. Don't you understand?" Then he added, with some contempt, "Poles, of course, have always loved Napoleon. They have always loved France. But now? France was bound by treaties to come to the aid of Poland if Poland were attacked by Germany. Did it? In September? It did not. This, I may say, was no great surprise to some of us. I have also lived in France. There are good Communists in France, and the French, after all, began the revolution. But they have allowed the class war to lapse; I would say that the French officer class is more fascist than the Polish officer class, and judging by my experience of your fellow detainees, that is saying a good deal."

The commissar looked over the desk for a response from Halperin. He gave none.

"No," the commissar continued, "the history to which we need to pay attention is the history unfolding now, not the history of the nineteenth century, although it was by studying the nineteenth century that Marx came to his irrefutable conclusions. These conclusions, these predictions which we now see developing through revolution into realities, do not, I repeat, concern individuals. They concern classes, as we have seen in Russia and as we shall see in Poland, in France, and even, one of these days, in England, where the revolution has scarcely started. The classes which falsehoods have sustained will be eradicated along with the falsehoods. The great mass of the workers of the world will prevail. I would expect that a man of modern education, of science and logic, such as you claim to be, would wish to join this future, would not wish to be stranded on the shore of the past, with priests and rabbis and Polish lords, as the tide of history advances up the beach to wash all away. There will soon be no possibility of rescue."

Halperin sat still, looking at his clasped hands. It struck him that the commissar wanted him to continue to argue. Why? He decided not to.

Then the commissar said, "Have you not often wished—in Poland, in Germany, in this prison full of Polish officers—to lose your Jewish identity, as in the Soviet Union so many Jews already have? Is not that a freedom to be desired?"

"I do not wish to lose my identity as a Jew. I do not wish to lose my identity as a person. The individual does count. Each of us, one by one, contains all the meaning there is." Why had he said this? Was he sure it was true? He returned to safer ground. "And it will never be possible to dissolve the distinction between Jews and others."

A patronising smile on the commissar's face. "Are you sure you are not a religious Jew?" The commissar allowed his question to stay in the air, and went on, "Whether or not you are, or have been, you are wrong. If religion withers away, as it is fast doing in the Soviet Union, no distinction is left to be made between Jews and others except the distinction inaccurately known as race. I can hardly imagine that a Jew who has lived in Germany at any time since the invention of the Nazi Party is likely to agree with Hitler that the distinction known as race is, shall we say, a useful one."

He wished it had been possible to prepare in some way for this interview. He was annoyed with himself because he felt unable to think clearly, now, here, when he most needed to, in this—he knew very well—deceptively welcoming room. He hadn't used his brain for months. But he had always been able to think clearly; mere lack of practice shouldn't have actually dulled his intelligence. And yet his mind felt clumsy, inarticulate, almost stupid. What annoyed him most was that he was aware of danger in this conversation but had no idea what the danger was. The accounts he had heard of these night interrogations had given him no warning of an encounter anything like this. He shook his head vigorously to dispel the dullness in his brain. The commissar didn't appear to notice and talked on.

"True socialism has dispensed with this distinction. That's the reason that the fascists—the Nazis of course, but also many educated Poles, including many of those detained here—regard all Jews as Communists and all Communists, clever Communists in particular, as Jews. They have a point. Clever Jews can do well in the Party. But only because clever people can do well in the Party. I am not a Jew."

Halperin suddenly felt angry enough to speak.

"In theory all that may be so. But in practice, a Jew, as always, may be dispensable because he is a Jew. Why was Litvinov sacked in the summer? No doubt to demonstrate to Hitler that Russia doesn't trust Jews. A Jewish foreign minister—could he have signed the pact with Ribbentrop? And Litvinov was born Meir Walach, as Trotsky was born Lev Davidovich. Why did these great Bolsheviks change their names?"

"The term 'Bolshevik' is no longer in use. And we do not mention Trotsky in the Soviet Union. Trotsky has deviated from the revolutionary path."

Ice across the desk. A mistake. But Halperin, who had seen what needed to be said, couldn't now stop.

"Religion is not withering away in the Soviet Union. Religion is being crushed out of people's lives by terror and murder. I have seen bullet holes outlining the shapes of dead men on the walls of the church here."

"Of course. We have had a revolution in Russia. Are you, a Jew who says he is not religious, telling me you have sympathy for corrupt and vicious priests who kept the peasants in the darkness of superstition for centuries, and for centuries encouraged them to hate Jews?"

"I am not. I am simply saying there is something in Christianity beyond the blindness of ignorant priests, something that terror and murder will not destroy. Christianity will not wither away, as you hope, and whatever is in it that is truly good will not die with the deaths of priests so long as in the souls ... in the souls of ..."

Now he was angry with himself. It was idiotic, he realized, to use such language to a Soviet commissar. Sure enough, the commissar said:

"Captain Halperin, you are a rationalist. Rationalists do not countenance the existence of the soul."

But Halperin was enjoying an old stubbornness he hadn't felt for months.

"They do not. I apologize", he said. "However ..."

"However?"

"I know little of Christianity. And yes, there are Poles whose Christianity appears to consist mainly of sentimental nationalism stoked with suspicion, or now more often hatred, of Jews. But there are many more in whom Christianity sustains courage and civility and a kind of trust in meaning and value which will overcome their own defeat and imprisonment—here, for example—and even death."

"Are you referring to survival after death? Eternity? The soul again? I would have thought you knew that all this is nonsense, nonsense contrived and maintained by churches and rabbis and the bloodsucking classes to keep the poor from rebelling. Religion is, and has always been, nothing but a mask for power. It is bourgeois chicanery, and the revolution is destroying it. This opium of the people was successfully supplied for centuries. In our time, in our generation, religion is over, finished. This is what we have achieved. The people have refused to be drugged any longer."

"I recognize what you're saying of course. For years I thought much the same. Now ..."

"Now?" There was a hard edge to the commissar's voice.

"Now I'm not so certain."

"Ah. You're telling me that you are what in Germany they call an agnostic. I despise agnostics. A man of your age and intelligence who cannot make up his mind is merely weak. You don't strike me as weak, Captain Halperin. It's time for you to make up your mind. If you are not with us, you are likely to be against us, and in present circumstances this is not a particularly safe path to choose."

How threatening was this? He looked over the desk into the commissar's face and read in it interest, resolution, and still some amusement. But coldness also, and calculation. Cruelty he could not see. Then he remembered the tears of the old general.

He had two options: silence, or continuing the discussion as if it were no more than a discussion. There were no others.

So he said:

"I would point out only that you will not kill religion among Poles by killing Poles. This is a practical, not a theoretical, matter. Catholic Poles are Catholic to the roots of their being, and you can't kill them all. I doubt if you will kill religion among Russians by killing priests and wrecking churches. And I am certain that you will not kill religion among Jews by killing Jews. Jews are born and die to safeguard their story. Their story lives in everything they do, sabbath after sabbath, festival after festival, meal after meal, blessing after blessing. Jewish religion will not wither away."

"We shall see. Meanwhile, what you say is precisely why clever Jews make such good Communists. They have turned their backs on one story and replaced it with another. But the new story happens to be true."

Halperin could see that the commissar was pleased with this. Clearly he thought he had scored a debating victory. Now he lit himself a cigarette, as if it were a little reward, and went on:

"I would be interested, by the way, to know what failed to convince you in the case for Zionism. Surely a land for the Jews, and not just any land but the land they believe is theirs, makes a fitting conclusion to the story you refer to, however illusory the story, in which Jews sustained their faith for so long and through so much persecution?"

"No. As it happens, it is not a fitting conclusion. The reason I could not myself become a Zionist is precisely because of the ancient story of the Jews, which has at its very centre hope and promise, not man-made fulfilment. The more I heard Zionists talk of the golden future in Palestine, of strong young men making the desert bloom like American settlers in the Wild West, the more their enthusiasm rang hollow. They are not interested in the old and frail, the poor, the sick—my patients in the Jewish hospital in Vilna. And their faith in a messianic future with no Messiah is not so very different from the Soviet future you are certain will come—or is it already here, perhaps, with Lenin as the Messiah? Well, Marx was a Jew, so this is perhaps not a coincidence. And what is the faith of the Zionists built on? What is its foundation? A divine guarantee of success with which God has nothing to do. That makes no sense. No. Its actual foundation is an opportunistic promise made by the English government twenty years ago, a promise the English government has since broken, abandoning to their fate the German Jews persecuted by Hitler. England and France at the Peace Conference after the war were playing imperialist games with the broken pieces of the Ottoman Empire and told the Jews one thing and the Arabs another. That promise to the Jews, by the way, gave all the European powers a welcome chance to shift what they call the Jewish problem to somewhere else, to a little corner of the Mediterranean coast, where they hoped the Jews would no longer be a problem."

The commissar looked hard at Halperin as he reached the end of this speech. What had possessed him to talk so much? How rash to talk as he used to talk to his friends at home, to this NKVD major about whom he knew nothing. He sat very still, silently cursing himself for exposing too much of who he was, what he really thought.

The commissar had been writing for a couple of minutes on a clean sheet of paper on which he had first scribbled a heading. Halperin couldn't read the Russian, upside down and at a distance of more than a yard across the desk.

The commissar laid down his pen and looked across the desk, again amusement in his eyes.

"Captain Halperin, you said you are not a religious Jew. It is clear to me that this is not entirely true. So often one finds this in intelligent Jews. So quick, so clever, so modern—doctors of medicine or professors of chemistry or physics, inventors of wonderful theories or machines or weapons, at the very forefront of the twentieth century's march of progress. Yet somewhere there is—what can I call it?—the fear of God, perhaps. Surely you know, Captain Halperin, that it's too late for that, much too late. There is in the middle of the twentieth century, more than twenty years after the revolution, no need whatever to fear God, ever again."

The commissar leaned forward, his hands clasped and his forearms flat on the paper on which he had been writing.

"What we need to fear now is being on the wrong side, on the side which is certain to lose, which history has shown to be certain to lose. These Polish lords, with their piety and their gentlemanly manners— they are evidently on the wrong side. About this, I suspect we agree. But you—you are not a lord. You are Polish only by chance. You are a Jewish doctor with a good life ahead of you, curing people, naturally, since that is what you are trained to do, but also, if you have the good sense to acknowledge which way the historical wind is blowing, furthering the cause of the revolution."

Even more earnestly, the commissar—though Halperin refused to meet what he knew was the intense gaze across the desk—went on, "Poland has been economically in advance of Russia, as Germany is far in advance of Poland. But it is Russia that has seized the historical initiative. Historically Russia is now far in advance of both Poland and Germany. Economically, industrially, now that it's in the hands of the workers, it will soon catch up. It will surpass Germany itself. Soviet Poland will be part of this development. It will need its doctors, certainly. Even more, it will need intelligent, resourceful workers for the revolution to assist in the establishment of its new socialist society."

He paused again, clearly to magnify the effect of what he was about to say.

"A few nights ago I had a Jewish doctor in here, younger than you are, a lieutenant in the Polish army. He said he wanted to stay in Russia once the present"—he hesitated, choosing his next word—"detention comes to an end. He wishes to care for the sick in a free, a socialist, country. We are delighted when such choices are made. He could, of course, have chosen to return to Poland. He chose the already-established Soviet state."

Another pause.

"I had high hopes for you also, Captain Halperin, a much more distinguished doctor, for such a role in the making of history."

Halperin blushed, and was horrified that he blushed.

"No", he said.

The commissar laughed, briefly.

"No. I had come to the same conclusion."

He put out his cigarette.

"What would you have expected to do, should you have been released from detention?"

"I would expect—that is, I would hope—to return home to Vilna and to resume my work as a surgeon in the Jewish hospital."

"Ah. You realize that Vilna is no longer a Polish city?"

"What?"

He had jumped to his feet. What might have happened to Else? The children? Josef's school? Else had said nothing in the three letters he had received. Naturally—she would know that one mention of politics would mean the censors' destruction of the letter.

He put both hands on the desk and leaned towards the commissar.

"What do you mean?" he said, very quietly.

"Sit down, Captain Halperin."

He sat down, sweating now, his heart drumming so that he could hear it.

"Vilna was returned to Lithuania at the end of October."

"Returned? Did you say 'returned'? What does that mean? What is Lithuania by itself, separated from Poland? A little country of peasants invented by President Wilson after the war—the Peace Conference again, playing games with people's lives in the name of nationalism. Lithuania has been remarkable, beautiful, civilized in the past. But it was all those things because it was with Poland in the old Common-wealth. The great Lithuanians—Kościuszko, Mickiewicz, Piłsudski, the Sapieha family—all of them were Poles. The Poles defeated the Bol-sheviks twice for Vilna after the war. If now you have 'returned' Vilna to Lithuania, it can only be to encourage the Lithuanians to love Soviet Russia. No doubt they will, for a while. But Vilna itself is Polish. It has always been a Polish city. I know Vilna very well; it is my home. I have rarely heard Lithuanian spoken in Vilna. You might hear it in the streets, among people from the country perhaps, working in the city for Poles—Lithuanian maids, coachmen, grooms. But the languages of Vilna are Polish, Yiddish, and yes, Russian, because of the imperial past, but Polish and Yiddish are the true languages of Vilna. What is the sense in calling Vilna Lithuanian now? Did you know that Vilna is also a Jew-ish city, where the Jews have been better treated than anywhere else for many centuries? Almost half the people of Vilna are Jews. The Great Synagogue, where five thousand can pray; the best Jewish library in the world; the Yiddish Scientific Institute—all are in Vilna. The Lithu-anians hate the Jews as much as they hate the Poles. What will become of Jewish Vilna in Soviet Lithuania? My own family ... are you going to release me?"

A heavy silence. Neither of them moved. Halperin felt the warmth of the wood and the stove and the lamps on their chains—the softness which had seemed to him benign, even friendly—move away from this NKVD desk to the shadowed corners of the room. A cold secret police-man was facing him after all.

"I see", the commissar said, in a voice that was now expressionless, without interest in him. "A little country of peasants. A country in which the workers will be enabled to seize power, property, the means of pro-duction. But you despise peasants—mere workers, exploited workers, servants speaking a language civilized people can't be expected to know. What a pity. Your instincts are those of an unreconstructed bourgeois. I took you for an intelligent man. But you are no more than a class enemy, probably a saboteur, possibly an agent of the fascists. Who were your friends in Breslau, I wonder? You will need to be watched. So will your family. It is even likely that you believe in God. I am disappointed in you. And I thought I had made it clear that in the Union of Soviet Socialist Republics we do not refer to Bolsheviks."

The commissar stood. So did Halperin.

"You are of no use to us. I am looking for brains. But brains without correct beliefs are worse than useless—they are dangerous. It is our loss, but also yours. Your German wife might have appreciated some security. The young doctor of whom I spoke earlier will not remain in Russia as he requested. He has already been returned to his family. As for you, go back down to your Polish lords. You belong with them."

The commissar marched to the door leading to the outer room and opened it abruptly.

"Anybody awake?"

No response.

"Come on!" he shouted. "Move!"

The young officer who had written the card, clearly woken from sleep, appeared in the doorway.

"Wake that sergeant and have him take the prisoner back where he came from."

"Yes, comrade."

The young officer, still half-asleep, turned back to peer into the room behind him.

"Get on with it!"

Halperin, putting on his coat, which he had picked up from the floor, and then his fur cap, walked to the door, not looking again at the commissar. Suddenly he very much minded leaving the warmth, the only warmth there was. The young commissar stood aside to let him through the door and then closed it behind them. In the outer room the drunk boy was fast asleep on the floor, his thumb in his mouth, as Halperin had last seen him. Nearer the door the sergeant, also lying on the floor, his bald head resting on his fur cap, was snoring. Out of his reach on the floor was his rifle. Halperin could have picked it up and shot all three of them. And then? Certain, instant death. The impossibility of his actually shooting them made him smile, as did the simultaneous sense of satisfaction that, like a good Jew, which he was not, he had never held a gun.

The young commissar bent down and shook the sergeant's shoulder. "Come on, Vasya. Work to do."

The sergeant growled a curse, sat up, looked round with puzzled eyes, cursed again, put on his fur cap, stood up, awkward with sleep, picked up his gun, and with it waved Halperin to the outside door.

"That the lot for tonight, then?" The sergeant nodded in the direction of the inner room.

The young commissar turned over the top page of the pile on his table. "Looks like it."

"About time."

Out of the door, down the steps, into the dark. Snow was falling, kind and silent. The night was a little less cold.

"All right, you. You'll have to follow me. Right behind me, mind", the sergeant said.

Following the sergeant's huge felt boots, which were all Halperin could see of him with the light from the torch shining only on the snow in front of them, Halperin was astonished at his sense of a fresh beginning.

What had happened in there, in that strange, peaceful room? What had really happened?

He knew he should feel desperately anxious about Else and the children. He did, didn't he? Yet already he was telling himself that Lithuanians with the Red Army behind them were nothing like as dangerous to Jews as Lithuanians with Hitler behind them—as, he knew, many Lithuanians would have preferred. Quick anxiety and quick reassurance. On the surface of his mind.

Beneath the surface there was calm, mixed with something close to joy; he hadn't felt like this since he left home in September. Had he ever before felt like this? Maybe when Else agreed to marry him? When Josef was born? Perhaps he had felt like this when his attention had been gathered, and his back and his feet and his shoulders and arms—the fingers of his right hand holding his bow, the fingers of his left hand precisely placed on the strings of his violin—had been balanced, just before beginning to play a piece of music he knew and loved, the whole piece present in his mind before a note was played. What else had reminded him of this feeling? The few minutes of prayer each night in the crowded, cold, uncomfortable church. But this calm mixed with joy, whatever it meant, was different, and better.

The inch of fresh snow on the ice beneath made walking downhill difficult. On the path, hard to be sure of between the trees, the sergeant, perhaps not wholly awake, was treading slowly and carefully. He didn't once look back to make sure Halperin was following him. Halperin could have stopped walking. He could have deviated—he smiled to himself at the word—from the path and vanished into the trees. He wouldn't survive long in the forest. He might not survive even the night.

No stars shone above them now. The snow was falling softly through the windless dark, lit only by the beam of the torch.

Through his head was running over and over again, like a tune except that the rhythm was only of words, a phrase he remembered from somewhere—some book? someone talking?—long ago.

"God is dead, and we have killed him."

Why now? And why this unfamiliar lightness, light-headedness, lightness of heart?

Because this was what the NKVD major was saying, over and over in different ways, and expecting, hoping, that he would agree. "God is dead, and we have killed him." He had discovered that he wouldn't, he couldn't, agree.

There were two alternatives, only two. Either Marx and Lenin and the NKVD major, and with them Voltaire and Hegel and Comte and Nietzsche and John Stuart Mill, were right, in which case Jews for three thousand years, and Christians for two thousand years, and, come to think of it, Muslims—there were a number of them among the indoctrinated guards, deprived of the God they had learned about as children, as now so many Christians and Jews were deprived—had lived wrapped in a fantasy of self-delusion. Or not. The secret policeman made him choose, as no one else had ever compelled him to. So he had. And now the sentence, Nietzsche's little refrain—surely it was Nietzsche's, and someone in those discussions years ago in Hofmannswaldau's flat in Breslau must have quoted it—sounded hollow, insolent, and high-pitched, like the refrain of boys in a playground taunting a child who refused to be cowed, refused to cry, refused to lash out. He was standing still, this boy, sure of something the others knew nothing of, and letting them chant their bullying words. By standing still and not reacting, not attempting to defend himself, while they shouted louder and louder and pressed round him in an angry circle, he might provoke them to hit him, knock him down, kick him. He didn't care. He was sure of something. Of what? Was it himself he was now sure of? Himself in relation to God, whose name can scarcely be spoken?

"God is dead, and we have killed him."

These were only words—presumptuous, foolish, stupid words. Nothing else. Chanting these words, the NKVD, the Red Army, the Communist Party, all the way up to the politburo and Stalin himself, had murdered Ukrainians, Poles, each other, the priests who had been shot in the church, thousands and thousands of people. Soon they might kill him. But tonight he had understood the price of joining them, even of pretending to join them, in order to save his life. The price was a foolish, presumptuous lie, flung at the night, the softly falling snow, the warm room that the clever commissar had prepared for his attempt at seduction, and he now knew, even though at the time he had not understood exactly the price that was being asked of him, that he had refused to pay it. He was glad—he was so glad that, almost by accident, he had refused to pay it.

When they reached the prison gates, the sergeant hammered on the small door set into one of the gates. Guards opened it, locked and bolted it behind them. The sergeant unlocked the door of the church and pushed him in, banging the door shut and locking it behind him. Halperin stumbled over clothes and shoes, feeling his way through the lines of bunks to his own, climbed up, trying not to wake the prisoner in the bottom bed, didn't bother to take off even his coat, and fell asleep at once.

Chapter 9

Six or seven weeks later—the weeks were so much the same that it was difficult to remember exactly how many were passing—he met Radek Dobrowski.

One early evening he had been playing his violin, as usual, with a few of the other musicians. Although perhaps thirty prisoners came to listen—not always the same ones—enthusiasm had faded for these efforts to play something resembling real music without either the right instruments or enough music. Seven or eight prisoners were now turning up to play; among them were the best players, and the evening usually ended with someone giving a solo performance of a piece he knew by heart. Halperin had been playing the first movement of a Brahms violin sonata, of course with no piano accompaniment.

A prisoner he hadn't consciously seen before came up to him as the players were putting away their instruments and those who had been listening were lining up the chairs for the hated lecture.

"Dr Halperin?"

How did this man know his name? But he liked the look of him. He was older than most of the prisoners and tidier than many, with a neat grey beard, spectacles, an engaging smile, more or less clean clothes, and a warm jacket—not Russian army issue, so someone must have sent it to him from home. He answered, "Yes, I am Jacob Halperin."

"I thought so. My name is Dobrowski. Radek Dobrowski."

They shook hands. Halperin realized he hadn't shaken anyone else's hand in the prison.

"A couple of weeks ago," Dobrowski said, "you saved the life of a friend of mine. He told me you were a violinist, so I came this evening, hoping to find you here."

"Ah, the ruptured appendix."

"Just so. How you did it I have no idea, in these conditions."

The operation had been like a nightmare. The patient had suffered acutely for days before he had said anything to a doctor. By the time they operated, they would have been unlikely to save him even in a properly equipped hospital. With no antiseptics beyond boiled water, coarse sewing thread for the stitches, and nothing but vodka to dull his pain, his survival had been as much a matter of luck as of medical skill.

"Your friend was very fortunate."

"I know. The power of prayer may have had something to do with it."

"Ah."

They were outside now, walking in the dark, damp evening, through mud with a crust of ice and piles of old snow beginning to thaw. It was past the middle of March, and the last couple of days had been mild enough for the arrival of spring to seem, if not yet achieved, at least certain to come soon. Relief from the months of winter cold had raised spirits in the camp.

"You are a medical man, and a Jew, I presume. Do you still believe in the power of prayer?"

For many years, until his interview with the commissar, he would have found this question from a stranger intensely irritating. Now he said, "Why not? There was enough pus in your friend's stomach to have killed most people before we operated. Something good, something in the universe that favoured him, now and here, cured the septicaemia. I would hesitate to name it."

The other man laughed. "Very proper and Jewish."

They had reached the door of one of the long wooden huts where prisoners ate in relays, four hundred at a time. The door opened and shut as people went in; from inside came a loud clatter of tin plates and spoons and talk, a thin warmth, and the familiar smell of cabbage and potato soup boiling in cauldrons that were never properly cleaned. Lately the soup had tasted worse; the potatoes had been thawing and rotting in the ground or in heaps somewhere in the camp.

For a moment they stood side by side near the door. Halperin wondered whether Dobrowski, whose face he couldn't see clearly in the twilight, might be as disinclined as he was himself to break off this conversation scarcely begun. He was pleased when Dobrowski said, "Let's give the soup a miss for once. I've got this and that to eat saved from the last parcel my wife sent. She's got very good at carving out the middle of books and hiding things. The guards don't bother with books on the whole."

"That's generous of you. Thank you." He was grateful for more than the food and knew Dobrowski knew it.

As they walked away from the hut, not in the direction of the church, Dobrowski said, "I used to play that Brahms sonata with my daughter, once upon a time. My ears and my fingers were remembering while you played. My daughter is a good violinist. Not as good as you are. I wish, I have so often wished, there were a piano here."

"Where is your daughter now?"

"She's a student at the Moscow Conservatory. I hope. How does one know? I haven't received a letter from her here of course, and my wife has heard nothing since October. We wanted her to study in Paris, but she set her heart on studying with David Oistrakh—I don't think she met him once in her first year in Moscow, but she was pleased to be near him—girls, you know—and by then in any case we couldn't really afford Paris. The Soviet Socialist Republic does educate talented musicians for nothing, as long as they're not from families regarded as abolished—we had to change her name before she went to Moscow for the audition. We made her the child of a friend of ours, a village school-teacher, a Belorussian, whose own daughter, about the same age, died shortly after she was born. Our daughter hasn't run into any suspicions over this—so far as I know. Ach!"

He stood still, and laughed, clearly to deflect emotion.

"How ridiculous it is, isn't it? On the one hand they train my child to be a great violinist—though I doubt, to tell you the truth, that she has it in her to be more than a good orchestral player—and on the other hand they lock up her father in this godforsaken place behind barbed wire and feed him potato soup. The same people. The right hand and the left, you could say."

His laughter was close to tears.

"Come along." He was walking again. "Let's raid my stores."

Twenty minutes later they were sitting in a corner of a room in a building Halperin had seen but never entered, an old, long, two-story brick building, white plastered with the plaster now peeling. There were good-sized windows, not broken, and large square rooms upstairs. In this room were a dozen bunks and as yet no one else, and they sat on the floor beside two lit candles, having eaten herring from a small tin, pickled gherkins from another, and some black bread Dobrowski had saved from the meal in the middle of the day.

"I wish I had some vodka to offer you. We get a little occasionally, one way and another, but it's no sooner got than it's gone."

Far from fretting over the absence of vodka, as many of the prisoners constantly did, Halperin had several times thought how much the Polish officers' behaviour, to which he had become accustomed in his weeks of training for the reserve, had been improved by the almost total abstinence from alcohol forced on them by life in prison.

"I can do tea, however", Dobrowski said. "Real tea." He began boiling water in a can on a spirit stove—"I know this can isn't exactly a samovar; it belongs to our colonel, but he's happy for any of us to use it"—and took a little tea from a box, hidden under his clothes by his bunk. The box was a small, red leather case, the black double-headed eagle of imperial Russia stamped on the leather. The case snapped open and shut and had once contained a row of medals. "I sold them for matches, a needle, a few buttons, a medicine bottle of vodka, and— wonder of wonders—a cake of quite passable soap, to one of the pedlars they let in. Tsarist medals. Not popular with the NKVD."

Halperin hadn't eaten so well in the five and a half months they had been in prison. He was impressed.

"Those windows", he said. "I expect you know how lucky you are to sleep in a room that has unbroken windows. In the church—"

"You sleep in the church? I am sorry. It must have been horribly cold at night in the deep winter. And all those hundreds of men crammed together. But I have also wondered whether the fact that it is a church is somewhat comforting; perhaps it helps a bit. Though of course for a Jew perhaps it's made things even worse?"

"No. Oddly enough, it's made them better. You spoke of prayer in connexion with your friend and his recovery. Before I was a prisoner I hadn't had much experience of prayer, except"—he laughed, remembering—"Except as spectacle: the synagogues in Vilna, the Orthodox at prayer. It was very powerful, but I couldn't engage with it. Probably because my father, a secular Jew, a doctor like me, took me only to see. He thought tradition important but not for him. But every night, here in the church, there is—what can I call it?—a pause for prayer, or at least silence, after the loudspeakers are switched off, before we try to sleep. Jews aren't accustomed to silent prayer." He laughed again.

"Come to think of it, Jews aren't accustomed to silence of any kind. We fill every void with words. But this silence every night—I suppose it began because of the building. And also because they took the priests away. I wouldn't have expected it to be good, but it is good."

"I'm sure you're right about the building. And I'm glad for you, and for all of you in there. It's a tragedy, you know, what's become of this place."

"I've often wondered what this place was. That big sign over the gate—I saw it when we first arrived. It was dark, but they had some kind of oil lamp above the gate, like the one above the door of the commandant's building. 'Maxim Gorky Rest Home', the sign said. That must be only since the revolution, in fact probably only since Gorky's death. Haven't they been pretending as hard as they can that they didn't kill him?"

"They have. And of course they killed him. Why? God knows. Naturally they'll have hidden their tracks, as they do. Poor Gorky. What a muddled life. You're right—the rest home is just a presentable revolutionary use they found for the buildings. They like to send exhausted factory workers on a holiday in the country for a couple of weeks in the summer—part of the preliminary arrangements for the Soviet paradise. No doubt they put up the huts for the workers to eat and sleep in and left the other buildings as they were, or sketchily repaired them so that they're more or less weatherproof. They repaired everything but the church, since Christianity is to be expunged from Russia—and Judaism too, it goes without saying—to make way for the worship of Marx and Lenin."

He picked up the can in which he had made the tea. "There's a bit more. Pity to waste it."

He shared it out between their tin mugs. By now it was lukewarm but still good—so good, the taste of real tea.

"This was a monastery—the Optina Hermitage. Have you heard of it?"

Halperin shook his head.

"Sixty or seventy years ago this was the most famous monastery in Russia. Have you read *The Brothers Karamazov*?"

"Of course."

"Well then, you know Father Zosima. This is his monastery."

"What do you mean? It's a novel, a story."

"Made up, yes. But made up of things and people Dostoyevsky had seen and watched, heard and listened to—among them Father Amvrosy, the great *starets* of this monastery. You know about the *startsy*?"

"The old men? No. Who are they?"

"Alas, the question has to be, who were they? Elders in the Orthodox Church. Every now and then in the Orthodox Church's long history there have been wise monks—kind and wise—who have become celebrated, not officially but among the faithful, for listening, for helping troubled souls, for understanding and absolving. In the last century there were several here in this monastery, a succession of them, one guiding and teaching the next. Father Amvrosy was the *starets* when Dostoyevsky came here, in despair because his little boy had just died of epilepsy. Dostoyevsky adored the child and felt to blame because of his own epilepsy. His conversations with the *starets* gave him peace. And Father Amvrosy became Father Zosima."

"Really?"

"Really."

He remembered, as if he had been reading the book the day before rather than twenty years earlier, the atmosphere in Father Zosima's monastery; how in the old monk's cell the novice Alyosha was so embarrassed by the behaviour of his family, the loutishness of his father, the nihilism of his brother Ivan, and the chaotic life of his brother Mitya; and the long account Father Zosima gave of the history of his soul.

After a minute or two, he said, "I've always felt ambivalent about Dostoyevsky—the fierce nationalism, the hatred of Jews, and of Poles too because Poles are Catholic. And yet—"

"And yet the marvels of the novels?"

"Of course."

"And the writer who could at such a deep level think and feel and above all suffer with such an array of complicated, damaged characters—how was he not, in the end, a lover rather than a hater? I know he hated Catholics, or thought he did. Really he knew nothing whatever about them. When he came here, he brought with him the young Soloviev. Have you heard of him?"

"I'm afraid not."

"An extraordinary man—a kind of innocent, though extremely clever and thoughtful. He saw no reason for Orthodox and Catholic Christians not to be reunited. He might even, later on, have become a

Catholic himself. Dostoyevsky thought a great deal of him, and there is certainly something of him in Alyosha Karamazov. So you see, Dostoyevsky was more complicated, even perhaps less prejudiced, than one might think."

"No. Yes. You may be right. I used to think Tolstoy the greater writer, but remembering *Karamazov* now, I think I was probably wrong."

"Tolstoy came here too. He also talked to Father Amvrosy. It didn't go well. Tolstoy exhausted the elder and then wrote dismissively of the whole idea of elders; if there were to be wise old men in Russia, I imagine Tolstoy wanted to be the only one. But then ... do you remember when Tolstoy died?" Dobrowski looked carefully at Halperin over the candle flames. "No, you would have been too young. I remember it vividly. I was still a naval officer then. I had a desk job at the Imperial War Ministry in Petersburg. The newspapers were full of it for days— the grand old man of Russian literature dying in a stationmaster's hut at the back of beyond, and Countess Tolstoy hammering on the door with her umbrella and not being let in. I heard later the most extraordinary story, suppressed by the so-called Tolstoyans, the very people who wouldn't let Countess Tolstoy see her dying husband. Tolstoy came to the monastery again just before his death. Between rushing out of his house in a rage and reaching the station at Astapovo, he spent three days wandering about, and he came here. They wouldn't let him see the elder—Amvrosy was dead by then, but he had a successor whose name I've forgotten—no doubt because the Russian Church had excommunicated Tolstoy, and the monks were probably frightened they might do the wrong thing with this half-mad old man at the gate. They gave him a glass of tea and sent him on his way. But it's quite a thought, isn't it, Tolstoy at the end of his life on some kind of pilgrim path, perhaps even wanting before he died to make his peace—with what? With the Russian Church? Probably not. But with something outside himself after all, even with God? And perhaps then he thought of the quiet room, Father Amvrosy's cell, Father Zosima's cell—"

"Tell me," Halperin suddenly said, "where was it? Do you know exactly where it was, the elder's room?"

"Oh yes. Everything about this place was famous, you know, in Russia before the revolution. The cell was the central room in the elder's hermitage. The hermitage was a little way from the monastery, for peace and quiet, and so that the peasants could come to visit the elder, as they do in *Karamazov*. It's a modest house, I believe, nothing showy, about five hundred yards up in the forest above the monastery. I gather the NKVD are using it to interrogate prisoners at the moment."

Halperin shut his eyes. In the dark, Dobrowski wouldn't be able to see his face. After a moment Halperin was able to say, "I know."

"You know? You mean you've been up there yourself? Were they ...? Did they ...?"

"Did they use force? Torture? No. But now I understand, or almost understand ..."

"Understand?"

Halperin stopped. He didn't know this man. However, it was impossible not to like him, impossible not to trust him.

"I had a curious experience up there. I discovered something about myself that I genuinely didn't know or that, I suppose, I had refused for years to consider even as a possibility. Now that you tell me about the elders and what they did to—how would you describe it?—perhaps rescue people from themselves, I think what happened may have had something to do with them, although they have gone, long dead and the last of them murdered no doubt."

Then he laughed, withdrawing from the seriousness of what he was describing.

"Or it may just have been the warmth."

"Hardly the warmth of the interrogators?"

"There was only one—I was surprised. No, what happened to me up there had certainly nothing to do with the interrogator's warmth, though it may have had something to do with his coldness. He was apparently sympathetic on the surface. But below the surface he was icy, calculating, highly intelligent, somehow ahead of me all the time. But the room was warm; there was a huge old stove. It was wonderful after months of cold."

"And you found that after all you were ahead of him?"

Halperin looked at this Polish stranger, astonished.

"Perhaps. Well, yes, in a way. It was good, in any case. Although for him, of course, I was a lost cause. If my brain had been working properly, if I'd been quicker to understand what was going on, I might have managed to get myself released—but only by pretending, by joining the lie, the set of lies that they ..."

"Ah."

Dobrowski didn't add anything immediately, showing that he understood. Then he said only, "What was he hoping for?"

"Co-operation in the future of a Communist Poland; spying on the Germans. He tested my knowledge of German. He wanted me to continue to work as a doctor while actually working for the NKVD. Something of that sort. He wasn't specific."

"I think that must have been Major Zarubin. About forty-five, spectacles, extremely clever?"

"That's him."

"NKVD top brass. He hasn't been here long. They must have realized their thugs weren't getting them far with Polish officers. Have you noticed that one or two of those sent for in the middle of the night don't come back?"

"Yes. I assumed they'd been punished, killed perhaps, for getting something wrong under questioning. But Zarubin told me at the end of the interview that one prisoner, also a Jewish doctor, had been allowed to go, even allowed to go home, because he said he wanted to co-operate."

"Yes. Well, that may or may not have been true. There were certainly punishments, probably even killings, earlier on. Since Zarubin got here, that may have stopped. And from what I knew of a couple of men in this house who didn't return, there's certainly a chance of getting something correct in their eyes and being released for some task in the construction of the socialist future. No, thank you. In any case, if you had lied to get yourself sent home, do you think Zarubin would have believed you?"

"I don't know."

The question had haunted him all through the weeks since the conversation with the commissar. If he had answered differently, kept his wits sharp and understood with enough mental agility when and how to lie, could he now have been at home? He saw his house in Vilna, the door on the street, Else opening it and her face as she realized he was back; Josef, who would have learned new pieces while his father was away, practising them to show that he hadn't been lazy while his father was in prison; little Rivka, five now since her birthday, which he'd missed, climbing onto his lap, her arms round his neck.

He shut his eyes. "What an idiot I was up there. Stupid, naïve . . . and slow, slow, slow to understand."

"Honest, perhaps?" Dobrowski said.

Halperin was angry, but not with Dobrowski.

"Isn't honesty in a situation like that plain stupidity? I could have lied. I could have continued to lie. I could have functioned as a surgeon, the one useful thing I know how to do. Where there is a doctor there are always patients. The rest of it I could have found some way through, lying, pretending, cheating, whatever. They don't deserve the truth. And now it's too late. I could have got myself released, and I won't get another opportunity, will I? O God!"

"They may not deserve the truth, but you do."

Halperin looked at Dobrowski across the guttering candles. He could hardly see him.

"Lying as a way of life is a dangerous game", the Pole went on. "And not just because you risk the vengeance of the NKVD. You risk the integrity, the coherence, of your own soul. I've seen it happen to friends of mine, professional naval officers, who thought they could work for Lenin and then for Stalin—Russia is Russia after all—and hold on to their own truth while knowing that the politburo is a gang of murderers, except perhaps for a few idealists whom Stalin has killed, and while knowing what happened to contemporaries of ours because they were the sons of landowners or spoke French or were caught wearing a holy medal. What happened to many of these officers was a sentence to exile in Siberia with no right of correspondence—meaning death.

"They thought they could hold on, but it turned out that they couldn't. Either they became genuine Communists or—it's difficult to describe—they somehow disintegrated, lost all sense of what is true and what is not. Faster and faster they skate, further and further from the edge of the lake as the ice cracks and then begins to melt, pools of water on the ice and the depths beneath too cold for survival. No, you are better as you are, and I mean that precisely."

Halperin thought of Zarubin's picture of the beach and the tide of history about to destroy them all, the former people.

"But I could have got back to my family. My wife ... my children are only young ..."

"Not necessarily, however cleverly you lied. They might have sent you to German Poland to keep an eye on whatever the Nazis are getting up to there. Most likely that's what they hoped to do with you. You couldn't have moved your family into Hitler's Poland, could you?"

Miserably, Halperin shook his head.

"And I would suggest that the choice you made there is better for your family, because it is better absolutely that you should hold on to your soul even if you are still in prison and they are having to manage without you for a while longer."

"Are we going to get out of here, do you think?"

"Oh, they'll have to release us sooner or later. Prisoners of war, which is how they must be classifying us, have to be released at the end of hostilities. There are international rules. I was a prisoner of war before, nearly forty years ago."

"Really?"

Halperin tried to think which war this could have been.

"The surrender of Port Arthur—1904. You must have been a very small child, so you won't have heard of it. It was a long way from Poland. There was a war between Russia and Japan, mostly a naval war. I was a young naval officer. Russia wasn't taking Japan seriously enough—who had ever heard of Japan as a serious enemy?—and we were soundly beaten. I was a prisoner for six months with my sailors, the crew of my ship. The Japanese treated us extraordinarily well. The whole experience could hardly have been more different from this. We all came safely home at the end of the war, the following year. Of course, whether Stalin will pay any attention to the rules of war is another matter. You might think that there's too much valuable knowledge, education, experience, professional skill, locked up here for even Stalin to waste. You might think they'll need us to run things in Poland, whatever absurd project of a workers' utopia they may be nursing at the moment. There's absolutely nothing any of us can do in any case. We can only wait and see. Let me find another candle. I should have one or two more."

The candles had both guttered out. Dobrowski in the dark rummaged in the kit bag hanging above his bunk and produced half a candle, which he lit with a precious match.

Dobrowski, Halperin understood, had given him time to pull himself together, so he had.

"Where in Poland is your home?" Halperin said.

"My wife is in Warsaw. She's probably safer under Nazi rule than as a Soviet nonperson. But Warsaw is not where either of us belongs. I grew up in Kresy. So did she, a few miles away. My father's estate, not enormous but so beautiful, I thought—I still think—was on the north bank of the Niemen, to the east of Grodno, not far from the beginning of the Nalibocka forest. The house and the estate were in old Lithuania all through Commonwealth times, so of course they were in Russia after the partitions. I was away at the war, the next war, in 1915 when the Germans arrived. They behaved reasonably well, it has to be admitted. But then, after the revolution, there was chaos for years. My old parents were still in the house, with my wife and our small children. First our little estate was in the Belorussian National Republic, a German invention that lasted a few months. Then we were in Poland—much rejoicing. Then the Red Army arrived. Then behold, we were in Lithuania, a new country, which hated Poles. Then, after Pilsudski's victory, we were back in Poland, but only just. My parents and my wife went to Warsaw for some peace and quiet after the Red Army was defeated. My parents died very soon after they reached Warsaw—my father had a stroke, my mother's heart was broken. This was all in 1920, the year I left the navy—left, deserted, resigned, depending on whose description you favour—and went home to see what had been saved from the Bolsheviks. The answer was, very little. The house was still standing but had been ransacked, emptied of almost everything. By the time I got back, my peasants were supposed to hate me. Some of them no doubt did. Some of them no doubt always had. But there'd been a great deal of propaganda about a golden future for the ancient nation of Belorussia—once the bloodsucking, bourgeois Catholic Poles had been got rid of. The new Belorussian Soviet Socialist Republic wasn't far away, and our peasants are Belorussian speakers. Keen young commissars had been going from village to village haranguing the peasants, sometimes leaving a wireless set, one for a whole village, for people to gather round and listen to the sort of rubbish they give us here day after day. But, you can imagine, although in theory they now thought of me—if they thought of me at all—as a wicked foreign oppressor, an agent of the capitalist west, the feudal yoke in person, when they actually saw me they remembered they had been quite fond of me since childhood, both mine and theirs, and couldn't remember why they were meant to hate me. So they didn't. The miller in the village, a splendid old Jew with about eight children, told me the young men in the village hated me only once, when they turned our house upside down. After they'd drunk the wine, they couldn't find anything else they thought worth having. My wife had taken her jewels to Warsaw, but the books, the paintings, the music, my piano, some old furniture—well, they broke up the piano and the furniture and carted away the whole lot, all the books, all the music, for fuel."

"Did you return to live there?"

"For a few years, yes. Some of the neighbours, and some of the peasants too, sheepish about what had happened, gave us a good deal of help, and we led a simple, spartan kind of life in the house, got the garden back to growing vegetables and fruit, borrowed a piano. But three years ago Poles, families we'd known all our lives, started disappearing from Kresy, over the border in Belorussia, arrested in the middle of the night—no letters, no news, no trace of them. We were not many miles away, and it was too close for comfort. Keen Belorussian nationalists were throwing grenades into people's houses. Moscow was encouraging them—and also killing them if they thought they were more nationalist than Communist. So we went back to Warsaw. My daughter, as I've told you, got herself to Moscow. My son joined the army in Warsaw last year. I have no idea what has become of him."

"I am so sorry", Halperin said, wishing he hadn't talked so much about himself. "I remember the chaos after the war, of course. I was a student in Vilna. It was impossible to predict which country we were going to be in from one month to the next."

"Ah, Vilna, our nearest great city. I remember it so well from when I was a boy—the 'third city of the empire', the tsars used to call it, although it was so very Polish, so very much itself, not in the least like Moscow or Petersburg, and not like Warsaw or Cracow either. What will become of it, I wonder? The Russians have used it as a bribe to keep the Lithuanians on Moscow's side against Poland—a bribe, like a few farms or a chunk of forest. What a terrible insult to an ancient, beautiful city."

"My wife and children are there."

"They should be safe enough. Soviet policy is to destroy Jewish life, not to destroy Jews. Jewish life, and Christian life, are to be blotted from the earth. They want to make it as though the faith of the ages had never been. Is your family religious?"

"Not my own family. My wife is from Breslau. But my sister is married to a rabbi, a learned Litvak rabbi, and she has become a devoted rebbetzin."

"They won't be happy with things as they are. But who is? Dedicated Communists perhaps, Major Zarubin and his like. They have convinced themselves that the word of Stalin is the word of history, that all the deaths they have ordered or allowed, or have hoped would take place in the deserts of Kazakhstan or the Siberian tundra, are necessary. Necessary for what? The times are insane. For a few months in 1917 I thought things in the old empire were going to get better, even for everyone. How long ago that seems. Now where are we, what are we, you and I? Poles at the mercy of Russians. Nothing new in that."

"What do you think they will do with us, those of us—it will be almost all, I imagine—who they decide are of no use to them?"

"Truthfully, I can't even guess. I said just now they should understand that they will need us in Soviet Poland. That was only a hope. I have no idea what they'll do with us, and I suspect that they have no idea either. After all, most of us haven't even been sent for by the NKVD up there in the elder's hermitage."

He sounded as if he would be interested rather than afraid if he were sent for himself. Halperin could sense Dobrowski picturing the possible encounter.

"We're so used to 'poor Poland'", Dobrowski said. "We drink 'poor Poland' with our mother's milk. But it's 'poor Russia' also, you know. Think of going from the tsars to Lenin and then to Stalin with scarcely an interval of hope in between the old terror and the new. The Cheka, and now the NKVD—where did they learn their methods, their disregard for any restraints of law or human decency? They learned them from Count Benckendorff's Third Section, from tsarist secret police since Ivan the Terrible's *oprichniki*. Young revolutionaries were thrown into prison, interrogated, tortured, starved, sent to Siberia—all lessons in oppression which the NKVD learned thoroughly. And look what's happened to the Orthodox Church—under the heel of the tsars ever since Peter the Great, then a few months of what looked like freedom, and then under the heel of the Party, which intends to destroy Christianity altogether. What would Dostoyevsky think? *The Possessed*—have you read that too?"

"Yes. It's a horrifying book, but somehow he had the fate of Russia in his bones, as we see."

"Indeed. Now the possessed invade even Father Zosima's cell. Dostoyevsky wouldn't be surprised."

"Poor Russia, as you say—as many Russians would say and, to do them justice, have said for generations, ever since Pushkin, anyway. But now we have to say 'poor Germany' also. Not since the Thirty Years' War has anyone said 'poor Germany'. But now—"

Dobrowski laughed.

"Well," he said, "I have to admit that it has never occurred to me to say, or even to think, 'poor Germany'. The Germans have always been so competent, so intelligent, so dutiful. I suppose that's because I'm accustomed to Russians. I have never visited Germany. But from what I have seen of Germans—can you imagine a German *Government Inspector?*"

"I'm not sure the Germans would even think it funny. They wouldn't recognize public functionaries behaving like that. Their own, so correct, so honourable, don't behave like that. Didn't behave like that. Until Hitler."

"My point precisely. On the other hand, an impartial observer—which of course I wasn't, since we had no wish, where I live, to lose one imperial master only to gain another—might have said 'poor Germany' in 1918. In just a few months the Germans plummeted from their triumphant peace with Lenin at Brest-Litovsk to the terrible humiliations France and England inflicted on them with consequences we can see now."

"That's not what I meant. I was thinking more of what my wife feels, reading about Hitler's Germany in letters from her family. She would have been loyal for the rest of her life, I have no doubt, to the Germany of her youth—Breslau; Goethe and Schiller and Heine; the excellent schools for girls; the emancipation of the Jews. And I was thinking also of German music. My wife does not play, unfortunately, but next to my family and my work, German music has all my life been more important to me than anything else in the world. And now—"

"And now appalling things are happening in Germany—and have been happening, one gathers, ever since Hitler came to power. They're copying Stalin and the politburo. Isn't this quite extraordinary? Germany copying Russia when it has always, always been the other way round. Hitler is clearly unhinged, and Stalin has shown him what it's possible to get away with. I do understand what you mean. Poor Germany indeed, sunk so low that Stalin has been willing to make a pact even with these capitalist fascists, his faithful imitators nonetheless, for the destruction of Poland."

Halperin heard Dobrowski take a sharp breath, as if in sudden pain, and, by the light of the single candle, saw him press a hand on his chest and drop his head.

"Are you in pain?"

He took a moment or two to answer.

"It's nothing. Just a bit of pain from time to time. It always passes." He took some deep breaths. "It's nothing." It was obviously not nothing.

When Dobrowski had recovered, he said, reverting to himself, "I expect they haven't sent for some of us because they regard Polish landowners and officers over a certain age, like me, as beyond Marxist redemption, dispensable relics of the past condemned to nonexistence by dialectical materialism." It had been a considerable effort for him to get this long sentence out. "Whereas you . . ."

"A clever Jew. Zarubin's phrase. Ripe for the picking."

"But you disappointed him. Good. And because of him you saw, you understood, something you hadn't seen before, something important. Even better."

"It was luck."

"What is luck? The hand of God? Perhaps. But you recognized it. That is the key, that we should be open to what is given to us so that when it is given we are ready to take it. So often that is how we fail. You did not."

Halperin was embarrassed. If he knew anything definite about what had happened to him up there with Zarubin, he knew that he deserved no praise. He tried to return to the ordinary.

"So do you think they will have to release us? In due course?"

"As I said, we can do nothing but wait and see." Dobrowski laughed. "Wait", he repeated, "and see. Wait until something is offered to you, and when it is, recognize it. That's perhaps all we can ever do. There's something Father Amvrosy wrote, the real Father Zosima. One of the old soldiers living here in this house at the moment was a student of philosophy and theology in Moscow, long before the revolution. He read books by Father Amvrosy. He wrote down for me a sentence he knew by heart from one of those books. I have it here."

He rummaged in a pocket of his coat and produced a very small piece of paper, folded.

The third candle was guttering in the empty bottle between them on the floor. Dobrowski unfolded his piece of paper and held it close to the dying flame.

"I can hardly read it, but I know what it says. 'Do not be greatly disturbed by the arrangement of your fate, but standing before God, await his help until the time comes.' There you are, written in this place, in the elder's cell. 'Until the time comes.' The time of decision, like the one you experienced up there with Zarubin. The time of death. We have no way of knowing."

Just before the candle finally went out, he put his hand as near it as he could to look at his watch.

"Wonderful", he said. "We've missed the film show or lecture or whatever it was this evening. Probably a film show. Too difficult to count heads in the dark."

"I'm glad." Halperin found it difficult to say even this.

"So am I, my dear fellow. So am I."

Halperin was ashamed. Why? Of what? How many years had it been since he had felt ashamed? Competence, confidence, exacting competence from others, inspiring confidence in others—that was where he had lived for so long. He stood up.

"I must go. The officers who live here will be back. They may not be pleased to find me here."

"Nonsense. Old prejudices fade in prison. Cabbage soup is a great leveller. Every prisoner here chose to serve in the Polish army, and every other prisoner knows that." But he paused. Halperin couldn't see his face in the dark. "In any case," Dobrowski added, "we'll hear them coming before they get here."

"I will go."

He hesitated nevertheless.

Dobrowski got to his feet, with some difficulty. He was at least twenty years older than Halperin. It was evident that he wasn't well.

"Here, in prison but also in the great Optina monastery, we are entirely in the power of the Russians, yes. What they will do with us, no one knows. But at the same time it is good to remember that there is that in us—call it whatever you like—over which they have no power. That, I think, is what you became certain of when you were being tested as a possible recruit to the NKVD by Major Zarubin. The sense of certainty will come and go. When it has gone, it is as if it has never been. Then all we can do is remember that it was, trust that again it will be. Waiting is all that is asked of the soul. Waiting, not for some decision of Stalin's—more likely, alas, to be cruel than to be kind—but waiting for a rescue into light and peace that can come only from beyond ourselves, from where truth and goodness and beauty are together. Waiting for God. I don't want to sound to you, a Jew, like a Catholic priest; I'm not a priest. I'm not even a very good Catholic. But there is one central thing that I hope, and will continue to hope, this side of death and, God willing, through death. And that is that waiting faithfully is not in vain. There's a psalm that says ... I know it only in Latin, and no doubt you know it in Hebrew ... in Polish it says, more or less ..."

He stopped. In the dark room there was absolute silence, no sound of the other prisoners coming towards the house.

" 'My soul waits for the Lord more than watchmen wait for the dawn. More than watchmen wait for the dawn, let Israel wait for the Lord.' You see? It's not only the best we can do; it's all we can do. And Russia and the NKVD and Stalin can't touch it. Nor can Hitler, who sees, correctly, that Christianity and Judaism are part of the same story."

"But how do we know? How do we know that ..." He couldn't finish the sentence.

"How do we know that the story has any truth in it? I don't know how we know. But I know that we know. So do you."

For a long minute the silence settled round them. Then Halperin said again, "I must go." Their eyes had adjusted to the dark enough for them to see each other dimly.

"Good night, Captain Halperin."

"Good night, Major Dobrowski."

They shook hands, for the second time.

Through the frozen slush of the spring that had not really begun, Halperin made his way back to the church as prisoners began to emerge from the lectures and film shows, blundering in crowds towards the buildings where they slept.

In the time of silence after the door was locked and the loudspeakers—tonight blaring a raucous Communist march sung by a military choir—were turned off, Halperin found himself listening for the first time to words in his head, Hebrew words he wouldn't have been able to remember if anyone had asked him, from synagogue long ago: "Give thanks to the Lord for he is good, for his faithful love endures for ever", words sung and repeated over and over by a single cantor's voice, far, far away from the marching Russian soldiers with their tramping boots. He thought of Dobrowski's quiet voice over the stumps of candles and the hot tea. He tried to think of the Pole's face, but he hadn't seen it clearly except when Dobrowski had come up to him after he had played the Brahms. It seemed a long time ago.

He noticed he was more comfortable than usual on his bunk, under the thin prison blanket and the heavy weight of his coat. He was even warm enough. He went to sleep.

He dreamed he was walking across an empty, snowy plain, a vast expanse of whiteness under a grey, snow-laden sky; a little figure in the white distance had to be reached. He walked, his boots heavier and heavier, the snow sticking to them as he walked. The little figure never seemed nearer. The figure was a boy playing a violin, alone on the white plain. The figure was Josef. He couldn't hear what he was playing; an icy wind was blowing in his face. He couldn't reach him; his boots were too heavy. He had to hear what he was playing. But to hear what he was playing he had to reach him. His boots were too heavy. It was too far. The wind was too cold, and roaring in his ears. He woke in tears. The roaring in his ears was his own pulse beating too fast.

Next day he remembered what Dobrowski had said about Dostoyevsky coming to the monastery because his son had died. After the coffee—made of chicory and heaven-knew-what but certainly not coffee—that every day was doled into their tin mugs after the roll call, he trudged several times round the whole camp. It was mild for the middle of March, foggy, damp, thawing fast. He walked under the old wall with its coiled barbed wire on top, miserable and angry—angry with himself, with Dobrowski, with Poland, with the Russians for cooping him up in this wreck of a monastery so that he couldn't look after poor Else, struggling alone in nationalist, anti-Semitic Lithuania, which would be crowing over the "return" of Vilna. Who would speak to her in German? Only Josef and Rivka. She knew some Yiddish and some Polish but not much. Naturally she knew no Lithuanian. Nor did Josef. Of course Else would be doing her best to keep the children as cheerful as possible. And Josef, eleven now, and a clever child—was he practising his violin? Of course; he was a good boy. But the dream—was Josef alone somewhere, needing his father to find him?

Halperin forced himself to calm down. Dobrowski had upset him. No, that wasn't fair. Zarubin had upset him. Not even that was right. Something else had happened in the elder's cell and had left in pieces the calm, the control he had assembled and sustained over the six months they had been here. The self-command he had been accustomed to, not just in the last six months but for the twenty years of his adult life, had disintegrated.

The white thaw fog was so thick that he seemed alone as he walked. Other prisoners appeared and disappeared, shadows in the fog. There were always too many people everywhere in the prison, so this illusion of solitude was good. And his sense of loss, of defencelessness, of vulnerability—was that good too? Whether or not it was good, it had come, and he was to accept it because there was nothing else for him to do. 'More than watchmen wait for the dawn.'

One of the things making him angry was the difference between being a prisoner here, knowing nothing of what lay ahead, and being a real prisoner who had been tried and convicted and sentenced. Real prisoners knew when they should be released. They knew that, eventually, they would be released. Even if they had been sentenced to execution, they knew that too. But here ...

He trod on something hard and broke it. He looked down. In the mixture of dirty melting snow, mud, and bleached grass that had been under snow for months, he saw at his feet most of a long bone, a human bone, broken where he had stepped on it. He shrank back. Then he bent down to look more closely. The bone was apparently a tibia, the tibia of a tall man. He looked round for anyone else to show it to. White fog; no one in sight; silence. He picked up a small rock that was lying close to the wall, and with it started to dig around the partly buried bone. It was soon clear that while the tibia alone had worked its way almost to the surface of the rough ground by the wall, a whole skeleton was buried here, in a grave only a few inches deep. There was no stone, no cross, nothing to mark the grave. With his rock he dug up a few clumps of earth; covered the two pieces of the tibia and the other bones he had exposed with enough earth and grass to protect them from being broken; and trod in more earth on top.

The monks who were here when the Bolsheviks came and ransacked the monastery ... the bullet holes in the walls of the church ... these monks had been shot and carelessly buried. How many of them?

He stood by the shallow grave of a man, perhaps a good and holy man though there was no way of telling—killed for no other reason than that he was here—and tried to remember the words of the Kaddish prayer for the dead. "Magnified and sanctified be his great name in the world which he created according to his will." He couldn't get any further. He thought of Father Zosima—Father Amvrosy, was he called?—who had comforted Dostoyevsky over the loss of his son. "Magnified and sanctified be his great name." His meeting with Major Zarubin, his meeting with Dobrowski—they had taken him out of himself, had taken him somewhere else, to a place where, as perhaps never before in his life, he had found some hesitant, faltering sense of the greatness of God.

He walked back towards the church and found he was praying as he walked, praying for the safety of Else and Rivka and Josef, and of Anna and her rabbi and her little boys. Prayer: he would, before, in the days of his rich familiar store of resourcefulness, have thought prayer evidently meaningless, a little self-generated comfort in a comfortless reality. In what he had discovered to be the poverty of attention, he knew that prayer was not nothing, not, after all, mere foolishness. Indeed, he now remembered from very long ago some more Hebrew words: "The fool has said in his heart, 'There is no God.'" That was it; that was it exactly. "God is dead, and we have killed him"—fools, all of them, however clever, quick, and resourceful, like Major Zarubin, or, in that very room, Ivan Karamazov, who, when Halperin first read Dostoyevsky, was his hero; fools, Marx and Nietzsche and Freud, and Lenin and Stalin and Hitler, who had said in their hearts there is no God.

He let them go, their names, from his mind, and found he was thinking of his father; his mother; his two-year-old brother, who had died in his mother's arms in the tsar's prison train; the nameless monk whose bones he had found in the shallow grave. Peace be upon them, he thought. He prayed. And that was enough.

Chapter 10

A few days after this, spring came. At dawn the sky was clear. The ground was soft underfoot; small birds had appeared flying and twittering among the bare branches of apple trees and birches inside the prison wall; and the air, even early in the morning, was sweet as it had not once been since they had arrived at the prison at the beginning of October.

Outside the hut where he had waited in line after roll call for his unfailingly disappointing coffee, Halperin met the captain who ran the prisoners' library and who played the flute.

"I've been looking for you, Dr Halperin", the young man said. "Are you by any chance a friend of Major Dobrowski?"

Something in the question chilled Halperin.

"Not exactly a friend. I do know him, yes. Why?"

"He's very ill, apparently. One of the other doctors said just now in our hut that Major Dobrowski had been asking for a doctor among the prisoners who plays violin and comes from Vilna, but he either couldn't say or couldn't remember the name. I thought it must be you."

"Where is he?"

"He's up in the small hut they use as an infirmary. It's—"

"I know where it is. Thank you for telling me."

"I'm glad I found you. How unlucky to be ill on the first day of spring, and at Easter too."

Halperin had already left him and was walking quickly towards the hut where he had dealt with the gangrenous foot and the ruptured appendix. Easter? He didn't register this at once.

He opened the door of the hut quietly, and a doctor he knew slightly appeared at the inner door and signed to him to follow him outside.

"Halperin, thank goodness someone found you. You are Major Dobrowski's friend?"

"I don't know him well. We had a long talk one evening."

"It's you he wanted to see. You may be just in time. He had a severe heart attack last night, and another, less severe but serious enough, this morning. He's in and out of consciousness. I'm afraid there's nothing we can do beyond keeping him as comfortable as possible."

"I understand."

They turned to go into the hut. At the inner door the other doctor stopped and put a hand on Halperin's arm.

"He was incoherent last night. Several times he told us to make sure to get the tickets for him to take his wife to the ballet. He's quieter this morning. He's asked for a priest. There isn't one in the prison. But I've got a Jewish doctor here who says there's a rabbi—transferred from another prison in the last few days, I gather. From what you know of Dobrowski, do you think a rabbi would be better than nothing?"

"Yes, I do."

"I hope you're right", the doctor said, as he opened the inner door, stood aside for Halperin to go in, and beckoned to a young, clearly Jewish doctor who was standing by the reasonably clean, reasonably comfortable bed, holding the patient's wrist as he looked at his watch. The young man bit his lip, put Dobrowski's hand down very gently, nodded to Halperin, and left the room with the first doctor.

There was a chair beside the head of the bed, almost as in a real hospital. Halperin sat down. Dobrowski's eyes were closed; his breathing was rapid and shallow; his colour was very poor. Halperin wished he had a stethoscope. He said, very quietly, "Radek, this is Jascha Halperin. We talked last week in your room, in the dark with some candles."

A flicker of the eyelids. Then a faint smile.

"Thank you", Dobrowski said, with an effort that was visible in his face. Then he said, "Tea."

"That's right. You gave me some tea."

His face relaxed and his breathing changed as he lost consciousness.

Let him go, or try to keep him till the rabbi comes?

Halperin took Dobrowski's hand and squeezed it a little. Dobrowski's eyes opened. Halperin, watching the effort he was making to focus his eyes, leaned towards him so that his own face was close but not overpoweringly close. He saw Dobrowski register his presence, or register a friendly presence at least. The sick man lifted his head a fraction, struggled to speak.

"Am I ... am I ... is this ... this ..."

"Yes", Halperin said. "You are close to death."

Dobrowski's face again relaxed, then creased with effort as his breathing quickened.

"I need ... is there ... would you ... before ..."

"A priest is coming. Very soon."

That this was a risk, Halperin knew perfectly well. The older doctor seemed practical and open-minded enough. There were no other Christians in the hut. Halperin hoped, without much confidence, that the rabbi, of whose presence in the prison he had had no idea, would have the sense to ... to what? Halperin didn't know what priests did for dying Catholics; on many occasions in the Breslau hospital he had left a dying patient alone with a priest. He knew only that dying Catholics needed the presence of a priest, if possible while they were still able to speak.

He watched Dobrowski closely. He prayed that the rabbi would come before it was too late. He had time to notice that what he was doing was praying rather than merely wishing. How strange the change in him, he thought. How easy, also.

The older doctor came in. He looked at Dobrowski, narrowed his eyes, and drew in a breath.

"Well, I've sent young Dr Feldman. I hope this isn't a mistake. In any case he may not ..."

He pulled a stethoscope out of his pocket, listened to Dobrowski's heart, made a face, shook his head.

"Not ...?" Halperin whispered.

"Not quite."

Halperin sat still, holding Dobrowski's limp, warm hand. The doctor stood at the end of the bed. Dobrowski's breathing had become more laboured. Some minutes passed. The doctor looked at his watch. Halperin saw him realize that this was pointless.

After what seemed like a long time but wasn't more than ten minutes, they heard the outside door open and shut. Dr Feldman opened the door; looked at the older doctor, who nodded; and beckoned in a tall, powerfully built man with a black beard and heavy black spectacles. He was wearing a major's uniform, as dirty as the uniform of almost every prisoner by now. He took off his cap as he came in, revealing a yarmulke on his black hair streaked with grey.

He looked at Dobrowski, wincing a little, then, swiftly, at Halperin, raising an eyebrow in a kind of greeting, then at the older doctor, with a question in his eyes.

"It won't be long", the doctor said.

Halperin pressed Dobrowski's hand again. Dobrowski half-opened his eyes but this time did not appear to be able to focus on anything. His eyes shut. His white, thin face creased with struggle as his breathing hindered his effort to speak.

"I need ... I need ..." The words were barely audible.

"Don't try to speak", the rabbi said in a deep, quiet voice. "If you can hear me, squeeze your friend's hand."

Halperin felt a very slight pressure on his thumb from Dobrowski's thumb. He looked at the rabbi and nodded.

"Good", the rabbi said. "I know you need to make your confession. I know it is too difficult for you now. Listen while I make it for you before God."

Halperin saw Dobrowski's face almost imperceptibly relax.

"I acknowledge before thee, Lord my God and God of my ancestors ..."

The Jewish prayer to be said by, or for, the dying. The rabbi was saying it in Polish. Halperin remembered his father's friend the rabbi saying it, of course in Hebrew, for him and Anna and his aunt just after his father's death.

"... that my death is in thy hands", the rabbi continued. "If my death is fully determined by thee, I will lovingly accept it from thy hand. May my death be an atonement for all the sins that I have committed before thee. Grant me some of the great happiness that is stored up for the righteous. Make known to me the path of life. In thy presence is fullness of joy, at thy right hand bliss for evermore."

"Amen." This was the doctor at the end of the bed.

Dobrowski's thumb again flickered on Halperin's—like a guttering candle.

"Deliver, O Lord," the rabbi said, "the soul of thy servant, as thou didst deliver Noah from the flood, Moses from the power of Pharaoh king of Egypt, and Daniel from the jaws of the lion."

Halperin saw astonishment on the doctor's face. This prayer must, however Jewish it sounded, be familiar to a Catholic.

Then the rabbi, coming a little closer to Dobrowski on the other side of the bed, said, in Polish, in his deep voice, "Our Father who art in heaven, hallowed be thy name. Thy kingdom come. Thy will be done ..."

Halperin looked across the bed at the rabbi's stillness as he spoke. A Christian prayer.

One more hard, rasping breath came from Dobrowski's constricted throat. Silence. The rabbi continued the prayer. Then a shallow sigh, the very faintest suggestion of a smile, and Halperin thought he felt the life leave the hand he was holding.

"... deliver us from evil. Amen." The rabbi finished the prayer.

No one moved for a moment. Then the doctor put two fingers to the side of Dobrowski's neck and crossed himself.

"He's gone", the doctor said. "How good that he should die so." To the rabbi he said, "Thank you for getting here in time."

The rabbi smiled. "Don't thank me", he said. "I'm only glad they decided to move me to Kozelsk when they did. Two days I've been here."

Halperin placed Dobrowski's hand on the blanket covering his breast, and then his other hand.

"We'll lay him out", the doctor said, "and do our best to get him buried tomorrow. Thank God for the thaw. I don't suppose there's any chance of a coffin. I expect the old admiral knew Major Dobrowski. I'll ask him to read the commendation—like a burial at sea. It's the best we can do here."

"Was he a sailor?" the rabbi said.

Halperin answered, "In the imperial navy, yes. As a young officer he was a prisoner of war in Japan. He was a reserve officer in Poland. He must have been over sixty."

Halperin stood up, looked one last time at the peaceful face of the dead man, and left the infirmary hut, opening the first door and then the second for the rabbi.

Outside in the sunshine everything seemed fresh, damp, alive with the possibilities of new leaves, grass, flowers, bees. The earth smelled of spring, open to the sun.

"Poor man", the rabbi said. "And yet ..."

"And yet it's possible we may come to envy his death? Delivered from the power of Pharaoh."

"Exactly so."

They began to walk side by side towards a stand of birch trees by the prison wall.

"Was Major Dobrowski an old friend?"

"No. We had one long conversation, a few nights ago."

"That is the way of prison."

They reached the birches, old, tall trees. A few had been felled some time ago, untidily, and had broken the branches of others as they came down. In the grass, bent and wan after months under snow, were snowdrops, the delicate white flowers beginning to open in the sun among the thin spears of their leaves, which, piercing the grass, were bright, clear green.

"Snowdrops", the rabbi said. "Harmless beauty. Lovely."

"And still here, not damaged. No use to the Bolsheviks."

"How fortunate for the snowdrops. Did you know that the Russians' name for corpses that emerge from snow and ice in the thaw is snowdrops?"

Halperin looked up at the rabbi.

"Really? How extraordinary. A few days ago I discovered one here, a corpse, further along the wall, a skeleton barely buried. One of the monks the Bolsheviks shot, I imagine. A snowdrop."

"Peace be upon him", said the rabbi.

After a moment they turned and stood side by side, looking back at the miscellaneous, untidy buildings, the dilapidated church.

"My name is Steinberg", the rabbi said. "Baruch Steinberg. I'm an army chaplain—for Jews of course, in theory. In practice, I also serve Protestants now and then, who sometimes in Poland might as well be Jews. Also, since the Russians have taken away all the priests who were in these prisons, I minister to whoever needs ..."

He hesitated.

"The reassurance that God is with them?" Halperin suggested.

"Yes. It's often all one can give."

"It's enough. It's a curious thing, but Dobrowski, a stranger, a Pole, a Catholic, gave it to me, a secular Jew."

"Did he?" The rabbi half-turned to look properly into Halperin's face. "But it was you who took it." He smiled. "Who are you, by the way?"

"I apologize. Jacob Halperin from Vilna. Surgeon. Captain in the reserve."

"From Vilna. So you are a Litvak. I am only a poor Galician."

This was merely traditional self-deprecation, and the rabbi, from his impressive height, from the impressive depth of his voice, laughed as he said it.

"Did you know that Moscow has given Vilna to Lithuania?"

"I was told, yes. All part of the great Soviet plan."

"It is dreadful, the new dismemberment of Poland. How long were we permitted to live in an independent country? After all the fighting and misery, less than twenty years. You may not have heard that they have also given Lwów to Ukraine, to the Ukrainian Soviet Socialist Republic. Lithuania hasn't yet been endowed with the dignity of a Soviet Socialist Republic, but no doubt very shortly it will be."

"I am sorry to hear about Lwów. I have never been there, but I have always heard it is a fine city, with a learned Jewish world within it, as in Vilna."

"Nothing in Lwów is as ancient as Vilna, but it is a lovely city, a Habsburg city, much fought over after the war. I studied at the university for several years. The city was good to me, kinder to Jews than Vienna, where I lived for a while as a boy. In the university in Lwów one in five of the students was a Jew, and probably more than one in five of the professors. But now I hear that the Ukrainians, with the Russians behind them naturally, are sacking the Polish professors and insisting that all teaching be done in Ukrainian—or, no doubt, in Russian. No Polish; no German. It's very sad. But probably worse things are happening, at least to Jews, in Warsaw and Cracow with Hitler in charge. Look at what was done to the Jews in Vienna two years ago. The city of Franz Josef—what would he think?"

"He would be horrified by Hitler."

"I remember when he died, the old emperor. To my parents' generation it seemed like the end of the world. In a way, I suppose it was, although the end of that world was really the war."

They stood in silence for a few minutes, watching the whole camp, where prisoners, alone or in groups of two or three, were walking, talking, moving aimlessly about.

"Have you been here since October?" the rabbi asked.

"Yes. It was much worse to begin with because there were twice as many men here. They let the other ranks go in November."

"That was also what happened at Starobelsk, the first prison the Russians put me in."

"Where is it?"

"Difficult to say exactly. They move you about in closed trains. It's in Ukraine, hundreds of miles south of here, towards the Black Sea. It's another sacked monastery, with two ruined churches, not nearly as large and grand as the church here, and other buildings, in rather better order than these. The food was a bit better too, and the climate of course milder. The winter must have been terrible here. Were prisoners dying of the cold?"

"Oddly enough, we've had hardly any deaths, and very little illness. But there's now serious malnourishment; an epidemic, of influenza or typhus, would make short work of the prisoners here."

They watched the prisoners for a minute or two.

Halperin asked, "Do you know why they moved you?"

"They moved all the chaplains—naturally there were many more priests than rabbis—out of Starobelsk just before Christmas. I imagine they didn't want the priests presiding over what they would have regarded as subversive demonstrations. I was in trouble in any case for organizing services, to which, to my surprise, gentiles came as well as Jews: prayers for Poland; psalms in Polish; readings from the Tanakh, which after all we share—that kind of thing. I don't know what happened to the priests. They took me to Moscow."

"To a prison?"

"Yes."

Halperin waited to see whether the rabbi wanted to expand on this. Had he been beaten? Tortured? Possibly. Halperin didn't look at him.

"I got into more trouble there. One week, a young guard, a Jewish boy, was bringing me my gruel every day, disgusting it was. I was alone in a very small cell—moss on the walls from the damp, no window. The second day, I asked him if he could bring me more water, and he did, which may have been difficult. The third day, he told me about himself. He had joined the Party at fourteen, along with his older brother. They came from a poor family—the mother widowed, no doubt delighted to have her boys in smart uniforms, going to summer camps, coming back fit and well fed, you can imagine. He was reasonably intelligent and literate, with a standard Jewish elementary education. He had absorbed like blotting paper the Party line on the revolution and the workers' state, and the abolition of property as the abolition of poverty, all that, so he found himself drafted into the NKVD and was sent to Moscow to guard prisoners. But he also had to take them down to be interrogated, bullied, and tortured to inform against their friends and families. He watched people obviously inventing names to satisfy interrogators and then being beaten until they collapsed, even died. He couldn't bear it. He cried when he was describing what he'd seen. He asked me what he should do. What could I say? He was nineteen years old, twenty at most. I told him that for his mother's sake he shouldn't make any sort of protest but see if he could find a way to change his work in the prison, volunteer for the least popular job—cleaning latrines, emptying slop buckets, whatever no one wanted to do. He thought that was a coward's way out. He wanted to tell them that they were wicked men and that he refused to be associated with what they were doing. I begged him not to."

He stopped, his eyes looking across the distant further wall of the prison to the blue sky above the forested hills.

"I didn't see him again. Two days later I was sent for. An NKVD colonel enjoyed telling me I had corrupted a fine young Communist, a commissar in the making, destroyed years of political consciousness-raising—what a phrase, by the way. The boy had deviated from the correct path and had therefore been shot."

Another pause.

"I was to be sent back to the Polish reactionaries with whom I clearly belonged."

"I am sorry."

"I was the one they should have shot. Not that honest boy. Peace be upon him."

Silence, for a minute or two between them.

Halperin asked, "Has it occurred to you that what the colonel told you may not have been true?"

The rabbi looked at him, raised his hands to heaven, and dropped them again.

"Of course. I have a good deal of experience of the NKVD. It may not have been true. They may have beaten him and sent him somewhere else, not wanting to waste all that consciousness-raising. But I believed that colonel. Why would he lie about that poor boy? They usually lie for a reason, though often you don't understand it until later."

"Yes", Halperin said, thinking he would never know whether Zarubin's story about the released doctor was true, though if it were a lie he could see why Zarubin had told it. He said only, "The colonel might have lied to warn you against behaving like a rabbi anywhere else."

"I hadn't behaved like a rabbi. I gave the boy only practical advice. I tried to save him from foolhardy heroism."

"I know that. The colonel didn't."

The rabbi groaned. "I sometimes think we are all living in a nightmare. Don't you, Dr Halperin? One day soon, shall we wake up to find that the world has returned to everyday, ordinary reality? Where truth means something, and means the same thing to everyone?"

"I'm afraid that that reality has gone, perhaps forever. I have understood this only here. One has plenty of time to think in prison. For the Party, as for the Nazis—I have lived in Germany—truth is what they say it is. So the so-called truth becomes no more than an instrument of power."

The rabbi briefly laid an arm round Halperin's shoulders.

"Yes. But you and I know that truth is part of reality nonetheless."

The warmth of the gesture, demonstrating the rabbi's sense that the issue was not abstract but deeply personal, brought tears to the back of Halperin's throat.

"Whatever terrible damage", the rabbi went on, "the Nazis and the Party inflict on their own souls and the soul of every person they succeed in destroying as a person by making him an obedient part of the mass—a tiny part of the single, monstrous machine which does as it's told and does not question—they can't hurt the truth, because the truth is in God. 'The Lord reigns, the Lord reigned, the Lord shall reign for ever and ever.'"

The rabbi said this, the opening of the prayer most familiar to all Jews, in Hebrew.

Halperin let the words go into the spring morning as he thought about what the rabbi had said.

After some time he said, "Before I came here I had no idea that there was any connexion between the truth and God."

"You are a doctor. You were scientifically trained. It's very easy for scientists to assume that the only truth worthy of the name is something gradually assembled by human beings by means of trial and error, hypotheses and experiments. Over hundreds of years the process is gone through, and behold, the truth. But these are merely facts that have been assembled. They are no more than provisional. If further experiments reveal errors, these supposed facts will change. People assume, and have assumed for a long time now, that science makes unnecessary the idea of God, makes indeed the idea of God nothing but a false notion sustained by nostalgia or fear, something for women and children and the old.

What these people have not grasped is that without our God as Creator of a universe that is separate from himself, that is itself not divine, science would not have been able to make the astonishing progress we see. Scientists have been able to assemble their facts not because the universe is divine but because it is intelligible. It is created intelligible; we are created with understanding.

"And truth is something different from all that. We see it only partially, as we remember only partially, and often inaccurately. But we know that truth is there. All of it is nowhere but in God, just as judgement that is whole and not partial, not fallible, is only in God."

Halperin thought about this for longer.

"So without a sense of God—a confidence in God, perhaps I should say—we cannot have a sure sense of truth, or a sure confidence in judgement?"

"I would say so. Would you?"

"Now, yes, I think I would. A few weeks ago, I doubt if I would have been able to agree." He paused. "No, a few weeks ago, I would definitely not have been able to agree."

"These Polish officers—you will not be as familiar with them as I am. I have been attached to the army for eighteen years, and a number of them have become my friends. They can be extraordinarily narrow-minded, romantically devoted to Poland's glorious past, sentimental about their Christianity, very unpleasantly sure that Poland has what they've learned from the Germans to call 'the problem of the Jews'. On the other hand, some of them are among the best people I have ever met."

"Major Dobrowski was such a man. He spoke to me as if ..." Halperin searched for words. "As if he knew that it was possible for a Catholic and a Jew to share ... to share ..."

He wasn't sure what he was trying to say.

"An integrity before God that is the result of loyalty to a tradition?" the rabbi suggested.

"Something like that. But ..."

"The traditions are too different? No. Of course they are different, and there are things—especially one central thing, the answer to the question, who was Jesus?—in each tradition that the other will find alien, impossible, historically pernicious, until the end of time. But the quality of loyalty is the same in a faithful Jew and a faithful Christian.

And out of one tradition came the other. They cannot be separated. People who hate Jews—viscerally hate Jews to the point of wanting to be rid of them, like Hitler and his friends—also hate Christianity, though it may not be politically possible for them to admit it. Those who hate Christianity, Stalin and his friends, also hate believing Jews. And there's more than that. In theory Communism has abolished the category 'Jew'. In practice it will take a great deal more than some fine words about equality to abolish hatred of Jews in Russia."

For a minute or more they stood together in silence.

"You are a rabbi. For Dobrowski you said a Christian prayer."

"Exactly so."

"This wasn't the first time you have been the only figure of religious authority at a Christian deathbed?"

"By no means the first. Prison, you know, mixes up the habits, the labels, with which people are accustomed to think, which can make it a place not only of isolation but of moments of reconciliation also. That Christian prayer—the Our Father, Catholics call it—is a Jewish prayer, and God is the father of Christians and Jews. Jesus was a Jew, telling his followers how to pray—in the spirit of his fathers, we would say; in the spirit of his Father, they would say."

Halperin was deeply impressed. He looked up at the rabbi's face. The rabbi was standing beside him, quiet and relaxed, his still gaze looking across the buildings of the prison and the groups of prisoners walking in the spring morning, to the cloudless sky. It was obvious that what he had said was not new to him, that he had thought it out and come to these extraordinarily peaceful and constructive conclusions over, probably, years.

"But if that's so," Halperin said, "why has it been so difficult all this time, Jews and Christians, so much contempt and hatred?"

"Because people are full of contempt and hatred. Christians call it original sin, the universal tendency of human beings to break, to spoil, to cover in filth, what they are given. Look at how, through the prophets, God reproaches the Jews over and over again for their disloyalty, their ingratitude, their betrayal of the unseen God for anything that glitters. Christians are the same. They say they worship Jesus because he is God. But they do not do as he said; they do not do as he did. If they lived as good Christians and we lived as good Jews, there would not have been these horrors down the centuries.

282

"There are always a few who do live according to what they have received. That they live so is enough to show that what God has given to the Jews and what God gave through the Jews to the gentiles in Jesus—did you know that, in one of the prayers Christians say every day, God's revelation in Jesus is said to bring 'glory to your people Israel'?—have been blessings for the world. But those people are few. The best of these Polish officers are among them, as no doubt are also the best of the Litvaks with whom you grew up."

"It's not enough, is it? What I mean is, there aren't enough of them, good Jews, good Christians. What can a man do at a time like this?" Halperin waved an arm at the prison, the prisoners as they walked, gathered between buildings, dispersed—groups of men of different ages taken out of their lives, deprived of enough food, of clean clothes and hot water, of the possibility of getting rid of the lice that tortured them, without any promise or undertaking that they might one day be released.

"There is very little a man can do", the rabbi said. "In a world where devils are abroad, there is very little someone by himself can do. But not nothing. He can refuse the devils his fear. He can pay attention to God. That is not nothing. And in any case it is always true that God is to be met, not to be discussed, although Jews have never stopped discussing, for three thousand years."

A long silence between them.

"Thank you", Halperin said, "for Dobrowski's good death. And for talking as you have."

"If I have been of any help to you, I'm glad."

The groups of prisoners were thinning and walking in the direction of the huts, where the midday soup was waiting for them.

Halperin and the rabbi began to walk towards everyone else.

"You know," the rabbi said, "tomorrow is Purim. Do you remember Purim, from when you were a child?"

"Not properly. My father several times took me to synagogue on the High Holy Days, but we didn't observe the other festivals in my family. What I remember of Purim is a lot of noise in the Jewish quarter where we lived—children in fancy dress, drunks in the streets."

The rabbi laughed. "That I can easily believe. It always was a bit of a wild celebration, I suppose because Purim commemorates the deliverance of the Jews from persecution." He laughed again. "There have been such rescues, from time to time. The one remembered at Purim concerns Queen Esther and the wicked Haman. Esther was a Jewish queen of Persia; Haman wanted to kill all the Jews in the Persian empire. Esther outwits him in the story and saves the Jews. There is, I'm sorry to say, a fairly bloodthirsty ending. The story is read at Purim, and children have a lot of fun shouting every time Haman's name is mentioned and rattling rattles. Haman is one of the devils let loose on the world. I doubt if the children in Germany and in Hitler's part of Poland will be allowed to shout and shake their rattles tomorrow. Jews drawing attention to themselves is dangerous at present.

"Tomorrow is also Easter Sunday for Catholics, the holiest day in the Christian year. With no priests they won't be able to make much of a celebration in the prison. And in the Soviet Union it's no safer for Christians than it is for Jews to draw attention to their religion. When I was with the army in Grodno a few years ago, a Polish officer I knew went home on leave to Belorussia and was shot because he had a rosary in his pocket. Your friend the major would have felt himself blessed to die on Easter Eve."

"I hope he knew."

"God knew."

They reached the door of one of the food huts.

"This is mine", Halperin said.

The rabbi chuckled, a deep, warm chuckle. "The day before Purim is a fast day. There's no problem observing a fast here, as there wouldn't have been a problem for the Catholics yesterday, on Good Friday. Where shall we all be this time next year, I wonder, when these holy days come round again? Well, whatever happens to us, they surely will come round again. Now I must find my own bowl of soup. Good-bye, Dr Halperin. It has been good to talk."

Ten days later, as had happened in November, a list of names was shouted out through a guard's loud-hailer after the early morning roll call outside the church. It was a very short list, only eight names. It was over so quickly that Halperin, and no doubt hundreds of others, faced the disappointment of not being on the list only a minute or two after it had been read out. The eight had been instructed, as the ordinary soldiers had been in November, to gather all their possessions together and go to the main gate of the camp.

Halperin soon saw that the eight summoned from the church were among the few older men who were not living in other, more comfortable buildings. They were slower than the ordinary soldiers had been to reach the gate: they had, by now, more possessions than the ordinary soldiers had had, though still very few; and convinced, because of the precedent, that they were about to be released, they were finding their friends to say good-bye to, and to encourage with assurances that if they were being freed, surely everyone else soon would be.

Outside there were more farewells, more embraces, slapping of backs and handshakes. It was soon clear that fifty or sixty prisoners altogether had been summoned—not the generals and the admiral, whom Halperin by now knew by sight though not by name, but the oldest of the professors, the doctors, the lawyers, who had joined the reserve either years ago to be part of Pilsudski's campaign against Russia or in the last year or two, like Halperin, to support Poland in what had seemed likely to be another hour of need. When ten or a dozen more prisoners appeared in clean, rumpled uniforms, kept for the moment of release and which now, after months of near starvation, were too big, the rest shouldered their kit bags and went back to their sleeping quarters to change.

This all took some time. When the departing officers were assembled inside the gate, in three ranks, with guards, looking sloppy in comparison with the prisoners, at the ends of each rank, the commandant appeared, not this time on his office steps with a loud-hailer but in front of them on the grass. Five NKVD officers surrounded him, among them—Halperin saw from well back in the crowd—Major Zarubin. A commissar read out all the names of the chosen prisoners, with each man saluting as he heard his own name. The commandant watched, a self-satisfied smile on his face.

After a pause intended to be dramatic, he spoke, loudly, looking over their heads. "Gentlemen," he said, "it is my pleasure to inform you that you have been selected for release this morning. Some provisions for your journey will be given to you as you leave the camp. I wish you good fortune."

He saluted. They saluted. He and his entourage turned and marched untidily back to his headquarters building, the crowd of watchers parting for them. The prisoners who were leaving turned as the gates in the wall were opened, and disappeared one by one, collecting as they went a packet, presumably of bread and perhaps more, which a kitchen orderly was handing out from a pushcart by the gate. They were gone.

Buzzing with excitement and speculation like a disturbed swarm of bees, the remaining prisoners milled about the camp in groups, every man able to say how much he hoped this was the beginning of a process of clearing the entire prison, no one, with the Poles' customary good manners, saying how much he hoped his own name would be on the next list.

Halperin, as usual by himself, walked to the distant opposite wall of the camp and stood by Dobrowski's grave, the replaced earth still fresh and a plain wooden cross at the head with his name and the dates 1879–1940 neatly branded on the wood. He had stayed away from the burial, not wanting to upset any of the Catholics by his presence, and he was glad that the place chosen was not under the same length of wall as the monk's grave he had stumbled on.

Poor Dobrowski. He might so easily have lived to go home, to see his wife again. Perhaps his son was at this moment, if he was alive, in a different Russian prison; perhaps he also would be freed to go home. And his daughter, the violin student in Moscow hoping to meet David Oistrakh—how would she learn of her father's death? He stood at the foot of the grave and prayed for them all. How simple, how obvious, it now seemed, to pray.

In the days that followed, the pattern of that morning, Wednesday, 3 April, was repeated. Many more prisoners, impossible to count but probably between two and three hundred, were released on Thursday, and about the same number on Friday.

The atmosphere in the prison was feverish. It now seemed evident that the Russians had decided to clear the camp. In tense silence the prisoners listened as the names of those to be released were called. Everyone no doubt did his best to be, as well as to seem, pleased for those on the list and to hide his own disappointment that he was not.

On Saturday morning there was no list. Was this the end of the release? Were all those not summoned, the great majority of the prisoners, condemned to the dateless confinement they had more or less got used to? If so, it was now going to be much harder to bear.

Then, on Saturday evening, the news spread rapidly through the camp that the most senior officers—the generals, the admiral, various brigadiers and a number of colonels—had been invited to what was called a "reception" in the headquarters building. As Halperin went to supper in his hut, he saw some of them, looking old and thin but as smart as they could manage, on their way to this ... what? Farewell party? Occasion of congratulation for the good behaviour of the prisoners? Ironic dismissal of any independent future for the Polish army? Possibly all of these. Halperin had never got the impression that the commandant was personally cruel.

The following morning fifty of the remaining prisoners formed a guard of honour for the departing senior officers, and all the rest stood in silence to salute them as they left. There was fear in the camp that day. Would the hundreds of remaining prisoners be forgotten, left where they were, or sent to Siberia, because their leaders, their spokesmen, with the weight to defend their interests, had all gone?

But on Monday morning the list after roll call was long. Fear subsided. The NKVD were clearing the camp.

That night Halperin couldn't sleep. The few minutes of silence that he had learned to value so much had disintegrated over the last five nights; tonight it hadn't even begun. No doubt it had failed partly because the loudspeakers hadn't been switched on at all for four evenings—someone had clearly decided that there was no longer any point in hectoring the prisoners with propaganda to which for so many months they had paid no attention—and the silent time had therefore lost its beginning. But the half hour when they were settling to sleep had changed in any case since last Wednesday; how much of their prayer had been almost hopeless hope? And now release was close, almost certainly closer every day for everyone left in the church. How much of their prayer, then, had been simply selfish?

The question upset him, as if he had been a child. Before he tried to answer it he set himself to dismiss, as even more childish, his conviction, which had been developing ever since Wednesday, that because tomorrow, 9 April, was his birthday, it was bound to be the day on which his name was called.

He lay on his bunk, wide awake, pleased that the bunk beneath him was now empty so that he could turn or shift his position on the creaking planks without having to try not to wake the man below. Although the two men had slept stacked one above the other since November, they had made almost no connexion; the other man was a lawyer, a reserve officer of about his own age, unfriendly. A formal nod of recognition if they met anywhere in the camp was the most he had ever given Halperin. Perhaps he found it difficult to have to sleep in such close proximity to a Jew. Now he had gone. Now he was free.

What was going on, round a table in the headquarters building over there, when the commandant and Major Zarubin and whoever else—perhaps a powerful NKVD officer sent from Moscow—decided who was to be on the next list? Apart from the choice of the generals and other senior officers who had been released on Sunday, there was no detectable reason for one prisoner rather than another finding himself on the list. Reason: wasn't the Party supposed to be a wholly rational enterprise? He felt furious to be at the mercy of pure arbitrariness; weren't they sitting round that table laughing as they knocked back their little glasses of vodka, and pricking names with a pin?

His fury had dealt with the idea that his equally arbitrary birthday was of any significance whatever. That left him with the question of whether prayer was, after all—as his father had always said—no more than a way of dealing with fear or pain or anxiety that delivered spurious encouragement. He bit the knuckle of his index finger to stop himself from groaning aloud.

He tried to remember why, only days ago, he had been certain that prayer was much more than this. Did that conviction that prayer meant much that was important, even essential to a sane life, really have any connexion with the commitment to the truth into which he had fallen, or thought he had fallen, during his interview with Zarubin in Father Zosima's hermitage? Hadn't it rather been merely stupid of him to think that commitment to the truth should outweigh advantage? Shouldn't he have had the speed of reaction to put himself at least on an equal intellectual footing with Zarubin, with equal potential for deceit, manipulation, power? Wasn't his failure to achieve such equality after all no more than his habitual pride in his own self-sufficiency, a fastidious and arrogant refusal to be mixed up in the lies of the NKVD? If that were so, he was the fool.

The fool has said in his heart there is no God. Or the fool has said in his heart there is God. Which?

And now none of it mattered anyway, since all the prisoners were, as far as anyone could tell, going to be released.

But wasn't it merely utilitarian to suppose that, even in prison, release or no release was the only question? Yes. There were questions that mattered more, much more. And the question that mattered most of all was the one he just asked. Which is the fool? Or, to put the question differently: whether or not the whole truth is somewhere, so in God, mattered infinitely, as it had mattered to the old rabbi, his father's friend, and as it clearly had mattered to Dobrowski, who had died before he could go home. He knew that it was because it mattered so much to Dobrowski that his death in the camp among strangers had not seemed even sad. Did that absence of sadness, that sense of a fitting peace, have something to do with the presence of Rabbi Steinberg and his strength, his confession on behalf of the dying man, his prayer for the safety of Dobrowski's Christian soul? How could he tell?

Then he remembered Dobrowski over the guttering candles saying something like, "You will lose it and find it again. Pay attention. That's all you can do." And he returned in his mind to Dobrowski's grave, where he had known for sure, as he knew now, that Dobrowski was not nowhere, had not been blown out like the dying candle, was not just the decaying body in the spring earth under the simple cross that would be pulled up and used for firewood by whoever next occupied the Maxim Gorky Rest Home.

He went to sleep, was woken by the siren at six in the morning, pulled on his clothes, and went outside for the roll call. The roll call took, as it had always taken, half an hour at least. Everyone stood, absolutely still, absolutely quiet, to hear the second list. Among about thirty others, his name was shouted out. He laughed with relief. He was on the list. He was to be freed today, this morning. He laughed also because it was his birthday and it had been after all a lucky day. He jostled his way back to his bunk among the others, who were laughing and talking, and pulled out his summer uniform, which had been for months rolled up in his kit bag. It looked terrible. He shook out the creases as best he could, put on the uniform, packed everything else, little enough, and his violin, into his kit bag, hoisted it onto his back, and with his Russian coat over his arm, patted the boards of his bunk in farewell and went back outside to wait.

A friendly guard had told someone days ago that the prisoners released each morning had to walk, not far, along the road they had walked in the dark in October, to the railway station at Kozelsk, where a prison train was waiting for them. This sounded bad, but the guard had said, "Don't worry. All the trains are going west." Towards Poland. Towards home.

They waited for an hour or so. It was raining, a mild spring rain; the growing daylight was soft and grey. No one minded getting wet. A few of those on the list smoked the cigarettes they had hoarded for weeks or months in case this moment ever came.

The commandant had stopped making speeches to departing prisoners after the first two days, so no ceremony of any kind marked the moment when a dozen guards appeared, and two of them unbolted the main gates in the wall.

While they were waiting Halperin had gone over to the top step at the church door to make a rough count of those who were being released—about two hundred, he thought. As he joined the back of the crowd heading for the gate, he was pleased to see ahead of him the tall figure of Rabbi Steinberg.

Each released prisoner was checked against a list by a guard as he went through the gate, and given a grey paper packet from the kitchen pushcart by an orderly. In the packet was a chunk of bread, two rolled-up pickled herring, and half an onion, the onion not even soft and mouldy, as was usually the case.

He looked back from the line, just before he was handed his packet, and saw Major Zarubin watching from the headquarters building, which had a light over its door. He was too far away to see the expression on his face.

It was shortly after nine o'clock on the morning of 9 April 1940 that Halperin left the camp. It stopped raining. The sky cleared. In weak sunshine the prisoners walked along an old, stony road, grass just beginning to look green between the ruts made by cart wheels. There were crows stalking about in the wet fields, not yet ploughed, and here and there smaller birds flying as if just unfrozen after the long winter. Guards led and followed the column, and half a dozen walked with the prisoners, but there was no attempt to make them march.

After half an hour they reached a small town, clearly Kozelsk, old, not prosperous, with a fine-looking church, its windows boarded up, and some two-storey buildings in the centre but on the edges low peasant houses with straw roofs—each in its little plot, some neat, some neglected—set back, behind picket fences in fair or bad repair, from unpaved roads with stinking ditches on each side. Women and children watched the prisoners go by from many of the open doors. A few of them waved. A handful of ragged boys tagged along with the column,

jumping and dancing, showing off but also both begging and mocking—
"Polish lords! Polish lords! Anything for us, Polish lords?" A prisoner
walking ahead of Halperin threw them a handful of coins, over which
they gathered and bickered like pigeons thrown a handful of corn.

They crossed a marketplace with stalls, barrows, tethered goats, live
geese and hens tied by the legs, strings of onions, baskets of turnips and
beetroot, and bundles of kindling from the forest. Halperin breathed
in the smell of animals, earth on fresh vegetables, Russian tobacco, and
relished the sounds of women arguing, small children playing in the dirt,
hawkers shouting their prices. He was struck for the first time by what
being freed from prison meant.

At the railway station on the far side of the town a prison train was
waiting. There were seven prison wagons, no locomotive. Halperin
thought he had prepared himself for this, for the familiar stench and
darkness of closed wagons, buckets, and jostling among the prisoners to
get close to slatted panels for a breath of air, a glimpse of the day, of the
country, some sense of the direction in which the train was travelling.
But after the pleasures of the walk along the rough road and through
the market, the disappointment was sharp. He had seen his mother and
brother die on such a train; he and hundreds of his fellow officers had
been herded into such a train six months ago. Twice was enough. In his
wagon, where there was at least rather more space than there had been
on both the other trains, and small barred windows rather than slats, he
looked for the rabbi, but he must have been in another wagon.

Nearly three hours went by before the train moved. The prisoners
grumbled, ate some of the food they had been given, saving the rest for
who knew what or when, and made no noisy protest; each man, no
doubt, was afraid, as Halperin was, of doing anything that might get the
decision to release them reversed. Some went to sleep, their heads on
their kit bags.

At last there was the sound of an engine approaching and then stopping, and a series of jolts as a locomotive was hitched to the train. They
left the Kozelsk station. Everyone in Halperin's wagon relaxed, smiled.
The first stage of their journey home had been achieved, without some
irrational cancellation from the NKVD, without anyone getting lost or
shot or taken back to the prison between guards.

The train travelled very slowly and often stopped, sometimes for as
much as an hour, while they waited in a siding so that an ordinary train,

what Halperin thought of as a real train, could pass them at a reasonable speed. Night fell. They finished their food, were careful with the water—of which there wasn't much left in the barrel—and lay down to sleep as far away as they could get from the now-almost-full buckets.

When Halperin finally woke properly, after an airless, restless night that several times had him longing for the draughts from the broken windows of the church, the train had stopped in a large station. Other trains were coming and going, hooting, shunting. There were shouts and the clink of hammers testing wheels. Everyone in the wagon woke. Someone standing beside a window, although it was still dark, said, "Smolensk. I recognize the station. And there are lights. Well, at least that proves we're going in the right direction."

Halperin looked at his watch. It was too dark to tell the time. Someone struck a match and said, "Just after four." Several people groaned. Too much of the night was left.

After half an hour, during which a few of the prisoners had managed to go back to sleep, the train set off again. It trundled along, as slowly as ever, for twenty minutes, twenty-five, thirty-five, and then stopped. Here there were no lights, nothing to be seen through the windows. But almost at once, a loud Russian voice was shouting, over and over from outside, along the length of the train, "All prisoners out of the train. Now. All prisoners out of the train. Now."

They fumbled in the dark for their kit bags, their coats, their boots if they had taken them off to sleep. The doors were opened from outside—crash, crash. They had to jump down to the cinders of the track, one man after the other, clumsily, as quickly as they could. NKVD officers with big torches were shouting and waving the torches to indicate where they had to go. The train had stopped in a siding at a country halt on what, because there were two parallel railway tracks, was clearly still the main line, the main line to the west because there was a faint grey suggestion of dawn in the sky in the direction from which they had come.

The only building appeared to be a wooden hut with two doors and a window on each side of the doors. A plank above the doors had painted on it in crude Russian capital letters GNEZDOVO, presumably a village that happened to be on the railway line. They couldn't have travelled more than ten or twelve miles from Smolensk.

NKVD soldiers, in smarter uniforms than those worn by the camp guards the prisoners were used to, herded them into a loose group in the station yard. Another roll call, their names read in alphabetical order. One by one, they answered to their names. Halperin heard the rabbi's name read out: "Steinberg, Baruch". He tried to see where the reply came from, but beyond the beams of half a dozen torches it was too dark.

Because he was close to the centre of the group he could, however, see that beside the officer reading and marking the list, pen in one hand, clipboard in the other, stood a junior officer directing a torch at the list, and on the other side an older figure, watching the prisoners, his hands relaxed, torch in one, revolver in the other. When he saw the gun, Halperin for the first time for months was really afraid.

After the roll call, nothing happened, for ten, for fifteen, minutes. The morning, chill in the April dawn, grew lighter. A few of the prisoners began quietly talking. "I don't like the look of this." "Do you think they're taking us to a labour camp?" "So far west? Surely not." "Then where?" "God knows." A young prisoner in front of Halperin, not much more than twenty years old, was shivering and biting his nails.

The sound of motors approaching. Two prison vans—"black crows", he knew they were called in Russia—were driven into the station yard, and stopped. Guards jumped down and unfastened the back doors of the vans by lifting the heavy bars that sealed them. The senior NKVD man walked forward. Standing in front of the crowd of prisoners to Halperin's right, he waved his gun in the direction of the black vans. "Fifteen!" he yelled. "And fifteen more. Now!" Some prisoners stepped forward. Fifteen and then fifteen more were counted into the backs of the vans. The doors were shut, barred. The vans were driven away.

The prisoners in the yard looked at each other. Silence, broken by a hard laugh—the senior NKVD officer bending down to hear something said to him by the man who had taken the roll call.

For half an hour, nothing. Some sat down and lit cigarettes. Over the fields beyond the station yard small birds were singing, as on the morning before. The sound of the prison vans returning. Halperin and one or two others moved so as to be at the front of the crowd from which the prisoners had been taken for the vans. Get it over with, whatever it was.

Again, fifteen and fifteen. He was in the second group. The inside of the van was foul, sticky with dirt, stinking, pitch-dark. The van rattled along a road, shaking them as it jolted over ruts and potholes. Beside Halperin sitting squashed on the floor of the van someone was shaking with sobs.

The van stopped. A pause. Then the bar over the doors was lifted with a clang, the doors opened, and they half-jumped, half-tumbled to the ground. The sobbing prisoner didn't move until Halperin took him by the hand and pulled him. He fell to his knees on the ground. Halperin took him by the arm and pulled him upright. He was the boy who had been biting his nails in the station yard. His face was just visible in the dawn light. He wiped his nose with the back of his hand, shook his head to pull himself together, and looked at Halperin with terrified eyes.

"I'm sorry", he said.

"Take a slow, deep breath", Halperin said. The boy obeyed. "That's better. And again."

They were in a grassy clearing in the forest. More birds. Two NKVD guards began to search them roughly, one by one, taking money if they had any. Each of them had to put his kit bag on the ground and open it. A guard kicked Halperin's kit bag, hit something hard—his violin—picked up the kit bag, flung it onto a pile, and then ran his hands down Halperin's sides and pulled open his collar. Nothing. The same guard kicked the boy's kit bag, left it on the ground, ran his hands down his sides, pulled open his collar, and grabbed a silver chain. The boy's hand went to his throat and clutched a small crucifix on the chain. The guard shrugged and let it go.

Then, not far away, a volley of shots, two or three cries, more shots.

Halperin was for a moment enraged by the elaborate deception, organized and carried out to keep them quiet. They were soldiers. They deserved to know when their courage was required.

The boy looked at Halperin again, his eyes calmer. He crossed himself.

"That's right", Halperin said. "They can kill us. They can't hurt us."

The clearing was in the forest of Katyn.

Epilogue

His letter, when it came, several weeks later than she had hoped, was not in his handwriting.

My dear,
You will see that I am not anymore in my flat and that I am not myself able to write this letter. A kind nurse here where I am is writing to you for me.

The address, printed at the top of the letter, was of a nursing home in Kensington.

I have had last month a stroke, not so bad, the doctors say, but bad enough that my right side does not work so well. Actually it works not at all. Very fortunately I am able to speak and, thanks be to God, am able also to read. So I have read many times your new story, the story of my father in Kozelsk. It is marvellous, what you have told of his last months in this life, and that I can believe what you have told of him is marvellous also. May he rest in peace. May they all rest in peace.
If it would soon be possible for you to come to see me here, this would be your last goodness to me, a great goodness.
With my many, many thanks,

J. H.

His initials were written badly, as if by a small child, so probably with his left hand.

On the morning she received the letter, she telephoned the nursing home and asked if it would be all right to visit him the following day.

"Of course. Are you a relative?"

"A friend. An old friend." They had met only that once. Nevertheless, in various ways, this was true.

"I see. You understand, he's very frail. But I'm sure he would enjoy a short visit. The afternoon would be best. His granddaughter sometimes comes in the evening."

"Thank you. Does he—do you allow flowers?"

"By all means. This is a private nursing home."

It was the last week of March, but the spring was late. In the grey, chilly streets north of Holland Park Avenue, with their expensive houses and expensive cars, the trees were still bare. Here and there the blossom on cherry trees looked pinched by the cold. She had bought him, in a flower shop near the tube station, two bunches of yellow tulips.

The nursing home was a large, grey Victorian house, the white stucco freshly painted, with tall trees in what looked like a big garden at the back.

"Mr Halpern?"

"Second floor. Number 12. There's a lift just past the stairs."

"The stairs are fine. Do you know how he is?"

"You'd better ask the nurse on the second floor."

"Thank you."

This was not the person she had spoken to on the telephone.

On the wide second-floor landing were a desk, two telephones, a computer, a lot of paper—but no nurse.

She looked at the doors, all closed. Shiny brass numbers—"12". His name was typed on a card in a brass frame, a neater version of the name beside the doorbell of his flat.

She knocked. Silence.

Very gently, she opened the door. He was asleep in a chair beside his bed, breathing quietly, very pale, a blanket over his knees and a shawl round his shoulders. He had a small white beard, neatly trimmed. She thought how much older than his father he had lived to become. More than twice as old.

The room was spacious, comfortable, very warm, as unlike a room in a hospital as it could be made, though on a white trolley were labelled boxes of tablets, a jug, a bowl, a thermometer, and other bits of medical apparatus. A sheaf of notes and charts was clipped to the foot of the bed. On the bed was a faded eiderdown, paisley chintz. Someone had fetched it from his flat. His granddaughter? A copy of that day's *Guardian*, untidy because it's difficult to fold a newspaper with one hand, was on his lap.

She shut the door. He didn't wake.

"Joe?" she said.

He opened his eyes. She stood without moving, facing the window so that he could see her clearly.

It took him a few moments to focus, to recognize her. He smiled, his smile crooked, the right side of his face not moving.

"You have come. That you would come I knew. And you bring tulips. Tulips I love. Come nearer." He held out his left hand. "I cannot move—as you see." The newspaper slipped to the floor.

She put the tulips in the sink, still wrapped in the florist's cellophane, dropped her bag on the floor, and took his hand in both of hers. Then she kissed him on the forehead.

"I'm so glad to see you", she said.

She had not forgotten his black eyes. They were undimmed.

"Still alive, yes. For how long, who knows? One arm and one leg I cannot move. And my right hand not at all. It is surprising how little is left that it is possible to do with one arm and one leg only."

"I'm so sorry."

She picked up the *Guardian*, straightened and folded it, and put it on his bed.

"No," he said, "do not be sorry. This is good. There could not be much time left, could there, by now, for me? And here, look ..."

He waved at the room with his left arm.

"There is a large garden for me to watch outside my window: daffodils, which soon will flower; pigeons; singing birds early in the morning. And sometimes even the sun does shine. But sit down, my dear child, sit down."

Did he know who she was? Of course he did. "My dear child" was truly for her. She took off her coat and sat in another high-backed armchair, facing his.

"How did—" she began.

"How was I rescued? Good luck again. The good luck of all my life, which you so well know. Or the God of Abraham, Isaac, and Jacob, kind enough to give me a little time to die."

He laughed.

"No, this is too grand an explanation for me. Let us stick to luck. It is a Tuesday I have the stroke. Ona comes, always she comes on Tuesdays, and there I am, on the floor. The kettle also is on the floor, which I would fill for coffee. If the stroke would come on a Wednesday or a Thursday, no doubt I will be dead. Then there was the ambulance.

Then the hospital. Then this room, so very fine, so very expensive. My son, you remember, is a rich man. And it is not necessary for me to feel guilty for him to pay these vast bills. I shall not be getting cured, the doctors say. They do not say that I shall not be living long. This I know myself. So my son will be selling my flat, my dear flat where I have been so long happy. He tells me it is worth a quantity of money I find it impossible to believe. But about such things he knows."

"And do you have good nurses? Are they kind to the patients?"

"They are kind to me. I have seen no other patients. One of these nurses ... perhaps you will meet her. Ah, I know—tea. You would like some tea?"

He pressed a bell that was resting on the arm of his chair.

"They make good tea, in a teapot, and they bring shortbread. I did not know shortbread till I was here, after fifty-eight years in England. Can you believe that? Coffee they do not understand."

A nurse came in, perhaps Filipino, middle-aged, with a friendly face.

"Mr Halpern, how are you today?"

"Carmen, good afternoon. I am very well, thank you. This is my old friend. She comes to London from far in the country to see me."

"With beautiful flowers. Would you like some tea, madam?"

"Please. That would be very nice."

Carmen left the room, not shutting the door, and returned a moment later with a pottery jug full of water. She unwrapped the tulips, took the rubber bands off the bunches, arranged the flowers so well that they looked like tulips in a Dutch still-life, and took away the cellophane and rubber bands saying she would be back soon with tea.

"You see, I am looked after very well."

"Is she the nurse you said ...?"

"No. I will tell you, when we have our tea. You know, when you cannot move at all, the cup of tea is an important event, a thing much to look forward to."

He smiled at her again.

"But your coming—that is a really important event. And your tulips—look at them there. They are so friendly, so golden. Thank you for them."

She turned to look. Carmen had put them on the white chest of drawers facing his bed and his chair, under a harmless blue painting of sea and sky, chosen by someone to be soothing.

The door opened again, and Carmen, pushing the door with her knee, reappeared with a tray: tea, milk, cups, sugar, a plate of shortbread, pretty china, white paper napkins. She put down the tray on the small table between their chairs.

"Thank you so much. That looks perfect."

"Do you need anything, Mr Halpern?"

"Thank you, Carmen. I will press the bell if I do."

After the door had shut, again he smiled.

"You know what she asked? Of course. I need help with everything."

She poured two cups of tea.

"Milk?"

"No milk. On the question of tea I returned to being a foreigner many years ago. Sugar, yes. Two lumps. Thank you."

She stirred his tea and put the cup and saucer at the corner of the tray where he could reach it easily with his left hand. She put a piece of shortbread on the saucer.

"So", he said.

He sipped his tea, cautiously because the right side of his mouth was paralysed. Cautiously he put his cup back on its saucer, wiped his mouth with a napkin.

He looked across the tray at her, his black eyes serious, his face still.

"How is it possible for me to believe what you have written of my father's last time in Kozelsk? The end time of his life? It will not be possible. This I thought for several days. Then I thought, how can it be possible for me not to believe? That is when I wrote, or my nurse Mira wrote, the letter to you. And I do now believe although neither I nor you will ever know exactly the details of what took place for him there. I do now believe what you have written because I believe that you have understood what my father was. He was careful—he stood back always, from so much. Always he wished to be himself sure before he agreed with the opinion of someone else. Always the conclusion he reached had to be his own. He was—there is a good English word—noncommittal. But always also he paid attention. He listened. He listened so well that as a child I would stop talking when his listening made me hear that my words were not after all making the meaning I intended to make. His friends had this experience also—I was old enough before he left in his uniform to notice that his friends would sometimes stop saying what they were trying to say because of the quality of his listening. There are not so many men like him."

He laughed, picked up his piece of shortbread, and took a bite. The left side of his mouth worked perfectly well.

"Very good, the shortbread. What a strange name—not bread, not short. This is typical of English, no? Like shortcake biscuits, which were favourite always in my shop—not cake, not short. But with most elegant scroll edges." He smiled, then put down his shortbread.

"No, there are not so many men like my father. In such a respect I am not like him myself. He did not care to please, and he did not care not to please, whoever was the other person. On the other hand, I try to please—too much, I think. Perhaps it is from so many years of pretending to be an Englishman. The English like to please. Or perhaps it is from so many years of selling things to people who actually might or might not want them. Would you try the shortbread?"

She shook her head.

"I couldn't." She sipped her tea. "But you're right. Their tea is very good."

He smiled again, his new, crooked smile.

"I am glad you are here. There is much I would want to say to you, you know, but my mind . . . it is not organized."

"I think your mind is in very good order."

"Do you? Well, it may manage a little longer. What am I trying to explain for you? Ah, yes." He paused. "You understand my father I think very well. So you understand the impression on him—the effect on him, I should say—of the people, whoever they might have been, that he would have met in the prison. It has not been possible for me . . ."

He stopped. He picked up his cup, but his hand was shaking and he put the cup down again, rattling it a little on the saucer. She saw tears in his eyes. He couldn't reach the box of tissues on the locker on his right, between his chair and his bed. She stood, took a tissue from the box, and gave it to him. He wiped his eyes, blew his nose, crumpled the tissue in his hand.

"Thank you. I am sorry."

"No. What is it?"

"It was—it is—the commissar. If my father would have been less brave—less himself, I think you would say—could he have agreed just a little to work for the NKVD? Could he therefore have come home to us, even for the time before the Germans came, a short time but actually more than one year? If he had done that, if it had been possible, my mother and my sister would not then have been taken to the exile train. So our family, for more than one year, could have ... and for that year we would not have known that the Germans would come, and so ..."

The tears were now too much for him. She gave him another tissue, putting the first in the lidded bin by the sink.

"I am so sorry", she said. "This is my fault. I shouldn't have raised that hope. It may not have been so. It may have been very different."

"No." He sniffed, long and hard, closed his eyes for a moment, opened them, and smiled at her. "No, it is I who should be sorry. You are right. You were right. What you guessed for him was right. If such an offer had been given to him, his reply would have been as you guessed. The truth for him was the most important. He would not have chosen the lie, even for more time with us—my mother, my sister, me. He would not have chosen it, even for the years that would have been if the Germans had not come—most of all for these years, because the lie would in these years have become heavier, all the time heavier, as the wise Polish officer did tell him."

She finished her tea, poured some more into her cup. She offered to pour him some more. He shook his head.

"You know," she said, "I don't think you are so different from your father. When the secret service wanted you to be a spy for them, you also refused."

"Ah", he laughed, restored. "No, that was not the same, not the same at all. That was my luck, which all this time I have found and never have deserved. Do you perhaps know what happened to the spies the British sent into Lithuania and Estonia after the war? I read in the newspaper not so long ago that they were betrayed, all betrayed. Mr Philby betrayed them. They were dropped, with their parachutes, and the partisans waiting there for them were not partisans at all but the NKVD. So my luck did save me. But also my fear. I did not refuse for the same reasons as my father—for courage or for the truth—but because I was afraid. So not the same."

He closed his eyes again.

"I am tiring you", she said. "Would you like me to go?"

"No. No, stay, please. There is more I have hoped ... but now ..."

He pressed his bell.

"You will excuse me a few minutes?"

"Of course."

As she left the room, Carmen appeared, smiled, went in, and closed the door.

There was now a nurse sitting at the desk in the corridor, younger than Carmen, serious looking, typing something at the computer keyboard, looking backwards and forward between the screen and some written notes.

"Excuse me. May I ask you about Mr Halpern?"

Without stopping what she was doing, the nurse said, "One moment." After a minute or two she stopped, looked up, pushed her spectacles up her nose.

"Yes? Are you a relative?"

"No, an old friend. Can you tell me how he is?"

"You have seen him?"

"Yes."

"Well, then. The paralysis from the stroke is irreversible, I'm afraid. He didn't reach the hospital for several hours. And there's always the possibility, the likelihood even, of another stroke. He's receiving the correct medication, of course, but ..."

She shrugged, but also smiled, without much warmth.

"He is eighty-three, you know, and he admits to being a smoker all his life. We are keeping him comfortable."

"I'm sure you are, and I'm most grateful. Thank you."

Carmen emerged from his room, holding something covered by a cloth.

"Mr Halpern would like you to go back, madam."

"Thank you."

"Oh, very good", he said as she closed his door. "You are still here."

"I wouldn't have gone without saying good-bye."

"Ah, good-bye. Every morning, you know, I wake up and I am surprised. Surprised to be alive. All night I sleep like a dead man because they give me this sleeping pill. So every evening I try to think good-bye. In case I do not wake at all."

He looked out of the window, at the grey London garden, at the grey sky.

"Will the sun come today? Not, I think."

He turned his head back towards her, his black eyes amused rather than sad.

"What was I saying—yes, thinking good-bye. I find it is not so difficult. I am grateful, as I have so long been, to chance, to luck, to providence, whatever it might have been, and to kind people. So now I can say, as all my life I could not quite say, I thank God. That is thinking good-bye, is it not?"

She put her hand for a moment on his left hand, lying now on the blanket over his knees.

"Yes. It is."

Then she said, "Shall I move the tray? Have you had enough shortbread?"

He laughed.

"I have, for today. Perhaps forever. This is how now I think."

She tidied the tray, put it on the chest of drawers by the tulips, sat down again in her chair.

"Tell me about your nurse. Was her name Mira?"

"Ah, Mira. She is a lovely girl—not so much a girl. I suppose she is forty or so. Older, even. At first I thought she is an Arab, a refugee perhaps from Yemen or Somalia, where the times are cruel. But her English is too good. So it turns out she was born in England. She is an Iraqi Jewess. Yes. You are surprised? So was I."

"I had no idea that ... what is the story?"

"It is a terrible story. This is no surprise. Another terrible story of the terrible twentieth century. Is it not good that we have left this century? But of course, in many ways we have not. Can you give me a little water?"

A jug, a glass, on the other side of his bed.

"Thank you."

He gave her back the glass.

"She told me the story one afternoon when she was not so busy. Both her parents came to England as children in 1950. They were Jews of Mesopotamia, Jews of Babylon. There have been Jews in Babylon since the exile. Do you know when that was?"

"Only that it was a very long time ago."

"It was in the sixth century B.C.—a very long time ago, as you say. A very long time already before there were Christians, before there were Muslims. Then, for a thousand years after the fall of Jerusalem, Babylon was the centre of all Jewish life. Did you know that?"

She shook her head.

"Nor did I. Which is a disgrace to me. But then . . . Ashkenazi history is another thing. Sephardi history also is another thing. So Babylon was the Jerusalem of the east, as later was Vilna the Jerusalem of the north."

Tears in his eyes again. A tissue. He blew his nose.

"I am sorry. It is weakness now I have, after the stroke I suppose. Also from talking to you."

He smiled.

"Which I love to do of course. I will tell you Mira's story because no one knows it—like my own, you could say. Until now."

He smiled again.

"So. A hundred years ago a third of the people of Baghdad were Jews. Also like Vilna. Now there are seven Jews, Mira tells me, in Baghdad. Her father's family and her mother's family left in 1949, with many thousands of other Jews, because after all that long, long time of living in peace among Muslims they have become the enemy. Why? Because the Nazis have told the Arabs in Iraq that the Jews are vile and horrible. Also because the Arabs are now afraid of the so new, so aggressive Israel. So they begin to persecute their own Jews they have lived beside without hatred for hundreds and hundreds of years. Even there are pogroms. So Mira's father and mother and their families go to Israel. Where else? So they think. Mira's grandfathers were a doctor and a lawyer. But they arrive in Israel with nothing. Everything has been stolen from them in Baghdad as if by the Nazis themselves. They live in tents in a camp. They are not welcome. They look like Arabs. The Ashkenazim in Israel—Jews from Germany, Poland, Russia—do not much like the Spanish Jews, the Sephardim, from wherever they were scattered to, but the Jews from Baghdad and further east they actually despise, as the German Jews always would despise the Jews from Poland and Russia. You see, it is another story of loss, of hatred, of the pain of people grating against each other when there is no need. This horrible thing *ressentiment*, which Max Hofmann told me about. So these families with much difficulty come to England, where things are better."

"And now?"

"Now Mira is an English nurse. She has an English husband who is a doctor. He is not a Jew. She has English children. All is well. But in the street now in London she is sometimes shouted at, spat at even, because the people who shout and spit think she is a Muslim, and Muslims now are as Jews were. This is no better; it is the same. Ach. A little more water? Thank you."

"You're getting tired. Are you sure you wouldn't like me—"

"To go away? No. Please stay with me a little. Or you have other things you must do?"

"No, nothing. Of course I will stay."

"Thank you. Yes, I am tired. But soon I shall be sleeping. Altogether sleeping. So to be tired is good, not bad. It is not the ... it is not the saying good-bye which is sad for me. You understand? That an old man dies is not sad but even happy. No, it is the world I say good-bye to which makes me sometimes sad. If I had died twenty years ago, I should have been sure the world was better to leave than the world I was born to find, in Vilna in 1929, when no one could know the terrible things that were to come for Vilna, for Poland, for Europe. Twenty years ago there was much hope, much light after the dark—in Poland above all. Should I return? This I asked myself then. No. To Vilna? Certainly not. Then maybe to Poland? Also not. In Poland even after so many years a Jew who returns is not welcome; he might claim what was stolen from his family. And in Vilna ... shall I tell you something I read somewhere?"

She nodded.

"I read it last year, perhaps the year before. There is a stone in the Ponary forest, near to Vilna, the forest where I should have died. This stone is to remember the thousands and thousands of Jews who were killed there. This stone, last year or the year before, is painted with huge red swastikas and 'Hitler was right' in huge red letters. No one objects. Nothing in the Vilna newspapers. This I read. It is a shock, even now a shock. Every year there are Nazi marches in Vilna, even up till now. They are permitted, honoured even. So, no. I have been right not to return to Vilna. But for Poland, even for Lithuania, I am glad that they are part of Europe, where they have longed to be, and that Soviet soldiers, Soviet tanks have vanished, and Soviet spies and the informers they love and bribe and blackmail have also vanished. Or have changed, one might say. Because it is surely again as it was in Germany after the war: suddenly there were no Nazis. After the war, in the east of Germany where Stalin ruled, good Nazi policemen and soldiers became good Communist soldiers and policemen in one week, one day. My friend Werner in Yorkshire—you remember him? So now in Poland: suddenly there are no Communists. But it is wonderful that Poland now faces to the west, that Germany after all is now friendly. Poland and Germany, the countries of my parents. This new Europe—not simple can it ever be. Complicated but also good. I wish England could understand how good. But England's memories of the twentieth century are always too different. So English people only complain about Europe. And English politicians—they have no idea of the fears, of the hopes. They worry about the *Daily Mail* and this new political party which says it is not fascist, and they have no idea. Even the English politicians who are the children of refugees have no idea. But then, nor does my son."

He paused and smiled.

"I talk too much. But it is good to talk. Too long I read and think to myself, and who is interested? My son? My grandchildren? Not really. Ona? Not at all; she is a good child who knows nothing."

"Please go on. I love to hear you talk."

"No. But you are kind. And intelligent. So . . ."

He looked out of the window again, perhaps to remember what he was saying.

"Yes, much that has been done in Europe is good. But in the world, what else is good? In these American wars, so stupid and so cruel, some bad men are killed or chased away. But nobody thinks what should next be done. So thousands and thousands of people who are not bad are also killed or chased away. And Muslims everywhere hate America as the result. There is so much hate in the world.

"And there is Russia. For old Jews of the Pale, like me, there is always Russia. The NKVD killed my parents and my sister. Twenty years ago I would have died hoping Russia was at last to change for the better. For example, at last Russia was admitting the truth of Katyn. But now this man who rules Russia has in his bones, as the English say—in his soul, I would say—the Third Section, the Okhrana, the Cheka, the NKVD, the KGB—this is a list I have known by heart all my life. All have told lies. Putin has said that Poland in 1939 was on the side of Hitler. And he has established a committee to prevent what is called 'falsification of the Russian past'. You know what this means? It means he forbids it to be said that the Nazis killed so many Belorussians, so many Ukrainians, so many Jews. After the war Stalin decreed that they were to be called

'Soviet citizens'. Now Putin decrees that they are 'Russians'. It is a lie. Millions of the people who died, the people I saw die and millions more, were Jews, were Belorussians or Ukrainians. Of course some were Russians. But all the rest are to be lost, into a history that must only be Russian. We should not forget to fear Russia. Nor should we forget to grieve for the Russian poor, the poor peasants, and as ever, the poor soldiers. When they killed my father and the Polish officers at Katyn, Russian soldiers took watches from the dead bodies. When that Polish plane crashed in the Katyn forest three years ago—which was, I do believe, truly an accident—Russian soldiers took credit cards from the dead bodies. *Plus ça change, n'est-ce pas?*"

He laughed. "You see, *après tout*, I know some French."

He paused, his eyes shut.

"But what is most of all sad for me ..."

He broke off and looked at her, a long look.

"What do you think I will say is most sad?"

"Israel?"

"Of course. Israel."

"Have you ever been to Israel?"

"Alas, I never did go there. I thought perhaps I would go when I sold the shop. I had some money. I wondered: shall I go to see Israel? I did not go. I was afraid—yes, I was afraid—of so Jewish an atmosphere. I have not lived a good Jewish life. At the same time I am not a good secular Jew, as they say. I was afraid of Jewish questions. Jews always ask questions. We are not quiet by nature. We are not—what is the English word?—reticent. But I, now ... I am more English, do you think?"

She shook her head. He laughed.

"No? You are right of course. I did not go to Israel also because since 1945 always I have been afraid to leave England—in case, you know, someone might not allow me to return. You understand? Yes, of all people, you understand. But now, Israel, what I read of Israel, is like a nightmare to me, a nightmare I wish to wake from but cannot."

He held out his left hand. She poured out some more water and gave him the glass. He held the glass, as if for comfort, without drinking any water.

"Yes, a nightmare. So wonderful, the Zionist idea, once upon the time, though we know how many Jews—for example, my father—had serious doubt. But my father and his friends did not know that the Nazis would overtake the Jews like a terrible tide. But what has become of the wonderful idea? Jews are the bullies now, with their settlements, their checkpoints, their wall, their guns, their tanks, their roaring helicopters. If anyone should know that this is not the way, Jews should know. Many, many do; of course they do. One, for example, has been for me a hero. Yeshayahu Leibowitz—what a wonderful name is this? A Jew from Riga. A great scientist. A great Zionist. He was educated in Berlin, in Basel, in the old times, when such things were possible. He went to Israel long ago, before Hitler's war. All through the years he watches what happens to Israel. He says it is necessary, already in 1967, to give back to the Arabs what Israel has taken. But no. So he watches. At last he says that the golden calf need not be made of gold—it may be called 'nation', 'land', 'state'. He is of course dead by now. But how difficult must it be for all the Jews who think as he did, who understand as he did, to live in Israel as it is? And what did make it turn out so?"

He drank a little water, gave her the glass.

"I have read much, thought much, about this above all. From the start there is muddle, even it may have been deliberate muddle: the British promising one thing to the Jews, another thing to the Arabs, now nearly a hundred years ago. That was the start. Then were the Zionist murders, assassinations, learned in Russia. As if killing would ever help. Already in 1924 Zionists are murdering Jacob Israël de Haan—you haven't heard of him? No. No one has heard of him. He was a good man who was making peaceful agreements with Muslims and Christians in Palestine. He is killed; his plan is dead. Ten years later Mr Churchill is telling Weizmann Palestine can be divided: a country for the Jews, a country for the Arabs. Then Zionists murder Lord Moyne, who is the British minister in Egypt and the friend of Mr Churchill. Again the plan is dead. Just as Palestine becomes what they have always wanted, Zionists murder Count Bernardotte and Israel is disgraced across the world. This is 1948; Israel is at last for four months Israel, and Jews murder the good man who works for peace. By now the muddle is very serious, and though now Israel is a country, a state, and the world has agreed, the wars that Israel wins make it worse, not better. In 1993 there is light, hope: Rabin recognizes the PLO; Arafat recognizes Israel; everybody gets the Nobel Prize for peace. Rabin and Arafat and Shimon Peres also. Ah, how sad it is . . .

"Shimon Peres is president of Israel now. Of course he is very old, some years, I think, older than I am. But he is a hero. You know about Shimon Peres? Yes. You do not know he was born in a little Jewish town in the Nalibocka forest. The forest we know, you and I. He belongs to the past, like me. So. 1993. Peace is perhaps possible after all. Then Zionists murder Rabin—that was truly a terrible day—and the plan is dead. The peace is dead. So, in 1993 there was this hope—exactly twenty years ago—before the assassination of Rabin. That would have been the time to die, you see."

He laughed, briefly.

"A little water. Thank you. So. Assassinations of important men have made again and again things always worse. But murder of people who are not important—the kind of murder which Stalin and Hitler loved—actually is worse. When we were in the forest in Belorussia, hiding, always hiding, the partisans would sometimes succeed in an attack. A telegraph line is cut in the night. A wagon carrying meat and milk for German soldiers is stolen and the guards killed. A car with German officers is blown up. Then comes the vengeance: a whole village, several villages, destroyed and all the peasants burned to death, in barns, in churches, hundreds of deaths. This I cannot forget. This happens again and again. Hundreds of villages. So thousands of deaths. Four years ago the Palestinians have killed thirteen Israelis with their mortars. So the Israelis kill thirteen hundred Palestinians in Gaza. The same. This is hard to bear, that Jews do this. Even so old as I am, or because I am so old. This is terrible. But worst of all are the settlements, as if Israel is two things, a good, a civilized, a free place for Jews to talk and think and disagree, really a democracy, and one is a colonizing monster of the nineteenth century. This I think of most, with my old man's sadness.

"America, the great, the wonderful, the so-called land of the free, is the example here, is it not? You take the best and the worst of Europeans. You put them in a new-found land. You pretend it is an empty land. And what happens? The worst, in the name of the best, shoot and kill, and say they are bringing civilization. In the desert of South Hebron now Jews with guns drive away the old Arab people of the desert as if the Arabs are Red Indians in a cowboy film. Hitler loved cowboy films, you know. He would chase the Slavs, the Jews, from his Wild East. The Germans are more civilized than these primitive people. They deserve

309

the land. They represent progress, a word never to trust, by the way. The Volga, Hitler said, would be his Mississippi. There is a name for this, an American name. Manifest Destiny. What it means you know, I know. It means History with a capital letter instead of people with a small letter, persons, one by one. All my life I know and hate this, if it is Marxist, if it is Nazi. How do they justify this in the good country Israel also is? Simple. They encourage fear. Like President Bush after 9-11: the War on Terror. It is easy to tell Jews they should be afraid. They have been always afraid. Now they have no need to be afraid. They are strong. They have the soldiers, the helicopters, the tanks. They have America. Even they have the atom bomb. The Arabs do not have any of these things. But tell the Jews they should be afraid, and they fear. So they make their settlements and they bully. Is this what it is to be a light to the nations?"

All through this long lament, he had looked not at her but at the glass of water in his hand. Now he looked at her, his black eyes deep and sad, and very tired.

"You know—probably you do not know—that the great prophecy in the Tanakh, where God does promise to bring his people back to their own land, says also that he will take away their hearts of stone and instead give them hearts of flesh. And now, look at what we see. He expected justice, but he found bloodshed. What would they be thinking, the old Litvaks in their study houses? You know, Benjamin Netanyahu is a Vilna Jew. Not only this. Benjamin Netanyahu's ancestor is the Vilna Gaon himself. This is what the twentieth century has done to the Jews. And now, even if there would be anything for me to do, to say, I do not ... have not ... the time ..."

His voice faded in his throat. The glass of water suddenly tipped in his hand. She took it just before it spilled. His head had dropped. She sat for a moment, chilled, the glass in both her hands, unable to move. Had he died? Had he talked himself to exhaustion and died? She should have stopped him. Why hadn't she? How could she have let him talk and talk when he was so frail?

She half got out of her chair, to ring the bell for the nurse. Then she saw that he was breathing, shallowly, without a sound. She put the glass down, very gently, on the locker.

She sat and watched him for perhaps half an hour. The room was very quiet. A large flat-screen television was on a table in the corner, facing the bed and the chair. She was sure he had never asked for it to be turned on. She did not remember a television in his flat in Shepherd's Bush. She thought of his piano, his violin. She thought of the shots that had missed him at the death pits of Ponary. She thought of the small boy going home from school through the ancient crowded streets of Jewish Vilna, where she had never been. She almost fell asleep herself.

When she opened her eyes he hadn't stirred. He was so still, breathing so gently, she thought moment by moment that his next breath might be his last. She looked at her watch, calculated some journey times to the station, to the train home.

She didn't want to wake him from such deep sleep, after all he had managed to say to her. Nor did she want to leave him without saying good-bye. She thought. She remembered his letter. Very quietly she got up and opened one of the top drawers in the chest of drawers. Only a new box of tissues and two pairs of socks. Socks. His feet, probably bare feet in slippers, were hidden under the blanket keeping him warm. She shut the drawer without making a sound, opened another. Writing paper with the nursing home's address; envelopes. Still quietly, though he showed no sign of waking, she found a pen in her bag and put the *Guardian* under a sheet of writing paper on her knee.

> *Dear Joe,*
>
> *You were peacefully asleep when I had to go, so I didn't want to wake you to say good-bye.*
>
> *I am sure you will understand how glad I am, so very glad, to have been able to talk to you today, to have seen that you are safe and well looked after, and to have been able to listen to everything you said.*
>
> *To have met you, to have learned something of your life, has been a great blessing.*
>
> *Don't forget what Max Hofmann wrote to you many years ago: God knows all our stories. Only God.*
>
> *With love and prayers.*

She folded the letter, sealed it in an envelope, wrote his name on it, and left it propped against the jug of tulips so that someone would notice it and give it to him.

Still he slept.

She sat, watching his tired, white face.

After quite a long time, she took another piece of writing paper and two envelopes from the drawer.

> *I would be most grateful if you could let me know if Mr Halpern dies. I am an old friend, but I do not know his family and may not hear of his death. I enclose a stamped addressed envelope.*
> *With many thanks.*

She wrote her name and address on one of the envelopes, found a stamp in her wallet, and put the letter and the addressed envelope in the blank envelope.

For a little longer she watched him sleep. Then she laid the *Guardian* on his paisley eiderdown; stood for a moment more, looking at the eiderdown; and then bent to kiss his forehead. His eyelids flickered. Very softly he said in German, "Gelobt sei Gott". Blessed be God. He didn't wake.

She left the room, shutting the door behind her without a sound.

"Mr Halpern is asleep", she said to the nurse at the desk.

"He sleeps a lot", the nurse said, looking at her computer screen.

She gave the letter to the receptionist at the desk downstairs.

"Could you very kindly see that this reaches the doctor who is looking after Mr Halpern?"

"Certainly."

It was cold, very cold for the end of March, in the almost-empty streets as she walked to the Underground station. The children were back from school, she thought with the surface of her mind, and their parents not yet on their way home, in their suits, with their briefcases, from the Central Line. Below the surface she knew she was leaving a whole world behind. She also knew that when she thought of him, although she would forget, probably, much of what he had said through the long afternoon, she would hear his voice, his old voice talking and talking in his stilted, formal English, for the rest of her life.

The letter came nearly three weeks later. A second, more serious stroke had proved fatal, and he had died peacefully without regaining consciousness.

That day she mourned him, without protest, for she knew he had prepared himself for death as well as he could, which is as well as anyone can.

She sat for several hours, as the afternoon became the evening, in the garden of her cottage in the country, a thousand miles from Vilna and far away from Yorkshire and even from London where he had lived so long. The doctor's letter lay on the table in front of her, beside a cup of coffee that was cold before she remembered she had made it.

The late spring at last had come. The air was mild and still, the daffodils were out, and the sunshine was warm enough to promise that the buds on the branches of the apple trees would soon unfold as blossom and leaves. One day there would be fruit. She looked at the familiar trees: the apples; an old damson tree, almost flowering already; an untidy plum tree, once neatly pruned and trained, growing against a high wall; at the end of the lawn an ash tree that would produce no leaves for more than a month. She thought of the larch wood on the side of the Yorkshire dale. She thought of the great Nalibocka forest, the immense wilderness of pine trees, birches, lakes, and squelching swamp; prickly undergrowth, ferns, moss, and fallen trees; the sound of invisible streams and of bubbles on the green surface of bogs; the unseen presence of beaver and deer and boar and wolves; the forest that had kept him alive. And she thought of the forest clearings of death, Ponary outside Vilna, the pits filling with corpses and the drunken Lithuanians shooting; and Katyn, where the Polish officers, among them Jacob Halperin, thinking until their last minutes that they had been freed, were shot in their thousands.

Towards evening the light thickened a little, as if with particles of gold, as the sun was going down. A blackbird was singing, further away a song thrush; further away still, pigeons repeated their soft call in the woods beyond the garden. Otherwise it was a gentle, windless quiet. She watched the bare branches of the plum tree. The wall behind it faced west; the stones of the wall were painted honey-coloured by the setting sun. Small birds came and went in the evening light, in and out of the motionless branches and twigs. She watched the branches, the shadows of the branches on the wall, birds and the shadows of birds.

Sometimes in a garden on a still autumn day you can hear the odd apple, the odd plum, drop to the grass, not because a wind is blowing or someone shakes a tree, but because it is time.

His death had been as quiet as the fall of a single leaf.

When the sun had left the garden, she got up, cold after sitting outside for so long, and went into the house. She put the doctor's letter in its envelope, addressed to her in her own writing. She wrote on the back of the envelope:

> Blessed be the Lord,
> who did not give us
> a prey to their teeth.
> Our life, like a bird, has escaped
> from the snare of the fowler.

She opened a drawer in her desk, put the letter inside, and closed the drawer.